BADLY
Behaved

MEAGAN BRANDY

Edited by: My Brother's Editor
Edited by: Fairest Reviews Editing Services
Proofread by: Lisa Salvucci

Want to be notified about future book releases of mine?
Sign up for my Newsletter today: https://geni.us/ BMMBNL

Playlist

Numb – Carlie Hanson

Distraction - Kehlani

Need Nothing – Verite

Vicious – Tate McRae, Lil Mosey

Empty – Olivia O'Brien

Honestly – Gabbie Hanna

Monsters – All Time Low, Blackbear

Runaway – Sasha Sloan

Fucked Up – Bahari

Love Made Me Do It – Ellise

LISTEN TO THE FULL PLAYLIST HERE:

http://bit.ly/BBMBplaylist

Dedication

This one's for the girls who break the mold.
The world needs more of you.

Synopsis

I'm a Monet.
A chameleon.

I'm whatever I must be.

And what I must be is a flawless daughter, a skilled socialite, and the perfect prize to the man who signed along the dotted line.

Not that I'm complaining.

I'm all for a contractual agreement, a quick and clean catapult into the next phase of rich girl life. One that takes little thought, less effort, and zero devotion.

It's exactly what I want.
An impassive life.
A calculated future.

Or, it was until the lights went out, darkness took over, and I learned what it meant to live.
To feel.
To fall.

But everyone knows what thrives in the night, burns in the light, and flames were among us.
There is no escape.
No turning back.

No ending within my control.

My mother always says our choices determine our consequences.

I hate it when she's right...

CHAPTER
One

JAMESON

*C*oastal party, alcoholic coma, repeat.

It took five days and seven pregame lattes to realize this was the practiced, yet unspoken mantra of the season for every rich kid here in Corona Del Mar who didn't spend their summer abroad.

Today being a party day means tomorrow's schedule is already penciled in, and it will be an eventful 'do nothing but rot in front of a giant television while feeding each other pain pills and swearing to *never drink again* day. And let's not forget the late-night dinner that is guaranteed to follow, which will more than likely end with someone screaming at their boyfriend for flirting with the waitress of the hour. Poor waitresses.

And my parents said life would be less predictable here.

I wonder if they can feel how hard my eye roll is from across the globe?

No matter how much they like to pretend they're not teetering at the tip of the dreaded hill every bad birthday card teases past the age of twenty-nine, they have no idea what being on the edge of eighteen looks like.

They're clueless, and to be honest, they like it that way. As if the dominating defense duo of Filano Law would bother themselves with meaningless matters such as wannabe boyfriends and zany-addicted daughters. Not that this is me acknowledging either of those issues, but are they calling me every night to make sure their ticket is well-punched and properly publicized? That's a hard no.

I'm not sure what's worse, that they don't check in or the fact they are aware they don't have to.

Thou shall not disappoint thy parents; words equivalent to downright dullness if you ask my peers, but I don't share their sentiment and they don't follow it.

Am I good at pissing my parents off? Yes, but where they do as they wish and bet on forgiveness later, I tread carefully at the start. Like an acrobat on a tightrope, I balance like a pro, never allowing myself to fall over the dreaded '*did you hear about the Filano's daughter*' line.

My sister, on the other hand, leaps without looking, unconcerned with the mess she makes on her way down.

If it were up to my parents, they'd have married her off to the former district attorney back in Naples when they learned he was asking questions they couldn't afford him to find the answers to, the whole 'keep your enemies close' and all that.

Ambitious, young women marry seasoned, older men, my mother's words echo in my ears.

I think she adopted such an idea after stepping into what, in many ways, was a man's world. Not that it stopped her.

She's the reigning queen and king of her profession.

My sister, of course, couldn't stomach my mother's desires and took things into her own hands by sleeping with the DA's son instead. And then she told him about it. It was a shitshow, cost them a fortune to rectify, but at the end of the day, it was done.

As for me, I find a contractual agreement airtight, and maybe this is because I don't want the things my sister does, but even if I did, it wouldn't matter.

My family requires something of me, and so they shall receive.

Are they assholes, far from a long hug when faced with a heavy dose of teenage 'the sky is falling'? Oh, hell yeah, but again... dominant defense attorneys. They are built to be tough and take no shit. Highly respected and hardworking. They've spent my whole life building what we have, and the result is right in front of me—a hundred-eighty degree view of the Pacific Ocean. I'm sure the paycheck my mother received after my bio-dad's suicide provided a nice cushion, but nobody dares to say so out loud.

Regardless, it's my job as a Filano to respect, protect, and secure a future for our name. So, I will, the bonus is I get to avoid the mess people face along the way.

It's a win all around.

"Classic Jameson."

I snap out of my thoughts, turning to lean my back against the infinity pool's edge and face my friend.

"Do you even realize how every party you manage to find the single spot nobody occupies and claim it as your own?" She smiles, offering me one of the two full champagne flutes she carries. "And always with empty hands." Her tone is teasing, and she holds her glass out, tapping its rim to mine. "Now drink up. You are officially two bottles behind."

I take a small sip, spinning when she approaches the edge and peers out at the endless darkness the ocean before us provides.

"Thank god for pool heaters, right?" She dips lower to

keep the breeze from hitting her wet skin.

"Right. Imagine the shrinkage in the package Jules would be getting served right about now without it."

We both sneak peeks to the far corner of the pool.

Jules and her man are tucked away, pretending none of us realize they're secretly grinding under the stone waterfall when everyone knows the truth.

Cali and I look to each other and she giggles.

"What a travesty that would be." She rolls her eyes. "Speaking of travesty, why are you not capitalizing on the open seat on Gentry's lap?"

"Which Gentry would you be referring to?" I glance her way.

Cali bounces in the water. "I told Jules his brother was checking you out the other night! So, spill." Her face lights up. "Did you bite?"

My nose scrunches slightly. "He's a little extra for my taste."

"Yeah, killing the music and gathering everyone into the gym for a dead-lift challenge *in the middle of a party* was pretty narcissistic of them."

"You think?"

She laughs. "Still, the youngest Gentry wouldn't be a bad way to pass the time. Gives you someone to fall back on for school events."

I press my lips together, tipping my glass toward her, entertaining the idea. "You might be right."

"Of course, I'm right." She downs her drink and looks at me expectantly. I don't inhale mine like she did, but I do follow her out of the water.

We slip our robes over our bodies and step into the pool house so she can get her refill, but as we approach the long table, her skinny fingers latch on to my forearm, squeezing.

"Holy shit, they're back. And here." Her brows furrow. "When did they get here?"

I spin to look, but her hands shoot up, catching my face and holding it still.

"Just scream we're talking about them, why don't you!" she hisses.

Humor tugs at my lips as I pull her hands away. "How am I supposed to offer an answer if I can't see who you're talking about?"

"You don't know them. They've been gone all summer." She subconsciously begins adjusting her stance—a little taller, a tad straighter, more staged than real.

"Maybe I do. I did live here all through elementary school."

"And they moved here in seventh grade, or at least two of them did. I think the other was here for sixth, but he was homeschooled or something." She swipes her hand in the air, deeming the details insignificant.

Her voice lowers even more. "Remember those guys I told you about, the ones who—" When I shift, she cuts off her words with a panicked frown. "What are you doing?"

I step around the long, tall table so that I'm now facing her and able to snap my eyes around the room when I'm good and ready to do so.

Cali flicks her eyes to the ceiling.

"You were saying?"

"Stealth, girl. Stealth." She pushes her hair over her shoulder and keeps going. "So, the story I told you about the guys who stole Ken Garretts parents' safe at the end-of-the-year party—"

"Says you."

"They were the only ones who showed up uninvited. Everyone else that was there had been there before, minus them, *and* one even screwed Ken's girlfriend earlier that week." She sips her drink with sass. "Ken kept her sorry ass, but still. It happened."

"That's hardly motive to lift a safe."

"Ugh." Cali sets her drink down beside her. "You are such a lawyer's daughter."

I roll my eyes. "If you're worried about them stealing, tell them to kick rocks."

"And then those *rocks* end up through the side of the pool and over the fucking cliff everyone in it goes."

Her dramatic spat has me pinching my lips as not to laugh at her.

She leans forward, speaking in an unexpectedly serious tone. "The safe issue was the last thing that happened, not the only. It's always something with them. They're psychotic. Unpredictable. Someone always gets fucked when they're around, figuratively *and*, well, literally." She takes a long drink.

I find myself trying to get closer, the need for some examples suddenly high, but before I can ask, or stop myself, my eyes snap over her shoulder, landing directly on the unfamiliar view not ten feet away.

Minus my mandatory 'hook the hunk' exploits, I've spent the last two and a half months with the same group of people. Every couple of nights, there were a solid five to ten newcomers, but it's at the point now where those who were gone for the summer have returned, so I've seen every face at least twice now.

Had Cali not pointed out the strangers' appearance tonight, I'd have spotted them eventually, and been fully aware this was the first party they graced with their presence.

And goddamn, is grace not meant to be given.

All freaking hail the trifecta of trouble straight ahead.

I start with the one on the end and slowly—very slowly—make my way along the others.

Hot, hot, and yep. *Hotter*.

No matter your flavor of choice, one is bound to hit your tastebuds just right. Probably linger along your tongue in favor of more.

I wonder if they're too high in demand for 'more'?

"Will you stop staring?!" Cali hides her lips against her glass.

My gaze snaps to hers. "Girl, chill, they're not paying any attention to us. They're otherwise *occupata*."

"Occupied by who?" Her eyes narrow, her curiosity and impatience equally piqued.

I lift a shoulder. "Guess you have to look to know for sure."

Her frown tightens and it takes effort not to laugh. Cali puts her elbow on the tabletop, purposefully jerking and knocking a napkin to the floor so she has an excuse to glance behind her as if this isn't her house and the rights not completely hers.

She straightens, repositioning herself in front of me with a full-on stank face.

"Poor taste must be contagious," she mutters under her breath.

Her annoyance has nothing to do with them and everything to do with the girl, I think her name is Sammie, who has placed herself in front of them. Two nights ago, we sat back while little Miss Thang stuck her tongue down Cali's ex's throat.

"I don't know, she's kind of hot," I tease and Cali flips me off. "So, who are these pretty party crashers?"

"Ransom Rossi, Arsen Agular, and Beretta Keller, but pretty isn't the word I'd use."

We turn to Scott Gentry as he steps up beside me, his attempt at a careless expression lacking in finesse.

"And what word would you use?"

"Trash," he says unapologetically.

I squint, tipping my head. "I'm pretty sure one of them is wearing fall Givenchy."

"I'm not talking money." He shrugs. "But while you are, they don't come from it. Those assholes are going nowhere quick. They're hardly passing, couldn't even make the grades enough to stay on the team. They're future felons, one already spent a summer in juvenile hall. They're around fucking things up and pretending they don't wish they were more like us, but then show for our parties and fuck with girls they have no business with. They're wasted air around this place, doing who knows what to afford to stick around. I don't know why anyone wastes their time with them."

"Maybe we should ask Ken's girlfriend?" I joke.

Cali laughs, choking on her drink.

He cuts her a quick glare. "Like I said, they fuck with girls they have no business with, playing their stupid games."

I keep my eyes on Scott.

So, he hates that they don't care to be in the cool kids' club. Noted.

I shift, positioning myself in front of him and a smirk hints at the corner of his lips. He takes my move as invitation to slip closer, his drunken gaze falling to the opening of my robe as if he has plans to unravel it.

As if he expects I'll allow him to.

Scott Gentry is the picture of privilege.

"What games?"

His brows furrow slightly, but he shrugs. "People call it 'blackout.'"

"Blackout?"

"They show up, the power goes out. Blackout," he explains, half in the conversation, half perving on me, his tongue unabashedly gliding along his lips for all to see, then his eyes come back to mine. "The gist, the lights go out and shit happens but it's not every time. Sometimes it's nothing more than a need to be remembered upon exit and they get their little fifteen minutes where they matter." Displeasure drips from his clipped tone. "Other times they fight, snag a girl to hook up—"

"Steal," Cali interrupts, full of sass, and pops an overly embellished brow.

I bug my eyes at her playfully.

"One time, the power didn't even come back on." Jules skips up, snagging the bottle from Cali's grasp. "A flame lit up the place instead."

"A flame?"

She smiles. "They literally lit Kay Kerr's parents' prize Bonsai on fire, and Kay couldn't even rat them out because she wasn't supposed to be in town when it happened."

My tongue slips between my teeth. "That's a drag."

"Yep. Now let's forget about the shadows in the back. Quit babysitting your drink, we went easy with champagne tonight." She looks to my flute. "And you, my dear, are far too sober."

"All I know is, if they pull some shit tonight, make sure my casket's amethyst and diamond-encrusted." Cali tops off her drink yet again. "We all know my mom will murder my ass if so much as a scarf is missing." She tears away from the counter and heads into the den, leaving us to laugh at her expense.

The conversation shifts to the events of the last gathering, and we move along the groups. When everyone's distracted enough, I break away once more, lowering myself onto the empty sofa near the open doors, and my bored-ass mind begins playing on an infinite loop, circling the party in search of some excitement that doesn't involve a half-naked couple or a shattered bottle that's slipped from a tipsy blonde's fingers.

This place is exactly how I remember it. A tight-knit community who look down their noses at any and all who don't fit the mold.

Obsessive fathers and aggressive mothers pushing responsibilities and expectations onto their children one second, pretending we don't exist the next.

It's not something only myself and my sister deal with, but a standard across the board in communities like ours.

The extent of it depends on your parents' position, and what they demand of you.

The Gentry boys, for example, they're to be carbon copies of their father. The oldest is already an intern while Scott is expected to follow, go to an ivy league, and he will, as his father and grandfather did—his parents' hefty donation will see to it. He'll be frat house president, without a care, paying people off for assignments, and then take his place in his parents' company when he's done.

Cali will sit like a waiting duck and take her pick of the litter and slip right into the socialite role her mother laid breadcrumbs for.

Jules, I don't even know. Her mom wants her to go to college, but she hates school, hates everything her mom wants her to do, period, it seems. *Maybe she just hates her mom?*

Either way, our lives are a series of Hallmark cards, written—and sold, if I want to look at my situation for what it is—by someone else, yet a perfect play-by-play of our reality, and that's pathetic.

Wash, rinse, repeat.

Boring, boring, boring.

Again, another reason why I'm eager for this year to come and go, because why not get right into what follows? At least some of the scenery will be different.

A heavy sigh leaves me, and I continue my people watching, and with each cycle of the room, I pause a little longer on the three who stand out above the others.

Maybe it's because they're the only ones who still have their clothes on, whereas everyone else dons a swimsuit. Or, perhaps it's the lax way in which they dangle the long neck of their beer bottles I've yet to see them drink from, rather than swirling scotch in a glass that costs more than summer highlights, with their pinkies half in the air.

It could be the hardened glare that's yet to leave the one with the deep mahogany shaded, tight cropped cut, even if it remains directed toward his drink.

It might even be the backward cap on the dark-haired guy, and the fact he keeps adjusting it, a full side smile on his flirty face, one that falls flat the moment he looks away from his friends.

Of course, not to be counted out is the ominous bronzy brunette with bone structure that could rival Colton Haynes on his worst day and how his sharp gaze continues to flick along the corners of the room. If I had to bet, I'd say he's searching for nothing, but awareness *is* key when hearsay has the potential to bury you alive.

Ah, the joys of Orange County.

A grin pulls at my lips at the refreshing sight before me.

The ripple in the rich little haven that is Corona Del Mar.

No shorts that hit above the knee, or open, windblown cotton shirts. No Loewe deck, yacht club must-have slip-ons or gleam of overused tanning lotion.

No, all three are wearing solid black, shoes included, giving you no insight as to the personalities within, assuming they're not as hardened as their expressions lead you to believe. And I was right, I do spot a Givenchy coat.

I'm far from surprised at how many girls have gravitated toward the three, a couple guys too, the need to stay with their happy endings of the night extreme, and even as these 'blackout' boys make their way from one space to the next, the others follow. Funny, though, while they stay within a few feet of the trio, they don't approach them.

Maybe they're hoping they'll be the ones approached?

I could almost laugh.

These guys must know they beam as bright as a knockoff in a country club, but perhaps that's how they want it?

Cali says they're crazy, yet these girls are practically foaming at the mouth for a split second of acknowledgment, their jerky movements and pursed lips telling the tale of how they've yet to receive their wish.

Oh, how the entitled hate to be ignored.

I chuckle to myself at the hypocrisy of it all. How those deep inside this world, the ones who live for it, feign disgust, annoyance or irritation. Put off the whole 'we're the only one in the room' vibe, when really, every move they make is for the benefit of those they hope are watching. It's a comical sight and playing out right in front of me right this second.

The age-old truth behind their masks, the one the fathers in our world likely hate the most but can't deny.

Every spoiled little rich girl craves herself a psycho, at least a time or ten.

"Girl, for real, you must have a death wish."

I shrug, turning to Jules. "I'm bored, what else is there to do but study new sights instead of the same ones we've seen for the last month?"

"Boredom is what ends you, got it," she jokes, taking the seat beside me. "You, my friend, are going to get murdered in your sleep."

Little does she know they haven't so much as glanced my way all night. My game of Susie Stalker is safe and sound.

"And *you* are going to get pregnant if you keep hopping on your man in the water," I deflect, doing as she prefers and switch the conversation so it's about her.

She laughs into the cooled air above us. "Honey, I'm all for it. That boy gets me pregnant, I'll be set for life. Besides, I love him, so win-win."

I shake my head, forcing a small smile, knowing she's dead serious. If you're not deemed ivy league status early, you're a token your family will later cash in on. This is how it goes for a lot of us trust fund girls. Minus the love.

Love is not something anyone should chase in our world.

Convenience breeds confidence and keeps the daily dosage down. Love creates jealousy and doubt and mental instability.

Love kills.

The two of us look up when Cali walks over, officially swaying on her feet. "I'm starved. Who wants to help me order—"

The lights go out.

"Oh shit," Cali hisses.

People yell in drunken numbness, some squeal and scream.

I roll my eyes, my fingers falling against the expensive leather at my sides, only to be pulled from it seconds later.

I frown, yanking my arms back.

"Jules, back—"

Something is slapped over my mouth as my hands are bound together.

What the hell?

A cloth is thrown over my head next, the soft fabric forming to my nose as my breaths quicken.

I kick, but I'm barefoot. I attempt to shout, but to no avail, and then I'm lifted into the air, not by one set of hands, but several.

I claw and scratch the muscles along the arm in reach, flexing as I do. When the cool night's wind stings my skin, alerting me I'm no longer in the house, I wiggle every inch of my body in an attempt to set myself free, but all I get is a firmer grip on my upper thighs. My muscles clench beneath a rough palm, and a dark chuckle wafts over my chest.

I squeeze my lids shut, a knot forming in my throat as my Barocco robe is torn from my arms, leaving me in nothing but a triangle top swimsuit and bottoms a decent parent would slay their daughter for wearing at a party—a gift from my mother.

All I can think is I'm about to be raped, murdered, or kidnapped.

The air around me grows chillier, my pulse kicks higher, and I'm five seconds from confessing all my sins.

Suddenly I'm dropped into a pile of sand, and not two seconds later, a wave threatens to carry me out to sea.

I push my palms into the thick, soft sand and drag myself to my feet before the water steals it from beneath me, running up and out as far as I can, only to trip over something, slamming onto the sand once more.

My chest rises and falls rapidly, and I wait for the assault.

For hands to bound around my neck or hips.

For something far worse I may never want to wake up

from.

But I get nothing.

The weep of the night's waves echoes around me, not a hint of another's presence with it.

With shaky fingers, I slowly reach up, and once I have the fabric in my grip, quickly tear it from my head.

I blink several times for my eyes to readjust, swiveling my body around in the damp sand to find I'm completely alone, nothing but the hint of taillights in the distance. The panic dwindles, my eyes snapping to my hands, and my shoulders fall.

A hair tie.

My hair tie, stretched around my wrists.

Pathetic, Jameson.

Teeth clenched, I angrily tear the tape from my mouth, surprised when it too slips off nice and easy, leaving behind a bit of a greasy residue.

With a heavy glare, I whip around, staring up at the sea cliff, and what do you know, the power suddenly kicks back on in Cali's house, the pool, once again, illuminated with LED lights, the music reaching my ears in the barest of tones.

A growl escapes me as I wrap my arms around myself, the coastal breeze freezing my saltwater-covered ass, and start back up the hill. The wind chooses to blow a little with my every step taken, and the tape I tossed to the side rolls up, covering the back of my ankle.

I kick the thing away, only to pause when the gleam of the ocean hits it just right.

My head tips slightly and I take a quick glance around before bending to pick it up. I shake off the excess sand and drag it closer, squinting at the floppy piece of shit.

Right across the front, written in big, bold, and, of course, red letters are two words that probably shouldn't make me laugh, but one flies from me before I can stop it.

With a shake of my head, I crumple their little love note in my palm and toss it in the bonfire on my way back to Cali's house.

Inside, it's as if nothing happened and nobody realized I was gone. They're drinking and talking and laughing like normal. And there's no point in making a scene or drawing attention to myself by calling everyone out on their lack of awareness, so I don't.

I'm the dumbass who let herself get dragged out of the party, carried down the hill, and tripped over a fucking log that Cali and I probably put there last night.

So, I pour myself that next round I was trying to avoid and bring the sweet treat of a drink to my lips. As I scan the room, I'm fully aware the three who popped in late were the first to leave.

With me dangling from their hazardous hands.

I scoff, watching the bubbles fight their way to the top of my glass, the words those guys felt the need to feed me dry on my tongue.

It's ironic to serve me with a tip that plays like a boomerang, only able to head in my direction if it initiated from theirs. Or vice versa—the 'who leaped first' is unimportant when two people end up at the bottom of the Pacific. All that matters is the key fact that led them there. They both jumped.

To be aware I was staring means one thing and one thing only.

They were staring, too.

CHAPTER *Two*

*J*ules giggles as she climbs from Dax's car, flashes him her ass through the open window, and then makes her way toward us.

"You're almost an hour late." Cali bites at the straw stuck between her teeth.

"It's called stamina, my friend." Jules walks up, and together, we spin, headed for the restaurant. "You should try to find you a toy who has some."

"Please, I don't have time for all that. Quick to the punch is more my style." Cali wiggles her brows, pausing in front of the door rather than reaching for it herself.

Not three seconds later, it's opened for us, the greeter, I always remember by his perfectly slicked hair, revealing himself on the other side.

"Ms. Marino." The man smiles at Jules with a small head bow. "Your table has been prepared on the patio."

He holds a hand out, ushering us past the group still waiting to be seated.

"Thanks, Korbin, Mimosas to start us off?" She smiles.

"Already on the way, Miss."

She blows him a kiss and we head out to the best seat in the house, right against the glass, overlooking the highest peak of the cliff.

Jules and Cali pull out their phones, snapping quick selfies for social media and tapping away while I watch the waves as they curl over the rocks below.

Farther out, I spot several surfers making their way in with the tide. They've likely been out there grinding since four this morning, and here we are, barely alive at a quarter to ten like a bunch of brats.

Or teenage girls, I guess.

Speaking of barely alive...

The waiter arrives with a large glass pitcher that no doubt holds their best-stocked champagne and freshly squeezed orange juice.

As he sets three glasses down and prepares to fill them, I decline mine.

"Miss?" He frowns from me to Jules, assuming he did something wrong.

"Sorry, but can I have a hot latte instead?"

"Of course, Miss. What flavor would you like?"

Pushing back in my seat, I shrug. "Surprise me."

He hesitates a moment, as if he heard me wrong, but when I nod, he bows, quickly disappearing inside the restaurant.

Once we order, it's no more than fifteen minutes and our food is brought out.

"So, should we park at the south end of the plaza, make our way down to the other end, and have valet cart us back to the car with our bags?" Cali pushes the last bit of egg whites around her plate with a fork.

"Makes sense to me, we're going for clothes, not jewelry and handbags."

"Speak for yourself." Jules grins. "I could use a new pair of earrings."

Cali smiles, but shakes her head. "Jameson is right, besides, if you wanted to look at jewelry, you should have invited Dax to come with."

"So true." Jules tops off her glass with a giggle.

I can tell by the end of breakfast, today is going to be a freaking marathon. These girls are tipsy and ready to max out their cards, with today's limit anyway. If I would have joined them, they would have gone for refill after refill, and we'd be ditching my car here, waiting for Cali's car service to arrive and head back to one of our houses, our shopping trip forgotten in favor of flirty 'fun.'

Once we've paid and are leaving the table, the waiter brings me a second latte to go and we're off to do some damage at the South Coast Plaza.

It takes less than fifteen minutes to arrive, and we're walking into the center within twenty.

"Oh, I was going to ask about the party Wednesday." Jules pulls her phone out, checking her lipstick in the camera. "Was anything missing after the power went out?"

My drink freezes at my lips as I look from Jules to Cali. *Uh, yeah. Me.*

"Nope. I searched that baby high and low, and everything seemed to be in place. Maybe Miss Skeptic's 'innocent until proven guilty' was right." She cuts a grin my way. "*Maybe* they aren't thieves after all," she mocks me. "Just psychos."

I scoff but look the other way in case a questioning squint is thrown my way.

Little does she know, joke's on her.

Or maybe it's on me since it was *me* they took.

"Okay, first stop!" Jules runs ahead, slipping through the open door of Brunello Cucinelli.

The next few hours are a blur of black cards and bag balancing.

I press the small help button on the inside of the dressing room that rivals the size of my own at home, and it takes less than a minute for the woman to knock her knuckle on the thick, wooden door. After letting her know the size adjustment and swap I would like, she promptly returns with said item in hand, and passes it off to me.

"Last one in this color, Miss." She smiles, her cheeks flushed.

Not five seconds after the door is closed behind me does Cali's voice reach me.

"Girl, we're going to scan over the shoes!" Cali shouts from outside the dressing room.

"I'm almost done, meet you over there!"

Carefully freeing the dress from its hanger, I tug the deep gray, thick strapped number over my hips and spin my body while keeping my head facing the three panel mirrors to see if it hugs in all the right places.

It's cute, form-fitting, but still, even in this shade, there's something about it that's not quite right.

I unzip and free my arms from the straps.

"That ain't the one."

I yelp, whipping around at the intruder's voice, but as the mirrors had already revealed, no one is there.

And then large hands grip the upper frame, a body slipping between the gap as another glides beneath it, all while I remain frozen in place.

With slow shuffles of his feet, the dark-haired one creeps closer.

We're near nose to nose and he tips his head, a slow grin forming on his lips as the sound of the door clicks, and in walks the third and final asshole from the party.

"What the hell are you doing?" I say, forcing my eyes to stay on the one in front of me, but the question is for all three.

"We haven't met." The smile I spotted the other night slips over his face. "I'm Beretta."

"You're a perv."

"Most days." The corner of his mouth hikes higher and despite the situation, a light huffed laugh leaves me.

I look to his forearm, and sure enough, the bit of damage I inflicted burns a deep red.

"Nice scratches."

His gaze flicks to my chest and back. "Nice paws."

My lungs expand with a quick breath.

I half-expected them to feign innocence, not instant, unapologetic, confirmation of what I already knew, but I don't know why. They wouldn't be standing in my dressing room right now if they gave two shits about, well... anything.

I frown, clutching the dress tighter. "How did you even manage to get back here?"

A rapt grin lights up his eyes. "We're quite persuasive, and that seamstress chick is *quite* repressed."

"I'm sure," I deadpan. "Now get out of my dressing room."

"Not until you get out of that dress."

My ribs cave, my attention snapping over to the guy in front of my shoulders.

I'm met with hard-focused, bright blue, iced-over eyes.

"Fuck you."

"Once you've earned it."

My stomach clenches, and he lifts his chin.

"But back to what you're wearing. Beretta's right and you know it." He boldly rakes his gaze over the length of the dress, which is nonexistent—it's a mini. The apex of my thighs is where his focus freezes. "It does nothing for you."

I roll my eyes and as if sensing the move, his snap to mine, a dark brow hiking high with slow surprise.

He kicks off the door, and as if his advance triggers an activate button, I'm suddenly the center of a cavernous carousel.

My pulse jumps with their synchronized movements, a hint of dizziness swathing over me as they loop around, and then I'm surrounded, the brassy-haired one having claimed the position at my front.

With the help of my heels, we're near eye to eye, lip to puffy, perfectly-shaded lip.

"The dress." His head falls back in full-on cocky boy quo. "Off."

I swallow, flicking my gaze over his aesthetically pleasing but basic, and, once again, all black outfit with a scoff. "What are you, some kind of fashion guru?"

He watches me intently, his gaze strong and commanding. "I'm a guy who likes what he sees... and you're ruining it."

Following his response, another comes from my left, right against the hollow of my ear. "Don't ruin it, Trouble."

I fight the urge to blow cool air down my neck, fully committed to hiding how my blood is heating beneath my skin, but the goose bumps are beyond my control, and they are not missed by the beastly boy sharing my air.

In an attempt to breathe easier, I turn my head to the left, but it doesn't help. Beretta stands too close to allow for a fresh inhale that isn't infused with unwanted invitation.

Friction tickles my exposed shoulder to my right, and my focus shifts that way, my palms pressing more firmly into my chest.

This one's yet to say a word, but his sensuous eyes

speak volumes. They're blue, as well, but darker, near navy in color.

"That's Arsen," *once you've earned it* says.

The back of Arsen's hand ghosts along my upper thigh and I pull in a long breath when his fingertips curl around the hem of the dress. He gives it a single, gentle tug.

If someone were to come to me later asking for an explanation as to why I allowed his hold to remain where it was, why I allowed any of this, all I'd have to offer is a weedy little shrug.

Especially when Beretta's firmer, far more unwavering grasp latches on to the other side, and my double-crossing body's response is to drop my arms in surrender.

I face forward, staring right into the eyes of the one in front of me while his friends work the fabric from my hips.

Those eyes, they don't fall as the dress does, and fervor threatens to govern my mind.

"Oh my god!" Cali shouts.

I jump away from the three, my head hitting against the triple mirrors at my back, knocking some much-needed sense into me.

"Are you seriously still in there, James?" she whines.

Pushing off the glass, I glare from one to the next.

"I am. I seem to have been held up." I pop a hip, and three smirks emblaze their devilishly attractive faces.

I cross my arms, and this time, all eyes fall to the strapless bra I probably should have gone a size up on.

All the girls have to do is look beneath the opening and they'll find four sets of legs. Really, they should have as they approached, but again... lack of awareness is a real thing among this group when they're perfectly unaffected.

"Okay, well, hurry up!" Cali's voice is already getting farther away. "I could use a smoothie or something."

With a huff, I bend, tear my romper off the floor and step into it, careful not to snag the material with my wedges.

I yank my purse from the hook and shoot forward, but the bossy one of the bunch catches me by the wrist with a glare.

One I give right back.

"What's the matter, blue eyes? Afraid to play in the light?"

His godly cut jaw sharpens, but his lips remain sealed, and when I jerk in his grasp, he concedes, releasing me.

I don't miss how they slip as far to the side as possible when I throw the door open as wide as the hinges allow and step out.

Only then do I realize how stupidly thoughtless a move it was, one the gossip mill would eat up and my parents would burn me alive for—I blame the twister of testosterone I was caught in the eye of.

But damn, how bold were they to creep in on me like that?

Maybe they are crazy...

I shake it off, bumping shoulders with Cali and Jules as I fall in step between them. "I've reconsidered my decision not to drink today. I could use one."

Or three.

I frown.

Jesus Christ.

Cali claps and at the exit, the doorman returns our bags and off we go to get drunk somewhere.

CHAPTER *Three*

*I*t's close to eleven p.m. when we walk into Dojo, a nightclub owned by Dax's parents, with an entire upper level dedicated to him and his friends, none who are of age. Well, maybe a few are. He does allow his fellow lacrosse players to lead the occasional strays up from the actual nightclub downstairs.

I thought to ask Jules if his parents were aware of this added space but decided it's another one of those unspoken rich kid things. Nobody wants their kids causing a drunken scene or getting caught on candid camera outside of paparazzi-powered venues, so might as well give them their own fake IDs, not that they're needed, and private hush-hush rooms, right?

I legit believe that's the thought process some of these parents use when it comes to their privileged spawns.

Give us what we want and out of your way we stay.

Kicking off the weekend by making an appearance, if not ending the night here, is yet another routine in the summer socialite party scheme. 'Club Friday,' I'm told, continues throughout the academic year where house parties die down in favor of school events, among other things that provide the guys and girls with the opportunity to one-up their peers.

This is one of those expected evenings I prefer, though. At least here it's more of a moving scene, a larger mix of people, rather than the same faces as always. Here, there's a blended crowd, students from the surrounding schools and others who know a guy who knows a guy who knows Dax.

I can see why everyone enjoys this place. The girls said it was decent, simple, but I'm guessing that was their way of 'warning me' it wouldn't be coated in gold and high-quality silver, because some require such a thing of the places they visit. I know they do, but I happen to like it.

The concept is wide open, the only seating being a continual leather booth-like seat that runs along three full walls, and a few curved couches, closing them in every five or six feet, with small circular tables wedged between them. The back side is left open for the bar, and a short hall that leads to the bathroom.

The lighting is teal blues and purple LED strips, all strung tightly in every crevice of the place, including the rims of the tables.

"Okay, drinks first and then dancing?" Amy, Jules' far more egocentric twin, who is easy to tell apart as her hair is cropped short and dyed blonde, suggests with a smile.

"Yes, let's go for it!" Cali hops up first and is quick to lead the way.

The bartender, who she went home with last weekend, zooms right over, but she loses his attention when Amy squeezes her way to the front.

I don't know what she orders us, but when something yellow with ice is passed over, I accept.

The girls get through two and are ready to dance, so I retire my half-full cocktail on the countertop and move to join them, but as I step away from the bar, my eyes are pulled to the entrance, right as a familiar sight slips through.

Beretta and Arsen lead the group, and visible over the curve of their shoulders, Ransom.

He never gave his name, but Scott provided three the night they showed up, so that must be his. I guess I was a little too distracted to realize it when he was standing right in front of me.

Their arrival, however, isn't the *familiar* I'm talking about.

It's the girl they enter with, the Sammie chick from the other night, and she's all smiles, with hair that walks a fine line between *I was screwed in the back seat* and *I didn't know we'd be in a convertible with the top down.* I don't know what they drive, so who knows the truth. She very well could have been fucked on fancy leather for all I know.

What I most definitely *do* know is Miss Sammie... is wearing the very dress the boys at her back slipped off of me not ten hours ago.

She leans against the countertop, and when she looks over, she pretends she's just realized I was standing here. "Oh, hey, Jameson."

"Sammie. Nice dress."

A chortled, swallowed laugh sounds behind her, but I don't look to them.

Sammie runs her hands down the sides of the gray mini. She looks over her shoulder at who, I don't know or care, and a superior smile covers her glossy lips. "It was a gift."

That drink I set down, I pick right back up, lifting it in cheers. "It was on sale."

As I turn away, I mouth 'what the fuck' to myself, but I don't have to question myself or them for long, because the girls are now joined by the guys on the dance floor and Scott is looking mighty fine tonight in his button-up and Balmains. Sure, he's as pretentious as they come, but at least he's far too into himself to ever want more from me. And he's pretty to look at.

He slips right up without invitation, wrapping his arms around the waist of my navy dress, and pulls me in.

We dance for several songs, the crowd growing fuller around us, and partners beginning to blend. The moment Scott is distracted, facing another girl from the group, a hand slides around my abdomen from behind, and hauls me backward, spinning me away from my friends and walking me forward a few steps.

I attempt to look over my shoulder, but pause as, in the same second, Arsen appears before me.

He doesn't speak, but pushes my hair over my shoulder, and the fingers along my stomach span out.

My core muscles clench in response, causing a small frown to slip over my forehead.

"So, it's Jameson, huh?" Beretta's low baritone fills my ear, his free hand landing on my upper ribs and pressing me into his body even more. "I like."

My eyes flick around the room, but everyone's so dazed, they've yet to notice us among the masses.

"Yeah?" I snap at Beretta, and Arsen swiftly brings himself closer, forcing me to take a deep breath. "Same way you 'liked' the dress?"

Beretta's smile is evident in his words. "I never said I didn't like it. I said it wasn't the one for you, and it wasn't." His taunting chuckle fans over my neck, his grip teasingly tight. "It was the one for *her*."

I tear away, slipping from between the two, only to spin on my heels and face them. "Classy. Now if you're done with me, go find another toy to play with, maybe one who's interested. I'm—"

I bump into someone, my head tilting up and to the side.

Wicked blue eyes slam into mine.

Ransom.

His large hands find my hips, and in one swift move, I'm spun and tugged into the firm lines of his chest. Yes, I can envision the hard cuts beneath his cotton dress shirt from the hasty graze.

"You're what..." he mocks, an arrogant brow lifting as he slowly dips closer. "Otherwise... *occupato?*"

I swallow, lifting my chin and putting a foot of space between us.

"So, you're a lip-reading stalker then?"

The corner of his mouth twitches but that's all I get.

I flick my eyes to the ceiling and shove past.

I'm surprised when they don't follow, and completely *unsurprised*, when my friends do.

All at once, the girls fire off questions.

"Um, hello. What was that?" Jules' bloodshot eyes widen in the fluorescent lights.

I force a short laugh, glaring at the bartender's expression when I ask for an ice water.

"I bumped into him," I lie, dropping a twenty on the counter out of spite, winking thanks at the chick behind it. "He told me to watch where I was going... and that I had a nice ass."

I chuckle at myself, and the girls gape.

Thankfully they're too tipsy to have noticed I was the fresh fruit in the center of a double-layered cake moments before that, and as Dax, Scott, and a few others slip up beside us, the entire interaction is forgotten.

I dance with Scott for several more songs, and when

his hands fall to my hips, my eyes close. Suddenly, it's not Scott's hands on me at all, but larger, rougher ones.

Or so my mind plays tricks.

It also convinces me not to spoil the sight until everyone decides they're ready to eat, and the time comes to leave.

We head straight out of the building, stumbling along the sidewalk and toward Cali's driver's car.

A loud revved engine demands attention, and several of us search the late-night fog.

Jules and Amy push me aside to slide in, the others following, but I stand there, gripping the edge of the door, the man waiting to shut it inching it closer in hopes that I'll soon climb inside.

Since my vision fails me, I join them in the back, and not two minutes down the one-way street, we're walking barefoot up the iron spiral walkway that leads to the entrance of Ocean's Pasa, a restaurant on the coastline that stayed open strictly for our service tonight.

The guys head straight for the private, dome-encased balcony and drop into our seats right as the chef comes out to say her hellos, but we girls hang back outside a moment longer.

They're perched and ready for a full-on photo op, duck lips, ass pops and all, as they prepare to bribe the busboy to be their cameraman, but I offer to be the one behind the lens instead. Of course, no one protests.

I snap a few shots, quickly passing back their phones and they slip inside, Cali's hand grabbing mine to tow me along, but once again, the roar of an engine purrs my name.

I pull free, glancing down the street, and this time, I find its culprit.

A sleek little sports car, matte black in color, rolls by me.

Tucked behind the wheel is Arsen, Beretta in the passenger seat, and when I look into the back, Ransom.

Ransom by his lonesome.

It's dark, but I swear all three sets of eyes flick up, finding mine through the darkness.

"Jameson, come on!" Cali calls.

I cut a quick glance her way, and when I look back to the street, it's empty.

With a low rasped laugh, I let go of the railing and make my way inside. Scott pulls the chair at his side out for me, so I round the table and lower myself into it.

He leans forward, grabbing the drink he must have ordered for me, and places it in my hand.

I accept, and he drapes an arm along the back of my chair as he jumps back into the conversation with his friends.

As I stir the clear liquor with the swizzle stick, the little sports car—a Camaro—flashes in my mind, and a slow smirk finds my lips.

Convertible hair it was.

CHAPTER
Four

I don't know how these girls drink day in and day out.

I literally feel like death rolled over twice and I had a fraction of what they did last night, as is the continual trend.

They like to give me shit about being 'unable to hang' as if such a statement is meant to be an insult. It's not, but they're not being assholes about it; it's safe to say my once elementary school besties realize we're no longer carbon copies of each other personality-wise. Five years apart will do that.

As I drive home from Cali's house, where most of us crashed last night, the music flowing through my speakers dies down, as my mother's weekly call comes through.

I look to the clock and press the button on the wheel to answer.

"Hey, Mom."

"How was your night?"

"You mean you don't want to know about my week as a whole?"

She says nothing and I shake my head. "My night was good, we went to Dojo again, had dinner after."

Same as last Friday, as well as the one before.

"You finished your school shopping?"

I put my blinker on, slowing at the red light. "For the most part, yes."

"Good, good. Gennie should have dropped off your essentials by the time you get in tonight."

"I told you I could get them."

"Nonsense. That's what she was hired for."

Sure, it was.

"So, what time are you meeting Anthony today?" she asks, as if she's unaware when she required, set up, and showed me how to manage a shared calendar.

"I'm supposed to go to his office at one. I think we're eating on the yacht."

"If he's not a gentleman, push him over the edge." My stepdad joins the call. "But make sure it's at the deepest point so the sharks take care of the evidence, huh?"

I roll my eyes, singsonging, "Hi, Dad."

He chuckles. "Your mom says you're staying busy."

As I turn into my cul-de-sac, a frown builds.

I slow, pretty much inching along, my eyes glued to the Tuscan-style home and the lone vehicle taking up the curved driveway.

Parked in front of the house, three doors from mine, sits the black Camaro from last night.

"Jameson?"

"Huh?"

I look to the open shutters on the home, but movement on the grass pulls my attention.

"Jameson, you still there?"

"Sorry." I turn away from the young boy wiping at his knees and face forward. "What did you—"

My eyes shoot wide, and I slam on the brakes.

"Oh shit!" The car jolts, my seat belt locking, as my bumper plays kiss the cat with something.

Someone.

As quickly as I freeze, I snap out of it, unbuckle and stumble from the car, my parents' shouts ignored.

I rush around the hood, my arms nervously bent at my sides.

On the ground is a male figure, curled up and unmoving.

"Holy shit." I drop, scraping my knees on the asphalt. "Oh shit. Oh no. Sir—"

I break off in a scream when I'm lifted from behind and swung in a circle, a loud laugh echoing in my ears.

As I'm lowered, the person playing dead rolls over, serving me a puckish grin.

Whipping around, I find Beretta taking slow, backward steps. He bends, grabbing an old football from the gutter, and my hands fall to my sides as my head tips back.

I release a long exhale, and then dart forward, kicking Arsen in the ribs with last night's heels. He catches my foot, of course, and tugs me down on top of him with a low chuckle.

"Ugh!" I smack at his biceps but knowing I didn't run someone over is such a relief, my forehead falls to his chest.

My car is on, parked in the middle of the street with the door wide open, but all I can manage to do is take a deep breath and push into a sitting position. I shake my head at the quiet, quizzical-eyed boy. "You're a dick."

Beretta's shoes slip into view, and I look up at him. "One that works well, Trouble."

He sticks out his hand.

With a low scowl, I slap my palm into it, allowing him to pull me to my feet.

"And you know this for a fact, do you?" I taunt.

Beretta's smirk is dark and devious and has my mind

swimming into murky waters I have no business being in.

He helps Arsen up next and tosses him the ball behind his back, right as three younger boys, the oldest appearing maybe fifteen or so, rush from the house.

The boys run out into the grass, and he sends the thing sailing.

The kids hop up, attempting to catch it, and each of them falls to the grass in theatrics when they miss.

A small smile finds my lips, but Beretta steps up beside me, so I wipe it away.

"His foster brothers," he offers when I didn't ask. "The couple in this house are damn near seniors, couldn't have kids, so they foster. Arsen's the oldest they've ever taken. He helps them out a lot, so they leave him to do as he pleases."

Cali had said they moved here not long after I left.

Has he been in the foster system that entire time or is this new?

"JAMESON JOLE!" booms through my speakers.

"Oh shit!" I rush around the car, leaning inside. "I'm here!"

"And seconds away from my calling Tanner!" my mom threatens. "What happened?!"

My glare swings to the right as Beretta steps up.

"Nothing." I push his face away with my palm when he sticks his head inside the vehicle. "I thought I hit a dog."

I thought I hit a dog?

What the hell?

"What the hell?" my mom drawls.

"Yeah." I force a laugh. "False alarm. I... ran over a ball."

"Two big balls," Beretta whispers, and I flip him off.

"Okay well, next time save us the heart attack and run over anything that places itself in your way, rather than jumping out into the road."

Beretta's brows jump. "Savage."

I frown, yeah, she's dead inside.

"Get home and be quick about it. Do not make the man wait on you. I'm sure you have yet to shower. After all, it is only ten." My mother's voice is slightly teasing, but she can never hide the disapproval completely, not that she has ever tried.

"Ah, yes. Sleep, my one and only." My finger hovers over the 'end call' button. "I'll talk to you later."

"Remember all of your training and do as you must."

"Yes, Mother. Any means necessary, got it."

"And Jameson?" I can picture her standing at the edge of her desk right now, her fingers running over her pearl necklace laying perfectly over her collar.

Kill them with Prada and pearls, she loves to remind me.

"Yeah?"

"Don't be late," my parents say in unison and then the call drops from their end.

I straighten, my hands finding the framing of the door, and look from Arsen, watching me from in front of my hood, to Beretta, who still stands in my way. "I have to go. Stay out of the road."

"I was simply getting a ball overthrown by an eight-year-old. You should work on not getting distracted while driving."

"You should fuck off." I widen my eyes like an asshole.

"Every other day, Trouble, at the very least." He flashes me his naturally perfect teeth. "So, who's Tanner?"

"A bodyguard who tails my sister when the parentals are feeling extra dickish."

"Nice."

"Not really, now move."

He grins but stays planted in the same spot.

I shake my head, sitting back in the seat, and I cut a quick glance around again, realizing they're missing a piece. "Where's your third wheel?"

"His... *parental* is feeling extra *dickish*."

My head snaps toward him and I can't help the small chuckles that escape. This pleases him.

"So, this 'man' you're meeting, who is he?" He folds his arms over his chest, eyeing me with a coy gleam in his hazel eyes. "Better question, does he know you're attracted to three assholes with respectable taste in clubwear?"

"Ha! Goodbye, Beretta." I close the door.

He doesn't stand there and trail my car to find out which house I end up at, which makes me assume they realized where I live before today, but claps his hands, ready for the ball to be thrown his way.

Just like that, their game resumes.

I pull into the garage and step inside, heading for the shower right away. I'm in no hurry, so I throw a deep conditioning treatment on my hair. By the time I'm out, fully dressed, and ready, it's time to leave again.

Before I know it, I'm gliding into a reserved parking spot, slipping from my car, and climbing a half dozen steps toward a seventeen-story glass building with a wicked ocean view.

Walking into Admiral Law is equivalent to the swimwear segment of a beauty pageant, all eyes on me, judging and sizing me up at a glance... as they do every time I stroll in. They know why I'm here, or at least they know it's not for a conference or consultation.

It helps that it's only the main partners and their assistants here on the weekends and not the full staff. Regardless, I'm here every week, a rewind and repeat mirage of myself with the ever-requested flushed lips, 'look at me' big barrel curls, and borderline Elle Woods wannabe wardrobe—gag. Add in how I'm the only body allowed to slip right past the Valde desks, and crystal-clear understanding is the result.

Still, I enter with my head held high, smile bright and never waver, as my mother coached.

Okay, I guess the entire process is full-on pageant mode—thank you to my fifth-grade nanny for the small, horrifying experience.

As I tap my knuckle on the large russet double doors, it's instantly opened from the other side.

Anthony smiles, reaching for my hand. "I've told you, sweetheart. You never have to knock."

My lips curve and I offer a one-shoulder shrug as I allow him to lead me closer.

He kisses my cheek, his lips lingering there a moment before he draws back to take me in further. "You look stunning, as always."

"Your suit's not so bad either."

A deep, low chuckle leaves him, and he leads me toward the cherrywood table in the corner. "That's nice to hear, considering it only comes off for bed."

I pull my lips in, and he nods, his chin falling slightly, but his eyes stay on mine. "I'm sorry, that was... inappropriate."

A demure grin slips over his face, but I don't buy it.

He's a successful, respected, and incredibly handsome twenty-nine-year-old man with a hefty bank account. There's no way he's timid with a woman.

"Hardly." I paint on a flirty smile. "And I get it, you're here more than you're not."

His hand still holding mine, he lowers us into the chairs. "Will that be a problem?"

"There's nothing wrong with being hardworking." I shake my head.

"I don't want you to see me as neglectful." He gauges my reaction, but I'm trained in the art of 'smile now, pout later.' Not that I will.

"I lived with not one, but *two* career-driven parents. I'm used to late-night dinners and canceled family vacations." I push my long brown hair over my shoulders, and his ocean eyes fall to my neck.

I know why I have to marry this man.

I know his business will boom once my name is tied to his.

My parents hinted at a second location for Filano Law, which would mean Admiral Law would be no more; they're already ruling over the East Coast, which is why we moved in the first place, and it seems Anthony will soon lead the way on the West.

I wonder if his business partner is aware of this?

Regardless, it would be negligent of me to pretend far more risqué reasons don't exist—arm candy goes a long way in the world of benefit dinners and government balls.

Slowly, he brings his gaze back to mine, a smile on his salmon-colored lips. "On that note, we won't be making it to the yacht today. I took the liberty of ordering in for us."

Right as he shares the news, a light tap sounds on the outside of the door and he calls for them to enter.

Four people usher in a cart swiftly pushed by one as the others make quick work of setting up a station for us to eat.

I'm not surprised when a bleeding steak with fresh roasted vegetables is placed in front of Anthony. It's exactly what I'd order for him if he were ever to run late and require my doing so, as it's the exact meal he's chosen every time we've gone out.

I expect a pile of sauce-drowned pasta or fresh risotto to be lowered onto my setting, but what I get is a pile of greens lacking any sort of dressing, not to mention the best part of a dreaded salad—fresh baked croutons! I'm convinced it's simply a starter, but as the group swiftly grabs their things and prepares to exit, I'm reminded that false hope sucks, just as this lunch is about to.

The woman who placed it before me sneaks an apologetic smile, begging me not to question the meal, so this time, I won't.

The rest of the meal is spent with me savoring cherry tomatoes while burying leaves of kale in the napkins, and Anthony stuck on his phone.

My cheek is kissed as I exit, and I rush out so my stomach doesn't decide to growl and give me away in his presence.

As I step inside the house, my sister is just emerging from her room.

"Hey." She lights a cigarette—her meal for the afternoon—and falls back on the couch, pointing a mocking grin at my outfit.

"Don't."

I quickly tear the itchy blazer from my body, tossing it to the floor, only to pick it back up, knowing if I don't, Gennie will be forced to when she gets here later.

"I was only going to ask how tea with the queen went?"

I flip her off and she giggles, stretching her legs along the cushions.

"A package came for you." She blows smoke rings into the air. "I put it on your bed."

With a huff, I tear a piece of French bread from the loaf I hid in the oven last night and make my way to my room.

On my comforter, a large rectangular box with a

blinging silver bow sits.

A small smile tugs at my lips as I pull on the silken ribbon.

I slip it from the ends and remove the lid.

My brows snap together when the item is revealed.

It's not a pastel or pallid.

It's a slinky, long-sleeved plunge neck dress that's ruched throughout. And red.

A deep, valiant red.

"Your favorite color, and a mighty contrast from the First Lady shit a certain fiancé-to-be sends over." Monti steps inside, lowering herself on the chaise at the foot of my bed.

I scoff, running my fingers over the delicate, daring piece. Gently lifting it from the box, I spin toward the mirror to hold it up in front of my body.

Without trying it on, I already know it will be a perfect fit, tight in all the right places and teasingly flashy. The fold-over dip that runs high on the left thigh is provocative and tempting on its own, and creates a flare of excitement within me, one that has me pulling in a long, full breath and holding it.

Monti comes up beside me, her eyes on the dress through the mirror as she whispers in a dreary tone, "It's not from him, is it?"

It takes me several seconds, but I meet her gaze.

"Who else would it be from?"

CHAPTER Five

*W*alking into school is far less exciting than the start of senior year should be.

Maybe it's because the year of possibilities and wonder that helps pave the path that follows is pointless for an eighteen-year-old girl who has the next decade fully mapped out for her.

As an honor student, like a solid eighty-seven percent of this school as well as my last, I have only three required classes, so the rest of my time is filled with pointless extracurriculars to help fluff my portfolio—again, pointless.

It does, however, help pass the time, and with the way summer got old fast, it's better this than that. Or at least that's the speech I give myself throughout the day, each and every time the desire to chop my own head off seeps in.

"Cali, what happened at your last party?" Amy asks, a bit of an edge to her voice.

My eyes snap to her.

"You were there, were you not?" Cali glances up from her phone briefly.

"I left early," she snaps.

Cali only shrugs, setting her phone beside her on

the tabletop.

"People said there was a blackout," Amy pushes further. "And guess who has been staring over here for the last twenty minutes?" She seems as equally annoyed as she does pleased. "I wonder why that would be?"

Cali's fork hovers over a slice of cucumber, her head jerking in the direction Amy indicated, and most of us around the table, including myself, follow.

Sure enough, there they are, tucked in the corner near the door.

Ransom is leaning back against the table, his legs lazily stretched in front of him, knees bent; Beretta straddles the bench seat at his side, and Arsen sits on the opposite side.

All three wear a frown of some sort, *all three* pointed this way.

Are there others around them? Sure, but they aren't the focus right now.

Beretta's eyes meet mine. While the frown stays strong, he delivers a quick wink, and I turn back to find Amy staring.

She quickly flicks her dull brown eyes away, but I don't. I wait her out, and her attention comes right back, this time with a frigid smile curling her bright pink lips.

The thing about Amy is... well, she's a bitch. She likes to state the obvious to make people uncomfortable, pretends her conversations are all random, so she can make sure others are aware of whatever it is she chooses to share, the kick her while she's down type. She likes gossip, loves attention, and loathes competition, not that she sees me as hers.

She's the kind of girl I make a point to avoid.

Pretty little pretenders' stakes are always razor sharp, within reach, and more often than not, shooting for the spine.

"You'll never know if you don't ask."

All heads snap toward me and Amy blanches.

"What?" She slowly straightens.

"You want to know why they're staring..." I lift a single shoulder, bringing my latte to my lips. "Ask."

"Ask." Her head has a bit of a roll, going for sassy, but her frustration is unmistakable, and she knows it. It only irritates her more. "You're the one who 'bumped' into them at Dojo, *you* ask."

My eyes narrow. "If I cared, I would."

A loud, mocking laugh slips past her lips, but when mine doesn't follow, the edges of her eyes tighten the teeniest bit. "Yeah right..."

I cut a quick glance around the table. It's the same people from summer, plus or minus a few who returned earlier this week from Paris. Curiosity draws their future Botoxed faces tight.

How will such a conversation end?

They can't read me, and I find that entertaining.

My lips begin to quirk, and not a moment later, a loud scoff leaves Scott. He glances from Dax to Amy to me.

He shakes his head, eliminating the space between us. "Man, fuck them." He throws one leg over the seat, his knee now knocking with mine under the table. "Let them have their fantasies," he says as if they could never fit in the world these people live in.

Amy and I meet eyes again, and the doubt flickering in hers pisses me off, but not as much as the inquisition behind them intrigues me.

What is it you're searching for, Miss Priss?

I hold her gaze for longer than she's comfortable with, then slowly draw mine to the boys of the hour and wait.

It takes several seconds, seconds I'm convinced are purposeful, and then Ransom's eyes are pinned to mine.

With a flick of my finger, I call him over.

"Oh my god, what are you doing?" Cali's panic is hidden behind her hand. "Jameson, he's going to cover you in your coffee."

I'll admit, my pulse jumps at her words; she knows him better than me, right? Still, I don't take my eyes off Ransom's.

No one knows about our few, short meetings, other than the five seconds they saw us speak at the club, which I covered up, and the people I met mere hours ago have no sense of what I'm about, so, yeah. I'm sure I come off every bit the overconfident girl their twisted brows insinuate they see me as in this moment.

To be honest, I half figure I am and wholly expect the guy to turn away and ignore me because who the hell am I? The kicker, though, is the hint of the sassy smirks dawning each of their lips. They're waiting to let them free and will the *moment* I fail to get Ransom to oblige, but those little grins are guaranteed to backfire as my sole reaction would be laughter, because again... who the hell am I and why would he come at my call?

Only Ransom doesn't snub me.

He pushes to his feet, and without so much as breaking eye contact, stalks this way in all his six-four sexiness.

Amy sits up straight, a weary expression twisting her face, somewhat mirroring the others around us, while I lift my elbow to the table and press my chin into my open palm.

Scott shifts closer.

The table grows tenser.

Ransom steps up behind me without a care.

His hands lock around the edge of the thick wood at my sides, and he bends, blocking Scott from me completely as he brings his mouth near my cheek.

"What can I do for you, Trouble?" He doesn't care enough to quiet his deep voice but allows whoever wants to listen in to do just that.

I tip my head backward, now inadvertently resting on the wide stretch of his shoulder. "You're staring this way." I don't point out how he's breaking the little rule their note conveyed.

"I am."

My lips quirk with his instant answer. "Why?"

His light eyes shift between mine. "I'm angry."

I cross my legs beneath the table, swiftly flicking my gaze toward Amy. I'm tempted to throw out her name but decide against it.

"Care to share your reasoning?"

Her eyes narrow and I move mine back to the entertainment of the hour.

Ransom pretends to mull over the question, and when he speaks, his words are delivered in a seductively coy tone. "I expected to find a wicked hourglass of red waiting for me... but that didn't happen."

Well, okay then.

There's the confirmation I didn't need, but confirmation, nonetheless. They sent me the dress.

Amy's frown deepens, even more so when heat sneaks up my neck.

She has no clue what he means; she couldn't possibly, but she sure as hell wants to.

"Damn disgrace, don't you think? Expecting a shade of the devil with long, dangerous... *forks* to show itself only to be disappointed by the sight of a crisp, blank canvas." He shifts the slightest bit, the small waves along his forehead grazing mine as he plays me like a matchbox, striking his lips across my cheek, leaving a low burn in their wake. "Shame really, it's my least favorite color."

My fingers twitch around my cup, and I freeze when

Ransom dips forward, the sharp definition of his jaw and stretch of his neck pulling my attention, the way his Adam's apple shifts as he opens his mouth. His mouth that now closes over the peaked swirl of whipped cream at the top. The ache that sparked grows, catching fire.

And then extinguishes.

He's gone, and I swear everyone at the table hisses a cut-short orgasm.

Following his exit, my eyes lift to Amy's.

"Well." I take a quick drink as an excuse to swallow. "There you go."

Thankfully the bell rings two seconds later and everyone pushes to their feet.

I don't miss the way Scott's gaze falls to my outfit as I slip away—a *crisp* all-white jumpsuit, even my leather slingback shoes share the same color or lack thereof, as Ransom chose to point out.

As I step into my cooking class, I'm greeted by the teacher's aide, a dark-haired guy I've yet to see until today who is channeling his inner Adam Levine and killing it.

He grins, holding the paper in his hands close to his trim chest. "Jameson, I bet."

"You should consider gambling."

He chuckles. "Yeah, my dad would love that. Station four."

With a quick thanks, I head where I'm instructed, and not two minutes later, Ransom, Arsen, and Beretta slip inside.

Arsen slips onto the chair at my side while the other two continue on to the far back corner station.

His entire body shifts, fully facing mine, and he stares, straight-faced, directly into my eyes. He waits for me to squirm, but instead, I lift a brow and he faces forward before his grin slips over his lips.

I shake my head, fighting my own, and look to the front of the room.

I try to focus on the teacher when he begins to speak, but I can't stop cutting quick glances toward my partner.

Or tracing the curves of Arsen's shoulders beneath his T-shirt.

With his forearms flat on the desk, one hand molded over his other closed fist, he leans forward, stretching the finely made cotton to its finest, fullest edge.

His skin is tan and like the mahogany in his dark blond hair, likely a gift from the sun.

He looks over his shoulder, the opposite way of where I'm sitting, toward his friends, and his neck shows its strength.

He's peeled a dress from my body.

He's tugged me on top of him.

But I have yet to witness the depth I imagine his voice holds.

Is it low and gravelly or crisp and clear?

Oh my god, why does it matter?!

I place my elbows on the tabletop and use my hands as blinders, blocking out any and all things from right to left.

The teacher has us watching a ridiculous film about the safeties of the kitchen, anyone with a decent set of parents or solid caretaker should already know, so I slip from class and head to the bathroom.

I text my sister to see how her first college class went, and all she sends back is a snooze emoji, so I know she doesn't have the time to help me pass mine. Stuffing my phone in my pocket, I step out the door, and come face-to-face with Beretta.

I jump, but quickly rebalance. "Okay. You really need to dial back this whole Joe Goldberg thing. It's getting a little weird now."

"Weird would be admitting I know what color your bedroom's painted."

My brows furrow, a subtle hint of panic curling in my abdomen and his far too mindful ass senses it.

His grin widens. "Ask me, Trouble, see if I'm bluffing."

"And give you the satisfaction of answering? Negative."

I shoulder past him, and his laughter looms in my wake. I swear it follows me clear into the hall, leading to the classroom, or maybe it's an illusory echo that's bounding off the walls as it cuts off completely when a tall, shadowy figure slips into my path.

Electric blue eyes collide with mine.

And then they snap over my shoulder, right as a hand closes around my mouth.

I glare, my fingers flying up to grip the ones forcing me quiet.

Arsen slips from the class door a few feet away, pausing just outside of it, my bag hanging from his fingers.

Ransom's strong and sturdy chest pushes into mine, driving me against Beretta at my back. "Come with us."

My 'fuck you' is a muffled, broken, and pretty pointless protest since they can't make it out, but I think he interprets my knee slamming into his nuts for what it is.

He growls, his left hand bolting down to grip his cock. He's so close, my outfit so thin, that the shape of his knuckles can be felt against my pelvis and my ass cheeks clench.

The palm over my lips twitches.

"I'll rephrase." Ransom's covert gaze sharpens. "Come with us or we'll post a spicy little picture on social media." When my brows furrow, he adds, "One taken in a dressing room bigger than my bedroom... right as a certain dress hits the floor..."

At first, I don't react and his hand disappears in his

pocket.

He pulls his phone toward his face, chuckling as I reach out to smack it away, a smug expression taking over him, yet something much darker is hidden in his liquid eyes.

"That's what I thought. Now." He steps back, tipping his head. "Close your eyes."

I attempt to yank free once more, but lips press against my ear in the same moment, and my body freezes in response.

"Do what he says, Trouble... or we might have to serve you some."

My toes curl in my heels, and I tell myself it's in uncertainty.

This is kind of fucked up, isn't it?

They're strangers and talk about coming on strong.

Not that I'm not used to it, with privilege comes, well, a warped idea that you can do as you please... but I'm not getting an 'above all' attitude from this group. More anarchist than anything.

But they're not murderers, right?

Even my mother would agree there's nothing wrong with hanging out with new people, granted they'd likely make the 'do not engage' list. And I *have* complained enough about days blending together. The fact is, now that school is in session, it's guaranteed to get worse until it's over, and the end begins.

What's a few hours with them going to hurt? Nobody learns anything during the first week of school anyway, and I've already submitted my summer essays for all my AP courses. I know what the reading schedule is.

Let's not forget the supposed picture. So really, this is not me agreeing.

This is me doing as my mother instructed and avoiding scandal by practicing her favorite motto.

By any means necessary.

As if sensing my crumbling resolve, that, let's be honest, isn't all that strong to begin with, Ransom's expression grows a cocky kind of confident, but he holds in his smirk well enough.

I lower my hands, latching on to Ransom's shirt, and close my eyes, even though I'm not sure what purpose it serves.

As quick as I do, he removes his hold, and only after they're sure I won't peek, does the hand leave my mouth.

There's a shift around me, a slight swoosh of rubbing fabrics, and then I'm lifted off the ground, cradled like a bride and bouncing around with forward steps.

I can't say whose arms I'm in, but I'm not sure it matters at the moment, so I simply hold on without thinking about it.

The sun warms my skin minutes later, letting me know we've stepped into the parking lot.

It's not until my ass is gently placed on cooled leather that I grow antsy, but before I decide to do as I want, the command is whispered around me.

"All good now, Trouble."

My eyes pop open, instantly snapping from one to the next.

Beretta winks from the passenger seat as Arsen pulls from the curbside.

We roll from the parking lot, the four of us tucked inside the two-door sports car, and as we pull onto Main Street, the top begins to fold back.

I trail it, watching as it disappears behind a sheet of metal, and run my fingers along the edge of the matte black paint.

A low laugh leaves me.

Ransom, who sits beside me, catches it, raising a brow,

but I leave him to whatever it is his mind provides.

I fish a rubber band from my bag and tie my hair back.

Here's to hoping they're not serial killers.

CHAPTER
Six

*T*he terms of my not yet, but future engagement, are simple *and* sensible. Both Anthony and I are to live our lives as normal until my graduation, then we'll link up officially.

We're to get to know each other slowly, while still doing as we please over the course of this year, with only one rule, no making headlines.

Unlike my sister, I have no room for failure. She might have popped a bottle to the fine print of her arrangement before *and* after breaking the single rule, but her situation was different. She had a fall girl.

Me.

But I'm the youngest, the last.

I have no room to fall.

When my parents talked to me about taking her place, I didn't argue or push back. I knew it was a possibility the day they sat us down to tell us Monti had become a tool of negotiations—they worded it differently, but we understood it for what it was.

My sister and I are similar in many ways, and polar opposites in others. She is a ball of feelings and vulnerability where I am not. She's all about finding her soul mate, running from one to the next on her way, where I can't fathom why anyone would ever wish to fall victim to emotions they can't control.

Simply stated, the girl is a mess, and it doesn't help that country is her music genre of choice. In my opinion, that was her downfall. I mean, can anyone honestly listen to a single country song without daydreaming or crying or having a literal mental breakdown? If they say yes, I'd call them a liar. Monti has that shit on repeat.

We do share a desire for excitement. The difference is I can rein mine in, she can't. Hers is driven by love and romance and thinking about such things makes me want to vomit.

When my mom crushed her spirit without batting a lash, we all silently suspected the ancient saying would ring true when it came to my whimsical sister.

There's no such thing as a sure thing.

She proved their safety measures right, and so the backup plan was in full effect—I was on the next plane home.

Growing up, my parents were unlike any of the others I remember. While they could enjoy a night or weekend out like Cali and Jules did, they weren't concerned with social order or country clubs and would rather be working than all else, including hanging out with me or my sister.

They would preach the importance of education, of independent thinking and demanded we stand up for ourselves where others were concerned. Nobody was to take us for weak, and what made us even stronger was our understanding of the world we lived in, one where our parents knew best.

And they do.

My mother came from the south side with nothing and now owns a forty-four-story skyscraper.

The day of my flight back to California, my mom drove me to the airport herself and left me with what she called her 'wistful notion.' I was instructed to 'sow my wild oats' as my old-school mother put it—gross, coming from her.

She knows I'm not a virgin, that I did my thing and had some fun throughout high school in Naples. She's the one who took me to get the Depo-Provera shot after all, but the only reason I have the freedom I do is because I am my mother's daughter and she's aware of that fact.

I have never had a boyfriend and I have no desire for one.

I never date as dating goes, but I'll hang out and go along for the ride. I go to dances and events, never alone, but that's where it ends.

Three to four 'hang outs' was all I allowed.

The first is an ice breaker, a fun and flirty night where you size up your companion. The second, when things go well, makes the curiosity rise. The third, sexual tension builds, and the fourth, you either give in to it or go home.

Either way, after that, you only see them again in groups, because that moment you go for the fifth, they want a quiet night in, with a movie to make things more personal.

That's not my vibe.

My mom always says you reap what you sow and it's true.

My family knows firsthand what happens when emotions take control, which is why I take after my mom and cut them from the equation.

It's the exact reason my parents' plan is perfect for me.

To hide the heart is to salvage the soul.

I learned that from my real father, and he didn't even have to be here to teach it to me.

"You're awfully quiet, Trouble."

"As are you three." I look to Beretta in the passenger seat. "Don't pretend you want me to annoy you by asking where we're going, all so you can say '*you'll see*' or '*wouldn't you like to know*' or something else along those lines."

His grin is widely idiotic. "I like you."

"Yeah." I nod. "You constantly being in my face sort of hinted to that."

An easy laugh escapes him, and he and Arsen share a small smile.

Ransom looks my way, so I give him my attention.

He holds my gaze steady for a long moment before he holds a vape pen between us. I make no move to accept, so he pulls it to his lips and looks away.

I have no idea what I've gotten myself into by leaving school with them today, but it's definitely not the smartest thing I've ever done. I've already done it though, so there's no point in dwelling on it.

All I can do is sit back and enjoy the fresh air.

We're on the road for well over an hour and when they finally pull over, it's onto the side of a long, winding, deserted road overlooking the ocean.

Beretta tries to grab my bag as we climb out, but I keep it tucked tight to my side. He laughs as the three lead me down a stairway of cement steps, half hidden by overgrown poppies. They curve to the right at the end, leading us toward a beach cave.

I slow, running my eyes along the spongy-looking rock arch, the opening, the shape of a gemstone; the inside, a shadowy pit of who knows what. There are a lot of these around here, different shapes and sizes, in various lengths from the ocean, some even half full of water.

The guys trek up the small trail to the entrance, turning toward me, and while it looks different from one to the next, humors marked on each of their faces.

Their premature judgment is misplaced but

understandable.

I'm wearing solid white and my heels cost more than all of their shoes combined. My hoops are large and solid gold, and yes, visually speaking, I can't deny I've got full-on spoiled, rich girl vibes, but I like to think that's only at first glance.

That's not who I am... but I can't expect them to know this.

I slip my shoes from my feet and climb up as they did.

I'm pretty much check-marking each and every line on the long list of 'never dos' by walking into a dark cave on an isolated beach, off a deserted road, with three guys my friends claim are crazy. Yet here I am, being a dumbass.

As I approach, the stereotypical expressions I had thought I first spotted reveal their true selves, and surefire grins curl their mouths.

Beretta slides backward, pushing his body into Arsen's chest and Arsen's arm comes over his shoulder. "Lead the way."

I turn to Ransom, who has yet to look away.

He glides closer, tugs my hair tie from my head and watches as my self-made curls fall around me, his middle finger flicking along the strap of my shoulder bag.

"She ties her hair back without a mirror, lets her silk soak in the muddy sand, and carries her own things." His tone is low, intensely sarcastic, yet somehow not mocking. "What kind of social princess are you?"

"Hm." I tip my head, playing along. "Wouldn't you like to know."

Beretta's knuckles brush my collarbone as he seizes a long lock, wraps it around his fingers, and gives a gentle tug. "I sure as fuck would."

I don't turn his way, and Ransom's haughty smirk

grows.

Making sure his chest brushes mine, he slips past me into the cave.

I follow behind, maneuvering around the narrow entrance, and my eyes widen with surprise.

It's not as dark and desolate as I imagined, but, in fact, quite the opposite.

A large diamond-like opening at the surface's top allows the afternoon sun to illuminate the space. Giant tree trunks, both cut and carved, are scattered all around, two creating a couch-like shape, the others offering simple stump-style seating. In the middle, a hole was dug, a deep cast iron crescent embedded there. It's lined with large stones, ashes speckled in the center as proof of recent use.

I don't have to look their way to know they're watching me, possibly waiting for that moment when my nose will lift high into the air or scrunch in distaste, but that's not going to happen. I lower myself onto the longest one and kick my feet up on the opposite end.

"I take it you guys hang here often?"

Slowly, they drop onto seats of their own.

"Maybe." Beretta grins, tearing into an M&M's packet with his teeth. "Or maybe it's where we bury bodies."

"Ah, yes, how could I forget, I became your target." I speak with playful energy. "How dare I watch you from across the room."

"More like, 'she dared to watch us from across the room'."

I laugh at Beretta's Shakespearean flair. "How bold."

"How rare."

My laughter fades and I look away to simmer the sudden curving of my lips.

"So." I cross my legs. "Which one of you looked me up

on social media?"

With unhurried movements, my gaze skitters across the three.

"What makes you think we did?" Beretta nods.

"I *know* you did. It's the exact reason I was threatened with a photo I know doesn't exist." I speak with confidence. "No phones came out to play in that glam room, I'm sure of it. You looked me up, found nothing... nothing but a way to get me here, and here we are."

"Odd for a girl your age."

I look to Beretta. "What are you, fifty?"

He ignores me, offering me some candy and shrugging when I shake my head to decline. "Your friends document everything from doctored morning pics to slinky new night numbers before bed, and you, Jameson Filano, have not a single account, on any platform, and there are no more than a handful of pictures of you on other people's socials. Boring ones at amusement parks and group gala shots."

"So, you are stalkers," I tease, humor lighting both my tone and expression. I know it's simply the way it goes. Everyone watches everything on social media; it's what it's there for. To make you feel seen.

"Social media is a shark tank. You swim, it's only a matter of time before you're bit in the ass."

"Do you not enjoy that?" Beretta's grin is broad and mischievous.

I roll my eyes, and Ransom leans forward, resting his elbows on his knees. He cocks his head, licks his lips, and as he desires, my attention becomes his.

With each passing second, his unblinking blues prod deeper with an unreadable intent, his words delivered slow but sure. "You're smart, careful and controlled. You're keeping your rep clean for a reason, I'm sure. Surprised you came."

"Surprised you wanted me to."

"Surprised you almost let your friends find us in your dressing room."

My eyes move between his, and his body dips closer, the corded muscles of his neck stretching as he does. "You weren't exactly in your right mind, were you?"

I hold still, staring into the sharp gaze demanding the truth of what he knows is an undeniable fact.

I had a momentary lack of sanity.

My lips curl into a smile before I can stop them. "Got that pen?"

His coarse chuckle is delayed, low and perfectly pleased.

Ransom pulls the Stiizy from his pocket and passes it off to Arsen, who pushes to his feet, walks over, and bends in front of me. He holds it near my lips, just far enough to force me to come to him.

I do, and his grin is just as satisfied as the boys behind him.

Unexpectedly, he tugs his shirt from his back, and my focus falls to his naked chest, holding there until he gives a teasing flex. I only get a hint of his smirk before his shirt is gently tossed over my face.

As it falls to my chest, he nods to the makeshift armrest, so I thank him, ball the thick cotton up and tuck it beneath my head as a cushion.

I know they're toying with me, testing my reactions, and that's fine. They can think whatever they want; it makes no difference to me. It doesn't change my reality or theirs, whatever theirs may be, but it does make me wonder if this is the way their game begins.

Do they entice, give a gift, then get inside?

So, I ask, and I think they're surprised by the question as all three silently stare.

After a few moments, Beretta decides to answer. "Believe it or not, Trouble, Sammie got the dress so we could see your reaction, and for no other reason than that. And she needed no enticing."

I roll my eyes. Of course, she didn't. It's like I said, rich girls love bad boys, even if only in secret.

I don't know if he's telling the truth or not and honestly, it makes no difference, yet to see what his response will be, I ask, "Why would you care how I reacted?"

"Because even though you gawked our way for half of that party—"

"I did not gawk."

"—you didn't try to get our attention. You didn't drop onto your back the moment we slipped into your dressing room, *and* you didn't find a way to slip us your phone number while pretending to act annoyed at the club."

"They really do that?"

"All the time." He laughs. "We're dirty little secrets they wish to have but refuse to tell their friends about."

I flick my eye to the blue sky above. "Now that you put it that way, it sounds about right."

Pathetic, but right.

Cali and Scott both said they use the whole blackout bit to hook up, so I'm sure there are many more 'Sammies' where she came from. Minus the dresses, or so Beretta claims.

We don't talk much after that, and before I know it, we're pulling up to my house, my car somehow already parked in the driveway.

My gaze slices to theirs, but all I'm met with are blank expressions.

I shake my head, fighting a grin as I gather my things,

but I don't ask questions.

Arsen steps out, and instead of lifting his seat, he reaches for my hands and motions for me to step up on the edge of the car. I do and his free hand finds my hips, gently lifting and setting me on the ground.

He pushes my hair from my shoulder, winks and slips back inside.

"Well, I owe you guys a thanks," I say with my eyes on my house, slowly looking their way once more.

Ransom's head falls back on the headrest, a single brow lifting. "For?"

I pull my lipstick out of the side pocket of my bag, quickly gliding it along my lips. I rub them together with a light pop and tap my palm on the frame of the door, redirecting their eyes up to mine.

"Good night, boys."

I turn and walk away.

Inside, I toss the little black tube in the air, catching it on its way down, and head toward my bedroom, but before I reach my door, my sister appears, leaning a shoulder on the frame of her own.

"Well, look at that." She crosses her arms with a grin. "She does smile."

Was I smiling?

I keep my shoulders straight. "Smiles are not rare, dear sister."

"No," she says lightly as I continue past her, but it's not until I reach my room that she adds, "only the real ones."

My muscles freeze, but only for the shortest of seconds, and I jolt forward. Tossing my bag on my dresser, I fly into the bathroom, yank the drawer open, and tear into the small glass box.

In the mirror, I stare at my own eyes, a hazel-like

color not all that different from Beretta's, at the maroon liner framing the black painted wing curved along my eyelids, a shade rivaling the natural highlights of Arsen's hair, at my lips... painted a rich, creamy red.

Kiss From The Devil, my go-to shade.

Ransom's favorite color, or so he claimed.

I lift the makeup remover wipe and swipe it over my mouth until every little hint of the lipstick is gone.

What the hell is the matter with me?

They're nobody. Strangers.

I spent the day with strangers.

I shake my head, turn off the light and walk out.

In my room, I open my bedside drawer with a glare and a prolonged exhale.

Two blue pills to the rescue.

CHAPTER
Seven

"**E**arth to Jameson."

My head snaps left, and the girls laugh.

"Girl, what's with you?" Cali passes me my coffee, but before I can grab it from her hands, she pulls back, a nasty frown taking over her face as she stares at the paper cup. "They can't even wipe the edges. If this shit would have dripped on my top, I swear to God."

"It's fine." I stick my hand out farther.

"You sure, because I can totally tell him to make you another one?" She speaks loudly, and I don't have to glance over to know the baristas are looking this way. "The least they can do is give us clean cups."

"As long as all my espresso shots are in there, I'm sure." I wrap my fingers around the lower part of the cup, and though she hesitates a split second, she releases it the next.

The cup is not 'dirty,' it simply has a small drip that slipped from the side when the lid was put on; it happens sometimes when you get extra shots but still want the same amount of frothed milk *and* an indulgent amount of whipped cream.

"Come on, let's go. We're already going to be late for class."

"Speaking of 'class,' remind me again why we agreed to go to your parents' benefit dinner this weekend, Cali?" Jules complains. "You said last week they could fuck off when they demanded your presence."

"That was before I found out my dad's gorgeous, self-righteous business partner would be making a surprise appearance."

"Wait, what?!" Jules grips Cali's elbow, stopping us dead in the center of the promenade. "Why is this the first I'm hearing about this?"

I look from Jules to Cali. "What am I missing?"

"All junior year, Cali was an intern under the guy, her dad's company had set it up. The guy told her he loved her on Christmas Eve, fucked her Christmas Day, and then left on some business trip, completely cutting her off, not twenty-four hours later." Jules looks to Cali.

Cali clears her throat. "And came to my parents' party on Valentine's Day... announcing he had a fiancée."

My jaw drops and the girls both laugh.

"Honestly, I'm over it," Cali swears, sounding as if she's trying to convince herself rather than us, and we start walking again. "He can choke on his future wife's cum for all I care, but that doesn't mean I'm not looking forward to him laying eyes on my birthday present." She wiggles her chest proudly, a boob job, a totally normal gift for an eighteen-year-old high school senior.

"Whatever." Jules sighs. "I guess we'll consider the dinner pre-gaming for the real party later that night. Our makeup and hair will already be semi-done, and we'll get a good buzz on."

Right, the Senior Kickoff, the first party of the official final year of high school, promising to be 'all sorts of epic,' or so the banners suggest.

The lunch bell rings the second we pull into the parking lot, so everyone is already seated or finishing collecting their materials from the kitchen area when I walk into cooking class.

"Look at you, you'll make a great servant one day."

Arsen's glare snaps toward me, but I quickly look away.

Okay, that came out wrong.

Honestly, I don't even know why I said it. Maybe my guard slipped far too much last night and now I'm on edge, I don't know, but that was shitty of me.

I focus on hanging my bag on the hook at the edge of the island-like table design, and with jerky movements, he heads toward the back again to gather the pans and utensils we'll need for today.

In senior cooking class, they leave us alone for the most part. Our grade is determined by how well we execute our menus. I think it's all a ploy for the teachers to see if we're completely silver-spooned or capable of problem-solving, ingenuity, and all that so they can laugh at our expense later when many of us are not.

Arsen comes back with a large bowl, a single whisk, and sets them down harder than necessary. He reaches for the menu, but I snag it first. Tilting my head at him.

He glares.

I narrow my eyes. "Sorry. I didn't mean that the way it sounded."

He crosses his arms.

"I had a bad night," I try again.

He raises a brow.

Now I cross my arms. Is he really going to try to make me confirm I'm not talking about our little impromptu trip? Because I'm not going to.

I give up, or sort of.

I resort to watching him from the corner of my eye while reading over the menu.

"And today's terror is... monkey bread. Wow." I nod. "I would bet this didn't go through the hovering mother committee for approval." I lean forward, flipping the thing over, but it's blank on the other side. "If it had, it would definitely be a sugar-free, gluten-free... god, I can't even think of anything that could possibly taste good when made in such a way."

I look to Arsen, who wipes the side grin from his lips as he meets my gaze.

I fight my own, pleased he's not punishing me for my thoughtless comment. He nods toward the measuring cups, so I move some things over and step closer to his side.

Once we get our ingredients into the bowl, I lift the whisk he brought over between us. "This will snap or get stuck, either way, it's a no-go. When you work with dough like this, you have to use your hands."

He eyes me curiously, but I spin on my heels, glancing at the other boys' table on my way back to the materials wall. They haven't even gotten past the flour, too busy laughing and joking between themselves.

Dropping the thick plastic item in the sanitization bin, I stretch over the countertop to reach for two pairs of gloves. As I pull out a pair of large ones, a body comes up behind me, pinning me in, and suddenly my hands are empty.

My head snaps to the side, fully expecting an entirely different pair of eyes than the ones I find.

Scott stands there with a grin.

I maneuver myself free of his hips, forcing him a few inches back when I spin to face him.

"What are you doing in here, Mr. Gentry?" I cross my arms, quirking a brow.

His grin widens. "Just passing by on my way to the office, saw you through the door, Ms. Filano."

"And at the perfect time, too." I lift my hands out slightly and he chuckles.

"What can I say, I'm good at spotting opportunity." He flicks the face of my belt, his gaze popping up to mine. "You're coming on Saturday, right?"

My conversation with the girls this morning comes back to me and I nod. "To the infamous seniors-only party, but of course."

"And so excited about it," he teases, slipping closer. "Save your dancing for me."

I shrug, going the intentionally dramatic slow blink route. "If you're lucky."

"Oh, if *I'm* lucky." He slides the latex of the gloves along my arm, his smirk overconfident and far too easily called on. "Interesting."

I grab a hold of the gloves, and he lets them go, his eyes following my hand when I extend my arm beyond his bicep.

Arsen steps up with an aura of confidence I should expect yet find myself charmed by.

Scott's glare is pointed right at Arsen, but he gives him not a moment's attention. His face remains blank as he takes the outstretched gloves and turns his body sideways, so he's now facing ours. His muscular arm glides beside my head to grab the size small I need for myself.

As he backs away, he decides it's time to go, and hooks his middle finger with mine at my side.

Arsen tugs me forward with his backward steps.

I fight a grin when Scott doubles down on his frown.

"I have to go." I slip past him, playfully whispering, "My partner needs me."

He doesn't find it funny, his body turning as mine does

and then we're facing each other again, but this time, he's the one against the counter while I'm three steps away and counting.

"What your *partner* needs... is to stay in his lane, and to learn when to keep himself out of a conversation." Scott's words are delivered with a nasty, condemnatory tone, making it clear he believes this lane he speaks of is several miles behind his own.

Arsen comes to a screeching halt, causing my body to bump into his. The finger curled with mine twitches. I glance down, finding I'm subconsciously running my thumb along his knuckle.

"Oh, that's right." Scott delivers a foul laugh, widening his shoulders. "Conversations aren't something he's capable of."

I jerk free of Arsen's hold and I'm in Scott's face before I know what I'm doing or why.

Threats are ready to spew from me like vomit, vomit he deserves to be served fresh and hot across his ridiculous shoes for calling attention to someone's disabilities, but I take a second to swallow, to heed the subtle warning in his eyes when what I really want to do is spit in them.

He and I, we run in the same circle, the one I was pulled into when my old friends learned I was coming back here.

Arsen, he doesn't even have a circle, but a triangle, and I don't doubt he's capable of handling anything thrown his way.

So why am I standing *in* his way?

I lick my lips.

"*Lucky* for him, I'm not a fan of useless conversation." I manage to hold the indignation at bay and hit him with a bored grin. "Catch you later, Scott."

Stepping out wide, I maneuver myself around Arsen,

and head straight for our table, but I'm caught around the wrist and yanked to a hard halt.

My eyes snap up to meet Ransom's.

His glare is instant and he shoves to his feet, his head jerking in the direction I came from.

His jaw flexes and he releases me, but I don't stand there to see what comes next and I don't know why my muscles have turned to knots.

I hastily slip the gloves on and dive straight into the mixing bowl to blend the ingredients, ignoring the ridiculous way my pulse beats through my palms.

I don't realize I'm basically strangling the poor dough until a solid chest meets my back, a familiar one that shouldn't feel familiar, and large hands slip inside the bowl, molding over mine.

His fingers do the work, entwining ours together and guiding us both, kneading and rolling the dough as if he's done this a hundred times when the whisk already gave away the truth.

His chin dips slightly, bringing his jawline to my cheek.

At my back, his chest rises and falls with long, full breaths, and my lids decide to close.

Suddenly his lips are at my ear, parting, but all that comes out is a half-exhaled chuckle.

"Ms. Filano."

My eyes fly open, and every other pair in the room is now on me, thanks to Mr. Gant's critical tone.

Arsen, in absolutely no hurry, removes himself as my blanket and steps beside me.

Mr. Grant crosses his arms, taking a few short steps into the main aisle with his focus on me. "Something wrong?"

I might be losing my mind.

I might feel hot all over with only a second's foreplay…

in the middle of a cooking class, with a guy I basically just met, like a practiced hussy.

Are those things 'right'?

I shrug to myself.

Hell if I know.

I look to the expectant man with gray-speckled hair and a mustache that would make Gomez Addams proud.

"Define *wrong*?" slips from my lips without thought.

Two memorable chuckles follow, as do a few others from around the room, but those come from people who are most definitely not on the same page.

Mr. Grant's eyes widen before he can stop them, but he returns to his desk with a simple, "See me after class."

As he turns away, I pull the gloves from my hands and toss them in the trash can near our feet. My eyes shift to Arsen.

His are already on me, a deep frown curved along his forehead, and the longer he stares, the deeper it gets. With a hint of reluctance, he looks over his shoulder.

Toward his friends.

Friends, I have a feeling, he'll have long after this year is over.

Or maybe not.

They'll probably fuck him over, or vice versa.

Every real relationship turns sour eventually.

Convenience and precise understanding are so much smarter, cleaner.

Necessary.

It has to be.

I don't look away from the task at hand until the bell rings and we're sliding our dough into our slot in the fridge.

Thankfully the teacher is occupied with another student, so I'm able to slip from class without a lecture on etiquette.

A second after my heels cross the threshold of the room, my phone dings with a text from Scott.

Scott: I'm wearing white on Saturday. You should, too.

And just like that, the self-proclaimed capo demands confirmation our little interaction was simply banter between rich kids with superiority issues.

With a long inhale, I do my part.

Better to pet a persistent dog than attempt to shoo it away, everyone knows it only makes them more eager.

Scott will get his dance, and he knows it.

Ah, how the circle of the high society goes round.

I frown at my screen, at the smirking emoji I sent back, and just before I press the little button on the side to turn the screen black, a sneer fans along my hair.

All at once, Beretta, Arsen, and Ransom are slipping past me. The first two keep forward, without looking my way, but not Ransom. He spins, walks backward down the hall with his head cocked the slightest bit, shaking it back and forth.

I swear a heavy breath escapes him as he reaches out, tugging on his friends' shirts before spinning and throwing his arms over their shoulders.

A girl walks by then, stepping out wider as they grow closer, and all at once, they jolt toward her, making me jump when a short scream flies from her mouth.

They chuckle, disappearing around the corner, and the girl growls, flicking her gaze their way in disgust. She recomposes herself, and I squash my grin as she breezes past me with a low mumbled, "Freaks."

I don't know why, but I push forward with rapid steps,

gliding around the corner they curved, and continue toward the exit it leads to.

I throw it open and step out, jerking in surprise.

I glare, but as quick as it sets in, an unexpected low laugh slips free. This time I'm the one shaking my head.

All three are right here, just outside the exit, each leaning against the wall with their heads turned my way.

Waiting.

They knew I would come.

Arsen kicks off first, stepping right in front of me. He dips his chin the slightest bit, and somehow, I know what he wants.

I close my eyes.

CHAPTER
Eight

A rsen and Beretta have been sparring for the last thirty minutes, neither pausing for air nor slowing their pace, clearly capable of going at it for much longer.

Ransom drops in the seat beside me, tossing his gloves to the floor with a bit of a pout.

"What's the matter, are you sad you're not getting your turn?" I tease, sticking my bottom lip out.

He surprises me when he jerks forward, ready to bite at it, but I pull back in surprise. My eyes must widen because his sudden grin is boastful. With a low laugh, we face the boys again.

Both drip with sweat, their broad smiles matching as they laugh and circle the makeshift ring. It's nothing more than a few mismatched, scuffed-up mats they dragged from the garage, rolled out over the sunburned grass and threw some quick tape onto to help keep them together. They're old, but they serve their purpose nicely.

Beretta bends at the knees, bringing himself lower as he spins, but Arsen whips around the opposite way, having expected his friend's tricks, and is now pressed to Beretta's back.

Arsen quickly hooks his elbows around Beretta's and tugs his arms backward, trapping Beretta's between his own back and Arsen's abdomen.

Arsen rushes them forward, pinning Beretta's chest to the side wall of the garage, and he holds him there, his chest to his back.

I grin, waiting for what comes next, unsure of what Beretta will attempt in order to get free, but neither of them moves, and then Arsen's hold loosens.

The moment his movements become lax, Beretta spins. First, it's only his shoulders and his upper torso, his abs constricting and showing their strength as he does. His lower half comes next, and then they're chest to chest.

Arsen doesn't back away, and Beretta doesn't force him to. They stay right where they are, eye to eye, grin to grin, and... I mean—

"Done?" Ransom's quick shout makes my eyes snap toward him.

I quickly look back to the others, but the boys are already headed this way, both reaching out to tap their knuckles together.

"You're getting faster," Beretta recognizes with appreciation.

Arsen's smirk is all too cocky, but he keeps it to himself, turning away as he drinks from his refilled water bottle.

I take a moment to glance around the yard, the entire perimeter lined with cactus plants of some sort, all different shapes and sizes. Some have large chunks broken off, others are cut clear across the tips in what seems like random fashion.

Beretta drops beside me. "Looks a lot different than your back yard, huh, Trouble?"

My eyes flick to his, but there's no mockery or anger there, only an easy grin on his lips, so I nod. "We don't even have real grass, let alone plants."

"No shit, turf or what?"

I shrug. "I guess, and a whole bunch of rock and cement."

"And a fat-ass pool."

I nod. Of course he knows this, you can see it from the beach below, just like Cali's.

"You ever tried it?" he asks.

"Tried what?"

His forehead wrinkles with amusement. "Cactus."

"I don't exactly have a green thumb."

The boys chuckle and I glance around.

"Take that as a no." He smiles, finishing off his water. "Stay here a couple more hours, and you will."

"So, this is *your* home, then?"

Nobody offered the information when we got here, and it didn't make a difference, so I didn't bother to ask. That, and I wasn't sure they'd tell me anyway. Especially since I assumed we were trespassing on someone's land when we passed the large home at its front and followed through to the back of a property line; where they had to get out to lift and move a metal gate by hand in order for Arsen to drive his car up to the house.

Beretta looks out over the land, where row after row of orange trees cover every inch of the dirt seen from this angle, and then toward the off-white house tucked about twenty feet from the garage we're parked in front of.

The screens on the windows are faded from the sun, the security gate rusted at the edges. There's some sort of tractor and on its opposite side, another identical house.

He shakes his head.

"Nope. It's not my home." He looks to his friends, then back to me.

A shadow covers his eyes, and he glances away, so I allow myself to drop farther against the wicker chair and admit what I'm thinking, as he did.

Only to myself, because saying it out loud will come off as crying rich girl syndrome, where nothing is ever enough, and always wanting more is the norm.

I don't want more, though, what I'm getting is plenty enough.

Still... I feel the same.

My house is not my home; it's temporary.

The difference is, I won't grow to find mine.

I'll be placed inside it.

"Can I ask a question?"

"No."

"Yes."

Ransom and Beretta look to each other, and Arsen chuckles, laying back on the mats with his arms folded behind his head.

"What's with the whole 'close your eyes' thing?" I pick up my watered-down smoothie, stick my straw between my teeth and wait.

And wait.

The boys don't say a word, just meet one another's gazes from where they sit on the mats for a shared, unspoken secret.

My brows lift. "Seriously?"

Beretta clears his throat, cuts a quick glance toward Arsen, and then rolls from his ass onto all fours. He crawls across the mat to where I'm now sitting on the open tailgate of the broken-down truck turned couch/bed.

He looks so ridiculous that I'm laughing before he's

even made it a foot closer.

"Why do we ask you to close your eyes..." His hands find my ankles and he uncrosses them, and nudges my legs open a little.

I fall back, catching myself with my hands. I'm on the verge of growing uneasy, but the others begin to laugh as he slips between my thighs, and somehow, my nerves are lulled.

He's not touching me, but he's damn close.

"We tell you to close your eyes..." Beretta lets his body fall flush with mine, his hazel eyes testing me with a tantalizing gleam. "Because everything is amped in the dark. Your want, your need, your... willingness. In the dark, you can be whoever you want to be. No fear. No judgment."

My left brow quirks high, and he chuckles, rolling off of me and sitting beside me.

I push up. "So, it's all about sex?"

All three of their heads snap my way and I laugh.

"What? I'm curious."

Ransom pins me with a fixed expression. "Why?"

"Why not? I've played your game three times now. Do I not have the right to ask?"

"Do you need an excuse to ask what you want to know?"

"Do you need to sound so condescending when you ask such a question?"

"Do *we* need to put you two in time-out, alone, in the dark?"

I glare at Beretta, but when Ransom simply laughs, I relax, even though I'm positive I've missed an inside joke.

A smirk covers my lips. "I don't think he could hang with me that long."

"Why, you all about girly, crybaby shit?" Beretta teases.

I look away, my eyes widening in mockery of my own damn self. "Yeah, that's me."

"Is it not?" Ransom wonders.

I shake my head.

"So, you're stone-cold then?" A hint of disbelief, or maybe it's disgust, deepens his voice. "No fire, no soul?"

"Sure, you can say that." I shrug carelessly. "Being all deep and devoted is senseless."

"I'm not buying it." Ransom frowns.

"It's true. It messes with your head, and it's all downhill from there."

"You've been fucked over then." A shadow of annoyance slips over him. "Loved and let go?"

"Hell no." I laugh. "And I never will."

"So you're scared?"

My gaze slices to his, narrowing.

He gets in my face, so I hop off of the truck and stand before him. His eyes search mine and a low huff leaves him. "Yeah, you're terrified of what would happen if you opened your pretty little eyes to more, aren't you?"

"I'm not scared, I'm smart."

"You think so, huh?" he scoffs. "What, mommy and daddy not love you enough?"

"Spoken like a scorned asshole." I tip my head. "What, desperate for something you don't have at home?"

His eyes turn to slate, hard and impenetrable.

I think I struck a nerve.

"Okay, yeah." He nods, detached. "I've got mommy, daddy, fucked-up sibling issues like the next blue-collar bastard, but tell me, Jameson, what's the point of this fucked-up world if you have no one in it?" His words drip of cold disdain, but something deeper strains beyond the surface. "Someone to lean on, to depend on, who can depend on you?"

I'm already shaking my head before he's done speaking. "What a fairy-tale world you speak of. You're setting yourself up for failure, thinking like that."

"And you're running straight to misery by not."

"I won't waste my life bleeding for someone else when I don't even bleed for my damn self."

His laugh is as cold as his eyes. "So, you cut yourself off from all that makes you human, like a true ice princess?" He slips closer, his tone lower. "How pathetic."

"*Pathetic* is to love someone so much that when they're no longer yours, you buy a one-way ticket to the bottom of the fucking ocean," I seethe. "*That* is pathetic."

He blanches, his face falling as he takes me in.

I hold back a swallow and straighten my shoulders.

Fuck him.

He licks his lips, creases forming along his forehead as the pieces fall into place. "Jameson..."

"Like I said." I purse my lips. "Love makes you weak."

A heavy sense of uncertainty clouds his features. "That's an unfair judgment."

"Yeah, well." I grab my bag off the ground and step toward Arsen's Camaro. "Me and my sister were the ones screwed in the end, so... kind of feels like I'm allowed to be a bitch about it."

I climb inside and slam the door.

Ransom is a dumbass.

Everything he said is what's wrong with this world.

People allow themselves to fall for such feeble ideals so carelessly that when they're hit with the unexpected and uncontrollable feelings that come hand in hand, their deepest regrets follow.

Unruly emotion always leads to irrational actions.

It's why I'm perfectly apathetic, agreeable to an arranged marriage, and looking forward to a contractual future rather than a precarious one.

When no one is looking, I slip a Xanax under my tongue and savor the chalky taste as it slips down my throat.

Feelings can go fuck themselves and so can the boys who shouldn't be able to bring them out of me.

CHAPTER *Nine*

This time, when they take me to my car, it's in the school parking lot, a note stuck under the windshield, one Ransom takes it upon himself to read, tear in half, and toss through my open window once I've climbed inside.

He pauses there beside me, waiting for me to pick up its pieces, but I don't.

I wait to read it when they are as good as gone.

Come by for a nightcap.
~ Scott

I take a deep breath... and head his way.

He's on his balcony when I pull in, so I start up the spiral staircase at the edge of the garden that leads to the entrance of his room. The place is basically a New York-style flat with a living room, kitchen and all.

It's a singular, large, and wide-open space with glossy gray flooring and matching beams running up the walls every four feet or so, the entire thing made up of black glass windows you can see out, but not in. It's extremely modern and screams bachelor. And his parents added it just for him.

He meets me at the landing with a grin.

"I wasn't sure you were coming, but perfect timing."

I give him a quick half hug, and he latches his arm around my shoulders, steering me indoors.

Leaving my side, he slips behind his bar, grabs a glass and empties the contents of the blender into it. My brows lift as I accept the slushie-like drink, knowing, without a doubt, he wasn't the one drinking it.

He notices my expression and chuckles, tapping his knuckle on his near-empty tumbler. "Jules and Dax came by for a bit. She made it and that's what's left. I was about to pour it out... and then I saw you coming."

I pull the glass to my mouth, allowing it to coat my lips so I can taste the red concoction. "Do you always sit around and stare at your security cameras?"

"Only when I'm waiting for someone to pop up on them." His smirk is a mix of triumph and assurance.

I cross my legs, my forearms resting on the cold granite. "You were so sure I would, huh?"

He nods, and the superior glint in his eyes is clear—he truly had no doubt.

I'm not sure what that says about me, or him for that matter, so I look away, push to my feet, and step out onto the back side, wraparound balcony. Behind his house is where his family's vineyards began, now relocated to a far larger estate, but enough to service the house and more remains.

"All this at your fingertips, and still, you go for the hard stuff."

"We leave the wine to my mom and her friends. Trust me, they go through enough without help from me."

"I don't doubt that." To love a good glass of wine is pretty much a prerequisite around here.

Scott turns his body to face mine, so with a long exhale,

I meet his move. His hand slips into my hair and when I don't pull away, he lowers his lips to mine.

I've kissed him before, on his yacht, when he blocked my exit on the stairs, and like then, he tastes of bitter bourbon and stale smoke, but most of all—privilege.

My fingers never leave my glass or the railing, and he doesn't give up the drink in his hand either.

He kisses me simply to remind himself he can, and I let him in hopes it helps me to forget, to bring the numbness back.

It doesn't and when he pulls back, it's with a grin of arrogant proportions, so I smash my lips into a smile for his benefit.

I pull away, taking a few backward steps. "See you at school?"

He nods, so I turn to leave.

"There's a difference, you know," he says, his tone crisp, yet calm.

I glance over my shoulder, and he continues, "In hooking up and fucking up." His eyes hold mine. "Stay on the right side of that."

I keep my face blank, but we both know I understand what he's saying.

Scott's so used to his whole crew eating up his every word and likely believes he's offering me some invaluable advice. Unfortunately for him, he's unaware that his words mean nothing to me.

I pull my lips in, lifting the drink in the air. "Thanks for the drink."

"Take it with you," he insists. "Finish it off at home."

I nod, and I'm in my car, pulling from the long driveway within minutes.

The roads are wide open where Scott lives, the houses

spread out by two and three miles, so I follow it down as I did up.

I don't notice the speed I'm gaining, the fog in my head rivaling the one from the ocean that's rolling up over the hillside.

A flash of yellow catches my eye, but by the time I slam on the brakes and jerk the wheel on impulse, it's too late to correct, my speed too high.

The car whips around, the passenger side crashing into a fire hydrant where the road ends and someone's land begins.

I gasp, my breathing harsh as my gaze flies out the window.

Water pounds against the side, taking the mirror clear off and spraying into the air. It beats down against the hood, splashing all around.

I managed to keep my arms firm on the wheel, my body only whipping slightly, and it takes effort to pull my hands from the leather. Inspecting myself quickly, I spot merely a few cuts and scrapes on my arms from broken glass maybe, but that's it. The airbag didn't even go off or else there'd be blood pouring from my nose, I'm sure.

My forehead falls to the headrest, a humorless laugh escaping me.

And then my door is torn open.

I scream, my hands flying to my chest. Instantly, I'm met with wide and wild blue eyes.

Ransom stands there, panting. The color is drained from his face and his brows are drawn in so tight they're nearly touching.

His gaze darts over every inch of me, his hand flying to my legs where he pinches near my knee. When it jerks in response, he falls to his ass beside my door.

"Ransom... what the hell?"

His hands come up and he drags them down his face, his shoulders sagging low.

I push up in my seat, but he freezes.

His head snaps up and he darts forward, latching on to my shirt, twisting his fist in the material and yanking me closer, his mouth now inches from mine.

His glare is heavy and hardens by the second. With jerky movements, he tears himself from the ground. "Get out."

My head tugs back. "What—"

"Get the fuck out of the car, Jameson," he barks.

He all but tears me from the vehicle, and I reach out to steady myself on the frame when my vision demands a second to catch up.

Ransom scoffs, attempting to hold me still, but I slap his hand away, and he growls.

The water has begun to flood the ground near my feet, hitting my face as it splashes off the hood, and back behind it, the lights inside the home flick on.

He growls, getting in my face, his lip curled in disgust. "You're lucky it was a fucking fire hydrant, or I'd tie your ass to the wheel."

"Excuse me—"

"Go," he cuts me off, tearing the glove box open.

My head pulls back.

What does he mean, go?

But then my ears perk, the haze in my mind clearing as the shriek of the sirens cools the blood in my veins.

Whipping around, I spot a hint of flashing lights in the sky a few miles away.

My hands fly to my head, and I spin around, but then they're covered with another pair.

I look up into Ransom's angry eyes.

"I said go. Fucking. Home." It's the last thing he says before roughly pushing me away to the point I almost stumble over my own feet. He slips into the front seat of my car. "Now, Jameson!"

The ambulance grows closer, police lights on its tail.

"It's... it's fine. It was an accident."

He whips around, his eyes bulging and then narrowing. He charges me, but the sirens grow louder and he stops in his tracks, a dark, disgusted laugh slipping past his lips.

He turns back to my car.

I growl, and without a second thought, I spin and run away. I run for blocks, and then walk for miles before I realize my purse is draped over my shoulder, my phone tucked inside, unscathed.

I lift it out, and as I do, I get a whiff of myself and freeze in my tracks.

The drink.

I'm covered in margarita.

You're lucky it was a fucking fire hydrant...

Ransom smelled the tequila on me.

"Oh my god." I would have gotten arrested, probably a DUI, even if I consumed none, and it would have been posted on the Orange County social media pages.

If Ransom hadn't shown up, I would be royally—

Wait.

My arms fall to my sides and I subconsciously glance in the direction I came from.

He just happened to be in Scott's neighborhood tonight?

I was kidding before, but maybe he really is a stalker.

Disoriented, I try to shake my mind free, and pull my phone closer. I scroll until I reach my sister's name, but once I'm staring at it, my thumb decides to hover there.

If I call, she'll ask questions, which is fine. I could tell her what happened, and she'd have my back if I needed her to, but who will have Ransom's?

Why is that my problem?

I squeeze my eyes shut a long moment, and before I'm forced to make a decision, my phone makes it for me, the battery dying.

Shoving it back in my bag, I walk the last two miles to my house.

My morning begins before dawn, courtesy of a hard knock on the door, two men in uniform on the other side of it. They ask me questions about my car and where I was last night.

I play dumb and claim to have been home since school the day before.

They let me know my car was totaled. Apparently, they found it in a ditch, every inch of it up in flames, and it appeared to have been chopped for parts, the stereo as well as navigation being the few examples they gave.

It takes all my effort not to smile.

Of course, he didn't simply wait there for the cops to arrive.

As my eyes lift again, one of the officers, the younger, beefier one, narrows his, and I square my shoulders in response.

It was 'stolen,' what is there for me to be concerned about?

"Miss Filano." He drags my name out as long as possible. "Mind if we see the keys, so we can note that you have them in our report. It will make everything nice and clear for the insurance claim."

Shit.

"Yeah." My response is a little rushed, and I nod, the door already closing as I begin to slink away. "Just... give me a second to grab them."

My back hits the wall the moment I close the cops outside, and I squeeze my eyes shut.

"Shit, shit, shit!" I hiss, flying into the kitchen, and begin to pace, my hands tearing through my hair, trying to think, when a flash of black catches my eye.

I whip around and my breath freezes in my throat.

The bay doors leading to the back are wide open, a light breeze carrying the curtains into the house, and just outside of it... Ransom.

His glare is heavy, angry, and tipped low.

Dirt lines his jaw, what looks like blood is dried to his right brow, and he's wearing the same clothes from the day before.

His arm comes up, his hand opening, and inside his palm, dangling from one finger... my keys.

My eyes widen and I dart forward, but as I reach him, reaching for them, his fist closes.

He backs away and a lump forms in my throat. I'm about to vomit, or scream, but then he tosses them against my chest.

A clipped huff leaves me, and I jolt, prepared to run back, but as I get a better look at him, my bare feet root in place.

His face is pulled tight, his body rigid, as if he's on the verge of... I don't know what.

A hard tap sounds behind me and I blink, keeping my eyes on him a moment longer, before running for the front door.

Yanking it open, I muster a smile, swinging the keys in the air in faux enthusiasm, and set them in the questioning officer's hand. The man at his side gives me a tight-lipped grin as if to apologize for his partner, and within ten minutes, they're gone.

As soon as the lock is clicked in place, I take a settling breath, flattening my palm against my forehead.

I head out back, but Ransom is gone.

Staring at the still locked gate at the far side of my yard, I lean against the frame, confusion bringing a frown to my face.

I may not have realized it right away, but he saved my ass last night in a big way, and again just now.

He went out of his way and he did it without my asking, without reason and for zero gain. I pretty much depreciated the situation and still he pushed me to go, as if it was his place, as if compelled.

What's most troubling, though, is the crestfallen look in his eyes, as if it killed him to do as he did. He tried to hide it behind anger and frustration, but I saw it.

Why did you have to go and help me, Ransom Rossi?

My shoulders seem to fall on their own, a long sigh leaving me.

Opening my palm, I run my finger over the golden J key chain my mom gave me for my birthday.

Shit, my mom!

I head back to my room to grab my phone, so I can let her in on what happened with my car, or the version the police provided me with.

I plan to talk to Ransom at school this afternoon, but I don't get the chance, because he isn't there.

None of the three are.

Not today, or the rest of the week.

It shouldn't bother me that I don't know where they are or why they stay gone, so I tell myself it doesn't.

CHAPTER
Ten

When Scott said wear white, I thought it was his way of being an ass and letting me in on how he connected the dots from the little 'devil' and 'blank canvas' nonsense at lunch on the first day of school, as if I hadn't noticed then.

Sitting here at the party, however, I now know it was simply his way of being ominous, leaving me to assume his true meaning—a purposeful mind twister, or it would be, for someone who cared enough to obsess over it.

The party is literally a black light party, so *everyone* was instructed to wear white, something the girls had to fill me in on when they called me on FaceTime to let me know they were on their way from her parents' dinner party—thankfully, my car situation gave me an excuse to get out of that. Had they not, I would have shown up in a hunter green dress.

So, I ran back into my closet and here I am, cloaked in white for the second day this week.

This time, though, it's not a pantsuit, but a thigh-hugging dress. It's not quite a mini, but I do have to bend at the knee rather than over at the hip to avoid a clear shot of what's underneath. It's a halter style that clasps around my neck, the thick straps crisscrossed over my shoulder blades.

Straps that Scott slips his fingers beneath and gives a gentle tug so that I give him my attention.

He smirks from his seat beside me. "Ready for a shot?"

I shake my head, wiggling my glass of water, and face Jules when she lowers onto the tabletop in front of me.

"Okay, the dinner party. You missed some major forbidden vibes. Her dad's business partner came alone!" Her eyes widen. "Still has the fiancée, I guess, but he showed by himself, *and* moved tables so he could be closer to ours."

"Or he moved so he didn't have to sit in front of the loud-ass speakers all evening." Cali rolls her eyes, but a smile plays at her bright pink and glowing lips.

"Honey, no. That man took his eyes off you only when he had to... which was when your dad stopped to talk to him." Jules' eyes sparkle, and it's not from the thick layer of glimmer she's lined them with.

A low laugh leaves me when Cali shrugs a single shoulder, slipping her straw into her mouth.

"Whatever, he's not here, so I need to find someone to entertain me." She grins, her perfect white teeth gleaming in the lights.

Amy bounces over with Sammie and a few other girls, and they turn their attention to them.

All of us girls had the same roundabout idea and added some sort of bright makeup that the black lights pick up with ease.

I went with my usual getup of a thick, heavy black wing, but framed it in with some bright purple glitter gel, and even painted my lips the same to match. My hair is in two Dutch braids on top, and I left a few long strands down in front, the rest waved and draped over my back. For a bit of added fun, I took some of my gel shadow and painted it along the curve of the braids, as well as down a few of the loosely curled strands.

I run my fingers through a small strand of hair that lays along my arm and listen in on the conversations around me.

Dax has an interview with *People* magazine on Monday, they want to know about his decision to turn down his full-ride to Notre Dame in favor of Michigan. He has to lie and claim it was his dream, when really his parents made the decision for him.

Cali wants to party on her parents' yacht next weekend and thinks she can blackmail her brother into agreeing to take it out of the peninsula and into open waters.

Amy can't stand the girl in the white crop top who is 'all over Teddy from chemistry,' and is looking mighty fine in her booty shorts and go-go boots. Not that Amy would dare acknowledge such an observation out loud. It's clear in her snotty tone she doesn't like that the girl is rocking the outfit better than she is, but her friends simply nod and agree and get her a refill when she downs the green drink in her hand.

I look around the place, a large, wide open vacation home rented solely for tonight's entertainment, likely put together by a team of prominent party planners who spent weeks preparing and days setting up.

Another day, another hundred thousand dollars.

I don't know how long I sit here, but the girls have gotten louder and lighter on their feet. The guys have busted out the second bottle of Scotland's finest, imported with ease and a hefty price tag.

I'm ready to call it a night, already planning my escape for the moment they lean in for refills.

But then my eyes are called toward the door as it's pushed open, and not to its fullest. Not by the guards or greeters on either side as every other person who set foot in this place tonight required.

With simple nods of acknowledgment and subtle shakes of their heads when the men at the door reach for the large iron handles, the boys slip inside without the need of feeling grand or important, all in favor of a quiet entrance.

My stomach swirls.

They don't pause in the doorway to look around to see who might have noticed their presence or decide what group to hit first.

They simply curve toward their right, headed for the far-left corner of the giant living room turned dance floor.

I play with my thumbnail, rubbing the pad of my fingers over the sharp tip.

I want to walk over, to talk to Ransom, to look into his eyes and see what I find staring back this time.

A frown builds along my brow at the thought, and I could almost roll my eyes at myself.

I sound ridiculous.

If I were to approach him, anyone could overhear, and I think it's safe to say, neither of us want that. I could leave and hope to catch them at Arsen's foster house again, as I tried to do several times this week with no luck, but the urge to go home is no longer there.

So, when the girls begin to talk about the final places they've narrowed their winter vacation destination down to, I lean in, but it's no use.

I was in my own world before, but now I'm fully zoned out, zoning *in* on the caged-up corner in the back as there's something about dark and devious that cannot be ignored.

It's fascinating.

They are fascinating, untamed and unapologetic.

It's as if there's this shadow that follows their every

step, one I'm not sure everyone sees, daring me to slip into it, to step from my own, and view the world through their eyes, if only for a moment.

Or maybe it's simply how Beretta has hopped up on the pop-up stage and joined the DJ behind her table that keeps me focused their way.

He smirks, allowing her to put her headphones on his ears and scoots over while showing him what she can do.

One thing about rich kid circles is they have no reservations when it comes to exploits and where to have them. The single ones all fuck each other, everyone knows it, but nobody talks about it, so the dance floor is already raging in racy rhythm.

Not that Beretta is paying much attention to that.

No, his eyes roam the room with a slow swivel of his head, pausing when his attention is pointed this way.

I squish my lips to the side to keep from smiling, but then he slips around the table, and in front of him, offering him a shoulder to grip as he hops down... Ransom and Arsen.

All three look this way.

Right at me.

People dance in the way, their faces coming in and out of view, their bodies blending into the stage at their backs.

But of course, black on black at a white wardrobe party.

Ransom lifts his chin, daring me to come closer.

I push to my feet, but before I can step toward them, they begin to curve left, leaving me to follow from my side of the crowd, down the hall and into a den-like room, set up as a designated smokers area—as if it doesn't travel all through the house.

They mold themselves around a tall table and I step right up to it.

"Well, well." I tip my head. "Ditch school but not the

party. I'm almost surprised."

"We had to let our lungs heal," Beretta jokes, pulling out a joint and lifting it up.

"Hm, right, so the smoking room with a joint the size of a tube of lipstick is how you accomplish such a thing?"

"Depends, is that lipstick as red as the one you wore for us?" He grins.

A smile slips over my lips and I shake my head.

I turn to Ransom and take a step closer, but I don't get a single word out before he's shaking his head, a firm look in his eye, even if he does refuse to meet mine for longer than a second.

As I expected, he's angry, and this isn't the place to have the conversation, but I had to try.

His attention shifts, now focused over my shoulder, and the muscles in his neck flex.

He glares at me in warning when he notices I caught it, but I turn to look anyway, finding Amy, Sammie, and a girl whose name I don't remember.

Amy flicks her eyes my way, offering a tight-lipped smile, and says something to her friends.

Unmistakable agitation radiates from the boys, and Beretta tries to erase it with a laugh. It's strangled and fake, and he hangs his head, lifting only his eyes to mine. "Uh-oh, Jameson. Abort."

I frown, already confused. "Abort?"

"Yeah and quick."

My mouth opens slightly.

I don't get it...

"Your friends, Trouble." He shrugs, his face going slack. "You better play it cool, make an excuse to slip away."

I blink and blink again.

Okay... wow.

Slowly, I push off the table, rubbing my lips together so I don't jump right to the 'fuck you,' but it does nothing to help, so...

"Fuck you." I take the drink from his palm, pour it into an abandoned glass on the tabletop, and slam it down as I back away.

I charge from the room, around the corner, but I'm caught by the wrist as I reach the dance floor. I'm spun around and jerked into Beretta's chest. Ransom stands just over his left shoulder, Arsen to his right.

His hands fall to my hips, and he walks me backward.

"Not so fast," he cautions. "What was that?"

My eyes widen. "Are you joking?"

As if pre-planned, Beretta slinks behind me, at my front.

It's as if he believes it's his, the place in front of me, he demands it time and time again.

Ransom's eyes, they burn in question, tension tightening the edges and radiating off him at rapid speeds, begging to be soothed, but why? And of what?

"Were we wrong?" Beretta whispers in my ear. "Does she do as she pleases?"

My blood warms, my body arching into Ransom's.

Pleased, the corner of his mouth lifts, but his eyes remain angry. His hands shoot out to grip my hips, inches up from where Beretta's fingers rest. Slowly, we begin to move to the music.

"Oh shit, Trouble." Beretta breathes and Ransom's eyes lift to his. "They'll really be watching now."

The second he says it, the DJ shouts the next phase of the night has begun, and I'm unconvinced it's coincidental.

The lights dim, and excitement erupts as the room fades to total blackness, leaving nothing but the neon around the room. There are no bodies, no shapes, and the sound, it adjusts as well. The tempo drops lower, the bass deeper, yet slower. It's a sexy sway of words.

"We're just dancing, right?" My voice is far raspier than it should be. "Like everyone else?"

"Yeah." His tease is heavy, and he presses himself into me. "Just like everyone else."

My arms come up to loosely drape over Ransom's shoulders, and his gaze locks on mine.

The three of us sway to the beat, our bodies following each other's and the room begins to warm.

Or that's how it feels.

My blood is pumping fiercely, my skin hot, and my body is in complete control of me now.

My core pulses heavily, growing wilder as my fingers slide along Ransom's neck, discovering the barren beat his thumps to, at twice the speed of mine.

My lips part, and the pads of his fingers dig into me, the heat of his hands felt beneath the fabric of my dress.

My ass cheeks clench and Beretta's hand comes around to grip my chin, jerking my head to the side so he can meet my eyes.

His are tight at the corners, narrowed, and flying between mine, but just as quickly, they snap forward to Ransom's.

Before he can release me, Arsen is standing at our sides, two shot glasses in his hands.

Arsen's knuckle glides along my jaw, guiding my head back, so I'm propped against Beretta's shoulder, my cheekbone lined with his jaw.

Arsen slips closer, and Beretta's arm wraps around his shoulder as he lifts the shot glass to my lips and waits.

I open my mouth and he pours the clear, warm liquid

down my throat. Beretta takes the other right after, his face grazing along mine.

With my head dropped the way it is, his lips are at the edge of my view, right there for me to watch as his tongue slips out, teasing the corner of his mouth, and I must attempt to reach for him, because the next thing I know, my wrist is caught in flight.

My head snaps upright and Ransom tugs me toward him again, but this time, he pulls my body flush to his.

There's no space to move, no air to breathe.

Or there is, but it's a shared air. A thick, asphyxiating air that allows no room for reason, only room for him.

His blue eyes blaze, bright and brilliant, drowning my own.

His chest rises and falls against mine, *with* mine, but then Beretta is behind him, wrapping one arm over his shoulder, his free hand locking on to his bicep. At the same time, Arsen slips up behind me, his head molding into the crook of my neck, arms coming around my middle, locking me to him.

His feet shuffle me forward as Beretta's shuffle Ransom's backward. I begin to protest, but then his teeth graze along my collarbone.

My hand flies down to his locked around my abdomen, and I forget to step when they slip lower, pushing into me just below my panty line.

I nearly trip, but he's quick, his palm flattening over my chest to save me from face planting.

His soft chuckle fans along my neck and I close my eyes.

Next thing I know, I'm staring into a dark room, black canvases framed over the windows to block out the light, a thick, neon green clay dripping from the center and illuminated by the black light above.

Arsen ushers me farther in, toward a black leather chaise in the center of the room, soft music flowing from somewhere, but it disappears as the click of a lock echoes in my ears, and all I hear now is my own pulse beating out of my skin.

My shins meet the cold seat and whip around, my chest slamming into Arsen. His hand shoots up, capturing the back of my neck, and he yanks me closer, aligning his lips perfectly with mine. But he holds there, impeccably still, a hopeful message in his gaze, one I'm not sure I understand, not that I get the chance, because behind him, a shadow calls to me.

My eyes break from his, finding Ransom tucked in the corner, his body rigid and gaze strained, Beretta still hanging on to him.

Arsen's exhale is soft and lulling. With gentle movements, he releases me, joining the other two in the corner.

The light above us cuts off, and the room grows dark. Black.

Blackout.

Goose bumps rise along my skin, but I don't move.

The soft rustle of clothing sounds, causing my toes to curl in my heels, and all at once, three pairs of eyes flash before me.

I gasp, loudly, my calves tightening.

There's no icy blue, no calming navy, and no earthy hazel, no recognition whatsoever as each pair, tucked as far from me as possible, glow the same exact shade.

A wild, wicked fluorescent, glow-in-the-dark, turquoise, only to be seen through the blackness they've placed us inside.

My gaze snaps along them as one by one, the only proof that they're inside this room with me disappears.

They've closed their eyes.

All that's left is breathing. Mine. Theirs.

Soft footsteps sound and I try to gauge where they are, but I can't think past the heavy thumping within my chest.

A hand meets mine. Instinctively, I withdraw, but only for a second, and with my next breath, allow the person to weave his calloused fingers with mine. The person shows his eyes, and I try to decipher who they belong to, who it is that slips closer, runs his free hand up my thigh, taking the hem of my dress with it... but I can't.

I have no idea who touches me.

But I don't tell them to stop.

My core clenches, a soft tortured sound fighting its way up my throat when a third hand comes around from behind, something cold written along it and burning against my heated skin. He, whoever *he* is, grips my neck just above my halter line, his lips coming to my ear, but only to allow me the sound of his heady breaths.

The person it belongs to comes up beside me, slipping half in front of me, his belt buckle biting into my hip as something just as solid strains against it.

The hand around my neck slips down, another joining and following the same path up and over the arc of my breast, curving beneath it and meeting in the middle, only to leave my body completely.

Two large palms find my lower back, sliding along the material there, and glide down to my ass.

The pads of his fingers dig in, squeezing once he has a handful, and a short cut groan follows.

My chin lowers as his forehead falls to my abdomen.

Hot, burning breath seeps through my dress and my hands fly forward, gripping on to his cheeks. Right as my fingertips reach the ends of his hair, my arms are yanked away.

They're lifted high over my head, and my body shivers as the palms snake along the edge of my forearms and biceps.

Locking gazes with mine, the person at my feet holds me hostage as he slowly pushes to his, molding his body to mine, but leaving just enough room for a hand to slip between us.

Two fingers press over my clit, and my ass crowds the groin aligned behind it, a low groan filling the air.

"Yeah." A low rasp melts against my skin. "She feels it."

All at once, I'm released, instantly cold, but able to breathe.

I search the room for a hint of a turquoise glow but come up short.

My voice has evaded me, my lungs too busy trying not to shrivel up and die from lack of oxygen, so I simply stand there, my hands finding my hips as sudden exhaustion rolls through me.

Note to self, add in some serious cardio!

I don't know what comes over me, but a low laugh suddenly creeps up my throat, right as the door's thrown open.

My eyes snap toward the noise in the hall, toward the low light flowing into the room, my mouth falling open as three black hoodies shuffle out of it.

I stand there for several seconds, my body slowly passing back the reins to my mind and oh my god, what in the…

My palm finds my forehead, and I whip around,

wringing my free hand out at my side.

Holy shit.

What the hell was that?

Better question!

What the *hell* is wrong with me?!

I spin, pacing the small space.

Shadows pass the open door, and my head snaps toward it.

Person after person passes in the hall, some headed left, others to the right. I shake my head.

I need to get out of this room.

I clear my throat, smoothing my hair just in case, and push it over my shoulder.

I walk out, and as I round the corner, I find the party hasn't paused in search of one missing girl but is just as busy and full as when I last looked around it, if not more so.

Thank god.

The dance floor is still dark and full, the drink area just as buzzing and the couches the guys sat at, still partially occupied.

Everyone laughs and shoves while animatedly talking, and I take a deep breath, moving straight for the bar.

On my way, I pass a mirror and freeze.

With small, slow backward shuffles of my feet, I bring myself back into view, and my eyes shoot wide.

Holy. Shit.

I turn fully, facing the mirror head-on, and a disbelieving laugh bubbles its way up my throat, but I quickly swallow it.

The cold hands, the chill that met my skin...

Paint.

Paint that can only be seen with the help of a specific type of light.

A black-fucking-light.

I look from the large, hot pink handprint on my neck, wide and strong and flawless, pressed and held there without so much as a protest, to the fluorescent blue finger trails that run along my chest. I shift slightly, a low curse leaving me.

Perfect palm prints cover my ass, both broad and curled, a shape one can only manage with a nice, full grasp, they're so perfectly placed.

My body heats all over again as I inspect their artwork.

Around me, people begin to slow their steps as the bright neon along my dress catches their eye.

You little fuckers.

This place may be dark as hell and they might have been blanketed in black, but it's so easy to see this little fun of theirs for what it is—their attempt to shift me into a spoiled girl's freak-out session. Little do they know, I don't exactly have one of those. It's one of the things that makes my mother crazy. I tend to brush things off—it's a waste of energy and time and worst of all, shit like that steals your sleep.

Screw that.

But the more I think about the why, the more unlikely it seems that three guys who don't care what others think about them would go through all the trouble of the beckoning and the seduction, just to make it a show of a conquest.

This feels a lot more like a challenge.

I can avoid sticky situations all I want, but can 'Trouble' get herself out of trouble?

It's with that thought that I take quick steps, hauling my ass back to the room they left me in. I throw the door open, flick the light on, and apologize to the couple now occupying the space.

I whip around, and sure enough, dropped perfectly in the corner where they had stood are three palm-size bottles of paint.

So much for a blank canvas, I can pretty much hear Ransom's thoughts.

"Well-played, assholes."

"Excuse you!" the girl snaps.

My eyes cut toward the glaring couple, and I toss them one, forcing the dude's hand to fly up to catch it. "Put it on your hands and go to town."

Without another word, I'm out of the room, through the hall, and with far more sass than before, I step back into the main party.

With one tube tucked beneath my arm, I pour some of the blue onto my palms and rub it in, slipping closer to the drink table where Cali stands with a group, and run my palm over her lower back, blowing her a kiss when she glances over her shoulder. She smiles and turns back to her conversation, and I continue on, placing my hands on someone's shoulder as I slip by, on another's hip as I squeeze between a few others, on my march toward Jules and the gang.

Scott, in his ridiculous white jeans, spots me coming, his words fading off as he glares at my dress on approach. He pushes to his feet, so I squeeze a fresh amount of paint over my fingers and rub it in.

I place one hand on his chest, and grip his bicep with the other, dragging it down his arm until I reach his fingers, where I steal his drink, downing it as my own.

Jules giggles from my left, her eyes bouncing over my outfit, and before she can ask, I'm handing her a bottle; she's got it on her hands and is cupping her man's junk.

Dax passes off his drink to me, so I down that one, too, and join Cali and a few other girls when they call me to the dance floor.

The last tube of paint is passed between them, and within minutes, everyone near is popping with a sexually placed flare of color.

When the way the girls move manages to get my blood pumping again, I laugh at myself, grab my shit, and go.

Clearly, I need to get laid.

The front door is pulled open by one of the guards, and I waste no time slipping out and down the porch steps, but before I make it to the sidewalk, high beams flash from the driveway across the street, the rev of an engine following.

A smirk curls my lips, but I don't play good little soldier and report to the general's call.

I stay exactly where I am, and what do you know...

They come to me.

CHAPTER
Eleven

The night is cool, but not cold, or at least it's not on the city roads we're cruising down. I'm sure their little cave is freezing right about now—the midnight ocean breeze is no joke.

I drop my head against the headrest, rolling my head to look at Beretta, who is behind the wheel this time.

His dark hair blows gently with the wind, and every few minutes, he runs a hand through it to help push it back.

It's not some vain attempt to keep his standard 'I wake up like this' vibe, but simply him, relaxed and rolling down old roads he must be familiar with, an easy grin on his face. I'm not sure where we're going, but I slipped into the passenger seat without pausing to ask, so I guess that means I don't care.

I probably should after what happened tonight. Not that anything happened, per se, but it could have.

Obviously, I was in no shape to protest.

Obviously, I didn't want to...

I hadn't even had a single drink before the one Arsen served me, so yeah, I was stone-cold sober.

Momentarily drunk on lust.

Again, I need to spend some time under the covers.

My eyes lift to Beretta's deep brown locks as they fall forward once more, the gust of the wind sweeping over the sides of the car as we turn left at a stop sign.

My fingers lift, gently slipping into his soft hair, swiping it out of the way for him, and he cuts me a quick glance, his grin holding as he faces forward.

As my hand begins to fall back in place, I catch Arsen's eyes in the mirror.

He holds mine for a few seconds, looking away in the next, and when I face forward, I realize we're pulling into a parking garage in front of a boarded-up, abandoned office complex covered in graffiti.

My features tighten as I look around, not another car in sight, and I'm about to ask what this little stop is about, but then he turns left, toward the giant 'do not enter' sign, where there once was an entrance. We curve around the lower level, the proof of the night disappearing as we're now underground, and not alone.

At least two dozen other cars fill the warm lit place, and my head snaps right when the echo of a door closing reaches us.

A girl, maybe nineteen-ish stands there, straightening her short blue wig before she slings a small purse over her shoulder, the box-style clutch meeting the skin of her thigh, her leopard print dress is so short. She looks to the car she climbed out of and pops her hip out. Finally, the passenger side door of the yellow Volkswagen opens, and a guy climbs out.

He doesn't spare her a glance, but she hooks her arm into his and together, they walk in a direction I can't see.

"Where are we?" I ask, slowly looking to Beretta since he's the one in the seat beside me.

His grin is deep, and he unbuckles his seat belt, so I do the same, climbing from the car as he does, the others right behind us.

They begin forward, the top to the convertible folding behind us, but I lean my ass on the door, crossing my arms.

It takes them three whole steps to realize I'm not at their side, and they pause, three glares swinging my way.

"Where are we?" I ask again.

"A... club." Ransom's frown deepens. "Sort of."

"Does this club happen to have black lights, too, because I'm basically an X-rated picture book."

Arsen laughs and starts walking again. Ransom is quick to follow after him and Beretta grins, his arm stretching out, so he can grip me by the wrist.

He pulls and with a heavy sigh, I follow. "No, Trouble. No black lights, though I'd love to see our work."

"I bet."

Beretta laughs, his fingers gliding down to lace with mine. For some reason, I let him.

A large 'out of service' sign is drilled into the elevator door, wires sticking out all over the place where the bottom should be located, yet somehow the thing opens and the boys begin to walk inside.

I attempt to yank free, but Beretta's grip tightens, and he yanks me forward, wrapping his arm around my body before I can scurry back.

"Cool, so you guys want to die."

"It's a deflector, to get people who wander this way to wander right back to where they came from."

The elevator is nothing but a black cube, and I'm unable to decipher if it travels up or down, but whichever way it's headed, it's toward a crowd.

Their laughter begins to invade my ears, the rich, creamy

sandalwood-like aroma from fresh smoked, inexpensive cigars lighting a small fire in my throat as it seeps into the elevator the moment the doors ding open.

While the chatter is loud and the music low, nothing is before us but a tiny hall lit up by streaks of light, a metal door at the end of it.

We follow the sound, push through the door and suddenly we're standing on a balcony that's seen better days.

The paint is chipped, and the railing has rusted over, but you can tell it was a beautiful place once upon a time.

The ceilings are high with intricate crown molding in desperate need of some attention, but as I step closer to the edge and look out, I would guarantee nobody here has noticed, nor do they care.

Like the girl from the parking garage, several others below wear bright wigs and loud patterns. Half of the men are in slacks and button-ups, the rest putting off more of a street vibe like the boys, jeans and T-shirts with high-top sneakers to match.

This time, it's Arsen who grabs my hand, leading me down the staircase, the other two on our tail.

Our feet hit the final step and no sooner than Arsen yanks me to a stop does a man with black curls covering the top of his head slip before us.

He eyes Arsen, the guys behind us, and then looks at me.

"Who's your friend?" His tone is short.

Ransom slips in front of me without a word and the guy softens, laughing lightly as he steps aside.

We follow Ransom down onto the main floor.

The people around here are chatting and smoking and lightly swaying to the music, but what was hidden from the view of the balcony are all the separated rooms tucked beneath it.

None of the spaces have doors, but the openings are as wide as French doors would be. Some have strange strands of beads hanging from the ceiling to the floor while others have some sort of Christmas lights strung across. There's even a tie-dyed curtain hung along one that may have been a sheet at one time.

There seems to be no real rhyme or reason for anything, but nobody cares, they are simply laughing and talking among their friends.

Tucked deep within the area closest to us is a wall of cabinets turned bar.

There is no seating, no loitering, no more than a walk-up counter with cocktail waitresses coming and going, full trays in hand. I realize they are the ones wearing the wigs.

We continue forward, coming up to what looks like a hookah room, a guy our age steps in front of us, blocking my view.

"What's going on, Freddy?" Beretta clasps hands with the Ken doll-looking guy.

"Oh shit, I didn't know you guys would be here. I'd have brought more cash."

Cash?

I realize then, there's a deck of cards in his hand.

The guy glances toward me, and with a grin, he extends his hand.

Considering how Ransom slipped in front of the last man, I cut a quick look his way.

Something flashes in his eyes but when he gives a curt nod, I accept, squeezing as hard as he does.

"I'm Freddy."

"I heard."

He grins wider, looking back to the boys. "No name,

okay then." He nods his head. "Well, come on, man. Let's play. I got first game."

Peeking at Ransom, I'm surprised by his smile. It's full, and he rubs his hands together, falling in line with Freddy, but not before connecting his eyes with mine.

Something low in my stomach swirls, but it's gone as quickly as it came. I turn to Arsen. "What now?"

He smiles and leads me to the right while Beretta stays talking to some other person they clearly know.

Arsen steps up to the man with a silver case, and as he pulls his wallet from his back pocket, his entire body freezes.

My eyes dart up to his.

His brows are dug in low, angry, but as fast as the anger appeared, it's replaced with fear. Worry.

"Arsen?" My voice is an accidental whisper.

But after I've spoken his name, it's called by another.

I straighten as a man with bushy eyebrows steps up to us. He's in his early forties maybe, a grin hitched high on his face, but it's one I recognize.

Fake, cunning.

Superior.

He reaches out, gripping Arsen's forearm, and clapping his shoulder with his other, but slowly, his attention turns to me.

"Well, well, now this is a sight," he says, facing me, but Arsen gently tugs me behind him.

The man, reeking of red wine and overused aftershave, only chuckles. "So, where's your little friend, he run into my boss yet?"

But nothing else is able to be spoken as Arsen's grip falls to my wrist. I'm yanked from the room without a second's notice, the man's drunken laugh following our exit.

"Careful, now," he shouts. "Wouldn't want him getting

into any trouble!"

I flip the guy off without looking back, my head slicing from left to right as we run and finally, I spot Beretta.

I wave as I whip past and he does a double take, shooting to his feet.

He catches up in an instant.

"Arsen?" he snaps, alarm laced in his low spoken demand, but Arsen doesn't pause.

He keeps forward, toward the direction Ransom was headed, as Beretta looks to me expectantly.

"Some middle-aged guy with full-on Mr. Beans brows walked up and—"

"Fuck," Beretta spits, cutting me off and yanks his friend to a stop, pushing hard on his chest. "You good?"

Arsen slaps his hand away, meeting his glare with his own.

"Right, yeah, let's get to him." Beretta nods, and together, we step around the final corner.

This room has a man at the podium-like desk in the front, a countertop stretching a few feet down and ending where a long, black curtain begins. It's effective, hiding what lies on the other side.

There is a long, high rectangular cutout in the ceiling that comes about two feet down, allowing the noise, smoke, and a bit of light to shine through. The clink of glass and soft chatter is all that's heard.

Ransom stands with Freddy, only inches from where one room leads into the next.

He chuckles, his shoulders lax, elbow loosely pressed against the banister on his left.

He seems calm, content, and my lips begin to curve at the sight, but then his eyes lift to mine.

His body goes pencil-straight, an instant frown forming,

one that grows deeper as he looks to the guys at my side.

We're in front of him in the next second, and Arsen grips his shirt, attempting to tug him, but Ransom grabs his wrists to keep them both there.

Freddy must understand their dynamics because he carries himself into the room without a word.

"What?" Ransom growls, his eyes on Arsen.

Beretta closes off our little square, and I can't help but notice the way both his and Arsen's stances widen, as if they're preparing for something, I'm unaware of, that's on the way.

"We need to go," Beretta says calmer than expected.

But the way Ransom's eyes narrow and the slight cock of his head lets me know there is a reason.

Beretta drops his chin. "Your brother's here."

My eyes snap his way, quickly shifting back to Ransom.

The sharp, always confident curves of his face, fall flat, and my brows meet in the center.

With a single blink, his expression flips.

Ransom jerks himself free, darting for the entrance, but Arsen grips the back of his shirt, yanking him so hard the thin cotton shreds, Ransom's steps strong and firm. But Arsen jerks forward, grabbing Ransom by the shoulder, and before Ransom can shove him off, Beretta is bumping him in the chest, locking his arms around Ransom's torso and it takes both of them to tear the angry boy back.

The three slam into the wall, shoving him repeatedly to keep him there.

I watch them, wide-eyed, and Ransom tries to throw them aside, but then Arsen's forearm shoots up, pushing into Ransom's neck, pinning him as hard as he can against the wall, Beretta right there adding force with his palms against his bicep.

"Stop, man," Beretta hisses.

"Fuck him, is he for real? He's here, as if he hasn't run through enough already?" he spits, his lip curled and body heaving. "He needs his ass handed to him."

"Yeah, and you're the one for the job, but not like this. There's no hiding, and he'll fuck you". Beretta is seething, right in his face. "That what you want? One wrong move, man, and it's over."

Curiosity is the only excuse I have for my forward steps.

"You're better than him," I hear Beretta say. "Fuck. Him."

My fingers curl around the cheap velvety material. I glide it over, and my nostrils are stung by a heavy cloud of oak and mint as the shoulder of two men slowly come into view beyond the silky smoke.

I vaguely hear someone say it's time to go.

I pull farther but am halted by a steely grip to my wrist, forcing me to release the thick curtain before I manage to move it a full inch.

My gaze locks with Ransom's, and my lungs squeeze.

He's the picture of rage. His forehead is strained with firm lines, his jaw thrust forward and clenched tightly.

His teeth are clamped shut, his grip tight and trembling. I should yank from his hold, but staring into his marble-like eyes, I can't.

There's something within them, a contrast of his expression, of his words and the tone in which he delivered them. This is deeper. This isn't about anger.

So, I nod, and walk backward, my fingers gently latching on to his wrist as he still holds mine.

He walks with me, and after a few steps, we're shifted, facing forward and stepping back onto the main floor.

Without another word, and with strong, confident strides, we leave the way we came, climb inside the car, and roll out into the night.

Ten, maybe fifteen minutes go by, before the tension begins to subside and Arsen, now in the driver's seat, turns the music on low.

I seek out Ransom in the side mirror, finding his eyes closed tight, head dropped back on the seat.

He seems tortured, at a loss.

Defeated.

"Where to, my man?" Beretta asks, but nobody answers.

Ransom makes no move at all, while Arsen looks toward the clock, a low sigh following.

Beretta pulls his phone out, but quickly locks it, glancing out at the night with a tight drawn frown and low fought groan.

I flick my gaze over them once more and something stirs beneath my ribs.

The time on the stereo reads two in the morning, and I get the feeling they either don't *want* to go home... or they can't.

We were about to start the night all over again, likely ring in the sunrise behind those doors, but the fresh energy we went in with converted to a heavy weight with our exit.

"Go to my house," I say, focused on the road ahead.

No one speaks the entire drive there, not even when Arsen pulls up to the curb in front of the walkway leading to my front door.

I unbuckle, grabbing my purse from the floorboard, and push the door open, stepping out onto the sidewalk.

I turn back, my eyes moving along the three, all staring right at me, and I raise my brows.

"Well..." I draw out. "Are you coming?"

There's a slight pause, a slow beat of silence, and then all at once, they're at my side.

We head inside my house.

"Game two, boy!" Beretta claps, high-fiving himself and bumps a shoulder into Arsen, who laughs beside him.

Shaking my head, I set my glass of water in the sink and grab my blanket off the couch, joining Ransom on the balcony.

He holds a vape pen to his lips, and this time, when he blindly passes it my way, I accept.

As I inhale, his eyes slide my way, but only for a second.

We stand there, looking out at the night for a few minutes, nothing but the ocean in front of us.

I spin, leaning my back against the glass and look at him.

"Don't." His forewarning is quiet and ignored.

His command could mean anything. It could be his way of telling me not to ask questions about what happened tonight, or it could be related to the last time he was here. It's probably his way for covering both, but we finally have a minute, so I take it.

"You had no reason to help me out with my car, but you did."

He frowns, looking straight ahead. "I said don't."

"And I don't care. I would have thanked you sooner had you been around, but you guys were never down the road when I tried, and apparently, school is low on your guys' list."

He scoffs, looking away. "Like B said, our lungs had to heal. Claim jobs make for a lot of smoke, and we couldn't exactly light it and leave it." His blue eyes find mine. "We had to make sure it was nothing but the frame when it was done."

I stare a moment. "The cop had said it looked like it was gutted."

He nods, a bit of a bite in his tone as he shares, "Sold the system to a guy in Irvine. Sold the gym bag in the trunk to a chick in Fountain Valley." His gaze tightens the slightest bit, as if he's looking for a reaction.

As if I'll be upset over the Saint Laurent my mother spent a small fortune on when she insisted my workouts go from three days a week to five.

Keep it tight and he'll still come home at night—laws of a loveless marriage.

"Well" —I look out at the water behind me, then back to him— "I hope you got a fraction of its worth."

"I did," he quickly confirms.

A small smile pulls at my lips and I shake my head, glancing inside the house at the other two.

Beretta tilts and turns his whole body as he plays the game, and Arsen sits beside him, calmly pressing buttons, chuckling at B, as Ransom called him.

"How'd you guys meet?" I wonder.

"Like most kids. At school."

"Did you go to Harbor Day?"

He scoffs, and we briefly glance toward each other. "No, Jameson, we didn't go to a private school. We went to Lincoln."

Right. "Were you in the same class?"

"Nope!" Beretta hops to his feet, gleefully interrupting.

Arsen stands too, following Beretta out to the balcony.

"Arsen, here, was getting his ass beat by a couple eighth-grade assholes," he shares, his hand on Arsen's shoulder. "Being the brave dude I am, I jumped in." He smiles. "Started getting my ass beat, too."

A low laugh leaves me, and I cut a quick look to Ransom, who grins at his friend.

"And there came Ransom, the motherfucking savior. He whooped all their asses, and then he turned and punched us both for getting ourselves into the situation."

The four of us laugh.

"We walked home from detention together that day, and every day after that."

"Friends at first punch. Nice."

"How about you?" Beretta pulls a cigarette from his pocket, closing the balcony doors so the smoke doesn't float inside. "How'd you end up with the trust fund kids? Is there like some sort of secret club you all automatically know how to join, submit your bank statements and all that?"

"Maybe." My eyes widen mockingly. "But if so, I couldn't tell you, could I?" I joke, and he grins, the stem of his Marlboro stuck between his full lips.

"No, I've known Cali and Jules, Scott and some of the others, since I was little." I look over the house, at the remodel I didn't even know my mom had done while we were gone and the complete layout change that had to cost a small fortune. "I was born here. My dad bought this house for my mom, and when she remarried, she kept us in it. We left at the end of sixth grade, but they kept the property, *just in case,* and, well..." I look away, remembering my mom telling me why we were leaving all of our furniture behind, not that any of it's here anymore. "Here I am."

The 'just in case' in full effect.

"And here they're not," Ransom guesses.

"My sister is." I cut a look toward Ransom, thinking of his reaction to his brother and his comment about his family issues the other day.

Seems we have some similarities after all.

He frowns, but shifts his gaze to the ocean, so I continue.

"We're both busy with our own shit, so we can go a few days without being home at the same time or we're both home, but one of us is gone before the other wakes in the morning."

Beretta nods. "She here now?"

"No clue." I shrug. "Maybe?"

He and Arsen walk to the far end of the balcony, looking down at the pool, lined perfectly with the edge of the cliff on the first story. Beretta starts talking about what he would do if it were his property and Arsen grins, nodding along.

"They're very protective of each other, aren't they?" I ask quietly.

"We are protective of all the things we care about, and of all the things we want."

I keep my head facing forward, moving only my eyes to his, and clear, steady blues stare back.

Something unfamiliar burns in my throat, but I swallow past it.

I'm not sure what he sees in my expression, but before I've even got my mouth open, he's shaking his head, and like before, I ignore him.

"Why were you on Scott's street the night I crashed?"

He doesn't confirm or deny he followed me, but he also doesn't look away.

"You read the note he left, so I think you wanted to see if I would go."

Again, nothing from him.

"I did, and you stayed. Why?"

"To see how long you would." This time, his answer is quick and honest.

I nod, figuring that as well. "To know if I was fucking him."

"I already knew you weren't," he fires back.

My brows lift the slightest bit.

"That so?" I wrap my fingers around the railing, and I shift to face him better.

"Yeah, that's so." He matches my move, facing me full-on, pushing closer until we're near chest to chest, his knuckles brushing mine on the cool metal.

I wait for an explanation, but what I get is a warning, the purpose buried beneath it.

His free hand comes up, and he presses two fingers against my neck, just beneath my jawbone and directly over my pulse point. My skin heats from his touch, under his darkened gaze, and I try to pull away, but his free hand wraps around my waist, forcing me still.

Forcing me to feel him.

To acknowledge the way my pulse climbs beneath his rough fingertips.

He dips his head. "Next time your little iron heart beats a bit harder than you want it to, give in..." He trails off, his thumb coming up, pressing firmly into the underside of my jaw, and tilting it up farther. "Or go the fuck home... not to someone else simply because you know he could never get under your skin."

My jaw clamps tight. His perceptiveness is as disturbing as it is alluring, but the way he insinuates my attention belongs to him is not good.

It's dangerous.

It's dangerous because my insides are suddenly dancing to a beat I've never heard, yet there it is, thrumming beneath my skin.

As if he's aware, his eyes seem to gleam, but he holds his frown in place, putting me on edge even more when he says, "You went there to regain control of your own mind, but you have no idea what jumping at Scott's call screams inside his."

Screw Scott, what the hell is happening here?

It's as if Ransom found a dark corner in my mind and took up shop there, discovering all my inner issues and blurring truths.

It's anxiety-inducing, so I pivot, call on my mother's training and hide all hints of humanism. I have to.

Stand calm, speak cold, and don't forget to smile.

"I can handle Scott Gentry." This time, it's me who moves closer. "And if I want to *handle* him, I can do that too."

His nostrils flare, and an angry little growl escapes, gaining his friends' attention.

Slowly, they walk closer, and Ransom nearly knocks me on my ass when his chest bumps into mine. "I should have let you get arrested, you deserved it the second you climbed behind the wheel."

My brows cave and he jerks away from me.

"If you ever think about drinking and driving again, don't." His words are a menacing command, low and deep.

He doesn't have to vocalize how I'll regret it; his words are dipped in the threat.

With erratic movements, he snags his sweater from the back of the chair, quickly tugging it over his head, and without a word, the others do the same.

They're out the door not thirty seconds later.

Just like that, I'm reminded they are a unit, and I don't have one.

It takes a second to remember that's the way I like it.

CHAPTER
Twelve

My phone alerts me that the Uber Eats driver has just left my coffee on the porch, so I throw my legs over the side of the lounge chair, but before I can push to my feet, my side gate rattles, and my head snaps that way.

Beretta hops over the fence with a wink, and I cross my arms as he opens the gate, revealing Ransom and Arsen on the other side of it.

Arsen smirks, holding up his hand, my coffee tucked inside it, an entire tray of coffees in the other.

Ransom grabs it along with another from the drink carrier and slips ahead of them, so I drop back in the chair and let the guy bring it to me.

He offers me both, and I gladly accept.

"Thank you." I tilt my head.

Ransom must be wondering what exactly lies behind the dark lenses over my eyes, because he pushes them up onto my head.

He frowns. "I'm not seeing anger."

I scoff, and bring my drink to my lips, reveling in the rich aroma before taking a small sip. *Delicious.*

I shrug. "I will never be angry when a hot latte is placed in my hand, and I have two."

The corner of his mouth tips up and my shoulders ease a bit.

"Listen—" I begin, but then he's pulling off his shirt, his tight body commanding my eyes to take inventory of each and every inch.

Ransom's body is something to be admired. His skin shines like the finest of silks, glowing a deep gold, and he's toned at every inch. The cuts of his abs are natural and deep. He's not burly by any means, rather tapered to precision, as are the sharp cuts of his hip bones pitted perfectly, inviting on their very own. I follow the length of the lines, and only then do I notice he's wearing swim trunks.

They all are, and at some point, the other two managed to discard their tops, too, both having already dropped in the chairs to my right, hot drinks at their lips.

Ransom claims the one at my left.

"You were saying?" He raises a brow.

A laugh sputters from me, and I push my glasses back down. "Yeah, yeah. Sun, swimming, and seriously delicious coffee it is, but only for a few hours. I'm busy this afternoon."

"Right, 'the man.'"

I point a brassy smile to Beretta.

Honestly, I'm surprised he remembered the day he eavesdropped on mine and my parents' conversation.

"Man?" Ransom pushes.

"Oh, you mean he didn't report back to you with every little detail from that day?" I joke, and Beretta chuckles. "Interesting."

Ransom's glare grows deeper and I laugh.

"I'm working on the next phase of spoiled rich girl, that's all," I mock myself before he can.

"And deeper into the pit she goes."

"I was born in the pit, Ransom. It's all about navigation."

"And you've got all the direction you need, huh?"

I give a simple shrug. "Some people go to college after high school, others go to the altar."

He looks my way, so I push my glasses up on my head.

After a short stare-off, in which his face remains blank, he scoffs, sips his drink and sits back, so I do the same, refusing to dwell on his little trip inside my head last night.

It's a new day, yesterday forgotten, so for the next couple hours, we simply hang out.

No one whines for fresh-squeezed orange juice to complete their mimosas, complains the water is too cold, or throws a fit over their hair getting wet. There's no hint of coconut oil in the air and no photo sessions.

It's pretty damn nice.

Right as I think it, a splash of water blurs my vision.

Arsen grips me by the hips and lifts me into the air. A quick squeal escapes me, and I'm forced to wrap my legs around his body for stability, knowing full well we're going in.

Sure enough, with me wrapped around him, he jumps into the deep end. His legs come up, crossing under mine, slowly allowing us to fall to the pool's floor.

At the bottom, he releases me, and we try to sit with our legs crossed as gravity sends us back to the surface.

Laughing, I swim to the opposite end, where we set up some snack trays with items we found in the fridge from Gennie.

I pick up a small crab cake and push the entire thing in my mouth as Arsen swims up, opening his.

I shove one in, laughing when he nips at my fingers and nods toward the pitcher of water, his empty glass in his free hand.

As I pass it to him, I catch Ransom staring, and he

doesn't turn away, but Arsen pats my thigh, so I refocus on him.

He nods toward the waterfall.

"Go for it." I laugh. "But you're on your own with that one."

With a grin, he takes off underwater.

His head pops up and he climbs out as Ransom lowers himself beside me.

He watches Arsen, a strained look in his eyes. "He likes you."

I study him a moment and then decide. "That surprises you?"

As if he's unsure my statement is true, his brows pinch.

"He doesn't sign," I ease, and Ransom looks to me. "Does that mean he can speak but doesn't?"

"As long as I've known him, I've never heard him say a word," he shares. "He saw some shit as a kid, things his dad did to his own mom. When someone finally called social services, his dad told him if he spoke a word, he'd find him and do worse. He told anyway and later, they gave him back to his dad, and the asshole made good on his promise. He couldn't speak after, and once he got better, he decided he didn't want to." He shrugs.

My muscles clench and I look to Arsen. "He doesn't need words. He speaks in his own way."

"He's fluent with you. Normally he just... stares or glares around other people, avoids as much as he can. Not with you." A small frown mars his forehead. "He motions, and you understand, without annoyance or pause or frustration. People aren't like that with him."

"People like Scott." I remember that day in cooking class.

When he doesn't speak, I look his way, and his eyes are

already on me.

"You're not like them," he says suddenly, a thick sense of certainty in his tone, and while I hold his gaze a moment, I'm forced to look away.

Sure, they're superficial rich kids in every sense of the word, preparing to live the lives their parents laid out for them, but am I not doing the same?

At least they're enjoying themselves as they wait, rather than watching the clock and wishing to get it over with already, like me.

Maybe I should be more like them than I already am.

Fact is, I *am* 'like them.'

A low sigh leaves me, and the corner of my lip pulls into a tight smile. "You're wrong."

"But you don't want me to be." His arm stretches out behind me, allowing him to lean closer, my shoulder nearly touching his chest now, his lips almost meeting mine. His breath is warm and minty, rich with a scent I can't place but screams *him*. "Tell me I'm wrong about that..."

If I tell you you're right, that means you see what you shouldn't and understand what no one else does, but that can't possibly be true. I've never failed at hiding and I can't afford to start now.

"I didn't drink and drive," unexpectedly flies from my mouth.

His brows crash in the center, and he slowly pushes himself upright.

Shit. Okay, I guess we're doing this now.

"That night, Scott poured me a drink when I walked in, and yeah, I tasted it, but by letting it wet my lips. I didn't take a single drink. He told me to bring it home, and for whatever reason, I entertained him, and did as he asked." I did go there to clear my head, but it didn't work. "I was speeding, and it was dark and foggy." I shrug. "When I crashed—"

"The drink spilled all over you," he whispers, his muscles settling, easing, but why?

He nods to himself, and slowly, he lowers his body into the pool, disappears under the water and joins Arsen at the opposite end.

I stare after him.

I knew he was angry over the alcohol after the crash, and had I not put it together then, he made it clear yesterday, but the relief that lightened his blue eyes just now was intense, it was as if that little fact somehow mattered.

"You only have the one sister?"

At his sudden question, I look to Beretta, but he too watches Ransom from where he lies on the lounger behind me.

"Yeah, why?"

He nods and kicks off his slides. "Yeah, he only had the one, too."

My brows snap together, and he finally looks to me, raising one of his, and it clicks.

Ransom had a sister.

He has a brother, but he *had* a sister...

A drunk driver.

I open my mouth to ask what happened, but he shakes his head and cannonballs into the water.

I sit back, watching as three young men act like little boys, knowing when they step out, they'll go back to their worlds, and I'll be here in mine.

Since they were children, they have fought for each other.

What it must be like to have someone in your corner.

I'm simply a charm dangling from a solid gold necklace, one appraised by my very own mother and traded by her just the same.

But it's for the best.

It fits my plan and helps my family, writes my future.

I won't have to think, plan, or prep.

I don't have to open myself up to false hope and broken promises.

To heartache and pain.

I simply have to be.

A low sigh leaves me, and I nod to myself.

It's for the best.

After a night of no sleep, it took a miracle to get myself presentable by Anthony's standards, so I had no energy left to put time into my outfit, so I kept it fault-free with a black pantsuit and shoes to match.

It's perfectly basic. Anthony should approve.

I slip by the reception desk as I begin to curve around the corner; I pass a coffee station and slow at the sight of the lovely latte button.

Scanning the area, I spot the cups and pull one from the top, placing it over the big red circle, but when I push the button, nothing happens.

"Can I help?"

I spin to find a young woman with brown hair and eyes to match.

"You mind?"

She smiles and steps up; within a minute, I'm thanking her and headed for Anthony's office.

He's on the phone when I enter, his back to me, so I round the room, coming up in front of him and his smile alone makes for a nice night.

Placing the call on hold, he lowers his cell to the desk

and steps around it. He grabs my hand, kissing my knuckles and his smile grows wider.

"Nice to see you, too."

"Trust me, the pleasure is all mine. Today has been a shitstorm." He chuckles. "Mind if I finish this call, it will only be another ten minutes or so?"

I lower myself into his chair, a tall back, mohair with molded wood, and place my hands along the fine shine of his desktop. "Do as you need, Mr. Blanca," I tease—playful banter is the second 'must do' on my mother's list, and with the way his eyelids lower, I'd say I'm not so bad at it.

He slips closer, grabbing my shoulders from behind, and leans toward my ear. "Thank you, Ms. Filano. I have a feeling you and I will be explosive." My eyes shoot forward.

Well, that was a first.

His light scruff brushes against my skin and my shoulders draw up slightly, his lips pressing gently to my cheek. "Enjoy your latte, sweetheart, only so many months before you switch to tea."

A laugh bubbles from me before I can stop it, but when I see his smile is kind, his eyes still warm, I swallow it, summon a smile of my own and then off he goes.

And he never comes back.

A half hour later, the pretty brunette knocks, only peeking her head in once I've called for her to do so.

"Mr. Blanca had an emergency meeting with his accountant, I'm afraid he won't be finished in time for your early dinner, but I can still call it in for you?"

I'm already walking around the desk before she's finished.

"No, that's not necessary, I can grab something on my way home," I tell her as I slip by, but as we make it into the hall, I jerk to a stop, spin and ask, "Do you mind making me another latte to go?"

Her smile is sly, but she tries to hide it, and when she hands it to me, it's with a wink. "Have a double."

As I walk from the hall, I pass a large glass room, Anthony tucked inside with two other men.

He gives an apologetic smile.

And I lift my latte in goodbye.

Give up coffee for tea, he said.

Yeah, right.

I mean... right?

———

Tanner, my sister's shadow, thanks to my parents, is still in the exact place I left him.

He sees me coming as I pass his window and he shoots from his door.

"Miss—"

"I told you, Tanner. No miss. And before you say you didn't expect me so early, it's fine. Get in the car, I can open my door."

I know he wants to argue, but I'm already tugging it open, so he slides back into his seat.

"Home?" he guesses.

I nod, looking out the window at the parking lot full of black cars and silver SUVs, the typical clean and clear choices of elegance. We won't even mention the 'I have money' models of choice, likely an unspoken requirement for the hardworking staff inside the building.

My mom owns a ridiculous Tesla Roadster in Florida, which was a gift from a client. She considers it average and hates it, but it stays parked in front of our house there, day and night. It's washed regularly but not by her because, well... image is everything.

Like her, I'd guarantee not one of the vehicles here belongs to the lawyers of Admiral Law—they couldn't possibly be bothered with driving themselves.

Imagine all the work they could get done in the back seat?

Sighing, I close my eyes, settling into the seat a bit and only when Tanner clears his throat, do I open them again.

Once we've turned onto my street, the first thing I spot is a familiar convertible, and Arsen and the boys who live with him in the grass playing catch.

So, the second I get home, I head for my room, change into a simple dress, and head for the safe hidden in the back of my closet.

My dad's dad was apparently a craftsman. He built custom safes, like the one disguised to look like my wall.

Like the one-of-a-kind lockbox hidden inside my father's headstone.

It's a bit outlandish, and completely undervalued since all that's in here is a small stack of cash and emergency credit cards.

I grab the one my mother advised I use and slip back outside, and straight down the street.

With a small scowl and slightly hurried steps, Arsen meets me halfway.

"You almost done?"

His shoulders ease as if he was concerned. He glances behind him, seeing the young boys pick up their water bottles and heading back inside the house.

He turns back with a nod.

"Want to help me pick out a new car?"

His smile is slow, and when he wraps an arm around my shoulder, steering me toward his Camaro, I hold in an entirely different kind of sigh, pretending his low chuckle isn't a settling sound.

But when our first stop is at a mechanic shop a few blocks away, the boys stepping from the door the moment we pause in front of it, I'm no longer capable of holding it in, not with all three of them here now.

My sigh slips.

CHAPTER *thirteen*

"**W**hy can't you valet like normal people?" Monti whines, one hand lifting to cover her yawn, the other gripping her coffee cup for dear life.

I put my car in park and push my door open. Swinging my legs out, I reach inside to grab my own drink, meeting her puffy, hungover eyes. "And have them go through my things and pretend they didn't? No."

I get out and the click of her heels matches mine as she drops her head back dramatically, looking up at the parking garage ceiling. "It's a brand-new car, J, there's nothing in it."

I laugh and we start forward. "You act like we're not within twenty feet of the entrance."

"You act like you don't know what it feels like to put on six-inch heels the day after a formal gala!"

I spin, walking backward, scowling at her as my mother would—tight-lipped, nostrils tucked, and head tipped, disapproving glint in my eye—and recite one of her lessons with her motherly tone of choice: annoyance.

"A smart woman follows up a six-inch with a four.

Trick your body into thinking it's getting a break, Monti, and tell your mind to fuck off."

Monti laughs, flipping me off. "And don't forget—"

"To smile," we say in unison, laughing as we step through the automatic doors and into the fresh smell of lavender and eucalyptus.

At the counter, an older woman with kind eyes and a bun a ballerina would be envious of, welcomes us with a smile.

"Monti and Jameson Filano." My sister throws her arm around my shoulders.

"Of course." The woman's spine straightens, and she keeps her smile high and clear, I'll give her that, but there's a shift in the air, one I'm not sure Monti is aware of as she follows up with a blinding smile.

The thing about my sister, she has the ability to swallow a room without any effort. She is so beyond beautiful that it makes others uncomfortable, she's that... perfect.

Her hair is a rich brown shade like mine, but fuller and shinier with a natural wave she doesn't have to touch if she doesn't wish to, though she never allows them to be seen. Her eyes, perfectly almond-shaped and the color of roasted honey, almost unrealistic in shade, are so mesmerizing, and framed with thick, curved lashes. Let's not forget her full, mauve-colored lips with a perfect heart's arch.

Don't even get me started on her figure.

All in all, if there was any woman in the world who could step out of the shower and directly in front of a camera with zero prepping or retouches to follow, it's Monti.

The sad part?

She's the most self-conscious person I know.

She spends hours in the mirror documenting every flaw, literally writing them down in a journal she keeps tucked in her handbag, and even more at the gym. She counts every calorie, and while she doesn't restrict herself from what she wants to indulge in, she does work off more than she consumes. Every single day.

But you would never guess any of that, and she makes sure of it.

It's not mentally or physically healthy, but how many of us can say we are?

People are supposed to be flawed, but how do you learn to accept such a thing when your own mother has convinced you your only attribute to the world is beauty?

My sister is so much more than beauty.

So much more than me.

"Right this way." The woman bows her head, and the doors to the left open.

We step into the hall, following it around the curved corner where another woman awaits us, fresh robes and booties in her hands.

Across from her station are dressing rooms with lockers, so we make quick work of changing and when we step out, she offers us a flute of champagne, but we both decline in favor of the coffees we brought in.

It's with a gracious smile she outstretches her hand. "Please." She motions toward another set of automatic doors, and when those open, it's with a heavy dose of steam.

My sister and I step through, into a rain-forest themed room.

Large leaves cascade from every inch of the walls, down the sides and hang high above, small lights threaded throughout, the soft sounds of showers filling the room.

Two large stone-like baths are set against the wall, a waterfall leading into the foot of them, a set of bamboo tables outstretched on the opposite side, steaming towels on top of them and a tray of fresh fruit in the middle.

Monti walks over, picking off a small piece of pineapple, and plucks it between her lips.

We drop our robes and slip into the steaming tubs, breathing in the steam and allowing it to open our lungs and pores.

"Seriously, I haven't done this in months." My sister moans, and I fight a grin when the masseuse who slipped into the room slowly backs out of it. "This is amazing."

She rolls her head along the back of the stone, her eyes meeting mine.

Monti and I didn't lose touch when she came here last year. We talked all the time, almost as much as when she was home, and we still do. I text her through the day or she me to the point where I consider us close, but close is subjective, and I think Monti might disagree.

She and I talk about the annoying guy who eats during her lectures and new items added to the coffee house menus or joke about what might be said when Gennie reports back to our mom each week. It's more chatter, easy flowing conversation that provides a sense of a connection, but at the surface is where we stay.

It's not for her lack of trying, but at the end of the day, I am who I am, which happens to be what my sister fears the most, my mother's creation.

A blank canvas to be filled and fussed with at the hands of another, without so much as a blink or care or concern. Taught to look without seeing, to smile without feeling, and to speak without interest.

I'm a Monet.

A chameleon.

I'm whatever I must be.

Monti doesn't judge, never condemns, but I know she

pities me. It's a waste on her part, not that I have to tell her that.

She's already aware.

"I've missed you, sister," she whispers suddenly, her eyes softening.

I give her a pinched smile and look away.

"I asked them to send me over a profile for all the masseuses. Naturally, I get the hotter, larger-handed man, and picked the one with hairy knuckles for you."

A laugh sputters from us both and just like that, she brings us back into our own kind of sisterhood.

Two hours later, my sister groans. "Oh my god, *what* does she want?"

I shake my head, not moving an inch, and enjoying the cool ice mask in contrast with the hot stones being used as my legs are kneaded and pressed.

"Hello, Mother." My sister's tone is silvery and fake as hell.

"Where is Jameson?"

I tense, and there's a slight pause, but then Monti laughs. "I knew you couldn't possibly have anything to say to me that would warrant a phone call."

"Is that why you ignored my last five calls?" My mother's voice is distant, forever only half of her attention given, a pile of work in front of her that takes precedence, I'm sure.

"We're at the spa," Monti tells her. "I'd say you're lucky I have my phone on me at all."

"Your sister," our mom clips.

"Mm, sorry. She's currently being groped and shown what a man with very large hands is capable of, but—"

At that, the hands on my body—not at all hairy, thank you very much—fly off, and I shoot up right in time for my mother to cut her off with a snapped, "Enough."

"I'm here, Mom." I widen my eyes at my sister, flipping her off.

"You didn't tell me you didn't spend time with Anthony yesterday?" She doesn't miss a beat.

I look to the masseuse, and he bows his head, he and his partner quietly exiting the room.

"Jameson!"

"I'm here, Jesus." I tilt my leg, smoothing out a spot of warm wax. "And I did go to Anthony's, but he got held up, so we had to cancel."

"Well, he's been trying to reach you for the last hour. He had to call *me* at work!"

"The audacity," my sister whispers, making me laugh, and I throw myself back on the table.

"He was worried, he said he didn't hear from you yesterday, I now assume he meant once you left, and when you didn't pick up today, well, imagine the thoughts that must have ran through his mind, especially when he learned your car was stolen, and from your own garage."

"Mom."

"He must have been—"

"Mother, please, no need to lay it on thick." I stand up, holding my robe together as I walk closer and try to take my sister's phone, but she pulls it back. "I get it. If you're calling to tell me to call him, I hear you. I will call him."

"Why didn't you tell him about your car?" She ignores me completely.

"Because I didn't see him long enough to get to the whole conversation part." Duh.

Is that not why she's bitching?

"You could have texted him when it happened."

Monti's eyes snap to mine, but I keep my face blank.

"Your job is to share your life with this man, Jameson. Don't make me teach you how to do so. Again. Men like Anthony have—"

"Billowing egos we must keep fed, yeah, Mom, I know." I shake my head. "I'll call him."

"No, you'll head home, fix your face and go to him, and it shouldn't take you long. I saw the charge already go through from the salon this morning."

Monti flips off the phone.

"Wait, now?"

"Right now. You had no school, being Labor Day. It's fitting, if you ask me."

"Well, no one did, so bye Mom!" Monti singsongs.

"Monti, if you hang up—"

My mother's threat is cut off as Monti powers down her phone, and I'm already tying my robe and reaching for the door.

"Duty calls," Monti teases.

"Fuck you," I call as I push through the door.

"Love you!" is shouted from the other side.

A low laugh leaves me and I head for the changing room, redressing and making my way to my car. As I get into the parking garage, my attention is pulled to a flash of blonde and I look to my left.

Ransom stands before a park bench, a wide, slightly crooked smile on his lips. He laughs and grins and waves his hands all around, speaking animatedly, with excitement and liveliness I've never seen from him.

I follow his line of sight to a shiny, golden head of hair. I can't see her face, can't see any other part of her outside of the gorgeous shade of blonde money can't buy.

My palms find the banister, latching on, my eyes sliding his way once more, and right as he points his grin to the sun in the distance.

He stands there, handsome without effort, the sunset creating a shadowy glow around him, making him appear gentle, vulnerable, unlike I know him to be.

His arms drop as he looks back to the girl.

His smile, it softens as he steps toward her, and he lifts a hand, cupping her face.

Something inside me tightens and twists, my brows digging in at the unexpected feeling. I push off of the cold cement and unlock my car door, quickly slipping inside.

I don't realize I'm holding my breath until I'm gasping behind the wheel.

My head falls back on the seat, but I lift it, slamming it back again because fuck. Something is wrong.

My stomach is queasy, my muscles suddenly too heavy for me to hold, but I don't understand why. I was revived moments ago, enjoying my sister's jokes and a massage and the lady had just taken our drink order. A steamy hot cappuccino was on its way.

I shake out my hands, but it does nothing, so I close my eyes, pull in a lungful of air, and when I open them, the weighted ache is gone.

I shift into gear and head home.

"Your mind is occupied."

My fork falls to my plate, my head snapping toward Anthony.

At his smile, a short laugh escapes me, and I reach for my glass of water.

Talk about triggered by word choice.

And why, all of a sudden, do people seem to notice?

Nobody noticed before when I would stare off into

space and answer with a single word or a fake smile. I would go as far as to say it was preferred. Who really cares to hear what's on your mind when it's not of benefit to the one forced to listen? No one, that's who.

Really, they're just annoyed they can't read your mind.

It's the quiet ones the people in this world of ours can't handle as they're so used to silence relating to sabotage.

It's one of those 'oh look at her sitting there, staring, watching, and studying. I wonder what she's up to?' And with the number of skeletons these people have waiting to come out of their closets, it could be anything, so, the uncertainty creeps in.

Anxiety, stress, and on the list goes.

It's no wonder the pharmacy here is always out of Xanax.

"Sorry." I dab at my mouth with a napkin and lie, "I'm a little tired is all."

He nods, reaching for my hand, so I place it in his and he shifts his chair to face me better. "Does it scare you, being in your home knowing someone broke in while you were sleeping?"

My mouth opens and I'm about to ask what he's talking about, but I catch myself quickly.

Right, my car was 'stolen' from my garage in the middle of the night.

Thank god I remembered to delete the Ring surveillance footage before I called my mom.

Am I supposed to say yes and come off as a helpless schoolgirl?

Am I supposed to say no and allow his wheels to spin?

Letting him draw his own conclusion sounds better, so I give a tight smile and lift a single shoulder as I bring my glass to my mouth again.

"You know..." He trails.

I know that tone.

It's the one all men use, leading and low, and I don't want to look, but I have to.

Sure enough, his eyes are hooded and focused on my wrists, his light graze following.

"You're eighteen soon." He looks to me. "We don't have to wait until next summer and rush when it gets here. We can... swim together now, set our own pace, so we're perfectly ready for the rest when it comes."

No.

Hell no.

I don't want to swim.

Swimming is slow and personal.

I want to crash face-first into my wedding, not plan it.

I don't even want to pick out the dress.

"I think a quick course will be exciting," I say instead.

Thankfully, he simply grins, nodding lightly. "I have no doubt it will be."

Together, we go back to eating our sushi, and when I leave, his focus falls to my car.

Creases form along his forehead and he rubs his lips together. "This is your new car."

I smile at the candy red paint, running my fingers along the glossy hood, up and over the windshield. I lift the top down so the crisp leather can get acquainted with the sun.

"What do you think?"

"When did you buy this?" he asks, rather than answering.

I turn to face him again. "Yesterday, when I left here actually."

His eyes still on the vehicle, he gives a slow nod, but when he looks up at me, he smiles. "I should get back to work. You'll make it home okay?"

"I will." Eventually. I open the door, sticking one heel in as I look over at him. "See you next Sunday."

The grin on his face answers yes, but the look in his eye says something different.

Only I'm not sure what it is.

CHAPTER
Fourteen

ifteen minutes before the lunch bell is set to ring, my teacher instructs me to grab my things, and sends me to the office with a pink slip in hand.

I figure it's the boys being silly, but as I round the hall, my foot nearly freezes in the air at the sight in front of me.

Sandy blond hair, perfectly parted, trimmed and tame. A devilish black suit and skillful chuckle.

What the—

I'm cut from my own thought as he spins, spotting me in the doorway.

I smile, maybe too wide, but Anthony smiles back. "Hi."

"Hi. I thought I would surprise you."

"I... mission accomplished." *Smile.*

He reaches back, grabbing his jacket from the edge of the counter, and nods at the administrative assistant, who excuses herself.

"I owe you a meal on the yacht. It's still off-campus lunch like it was when I was here, right?"

The curl of my lip takes a little less effort this time. "I don't know, that was a really long time ago."

He chuckles, slipping closer. As he does, his eyes lower and they take a long time to come back up.

Yeah, the girl he's looking at isn't the same one who visits him on Sundays.

My skirt doesn't reach just above the knee, and I'm not wearing nylons or blazer or a crew cut top.

My heels are dipped in rose gold glitter, my top a draped crop cami and my skirt leather. My hair isn't curled but silk straight and parted down the middle. The large hoops in my ears match my shoes and my eye makeup is heavy.

Basically, I look like a basketball wife, a far cry from the duchess he signed on for.

But six days of the week still belong to me, and Tuesday is one of them. I'm allowed and he knows it.

And I think he likes it.

Thank god!

A teasing grin covers his face, and he lets out a low whistle, his eyes coming back to mine. "You're exquisite, Miss Falino."

I link my arm in his when he offers it, allowing him to steer us toward the exit. "And you're far from average, Mr. Blanca."

He chuckles, leading us toward his driver, who is parked at the curb's edge.

We slip inside and Anthony has a carafe of water waiting.

I tilt my head, accepting a glass as he passes it over. "Since we're eating on the yacht, can we stop at my car? I have a coat in the back."

He nods, glancing toward the driver's window, who must have heard perfectly, and already knows which vehicle is mine, coming up behind it in the senior parking lot without direction.

Handing my water back to Anthony, I slip from the car, taking my book bag with me. I grab my jacket off of the seat and lay my school stuff in its place. I reach toward the center console for my sunglasses, and something on the windshield catches my eye.

After locking my door, I reach up and over the hood, freeing the folded piece of shredded binder paper from under the wiper.

Because I know you'll fail without me... this is me letting you know not to panic. I'll be in class, but a little late. Have more than a coffee for lunch, Trouble. ;)
~ Arsen.

My hand is frozen, the note stuck between my fingertips. I read it again. And again.

Arsen.

A light laugh leaves me.

This is his voice... flirty and teasing, as I know him to be. Well, for the most part.

And look at that, the boy has jokes.

A lightweight sensation swims through me and I turn, jolting to a stop when Anthony is standing outside the door, watching.

I go to open my mouth, to provide a quick and clean, and hopefully witty... something as I drop the note in my purse, but I don't have to because Anthony smiles, holding his hand out for me to take.

So, I slip mine in his, and then we're headed for lunch.

"It's this one here." Anthony gestures toward the black Vendetta yacht with a single white and red pinstripe lining the upper edge. "I know your lunch isn't long enough to take her out, but I thought it would be nice to eat on the water, make fun of the tourists in the pontoons?"

I laugh, running my fingers along the original wood framing.

Anthony stares. "It was my grandfather's."

"It's beautiful."

"It needs to be completely redone."

My hand falls.

Of course, it does.

I hang my bag over the back of the chair and look to Anthony. "Restroom is below?"

He holds my eyes, nodding, so I excuse myself to quickly wash my hands; I don't take the time to look around since I only have an hour, or a little less than that now, and meet him back up top.

I lower into the seat across from Anthony. "So, what's for lunch?"

He nods, looking over my shoulder. "Elena, we're ready for you."

Elena, the woman from the office the other day, comes from the cabin, two dishes in her hand.

"Anthony said no time for appetizers, so I hope this is okay."

She places a seared salmon over a miniature pile of brown rice in front of me, and my mouth begins to water.

"This looks amazing, thank you, Elena."

Her smile is wide, but when she looks to Anthony, it vanishes and she nods, excusing herself.

He takes a drink from the glass in front of him, a slight scowl along his brow.

"So." Anthony lifts his napkin, pulling his knife free. "What classes do—" he cuts off mid-sentence when something falls from the folded cloth, landing directly into the melted butter concoction at the edge of his plate.

The oily liquid splashes up, wetting both his suit jacket as well as the tip of my knuckle.

His frown is instant.

I lift my chin, trying to see better as he takes a spoon and scoops it from the small saucer.

He lays it out on the napkin and in a puddle of grease, the same shade of the napkin beneath it, a soft white pearl sits.

"That's odd—"

"Get up."

My eyes fly to his, my water spilling over and pouring into my lap as he jumps to his feet.

I gasp, pushing back.

"I said up!" he snaps, tugging on my arm. "Elena!" he shouts, pushing me toward the portside exit.

She comes around the corner, and as I glance over my shoulder, her wide eyes take us in, his grip on my arm, the way he's pulling me forward, and she hurries behind us without a word.

As he rushes us onto the dock, I almost lose my footing, catching myself on the wooden post when he shoves Elena into me and out of his way, as he quickly whips around to face the yacht.

Elena rushes toward the road, waving her arm in the air as she shouts, "Pull the car up!"

I stand straight, smoothing my skirt down.

Anthony wipes at his mouth and takes a step forward, only to take one back.

"Anthony, what—" I break off in a scream when the yacht explodes before us.

Small shards of debris fly around and I spin, ducking as Anthony hits the ground. Heat warms my back and as the thunderous sound begins to fade, I peek.

My fingers lift to my lips as the flames billow over the edges of the yacht. They roll in unison, up and over the top, into the air and then quickly shrink. The polished wood crackles and splits and pieces fall into the ocean water beneath it.

Voices begin to shout in the distance, but I'm stuck staring.

I was sitting on that thing not even a minute ago.

I...

A frown pulls at my brows when something warm meets my fingertips. I pull them back, looking down to find a thick droplet of blood coating my nail, and rolling down the back of my hand.

I reach up, gently swiping along my cheek, and when I look to it, smears of blood cover my palm. My face falls, my stomach sucking into my ribs. My knees begin to wobble, and I swallow.

And then Anthony is in front of me.

My gaze snaps up to meet his when he reaches out and he gently cups my neck, holding me still. I lift my hands, grasping on to his wrists and take a deep breath as he does.

I close my eyes for a long moment, and when his thumb glides along my jawline, I open them, my lips beginning to curve the slightest bit.

The pad of Anthony's finger glides along my chin.

He holds perfectly still and whispers, "This better not leave a scar."

And then he's gone, and I'm alone on the dock, my muscles frozen in shock, vaguely registering his clipped tone as he barks into his phone, "Tell me the yacht was insured."

I'm not sure how long I stand there, blood dripping down my cheek, my hands half-suspended in the air, but when

Elena appears with a coat that's not mine and the handbag that is, I jerk.

Her smile is soft, pitying, and it's enough to steel my spine.

"He's stressed and—"

"Thank you for snagging my bag," I cut her off, spin and head back for the car.

A second driver is already rolling up beside the one that brought us here and just as my heel meets the asphalt, Anthony's closing himself inside his, leaving me to find my way to the other.

People call out, asking if I'm okay, shouting how I can't just leave, but I ignore them, ignore the blood splatting against my collarbone and ruining my top. I don't respond to the driver when he speaks to me as I reach the door, but slip into the back seat, staring straight ahead.

I do tell him to take me home rather than to school once we're on the road, but it's obvious he has no intention of listening when he makes a right rather than a left at the intersection, so I text my sister, letting her know I need her to meet me at the school and sit back.

I don't allow myself to shrink into the seat, not with his eyes continually flicking to mine in the mirror.

I keep mine trained on his until we're pulling into the school parking lot. Thankfully my sister answered my call and was close, so when we pull in, Tanner is already blocking the entrance. The door opens and my sister is waiting beside him.

Thank god lunch is over and the area is a dead zone.

The man frowns when I swiftly push the door open before he has a chance to climb out and do his job.

I don't know if he watches as I walk straight for my sister, but I sure as hell don't look back to find out.

I hold my head high, keep my face blank, and my spine straight, even when Monti's hands fly to her mouth as she lays eyes on me.

She quickly moves out of the way, and I climb right in.

We're on the road in seconds.

I don't speak and she doesn't push and only when her hand latches over mine, do I realize we've pulled into the garage.

"I'm fine." I look to her, finding tears in her eyes.

Monti pulls her lips in and nods, because what else can she do?

Absolutely fucking nothing.

It's a little after four when I have Monti take me to get my car, and I regret it the second the school is in view as there are only two cars left in the senior parking lot.

Mine and the black Camaro parked by it, blocking it in from behind.

Ransom leans against the passenger side door with his arms crossed, his eyes pointed at the ground, while Arsen lays along my hood, his arms folded behind his head. The legs sticking out slightly over the side panel near the back seat can only belong to Beretta.

Tanner slows, spotting them just as I have, and hardly allows the car to roll forward.

My sister snaps out of her own little world as we cross into the parking lot.

She shoots up in the seat, her hands on the window frame like a child pulling into the Disneyland parking lot and opens her mouth to speak.

"Don't," I stop her.

In my peripheral, her head yanks my way, but I don't

look away from the three we creep closer to.

They heard the crunch of the tires against the asphalt as we pulled in. Beretta grips the headrest, yanking himself up for a clearer shot, while the other two remain unmoving, watching. Waiting to see who is inside.

That is until we've stopped a few feet away.

All at once, they jolt.

Beretta hops from the back, Ransom pushes off the side, and Arsen shoots into a sitting position, his right foot planting firmly on the ground.

I don't realize my lips have begun to curl until I blink, finding Monti's staring at me.

"James—"

"Monti." I turn to her.

She nods, and then shrugs, her eyes moving back to the boys. "K, fine, but like... don't be stingy."

She grins playfully and a low chuckle makes its way up my throat.

I grab for the handle, but Tanner flicks the locks.

He glares at my sister before focusing on me and reaches between the seat for his weapon, but I roll my eyes, shaking my head.

"Open the door, Tanner."

When he hesitates, my sister kicks the seat. "Now, Tanner."

With a low growl, he does as he's told, and I push my door open.

My sister laughs when all three of the guys are suddenly standing shoulder to shoulder.

"Should we wait?" she asks, but I shake my head and step out.

No sooner does the door close, than they pull away, and I don't make it a foot forward when I'm flanked.

"There she is." Beretta smiles, but it's short-lived and the air shifts. "What the hell?"

Ransom comes right up to me, a heavy frown over his forehead, his eyes glued to the clean slice along my cheekbone. He darts forward, one hand pulling on my lower back, to keep me still or move me closer, I don't know, but he manages both.

His free hand grips my chin, tipping it sideways and his nostrils flare, his face painted with anger, but his touch is gentle, as the last man to touch it was.

But this is different, as are his words.

"Are you okay?" He grips me tighter, his voice strained and body stiff.

I swallow, and when my hand begins to shake, I ball it into a fist, but he either notices or senses it and covers my knuckles with his palm. I'm not sure if he realizes it, but his hold on my chin has softened and slipped back toward my hair.

He dips closer and my lungs decide they can finally open, my nerves come back to life, and I suddenly feel the sting of my skin, the pounding of my head.

"Jameson." My name is a mix between a desperate growl and harsh whisper.

My eyes flutter closed, my body deciding it needs no permission from me to mold to his.

"I'm fine, it's nothing," I breathe.

Fisting my hair, his exhales warm my skin, and an ache forms between my ribs, my lips parting.

His gorgeous blue eyes are sharp, hooded and desperate for something—relief, connection... answers.

But I'm not sure to what questions.

Tension builds along his brow and he swallows. My muscles coil low in my stomach as his attention falls to my mouth, only to snap back up to mine. They're lower, darker, and I'm witness to the desire raging behind his gaze.

I hold my breath as his tongue pokes out to wet his lips and I swear he wants to kiss me, but instead, he tears away, taking my breath with him.

He throws himself in the passenger seat, and pulls his hood up over his head, pointing his glare the opposite way.

Instantly heavy, my shoulders fall, but this is an entirely different kind of weight, a denser, full-body exhausting kind.

A mental one, pounding at my temples and ribs and wrists.

It makes no sense.

When Beretta's hand falls on my shoulder, I look to him.

He gives me a little shake. "We were just gonna fuck with you, start trouble for whoever you ditched with for the fuck of it. Didn't think it would be your fam and didn't know you had an interview with the Joker."

A small smile finds my lips and I glide my finger along my skin below the cut, fluttering my eyes. "I'd say the position is as good as mine, what about you?"

He chuckles, walking backward toward the car. "You're committed, that's for sure," he teases and reality slams over me once more.

Committed.

I'm committed.

I belong to a man who looked into my eyes while I stood cut and bleeding before him, his only concern if his trophy would no longer be posh and polished.

He didn't apologize or exhale in relief that we made it off the yacht before it blew the fuck up. He didn't ask if I was okay or offer comfort as I remained there, unmoving and maybe in a bit of shock.

He was cold. Showed no emotion.

Not an ounce of fucking care.

Just as you wished for, Jameson...

I don't realize I've closed my eyes until a forehead meets mine, and I open them to find Arsen has stepped into me.

His arms are gentle and wrap around my body, hugging me to him.

My features smooth out as I look up into his dark blue eyes. My hand falls to his chest, and a soft smile finds my lips.

"It was an accident," I tell him, shrugging one shoulder. "I slipped getting out of the bath."

It's a lie and doesn't explain why my car is here and I wasn't, but my hair is wet from the shower. And like Beretta pretty much pointed out, I left my car here like this when I ditched with them the last time, so maybe I left with someone else today.

Arsen's eyes are tight, and he doesn't believe me, so I curl my lips up higher.

Never forget your smile.

"I saw your note."

As if he forgot, his face transforms, a sly little grin slipping over him.

"And I know you wrote that very first one, too. I have to admit, I like your voice," I whisper. "It's sexy, or so I imagined."

He chuckles, and my attempt for much-needed space but my inability to take it on my own works.

He releases me, stepping back a bit.

But he's intuitive, and he reaches out again, cupping my face.

He nods slightly and I nod back.

I'm okay, Arsen.

He doesn't believe me, but he does join his friends inside the car.

I step around mine, slipping into the driver's seat with conscious effort not to glance in their direction. I know their eyes are locked on me and I know they are waiting for me to give them more.

I know because I can feel it.

It's a tragic, unwelcome warmth, one I'll freeze out with my mother's favorite mantra: by any means necessary.

Maybe even tonight.

But since I'm not yet in my right mind, and apparently still a glutton for punishment, I dig Arsen's note from my purse to read it once more.

Only I don't get to.

Because it's gone.

CHAPTER *Fifteen*

ot, sweet, *cheap* whiskey burns its way down my throat and I welcome the sting, then pull the second shot glass to my lips, experiencing it all over again.

I take a deep breath, finish off half of my glass of water, my mind flashing to the ocean waters from earlier this afternoon.

It was beautiful and blue.

As was the yacht that exploded four feet from me.

I wince, tearing my hand from my face when I realize I had subconsciously reached up to touch the cut on my cheek, currently buried beneath my best layer of makeup, yet is still visible enough to make the bouncer warn me that 'spousal drama isn't welcome in this place.'

What made Anthony decide to come to the school when we have never even spoken outside of our routine? He or his receptionist emails me Sunday's plans, sometime Friday afternoon, I add it to mine and my mom's calendar and show up when and where I'm told. That's it.

And then there's the yacht...

I growl, running my hands over my hair and

planting them on the bar top a moment later.

Screw this, I didn't come here to think.

I came for the opposite.

I turn to the dance floor, getting myself as deep into the crowd as possible.

No matter what angle I shift toward, there's no more than five inches of space between me and another person. It's exactly as I want it to be.

Loud enough to block out my thoughts and dark enough to hide my existence. Unruly and crowded, perfectly suffocating.

I can't think or hear anything outside the too-loud music, but I can move.

Allowing my hips to lead, I roll in tight circles, jutting my ass out every few times to stay with the beat, and the rest of my body plays as the after wave, following the same path, every part of me lost to the wild beat.

A few songs in, I begin to sweat, so I pull my hair into a high ponytail at the top of my head. As I pull on pieces to tighten it, a guy with short dark hair slips in front of me with a half grin, so as I bring my hands down, I string them around his neck.

His grin turns to a smirk and he grips on to my hips, allowing me to move as I wish but staying close for the ride.

When his touch slides higher, I step into him more, my hands running down his neck, and staying there. One of his palms moves along my back, down the curve of my waist, and pauses there, his fingertips teasing the curve of my ass. He's waiting to see if I'll protest, but I do him one better and smirk up at the golden-eyed guy.

He chuckles, bringing himself closer when I fist his shirt.

Anthony's eyes flash in my mind right then, and I squeeze mine shut, pulling my partner closer.

He skims his lips along my jaw.

This better not leave a scar...

I bite into my cheek, tilting my head in invitation, and the guy accepts, dipping into my neck, his lips pecking me there. He cups my ass now, his mouth hovering over mine, teasing, but teasing isn't going to help.

I grab his face, my brows caving as I press my lips to his.

His other hand glides up my arm and he deepens the kiss, his tongue fighting for entrance I'm prepared to give.

But then his sharp cry of pain shocks my mouth.

No sooner than I get my eyes open, spotting my dance partner rubbing at the back of his head and spinning around in rage, am I yanked backward like a fucking bungee cord when stretched to its fullest or tightest point.

I trip over my own feet, fighting for balance on six-inch stilettos as I stare straight ahead.

Blood drips from the back of the guy's neck, soaking into his gray shirt as he raises his hands, but they don't make it halfway into the air before he's swallowed by two figures, dragged through the crowd and out of sight.

My eyes shoot wide, my feet darting forward, but the hand gripping the band of my bra through my dress reminds me of its presence and doesn't allow it.

I'm shoved forward, spun, and pinned to the edge of the stage.

I suck in a large breath.

Wild angry marble blues with shaky lids glare into mine.

His jaw twitches, his muscles flexing and releasing over and over again. He shoves at me, even though I'm already flat against the wall, and pushes into me even though he's already as close as possible.

And then he growls and tears away, but not by much.

It takes me a second, but I stand tall and now I'm pissed.

I push him, but he doesn't budge, so I try again.

Ransom grabs my arms, locking them between his, forcing my elbows to bend, so now we're eye to eye.

"Get the hell off me," I growl, jerking in his hold to no avail.

"What the hell are you doing?" he growls back, lip curled high. "Huh?!" he shouts louder, angrier. "What the *fuck* are you thinking, Jameson?!"

"I'm not!" I yell instantly, and he blanches, but only for a split second. "I don't fucking want to! I want to do whatever the hell I want!"

"This isn't the place!" he barks, tossing my hands away.

"It's the perfect fucking place!" I throw my arms out wide.

I'm practically hyperventilating, waves of shit I don't want to think about or acknowledge crashing back in like a fucking tsunami now that I'm standing here, forced back into my reality by an asshole that shouldn't even exist in it.

I look around at the average men in jeans and sneakers, to the plastic 'Bride' tiara in the distance and the 'Finally Legal' paper sash proudly worn to my right. No one knows more than the person to their left and nobody gives a shit who you are.

There is no expectation, no dress code.

It's nothing but a busted-ass bar pretending to be a nightclub at the edge of an alleyway not far from a tourist corner.

I scoff, a low laugh leaving me as I give myself some space, my eyes hardening and moving back to Ransom, who has yet to look away from me. "This is the perfect fucking place."

He hears it in my tone, the heavy, the pathetic hint of misery, as do I, but only once it's too late to change or charm up.

His eyes narrow on mine, before darting to the wound on my cheek and pausing there.

His chest rises and falls rapidly, his nostrils flaring, and before I can think to move, he's grabbing me again.

He hauls me into him, anger and frustration and something I can't quite name driving the creases between his brows deeper, the edges of his gaze tighter.

And then his hands are on me, rough and tight and dare I say possessive.

Heat pulls low in my core, but I force my arms still at my sides.

This isn't what I wanted tonight.

I wanted a stranger.

I *needed* a stranger, and the guy in front of me should feel like the perfect one.

But he doesn't.

I hate it.

Ransom's palms run lower, moving over my hips, and framing the curve of my body over the strings of my thong. He squeezes, shifting, his mouth now aligned with mine.

I attempt to pull away, swallowing my own breath when his hand flies up to my jaw, keeping me where he wants me.

His eyes are furious, desperate, and narrow when my tongue sweeps out to wet my lips. He starts to shake, his entire body radiating with heat and power, with frustration, and any fight I had in me vanishes.

Do it.

Kiss me.

Bite me.

Want me.

He's close. To me, to doing exactly what my mind has no right to cry for, yet is. The shake of his grip grows wilder, undeniably noticeable, but he doesn't take. His hands drop, a wall slamming over his eyes.

My shoulders begin to fall, but then a bruising grip wraps around my upper arm from behind. In one quick move, I'm whirled around, pulled forward as my head is yanked back, and Beretta's there, his lips hot on my neck with zero hesitation.

I gasp into the dim-lit space, shock compressing my muscles.

Beretta is a savage. He greedily kisses, sucks, and flicks his tongue over my skin, my entire body trembling in response.

A chest slams into my back, nearly knocking the air from me, and forces my steps forward as Beretta blindly shuffles backward, bumping a random couple but nobody pauses to care. They move out of our way, the space becoming ours.

Large hands come around, pressing against my lower abdomen, driving my ass into the very hard cock aligned with it.

"Bite her." Ransom's raspy demand burns low in my stomach, and Beretta does as he's told. "She deserves it."

He bites, and a hissed whimper slips from me, my head falling onto Ransom's shoulder.

He growls, his hands running lower, down to mid-thigh, taking my dress with them on their way up.

Half of my ass is out, right here in the dark corner of the dance floor, but I couldn't care less.

I need more.

I want more.

"Arsen," Ransom suddenly snaps, a strangled sense of desperation in his tone. Arsen is there in a flash as if he was waiting to be called on.

Hoping to be.

Dazed, I look to him, and he the others.

They have an entire conversation without words while I remain suspended between them, arched and curled like a snake. Three short seconds pass, I blink once, and we're leaving.

My body is on fire, my mind gone and suddenly we're outside. Parked the furthest row back of the dark parking lot with the hood still down, is Arsen's car.

I'm spun and shoved against the trunk, my heels allowing my ass to reach the very edge.

Ransom stares a long moment. Then with slow movements, he reaches inside his back pocket, pulling out a black bandana.

Beretta slips in front of him, his hands starting at the sides of my breasts and gliding down to my hips.

His eyes hit mine and he lifts me, the cold metal making me jump slightly with contact. Despite the chill, I'm sweating.

Anxious.

Ready to tear away from my own skin.

I need a night to flip off the fucking world.

A night to want everything I shouldn't, be all I'm not allowed to be, but I don't have to say it out loud.

He knows.

I try to find the logic in that, to understand how, but maybe there is none? Maybe there doesn't have to be.

Maybe we're the same, fighting ourselves for reasons we don't share.

Over Beretta's shoulder, Ransom's eyes burn, a brilliant

baby blue, and he finds his way in front of me again.

His chin lowers, the bandana rises, and my toes curl in my shoes.

I pull in a full breath as he ties it over my eyes, snug and tri-folded, forcing my lids closed behind it.

His hand glides down my neck to my chest, and he pushes, my body breaking out in chills as my shoulders lower to meet the metal behind them.

All at once, their hands come forward, gliding and massaging, and my core muscles clench.

My chest rises and falls in rapid speed as my dress is guided up and over my stomach. Instinctually, my legs pull closed, but when the hands on me freeze, I take a deep breath and open them.

My ass is tugged to the end of the hood, two sets of hands following the same exact path down my legs. One is rough and massaging, the other gentle and fluttering, both making me shake and warm and holy shit. This is...

A hand presses over my underwear and I moan, my muscles relaxing.

My legs are lifted, the point of my heel placed on the bumper, and I shiver as the wind blows over my exposed skin.

The hand cupping me dips lower, pressing over the wet spot in my underwear and my ass cheeks clench, my hips arching, begging for more.

"What do you think?" Beretta rasps from somewhere to the left, and fingers slide beneath my underwear, meeting my bare center. Someone groans. "Off or to the side?"

My hands come down, pushing at the silky fabric, but they're captured, kissed, and threaded into another.

I sigh, jolting when a finger is slipped inside me.

"Oh my god," I rasp, clenching around it.

"Off," Ransom answers, his voice so low, so rough, it's

almost missed. "Quickly."

Teeth nip at my hip seconds later and I squeeze the hands locked on mine, pulling him close, and whoever *he* is, comes to me.

Full, plush lips glide along mine, a tongue teasing at my bottom one as the shred of silk heats the air.

My mouth opens and those lips come down hard. I kiss him back, trying to tear my hands free, to wrap them in his hair and force him closer, but he doesn't allow it.

The finger inside me begins to pump in and out, slow at first, then faster. Another.

My hips begin to roll, the kiss is broken and hands glide under my dress and bra, my breasts now heavy in calloused palms.

I moan, my lips parting as the fingers inside me disappear.

The hiss of a zipper hastily torn down creates a spasm low in my belly and I reach out.

Someone comes to me, buries their face in my neck as a cock buries itself inside me.

A desperate groan echoes and heavy panting fills the space around me.

"So fucking sexy, yeah, Arsen?" Beretta's words are strained, the hands on my hips holding me steady, twitching.

My nipples are pinched, my neck kissed.

I'm fucked slow and deep, the pace spiking with my pulse.

I moan into the air, my legs widening, stretching.

The need is building, deeper than anything I've ever felt, and my pussy is rocked over and over.

Heavy grunts have my fingers curling, hands overwhelm me, and I'm crying into the air.

"I need... fuck I—" I break off in a moan, my back

arched high.

The cock inside me flexes, holds, and tears away, but only seconds pass and I'm filled again.

My legs are pushed back, held up, and I thrash along the hood.

"Fuck, she's about to come."

"I know."

"Kiss her. Claim it."

A mouth falls hard on mine.

It's rough and punishing, possessive and commanding, and I gasp, my body shaking, my tongue diving inside, tangling with his.

My pussy convulses, his cock twitching as I do, and he rolls his hips, pressing deeper.

A finger comes down over my clit, applying pressure, and I squeeze his cock tightly.

He slips out, the sound of jeans being shuffled, belts being fastened filling the air around me, and then I'm lifted and held, my muscles limp beyond my control.

I'm pulled against someone, my bare center flush with his cotton shirt, my cheek placed on his strong chest.

The wild beat of his heart soothes my own, my breathing growing lax along with his.

I jolt, attempting to pull free when the back of his knuckle comes up, sliding beneath the cut on my cheek.

The cut I came here tonight to forget, along with the man in front of me when it happened.

Along with the difference in reaction from the ones I'm with now when they saw it.

He doesn't allow me to escape, though.

He holds me there, gently rubbing at my skin as if he sensed I was scared.

As if he's aware I needed comfort.

As if he knows those very things left me angry with myself and landed me here.

As if he's telling me all of that is okay.

And letting me know he's willing to be whatever I want him to be.

But the best part is *he* doesn't confirm who *he* is, allowing me to pretend everything he's saying with his touch... means absolutely nothing.

As it should.

I lift my head, and I'm slid down, my body still flush with the one holding on to me. With one last touch to my cheek, the hand drops to my dress, stretching it back into place, and I'm released.

There's some shifting around me, but only when the exhaust kicks on, heating my leg, do I reach up, freeing the bandana from my face.

An unexpected hesitance swirls in my stomach, and I glance over my shoulder. Ransom and Beretta drop into the back seat, Arsen behind the wheel. They aren't staring or smirking or laughing.

They're simply allowing me a moment, waiting for me to be ready to join them. Slowly, I spin, the front of my body now faces the car.

I glide my fingers along the trunk space, and my lips twitch, my chest rising with a heavy inhale.

And then I'm laughing. A full-on, stomach clenching, abs aching laugh, and the boys look to me.

At first, they're unsure, but then low chuckles slip from each, and Beretta shoots up in the seat, grabs me over the trunk and hauls me forward. I squeal, flying forward, and landing across his and Ransom's lap.

His arms spread out along the back of the seat, and Ransom unclasps my heels from my feet, tossing them to the floorboard before leaning over, grabbing my hands and tugging me toward him.

His arms wrap around me, and I shift so I'm sideways in his lap, my knees bent and feet flat on the middle seat. His left hand falls to my thigh, the other drumming along the outer edge of the Camaro, so I drop my head back, resting it on the bend of his elbow.

Arsen turns up the music and we pull from the parking lot, my eyes on the stars above us.

Oh, what the September skies have seen.

My mother would murder me.

I close my eyes, grinning at the thought.

CHAPTER Sixteen

S tepping from my car, a hand comes around my shoulder, swiftly stealing my coffee from my grasp as a second pair wraps around my hips, driving me against my door.

I'm held still, warm, wet lips gliding along my cheek, pausing at my ear. He inhales, a low rasped whisper following, "'Morning, Trouble."

Mint and clary sage assaults my senses and I exhale. "Ransom."

His lips press harder, twitching as if he wants to kiss me, or say more, but holds back.

He squeezes, and then he's gone.

My hands fall to my window, and I pull in quick breaths, a low chuckle escaping me as my chin falls to my chest.

My god, I'm a mess, and clearly, easily enticed.

I lock my car, glancing around to find other students shuffling from their cars toward the school.

Only then does my mouth fall open as I spin around, searching for my coffee, but I don't find it.

Oh, hell no!

I stomp my ass to the main building, into the corridor, and cut the corner leading to senior row, where all the senior lockers are located.

I wave at a few people as I pass them, spinning to answer Keri Morgan's question about a quiz we have in English today, but I keep moving forward.

Scott and his teammates are grouped together in conversation, and I manage to slip by them without having to pause to engage.

I spot the three pariahs near the end, stuffing their backpacks inside their lockers without so much as pulling a single book out.

I sneak in quickly, snagging the paper coffee cup from Ransom's hand as he did mine.

I step out, spinning around as he's *whipping* around to face the thief, but the mischievous gleam in his eyes tells me he knew exactly who it was. And that he was waiting.

Taking backward steps, I bring it to my lips and raise a brow.

Ransom chuckles, falling against the locker, a discreet little smirk curving his lips.

Yeah, he knew I'd come for it.

He's playful. I don't know if I anticipated that...

I swallow beyond the small tizzy in my throat.

My back meets the double doors, and I push through, my eyes bouncing to the right before I step away.

Amy stands beside Dax and Scott, her gaze locked on the boys in black, and the second Scott and the others see her staring down the hall, they turn to see what has her attention.

I laugh to myself and head for class.

The next few weeks are full of the same little amusement.

Ransom snags my coffee and runs or replaces it with one he brought for me instead; they sneak up on me in the halls for quick scares and he's never not watching me from wherever he is. This past weekend, they snuck into my garage and filled my car with softball-size balloons. I had to lie and say they were for a school project when I opened my trunk in front of Anthony on Sunday to grab a jacket when he waited for me to arrive, just to tell me he had to cancel, and a half dozen of them flew into the air before I could get the damn thing closed.

Yesterday, they moved my car across the parking lot, parking it directly beside Arsen's. So far today, they've stayed out of sight.

It's Thursday and the girls decide to stay on campus for lunch again, but they opt to eat outside in the cool air instead.

Southern California can be a lot like Florida when it comes to weather. The sun shines most of the time, even through fall and winter, though we do have chilly nights almost all year long. For the most part, living here is a mix of long-sleeved shirts with exposed legs or vice versa. We're sweating at eighty-five but freezing at sixty.

It's nearly mid-October and while the gossip magazines are covered with flannels and turtlenecks, we're still in open-toed heels and swimwear on the weekends.

Speaking of weekends, there's only a few more until my eighteenth birthday as my mother felt the need to remind me in her text this morning while asking what I wanted her to arrange in celebration.

She wasn't too keen on my single-word response.

I finish off my smoothie, looking at the sticky strawberry mess on my palm from the cup, and turn to Cali. "Watch my bag?"

She nods, going back to her conversation with Jules, and I head for the girls' powder room, but I don't make it a step through the door before I'm pushed farther inside.

My eyes flash to the mirror, just in time to catch a glimpse of Ransom's face, hardly registering the others behind him, when the lights go out.

My stomach flips, and my head is tipped to the side, warm, greedy lips lighting my neck on fire as not a second is wasted.

I grab the countertop, wobbling slightly as my legs are nudged wider, the rough texture of thick jeans scratching against my upper thighs.

"What, have you been waiting for me to slip in here?" My voice is hoarse and cracking.

"No," Ransom whispers in my ear. "Waiting until I could slip in here."

I gasp when his fingers, skillfully and without direction, dive past my underwear and drive inside me. I moan, clenching around him, but when I tip my head, searching for his lips in the dark, he pulls back, lowering his forehead to the nape of my neck.

His fingers inside me swirl with every pull back, his breathing burning me through my cashmere long sleeve, growing deeper each time he pushes back in. He's slow and deliberate. Reveling.

My whimpers grow louder, and he begins to shake.

I feel his muscles lock behind me and his hand swiftly pulls back, but then the heat of another's finds my thighs, gripping on to Ransom's wrist between them.

Slowly, his muscles ease, and then there's another figure, now at my right.

I'm surrounded, barricaded.

My hands are gently pulled from the counter and crossed, my fingers wrapping around the biceps caging me in.

I squeeze, opening up more, and the fingers between my legs move once again.

Heavy breathing fills the room, low groans flowing around it and as lips meet my shoulder, the sound of clashing tongues burns in my ear.

My eyes shoot open wide, seeking confirmation of what, I don't even know at this point, but it's pitch black in here and they know it.

My blackout boys.

I freeze, my blood running cold and locking my limbs still.

No, no.

Not mine.

They're hardly even my friends.

They—

"Stop," is growled into my ear, and then my chin is gripped and yanked to the side.

Heavy, hard lips find mine, and my body decides to melt, to cave, to form to the one behind me.

"Give her more," Beretta rasps. "Help him."

Suddenly my hair is tugged, gently yanked and held back, massaged and pulled on in every manner possible, my head rolling, my eyelids fluttering.

I start to shake, everything inside me tightening.

"Kiss me," I whisper, but I'm bitten at the base of my neck instead.

I shiver.

I come.

Right here in the girls' bathroom that doesn't lock and is accessible to all.

I'm given no time to come down. I'm gently spun, leaned against the counter as the door opens and the lights flick on.

It takes two seconds for my eyes to adjust to the brightness, and it's long enough for them to disappear.

I brace my hands on the cool granite, flattening my palms to soak in the chill it provides.

I huff a laugh, my head falling back to rest against the mirror.

Oh my god, I'm an idiot.

And they're dangerous.

Still, I laugh, wash my hands as I came in here to do, and when I meet my eyes in the mirror, it doesn't wash away.

But it does when the stall to my right opens, and Amy steps out.

Shit.

I try not to swallow, to hide the shock or care, but heat is creeping up my neck, and I can't hide it because how fucking embarrassing!

But the superior pinch of her face, the way she's pursed her lips and lifted her nose in the air is enough to shake me out of it.

People hook up in the same rooms, cars, and hot tubs all the time.

I've heard Dax and Jules come more times than I care to admit, several others too, because at the end of the day, teenagers will get theirs wherever they wish, and their 'friends' don't bat a lash.

The problem?

Amy isn't my friend, even if she pretends to be in her passive-aggressive ways.

So, as she reaches the counter with her one foot in front of the other catwalk-like strut, I stand tall and dry my hands.

She washes hers as I reapply my lipstick.

When she doesn't speak but meets my eyes in the mirror. I stare back, popping my lips once I'm done, and spin. I lean against the sink, cross my arms and wait.

I know she's got something to say, and she will.

She's incapable of silence.

Rather than grab a paper towel closest to her, she steps in front of me, reaches over and slowly pulls one from the dispenser at my side.

"So, you're the new plaything." She tips her head, takes in my outfit, and her mouth forms into a judgy little grin. "I have to admit, I wondered, but I didn't think you had it in you."

"Pun intended?" I pop a brow.

Her eyes flash to mine, narrowing, but she catches herself as quickly as she can. Her hundred-thousand-dollar dental implants beam as she smiles, big and fake and purposeful. She laughs, shakes her head, and begins to walk out, but of course, she has to pause for the dramatic exit.

"Just remember, toys are only fun when they're first opened, but they grow old fast, and then to the bottom of the barrel you go." She delivers her closing statement.

And it's a shitty one.

I grin, but the difference between mine and hers, is mine's real and she knows it.

Her smile falters as I approach, tipping my head as she had, my eyes three inches above hers, thanks to today's pumps of choice.

I place my hand beside hers on the door, lean in close, and I whisper with a laugh, "I'm counting on that."

Her face falls and I walk out with my head held high.

But even as I return to our table, Amy doing the same not three minutes later, I'm forced to face what she's said as well as my response.

I was being honest; I am counting on being tossed to the side.

"You look flushed, Jameson." Amy's cheeky tone calls out, and my eyes dart to hers while everyone else's fly toward me. "Are you feeling okay?"

I can see it, the instant regret at her choice of words, and my smile spreads slow and wide.

I laugh, nod, and push my hair over my shoulder. "I feel fantastic, satisfied even." I lift my water bottle to my lips, pleased when hers pinch tight. "Thanks for asking."

Bitch.

CHAPTER Seventeen

"Your birthday is almost here." Anthony lowers his fork to his plate, sitting back in the chair. "I could throw you a party, be your date?"

I nearly choke on my pineapple juice, my fingers flying up to cover my mouth.

It's not easy to recover from, to hide the shock of his suggestion, but I smile through it, as does he, though his is a little more strained.

"I wasn't really planning to celebrate."

He nods. "We could keep it simple, just go to dinner." He flips his phone from front to back, over and over against the tabletop, staring at me.

It's obvious how hard he's trying not to look at my cheek. He didn't last time I came to see him either, though, he had rushed me out as quickly as I had arrived. He hasn't acknowledged that day once, and I'm not about to bring it up.

I am tempted to tilt my head to show him the cut is still visible. It's on the mend and I've been using creams to help, not because of his scar comment, but because I sure as hell hope it goes away myself.

Anthony shifts slightly. "You could invite your friends."

I smooth the napkin on my lap for something to do, then force a small laugh. "Trust me, my friends would bore you."

"I want to meet them."

His quick response has my eyes returning to his.

Smile, Jameson.

"That's sweet, I'm glad to hear." I pick up my drink, finishing it off, and finally, Anthony picks up his silverware and continues to eat.

He offers a small smile, and the rest of the meal is spent in silence.

After eating, he takes me out to the garden in the back of the building, shows me the fountain they added, and when we slip back inside, he follows my every move as I grab my bag.

As I walk toward the door, he heads for his desk.

"I think I like Jamie."

My eyes fly to his, and he takes his sweet time sliding his to mine. He rolls the cuffs of his white button-up and slowly lowers himself into the chair. "It's far more feminine, Jamie." He says the name as if to test the sound once more.

Or maybe it's to test my reaction.

"Do you agree?" He cocks his head.

I open my mouth, my fist clenching the handle.

Any means necessary.

I smile wide, welcoming, as if I would be happy to oblige, to erase the one thing that's truly mine. "It is a pretty name." *Smile through your lie.* "See you soon."

He nods and I get the hell out.

Behind the wheel of my car, my body begins to shake, but I wiggle in my seat, taking a deep breath and blowing it out just as quickly.

The second I get out of the parking lot I call my mom.

"Date over so soon?" she answers.

"Did you tell Anthony I didn't have plans for my birthday?"

"I might have mentioned something about it approaching rather soon."

I shake my head, switching lanes. "Mom... maybe we should cut our Sunday things to once a month. It's only October. We have months before anything changes between Anthony and me."

"Oh please, you would simply be lounging or shopping or some other useless endeavor that in no way assists your future."

"My future is set, Mother."

"And you only cement it further with every bat of your lashes. Listen, I have to go, but you have to get a handle on yourself and learn how to work for things sometimes," she says as if I don't already. "Not everything will be handed to you, Jameson."

No, just my life in an itinerary.

My mother hangs up.

I don't remember the drive here, and I have no clue how long I've been parked in front of the driveway, blindly staring at a house that's not mine.

I'm only jostled from my numbed state when a pair of dark blue eyes find mine through the windshield, and that's when I realize it's Arsen's foster home that I'm in front of, my own house in view but clearly not where I want to be.

My lips curve to the left and I follow Arsen's steps to the driver's side window.

I sigh, my head drops against the seat. "Hi."

His mouth lifts in the corner and he tips his head.

"My morning sucked."

He nods, reaching beyond me to put the top down on my convertible. He jerks his chin toward the passenger seat and I not so gracefully climb into it.

He lowers himself behind the wheel and then we're on the road.

We listen to his favorite playlist and within a few minutes, I recognize the direction we're headed. It's toward the cave the boys took me to that first day I slipped inside their car.

God, that day seems like so long ago when, in reality, it wasn't.

It's a shitty reminder that time flies.

We park where we did before and walk down to the cave.

There are blankets and what looks like a bag of garbage in the corner, the firepit now has half-burned wood inside it, and there's a tiny piece of a take-out box that didn't char sticking out on the side of it, indicating they've been here recently.

I almost wonder where I was when they were here, but I shake it off and turn to Arsen when he jerks his chin.

He's grabbed a backpack that must have been stuffed somewhere and we slip out into the open air again.

He starts to remove his shoes, so I do the same, and he stuffs them inside the pack, my purse and keys with them.

Together, we walk along the beach, and it's the most relaxing of silence. As we reach the curve of the hillside, the pier in the distance comes into view and a smile breaks free.

"Oh man." I follow the length out into the ocean. "I haven't been over here in years."

Arsen looks to me and I shrug a shoulder.

"The girls say it's too crowded, vacationers and

whatnot."

He nods, slips his hand in mine and with quicker steps, leads us straight for it.

Just before the pier, there are several small stores and privately owned restaurants. Arsen gets in line at a small deli for something to drink, so I snag my wallet and pop into a board shop next door, buying an outfit my mother would die if she saw. A matching sweatsuit with 'California' printed along the chest and down the left leg. I even grab some flip-flops to throw on with it.

It's a total tourist purchase, but I couldn't wear my "Anthony approved" nylon skirt and blouse any longer. This is comfortable, and apparently, that's what I need right now.

Comfort.

The store owner is nice enough to let me wear it out, and when I reach Arsen, he laughs at my outfit.

"Hey, it was either this or a tie-dyed onesie with a giant marijuana leaf on the front, okay?"

He lifts his hands, fighting a grin, and I steal one of the lemonades from his hand, shoving him with my other. We stuff my wallet and clothes with my other items in the backpack, and then his arm comes around me and he steers us toward the pier.

Walking all the way out, we look over the edge at the deep dark waters, but then he curves us around the other end.

The moment we do, I spot two familiar figures.

Ransom and Beretta, among several others, are tugging on a large red rope. They each seem to have their own and as the ropes pile higher on the wooden dock beneath us, a loud clanking fills the air. An aluminum cage of some sort comes into view and they lift it up and over the railing.

My mouth drops open when I spot the half dozen crabs inside.

"Holy shit," I say out loud, and at the sound of my voice, both their heads jerk our way.

Ransom frowns, looking from me to Arsen, but then his eyes come back to mine and lower. It's Beretta who laughs first.

"Don't even." I chuckle, stuffing my hands in the pocket in the front of the hoodie.

Wiping the sweat from his forehead with the sleeve of his shirt, Beretta empties the contents of his cage into a large ice chest with holes in the top and then tugs his gloves off, tossing them to the ground, while Ransom moves over to the next station, helping them with theirs.

Beretta's grin is wide as he walks over. "Hey, I'm into it. You almost look like you belong."

"Uh-huh, sure." I look beyond him at all the crabs Ransom shakes from the little trap box.

"Pretty cool, huh?" Beretta asks.

"Yeah, I never would have thought. Is this, I mean, is it—"

"Legal?" He raises a brow, fighting a grin.

I nod.

That's a solid five-hundred dollars' worth of crab, if not more, and that's just what's in front of me.

"It is, but there're some restrictions," he shares, looking around at all the others, some fishing, some doing as he was. "It's how a lot of people around here feed their families."

"Well, they eat well then."

He licks his lips, coming closer, his voice lowering. "They don't eat them, Trouble, only sometimes for special occasions will they do this for themselves."

I frown and he adds, "They sell the crabs for way too fucking cheap if you ask me, but a buyer is a buyer. With the money, they get the things that make more sense for their households: rice, flour for bread and pasta. Things that can make more for less."

Embarrassment colors my cheeks, but Beretta only grins, coming in to kiss my temple.

"Give us five, we've been here long enough." He looks to Arsen, gripping his bicep before he turns back.

The two of us step around the group, making our way to the start again, but Beretta slips between us before we're even halfway there. "Ransom's coming."

"I feel like an asshole," I say instantly, and he grins, throwing his arms around both me and Arsen's shoulders.

"You're not an asshole. If you've never been down here to see, how would you know?"

I frown, facing forward.

"Here, come on." He tugs us to the right, off the pier and toward a little roller cart a woman is frying what looks like diced green peppers on.

He orders and pays her four dollars for a giant bowl.

It looks delicious. Some sort of greens topped with tomatoes, cilantro, and crumbled cheese.

He holds it out for me to grab the spoon.

"What is it?"

"Cactus."

My eyes bulge, and he laughs.

"Cactus," I deadpan. "So, when you asked if I ever tried it you meant—"

"Eaten, not grown."

I cover my eyes, shaking my head. "I'm so embarrassed!" I look to him.

He chuckles. "It's all that fine dining, Trouble. Stick with us and you'll learn a whole bunch of new, average joe shit." He scoops a spoonful and holds it out. "Try it."

I open my mouth and take the bite.

It's a little slimy, but also crisp, like a partially cooked pepper, but the flavor is all in the spices.

I have no clue what they are, but it works.

I take another bite.

Beretta grins, his eyes cutting over my shoulder, and I glance the same way to find Ransom leaning against the ledge, watching us.

He frowns and looks away.

I face forward and Beretta looks from him to me, but I ignore the flair of frustration in my chest and turn to Arsen.

"Can I have my phone from your bag?"

He shakes his head no, backing away slowly.

My mouth falls open and then he darts off, I don't know what possesses me to act like a child, but before I know it, I'm chasing after him.

He spins behind a bike rack, juking left and right, so I wait, cut around the second he breaks free, but I bump into someone, stumbling slightly.

Hands wrap around my biceps, steadying me, and my smile lifts to the skater boy I ran off his board.

"I'm so sorry—"

I cut off when Ransom's arm darts between us, and he grips the guy by the shirt, twisting the thin cotton in his fist. He yanks him forward only to toss him back.

The guy stumbles over the curb, falling into the sand beneath it. "Yo, what the fuck, man?"

My eyes widen, flying to Ransom, but he glares at the angry guy on the ground.

"Oh my god, I—"

I try to apologize again, this time for Ransom's antics but then his hard eyes find mine and I snap at him instead. "What the hell?"

His jaw is flexed, but he says nothing, tearing away and

stomping down the beach.

I turn, but he's already up and spun for his skateboard.

Arsen hands over my phone with a tight-lipped smile and jogs off to catch up to Ransom, Beretta and me slowly following behind.

"Someone is in a mood today." I sigh, and Beretta bumps his shoulder with mine.

We head back to the cave, both sticking to our thoughts, which sucks, and once we reach it, Ransom is standing outside of it.

He steps in front of me, blocking my path, his light blue eyes staring into mine.

It's funny, I'm always in heels, but standing here like this, the flip-flops I bought dangling from my hand, I realize he's even taller than I thought. He's irritated, so I should leave him to himself, but for some reason, I reach up, brushing a little bit of sand from the edge of his forehead, and his frown deepens.

It's as if he's waiting for something, but I'm not sure if it's from me or from himself. Either way, it never comes.

He growls and walks away.

I spin, facing the water, and Beretta comes up behind me, wrapping his arms loosely over my shoulders.

"He's got a lot of shit going on, that's all." He excuses his friend.

I scowl at the ocean.

"His uh, his brother's a dick," he shares, and my ears perk up. "Uses him when he needs to, but it's all to keep a leash around his neck. It's fucked up, but it was that way with his parents, too. They didn't like him, they might love him, I don't know, but they didn't like him."

He pauses and I know he's trying to decide what else to say, so I wait and eventually more comes.

"They're addicts, like my dad, but harder stuff," he mumbles. "Been gone for a few years now. His brother stepped in like he was being noble, doing what was right and all that other showboat shit, but he only wanted what his mom tried hard and failed to get after their sisters' accident."

"What was that?" I ask quietly.

His chest inflates against my back, and he holds his deep breath in for a long moment.

"A little bit of hope his granddad left them," he tells me. "It's not a lot by the standards of people here, but for them, it's more than enough, just like it was enough to get big brother to pretend to play nice for a minute."

My chest aches.

Money is the devil of this world, and power is its son.

Beretta's chin falls to my head, and he speaks below a whisper, just in case. "His sister...she's alive, Trouble."

I tense, my hands coming up to grip his forearms. I'm tempted to look over my shoulder, but I'm not sure I can look at his face right now.

"But you said... or I thought..."

"She's partially paralyzed now, and in a home," he murmurs. "It's really hard on him, but he's helpless right now, at his brother's will. It's tough, seeing him fall apart. She's been the most important person in his life since I've known him. It's not for me to say how he's feeling, but he's not the same as he was. He tries, but his world is different now."

How could he not be forever changed?

The weight of his words is too heavy, and my body sags against Beretta's and he gladly accepts the burden, his stance widening in the sand to hold me up.

"His brother's a piece of shit, parents are who knows where." He's quiet for a long moment before he adds, "He has no one, Trouble, just us."

I pull in a lungful of air. "Maybe that's enough."

He shifts, leaning over slightly so he can meet my eyes, a sorrowful look in his. "No," he says. "There's still something missing."

We hold each other's gazes a long moment.

"The blackouts, the hiding in the dark," I mumble. "How you guys hid in the corner of my dressing room that day..."

"He gets in any trouble and it could ruin things for him, his brother will only make his life harder, send him back to jail." He nods, a somber look in his eye and I know there is more than he is sharing. He grins suddenly. "What's that Cardi B song say, 'no face, no case'?"

An instant laugh escapes me, but it's thick, and while Beretta smiles wide, it's weighted as well.

The heavy eases the smallest bit as he steps closer, now holding my chin between his fingers. A low sigh leaves him, and he speaks a truth I'm not sure I want to hear.

I'm not sure I should.

"You're more alike than you think, Trouble," he says softly. "Just look where you landed after a long day."

What he means is after a shitty day.

Look where I am, look where Ransom is.

Here, with them.

Where existing is easy and not a series of well-practiced etiquette.

It's strange, the dynamic we have.

How they can sense what's going on with me, how Ransom can see right through me. How comfortable I am around them when I don't even let my hair down, so to speak, around my own sister. Around Cali and Jules.

It's as if, when they're near, this little voice is on repeat inside my head, whispering to me, but I can't quite hear what's said because it's just out of reach, and then comes the need to slip closer.

To be closer.

It's not smart of me, but it's true.

CHAPTER
Eighteen

Arsen puts the last layer of green onión on top of our dip, his hand raising.

I pop a brow, pulling my gloves off and tossing them in the mixing bowl. "Seriously?" I fight a grin but meet his palm with my own.

He locks his fingers around mine, tugging me in with a teasing gleam in his eye, but steps back with a laugh a moment later.

"I think the last time I high-fived anyone had to be when I *was* five."

He bumps his shoulder with mine, tossing the can opener into the bowl, and starts wiping the counter, so I carry our trash to the back of the classroom for sanitizing.

Passing the boys' station, my eyes meet Ransom's, and a smirk covers my lips when I find, of course, he was already staring.

I toss the gloves in the trash, the utensils in the bin, and the bowl in the sink, taking my sweet time washing my hands.

I don't look back as I reach up for a paper towel, drying them, and only when I have nothing left to do, do I slowly spin around.

He leans against the counter, his knuckles flexed around the gray granite, head tipped to the side, watching me.

He glances behind him, toward Arsen, and back to me.

He opens his mouth to speak, but a few other students are suddenly here, putting away their own materials.

Ransom shifts and the girl setting her things on the table beside him jumps.

A chuckle slips from me and her eyes flash to mine, narrowing, but I simply roll mine.

Ransom shakes his head and walks away, but I follow, stopping beside him at his station.

Beretta looks up at us and a grin covers his lips. "Aw, are we in that after hookup, pent-up and repressed stage?" he teases, so I follow his mood.

We need to lighten things up a little.

"I don't know, are we?" I put my elbow on the table, my chin resting on my palm and flutter my lashes at Ransom.

His palms flatten on the tabletop, and he leans in with a blank expression. "I want to make sure you understand."

"What, you think I need a proposal after two finales?" I tease, keeping my voice down. "Sorry, but I already have one of those, remember?"

Beretta chuckles beside us, pouring M&M's in his mouth.

Ransom's eyes flash, creases forming between them as he dips lower.

"Come on, blue eyes," I whisper. "What is it I need to understand?"

"*Understand* Arsen isn't yours for the taking."

Beretta chokes on a piece of candy, slowly pushing to his feet.

My eyes snap to his, but his are focused beyond me, toward Arsen.

I look back to Ransom and take a deep breath, a nasty little swirl of something agitating my stomach. I stretch through it, pushing to my full height, and the grin I give him is forced, unlike the others I've worn when my eyes are locked with his.

He spots it, and he too stands, but he does so, taking a step toward me, pausing when I shake my head.

"I thought you heard what I said before, but maybe you forgot." I lift a shoulder. "I don't want anything, I need nothing, and I expect even less. If you are hoping I'll challenge you here, I won't, so make sure you're saying what you really want to say, or it won't be effective."

His face contorts as if he's angered, tempted to explain, as if there is something *to* explain, but if there is, something stronger holds him back.

A guy goes to step around me, so I move to the side, and it must annoy Ransom because he jerks forward, shoving our classmate in the back.

The guy stumbles, catching himself on a nearby table, and whips around with a glare.

Ransom puffs his chest out and a few near us, who saw the interaction, stare, waiting, but the guy only shakes his head at Ransom, flicking his gaze over him, as if deeming him unworthy of the argument. The guy walks away.

I shake my head, returning to my table as well.

The moment I step up, Arsen's grin hits me in the chest, and a light twinge of discomfort follows. I quickly look away, grab my things, and dodge his hand when he reaches for me. I get the hell out, knowing he can't exactly call out in protest and feeling like shit for leaving him with my half of the cleanup to add to his own.

I book a session with the personal trainer at the gym for this evening and the minute school is out, so am I.

My chest had no permission to ache, and to remind my brain of such a fact, I'll make sure my entire body does too by the end of the night.

"This is amazing." Cali closes her eyes, leaning her head back on the ledge. "My muscles are so tense right now."

We kept the jets in the jacuzzi off so our hair doesn't get wet since we agreed to show up for last call at Dax's club tonight after their team gets back from their away game.

I nod, my eyes closed. "Same. Monti met me at the gym just before I was coming home and made me do leg circuits all over again."

"Where is Monti?" Jules slips, splashing us both by accident. "I haven't seen her in forever." Half of her words are drowned out by the glass at her lips.

I frown, my eyes roaming over her. "I don't know. Busy, I guess."

"God, how I wish I didn't know every little thing Amy did all the time." She glares at the water, downs her glass and climbs out, nearly losing her balance. "I'm getting a refill and more sushi. Who wants?"

"We're good, Jules." Cali watches her go and turns to me.

"She's off the hook lately," I say what we're both thinking.

"We were late yesterday because she was drunk when I went to pick her up for school." She keeps her voice low. "I had to throw her ass in the shower and shove half a loaf of banana bread I snagged at the coffee house down her throat."

"Did it work?"

"I'm pretty sure it was the first time she had eaten carbs in like two years, so yeah, it worked." She nods, a light laugh leaving her but concern is there too. "You haven't been around as much as you were this summer." Her eyes slide to mine. "I didn't think you noticed."

I look away and sigh. "I noticed, Cali."

I don't make an excuse or add a lie to make her feel better.

I give only the truth, and she accepts it.

"I think she's stressed over her mom or something. Our girls' day, sans alcohol, will help." She nods as if she's sure when she's not.

"Cali!" Jules shouts from the island in the kitchen, a half-chewed bite of sushi in her mouth. "Dax says Marcus from sophomore year was at the game! He's following them back to his house. Want to go there first, get reacquainted?" She laughs.

Cali chuckles, rolling her eyes playfully as she climbs out.

"Of course, I do!" she shouts back, turning to me. She sighs but then smiles. "You're off the hook tonight."

"Who says I want to be?"

She laughs, grabs her towel and looks at me over her shoulder. "Uh-huh. See you tomorrow, girlie."

They're out the door and not five minutes later, my gate rattles.

I don't have to open my eyes to know who's stepping through—I never bothered to put the lock back on.

Footsteps grow near, and then the water sloshes as one of them steps inside.

Apprehension curls beneath my ribs and I half hope I'm imagining the person before me.

I'm not.

I'm lifted from my little corner, my eyes opening to find Ransom before me. His arms around my waist as he guides my legs around his, lowering us to our shoulders in the heated water.

I stare, unease pulling at my muscles, and he reaches behind me, coming back with an iced latte.

He holds it out, waiting for me to wrap my fingers around the clear cup.

The moment I do, his mouth curls to one side.

I don't allow myself to react, but ask, "What?"

He pulls my body closer and I have to lift the coffee higher, so I don't spill or smash it between us.

"Coffee is in your hand." He leans back until his neck meets the concrete while he remains sitting on the seat's edge. "Rule is you can't be pissed now, right?"

It takes a moment to understand what he means.

I give a slow nod. "I did say such a dumb thing."

His blue eyes move between mine, his expression grows somber fast, and a knot forms in my throat, threatening to close it if I don't find space to breathe. I try to pull free of his grasp, but he holds me tightly and my stomach caves.

"Stop," he demands, his voice is low, strained yet strong.

"Stop what?"

He glares. "Fighting me."

I scoff, angling my upper half as far back as he allows, which isn't far.

That's rich coming from him.

"You lied today." He gauges me. "Tell me you did."

"This is ridiculous." I try to get free again, and his hold on me tightens.

He rubs my skin, massaging my muscles beneath the water. Waiting.

I glare, setting my drink down. "I didn't lie."

"Yes, you did."

"No, I didn't—"

"I said stop," he snaps.

My stomach begins to turn, and I look away, but his hand lifts, gripping on to my chin and bringing it back so I'm looking at him.

My eyes meet his and my tongue presses against the roof of my mouth, my teeth clamping together to the point of pain. My breathing picks up and something outside of myself takes over. Rather than shoving off his chest, as I should do, my hands decide to glide along it, and while his pecs flex beneath my touch, he doesn't push me away as I wish he would.

He's like a mannequin, flawlessly shaped and cut, intended to draw maximum attraction, to create envy and desire with every sharp, refined angle. He's soft and warm, has abs without flexing and his biceps fill the sleeves of his shirts to a T.

But his face...

My hands pause at the center of his chest, my fingers spanning out and pressing into his smooth skin.

His face is not one to grace the cover of a magazine; he's too harshly handsome. Sharp, darkened angles and tortured eyes.

He's more the unexpected stranger who lives in the deepest parts of your mind, only to appear in your dreams. The guy who vanishes when your fantasy-killing alarm clock rips you awake and you try to fall asleep again for a few extra minutes, just in case he comes back. But he doesn't.

Because as dreams go, the guy within them is a figment of your imagination.

He's raw but not real.

In reach, but untouchable.

Not even if you're touching him now?

My eyes, reluctantly, pull from his chest, meeting his magnetic blues.

Something aches low in my abdomen, high in my chest, deep in my conscience.

"You're human. You do want." His palms wrap around my outer thighs. "And you do need." He squeezes and whispers, "I've felt your need... just like you feel mine now."

He lifts his hips, pressing them against me beneath the water and I swallow, staring. He's hard beneath me.

The spa light illuminates half of his face while shadowing the other, making him appear dark and dangerous.

Like a bad decision.

Like trouble.

"Jameson," he rasps, a note of desperation adding weight to my name, weight that wears within me.

He brings me closer, his lips now an inch from mine, and I hold my breath as his fingers glide into my hair, tightening.

I don't know what he's doing, but I like it and the sound that slips from me is proof.

He growls, and I swear he's ready to take whatever he might want, but then his eyes squeeze shut, his muscles tensing.

He spins us, now hovering over me, the veins in his neck strained and angry, and then he's leaping from the water.

He stomps away, but his friends are there, waiting, blocking his escape. One of each of their shoulders press into one of his, his chest facing away while theirs face me.

Talk about fighting something...

Beretta whispers something, and Ransom's chin falls to his chest.

Slowly, he glances over his shoulder, and suddenly, all eyes are on me.

There's a plea there, written along the three faces

before me, but my headspace is fucked up and far from what's necessary for my own good, so even if I know what they want from me... I don't give it.

I climb from the hot tub, but instead of walking forward, I turn my back to them, head for my room, and quickly pull myself together. Throwing myself into my car, I pretend I don't care if they're still standing where I left them.

I head for the club for that last call I promised the girls, but I only make it five feet inside the door before I stop in my tracks.

Looking around, I note the enjoyment everyone seems to be reveling in.

They laugh and joke, drink and dance and why does none of it look appealing?

It should be, right? This is my world. I should like the things they like; do the things they do. Want the things they want.

My leg bounces where I stand and I try to find that sense of ease, the giddiness I'm witnessing, but it simply isn't there.

Was it ever?

Annoyed with myself, I spin on my heels to leave, but jolt when I come face-to-face with Amy.

She tips her head, pulling her drink to her lips as her bloodshot eyes trace over every inch of me. She takes a small sip from her glass, her fingers coming up to cover her lips. "Leaving so soon, are we?"

"Hey, Amy?"

She straightens, a smirk playing at her pink lips. "Yes?"

"Fuck off." I shove past her, thanking the bouncer at the door when he opens the rope for me to pass.

I step into the cooler air, taking a deep breath that does nothing to settle my mind.

I get to the curb, two spaces from where I parked and stop.

Leaning against my car with his head angled toward the curb and arms crossed over his chest is Ransom.

My heels click with another step forward and his head lifts, his eyes catching mine.

He pushes to his full height and I keep walking until the tips of my heels meet the toes of his sneakers.

Our eyes and bodies are aligned, and his hand lifts, pulling my hair from the high pony I put it in, in a rush.

It falls around my shoulders and his fingers bury into it.

His forehead falls to mine, and I close my eyes to get away from the strangled look in his.

He says nothing, but stands there, hanging on to me, and I don't know why I let him. A hand meets mine, and I open my eyes to find Beretta.

He nudges my palm open, pulling my keys from my grip.

He nods, unlocks it, and Ransom leads me into the back seat as Beretta slips behind the wheel.

The top rolls back as a second engine roars and I turn my head to find Arsen has pulled up beside us.

He winks and slowly rolls forward.

Beretta pulls out behind him and off we go.

I don't know what the hell is happening or why I go with their every move, but I do.

And I can't bring myself to regret it.

At least... not yet.

CHAPTER
Nineteen

*S*equins and Satin and Diamond Studs, oh my. Literally, the chaises are covered, the garment racks overflowing, and the seamstresses are working on overdrive to keep their smiles on their faces when, really, they're wondering if they can get away with letting a pin slip and call it an accident.

"What about this one, can it be taken in, extended at the hem and the back twisted rather than crossed? Maybe even dyed a shade darker?" Amy holds a gown to her front, shifting from side to side.

"So basically, can the dress you're holding be completely redesigned to create an entirely new one?" Jules snaps, swapping out the purple disaster in her hand for another.

Amy cuts a glare toward her sister, her eyes flitting past mine but coming right back when she catches me staring. She folds the gown over her arm and a woman comes up beside her, quickly taking it and smoothing it out.

"Not trying anything on today, James?"

I shake my head.

"Skipping the Fall Ball, are we? And what, might I ask will you be doing instead?" There's a hint of accusation in her squeaky little tone, one that has me sitting up slightly.

"Oh, my god, you're not going?!" Cali whips around with a frown.

Jules and a few others are staring now too.

Amy smirks, her chin lifting a little higher as she grabs for another dress.

"I never said I wasn't going."

Amy's movements falter.

"I said I wasn't trying anything on."

"If you wait any longer, your dress will never be ready," Jules stresses, hiccupping and reaching for her wine glass as if it will help.

"I already have mine settled." As I figured it would, that gets Amy's attention. "It's on its way."

It's a lie, but I know exactly why Amy suddenly wanted to join us in Los Angeles today. She wants to see for herself what I lean toward as far as style, so she can one-up it.

It's been a constant over the last six weeks, ever since the first day of school, when she tried to bid on my bluff and failed when I called Ransom to our table.

My mom had sent me a new prototype handbag from one of her designer friends and she insisted I use it for a set number of days to test the 'audience,' so Amy went out and tracked down a limited-edition Louis.

Days after I showed up with my new car, she traded hers in for a foreign one, a darker version of red than mine, one she likely had to pay a shitload to have expedited.

I didn't care, considered it a coincidence in my head, which is ridiculous in itself, but yesterday, I had a hair appointment right after school. I added some darker streaks into my hair, which she saw at the club last night for a whole five seconds, and what do you know... someone showed up with a new do today.

She must have her people on speed dial.

Not that we all don't.

I should pull a Britney and go bald, see what she does then...

A smile tugs at my lips at the thought, but I rein it in when Cali speaks.

"Good, because I was about to say." She laughs. "I'm tired of you being MIA all the time." She poses in the mirror, smiling as she would for a camera. "And since you already have yours, don't let us buy the same color! I don't want to walk in looking like some twister sister shit."

I wiggle my brows instead of responding, pulling my phone from my purse when it vibrates. It's a text from Beretta.

Beretta: we're outside.

My brows pull and I slowly sit up.

Outside?

Beretta: dress-up ended an hour ago.

A laugh spurts from me, and I type away.

Me: dress-up never ends around here. I thought you knew?

Beretta: educate me.

Beretta: when you get in the car.

My lips quirk.

Me: I didn't even tell you where I was going...

His name flashes across my screen then, and I push to my feet.

I walk over to the window, scanning over the street ten stories below, as I bring it to my ear.

"It's cute, in an annoying way, how you have no idea the power social media gives assholes like us." He pauses a second, and then says, "There, look at what I sent you."

I pull it from my ear, my eyes cutting up to the girls

briefly.

The photo is a screenshot of Jules' Instagram Story.

It's a picture of her and Cali standing back-to-back, blowing kisses at the camera, the words at the bottom reading "Lovely in Los Angeles."

I pull it back to my ear, snagging a melon ball from the hors d'oeuvre table, and gliding my teeth along the silver pick. "It's a big city."

"Yup, and we might not have found you if your girl hadn't hashtagged your location along with 'girl gang.' Think she knows what a gang is?"

I chuckle. "Only what can be learned from *Riverdale*."

His laughter is loud, and I smile.

"Come on. We're bored." His grin easily heard. "Entertain us, Trouble."

"And there it is." I tip my head, trying to see farther down the road, but don't spot them.

"Not the way you're thinking. Your boy ain't here. It's just me and mine."

My head jerks to the side, my mouth opening, but nothing comes out and his airy chuckle fills my ear.

"My car is at Cali's."

"We'll grab it. Come on, get down here before we get a ticket for parking in a red zone. It won't exactly be believable if I tell a cop we're both color blind *and* one of us is a mute."

I laugh, turning to look at the girls when their giddiness grows louder.

Cali beams at the mirror in a floor-length, chiffon gown, Jules clapping at her back, her wine spilling over her hand and making her laugh louder while the seamstresses appear about ready to have heart attacks.

So much for keeping the alcohol from her today—the girl brought her own bottle.

"We don't get you next weekend since you'll be playing royalty at the dance with your fake friends. Give us today, you know you want to."

I take a deep breath, grabbing my clutch off the seat. "On my way."

I say a quick goodbye and step into the hall, onto the elevator and hit the button for the bottom floor.

The doors begin to close, but a hand shoots out, and they reopen, Amy standing on the other side.

She stares, laughing as she tilts her head. "God, you must have serious daddy issues to be playing the game that you are."

"And you must be mistaken if you think for a second anything that comes out of your mouth bothers me in the slightest."

"Not a rebuttal, interesting." Her smile surprises me, but I don't show it. She steps back, waving her artificial fingernails at me. "Enjoy the scraps they're willing to give, Jameson. I can't wait to watch this blow up in your pretty little face."

The doors finally close, erasing her from sight, and I bounce my knee as the elevator dings floor by floor until I'm stepping from the smothering box.

Not a second after I arrive in the lobby, into view through the large glass window, does a horn honk and hold.

Beretta stands outside the black convertible, the door held open as he crosses an arm over his chest, bowing to play chauffeur, Arsen perched high on the driver's seat, grinning from him to me. The actual doorman is trying to get them to move, or to at least acknowledge his attempt, but they don't, and the man turns to me.

I shrug, chuckle, and push out the door.

I take Beretta's hand and climb into the back seat.

He doesn't join me but falls into the front, and then we're driving away.

Beretta catches my eye in the mirror and pointedly looks to the empty space beside me and back. "More of that family shit."

I shrug because I didn't ask.

Even if I sort of wanted to.

I'm laying across the plethora of blankets piled on the old mattress in the bed of the truck at Beretta's house, laughing as he acts out a scene from some movie called *The Night at The Roxbury* that he swears is a 'classic' and almost had a fit when I told him I'd never heard of it.

He's dancing like a fool on the open tailgate, his hands, arms, and legs flailing all around as he bumps his chest against Arsen's, who laughs with me.

His tone is soft, but strong, maybe a little gruff, as his voice must be.

He doesn't move but is fully entertained by Beretta's antics.

Nobody I know would have the confidence or comfort to act so silly out in the open like this. I know I don't.

It's addicting, the freedom they walk with.

Beretta spins, his grin wide as he shouts, "Emilio!"

I laugh, shaking my head, but then he turns serious, straightens, and hops off the bed of the truck.

"This can't be good," he mumbles, taking a few steps.

Arsen hops down next, both walking around the truck.

I lift onto my elbow, looking over my shoulder through the back and front windshield to spot Ransom slipping through the gate on foot.

His hair is pulled at its ends and chaotic, his eyes dark

underneath and shirt torn at the neckline.

"Hey man," Beretta says cautiously, but cuts himself off.

Ransom darts forward, gripping the edge of the folding table set up next to the garage door and flips it.

He picks it up again, tossing it against the wall and it snaps in the center, the cheap plastic no match for his wrath.

He jumps on top of it, stomping, and picks up a nearby wrench off of the top of a small safe tucked in the corner, heaving it across the yard. It crashes into something, clanking hard as it falls to the ground.

"That motherfucker!" he bellows, growls, and spins. "That sorry piece of shit!" he shouts, then bows, screaming nothing into the air.

Ransom lifts a chair until it reaches the high point above his head. He prepares to send it flying, but as he lifts, his eyes lock onto mine.

His body turns to stone and whether he intended to or not, the chair falls behind him, nearly ripping his arms backward, his torso twisting and throwing him off balance.

I push up into a sitting position and offer a tight smile, because what else can I do? He came here to lose his shit in front of the people he trusts to help him pull himself together, something most people don't have and here I am, the 'plaything,' invading the space he requires.

Shame burns beneath my skin as his own flashes across his face, but it's quickly replaced by sheer anger, and he charges toward me. He pulls on the top blanket, yanking and yanking until I'm before him.

His nostrils flare, his jaw flexing repeatedly.

I shouldn't, but I know what comes next, and it takes effort I refuse to acknowledge to keep my shoulders high and my face blank.

Ransom stalks away.

With a low exhale, I climb from the back of the truck and step toward my car, but Beretta catches my arm as I pass, halting me.

"You can't leave." He frowns.

"Beretta, seriously?" My eyes widen. "I shouldn't be here right now."

"He doesn't want you to go."

A scoffed laugh escapes before I can stop it and his gaze narrows farther. I falter. "Please tell me you're joking."

He says nothing and I tug my arms free, glancing where Ransom disappeared and back. "Beretta..."

"If he wanted you gone, he would have no problem saying it." The creases framing his hazel eyes deepen. "Just... give him a minute. He gets like this when he's forced to go home."

Forced to go home?

He doesn't go home?

Where does he...

I glance over my shoulder at the mattress and blankets I just climbed off of, remembering the ones tucked into the corner of the beach cave. The take-out boxes and recent fire.

He can't... no.

I shake my head, looking away, but when a light knock echoes to the side, we both follow the sound.

Arsen holds a paddle board in one hand, the paddle in the other. He shrugs.

"Yeah, perfect. It's been a minute." Beretta grabs my hands, pulling me to him. "You're in, right? Ransom loves the water."

He does?

Arsen lifts and carries two boards toward his car, and I watch as he wedges them into the back seat, the ends sticking over the side.

"Jameson."

I shake my head. "Look, I—"

Ransom comes from behind the garage.

He avoids everyone's eyes, but heads straight for where the other boards are leaning against the wall. He grabs two, walking toward Arsen's car, and as he passes, his eyes flick to mine.

I don't realize I'm nodding until Beretta claps beside me.

I guess we're going paddle boarding.

Within minutes, we're off.

Beretta rides with me and when he tells me to turn onto Nineteenth Street, where the most commonly used loading dock in the peninsula is located, I do, but not without hesitation.

He senses it, glancing from me to where several men with power scooters are delivering a load of boards to the vacationers.

"What's wrong?" he pushes.

A yacht blew up seconds after I climbed from it twenty feet ahead.

I park, get out, and say, "Nothing."

Without my asking, the boys carry my things into the water while I open my trunk for a swimsuit and slip it on beneath my dress before peeling my heels from my feet.

I don't bother swapping for my spa sandals; I just walk toward the water.

Beretta has already stepped out and onto his board, but he's yet to start paddling. He waits for Arsen, and once he's ready, they both look to me.

Ransom hasn't said a word, but silently peels his clothes from his back, and slowly, the others begin to paddle right.

I strap the board to my ankle and start in a sitting position, getting myself a few feet into deeper water, the paddle carefully tucked between my feet. I start to pull my hair up, wrapping it into a bun on top of my head when a hand grabs at my elbow.

I look over my shoulder.

Ransom stands there, his body half hidden beneath the cool ocean water.

I hate that I know what he wants, and more that I give it to him by allowing my hair to fall to my back again.

He pulls a small strand into his hand, running his fingers along the newly added peekaboos, two times darker than my natural shade, and I don't know if he realizes it, but the corner of his mouth hitches the smallest bit.

We stare at each other, but after a moment, I have to look away, and for some reason, I slip forward on the board. Though he has his own, Ransom pulls mine closer to the shore, and I grip the sides as he climbs on behind me.

I stay sitting on my knees, passing him the paddle, and he stands, directing us out into the peninsula.

Instead of following the others' path, he cuts straight across the water, where the yachts are tied down in the center, and weaves us in and out.

The board wobbles beneath us when he lowers himself. When it stops shaking, I peek at him.

Ransom lies on his stomach, his arms folded beneath his head, his lower half hanging in the water.

Sensing me, his eyes open, and I maneuver my body to mirror his, but I prop myself up on my elbows.

"Do you ever want to do the same?" he asks suddenly, slowly gliding his eyes my way. "Buy a one-way ticket to the bottom of the ocean?"

Panic wraps around my shoulders, tightening, squeezing

at his reminder that I angrily shared more than intended.

He's not supposed to remember.

To bring it up.

To ask.

I lift my chest from the board, ready to push off, but his leg meets mine, his shin gliding across my skin.

Something in his gaze holds me still, but my throat remains thick, my mind guarded, though my mouth decides to open, a low 'no' leaving me.

It's the truth.

I haven't, but I have wondered that if something were to happen, how long it would take my mom to notice—probably whenever the next Sunday rolled around. I wonder if I would be missed, *truly* missed, for me, not for what's needed of me.

Monti would miss me, wouldn't she?

A pontoon boat blaring Taylor Swift cruises by, the wake wobbling the board beneath us, and snapping me from my thoughts.

I sit up, swing a leg over and straddle the board, glaring at Ransom who still has his head rested on his hands, eyes on mine, though they did flick to where my swimsuit bottoms have met the hard epoxy.

"Who was it?" he asks, guessing when I don't answer. "Your bio-mom or bio-dad?"

Angry, I set it straight. "My dad."

"She kept his name, didn't she?" He eyes me, a tortured look in his. "Filano was his last name?"

"She made her name as a Filano, she had to keep it." I frown, a deep twist behind my ribs. "Why?"

"That's why you're so quick to help her, to be what she wants. To help hold on to the name. To your dad's name."

"No, it's not." My spine shoots straight. "I didn't know the man; all I know is he was weak. Why would I care?"

"You try *not* to care, period, because of what he did, but even cutting off your emotions can't erase the fact that your name is the only piece of him you have. You want to hold on to it."

My stomach leaps then drops. "What are you doing?" I snap.

He pushes up, confused, so I clear it up for him. "You're asking questions you shouldn't."

His eyes narrow. "And why shouldn't I?"

"Because it's none of your business."

He lifts, swinging one leg over, so he's straddling the board, the paddle laying across his lap. "So, you *don't* understand."

My head pulls back. "I don't want to understand. I want you to stop talking, or better yet, *start* talking."

He raises a brow.

"Why did you help me the night I wrecked my car?" I put him in the hot seat. "You were angry because you thought I was drinking and driving, but you could have gotten caught, gotten yourself in trouble. Still, you fixed my problem. Why?"

"Who else was going to?"

"No one." I shoot back instantly, leaning forward. "That's sort of the point. It's no one else's job."

"So, I should have let the girl who doesn't live in order to keep a low profile drop when I had the power to hold her up?"

My chest tightens and I shake my head. "You shouldn't have been around to have to do either."

"But I was. I was there when you crashed physically, and I was there when you crashed mentally."

I clench my teeth together, my jaw muscles aching from the contact.

The club.

"Who knows what would have happened if I hadn't followed you that night."

I scoff. "I probably would have fucked someone else on the hood of their car."

His face hardens. "That's not fucking funny."

"It's not supposed to be. It's the truth." Maybe, I don't know, but I shrug anyway. "Why did you follow me? Why *do* you follow me?"

"I told you before. We're protective of the things we want." He glides closer on the board, frustration building behind his light eyes. "*I* am protective of the things I want."

My mouth runs dry, but I refuse to swallow while he's so close, staring so intently. Waiting for a sign I heard him, for a sign I 'understand,' knowing I'm sitting here, forced to face his words, head-on.

He's protective of the things he wants.

Ransom Rossi wants me.

Sure, he doesn't indulge when his sexy time playmates aren't in on it, but group play or not, he's had me, has he not?

In his hands, at his will...

What more is there?

Nothing that you can give, Jameson.

A softness flickers across his face and he reaches out, his knuckles trailing over my swim top.

"Ransom..." I don't mean to whisper, but that's how his name leaves me.

His knuckles continue their way along the seam of my suit.

"You know nothing lasts forever, right? That wanting and having has nothing to do with keeping? Protective or not." Possessive or not.

That's what his touch is.

Possessive.

Claiming.

Calming.

His thumb comes up, gliding along my jaw, my lower lip, where it presses gently.

I swallow.

"My world, it's different than yours."

His eyes lift to mine, and I nearly stop breathing when he whispers, "Is it?"

CHAPTER Twenty

"This is most definitely not the way to La Parilla." I turn toward Anthony, finding his eyes already on me. "Change of plans?"

He nods from his seat and I don't have to force a smile because the news is thrilling enough. It would have been the first time we went out somewhere and I'm not in the mood to call on all my finishing school skills right now.

"So where to?"

His critical eyes scan over me, and slowly the corner of his mouth lifts. "I want to show you something."

I twist my body slightly. "I'm intrigued."

He nods and looks away.

If I didn't sense the obvious weight in the air the moment we climbed into his town car, it's undeniable now, but it's not my job to worry about his problems quite yet.

His ego, absolutely.

His issues? I have several solid months before those roll over as mine.

He was no sort of gentleman following the yacht fiasco, but in his defense, he's never truly had to be, so

I don't know if I can fault him for it. The guy is gorgeous, up and coming in his career at his young age and could easily win a bachelor of the year contest.

He's never been tied to or even photographed with a woman outside of his own staff—sure, he probably screws them behind the scenes, as my mother pointed out, but a girlfriend? Not once. I can be pissed off over his lack of concern, sure, but it makes more sense to respect him for focusing on what his desires are rather than faking emotion— he desires an attractive wife, not a needy one.

The driver turns down an unfamiliar cul-de-sac, nothing around but homes similar in size to mine, and as Anthony leans forward, preparing to exit the vehicle, I realize where he's taking me.

Unease wraps around my ribs, but I don't show it, smiling politely when he steps out, reaching in for my hand.

I could almost laugh at the stone walkway, my legs suddenly seeming to weigh the same. If he wasn't holding on to me, reminding me to put one foot in front of the other, I would likely be frozen in place, staring up at the mini mansion.

The home is as wide as it is tall, a deep gray in color. Large bay windows make up the center of the second story, a black iron patio railing overlooking the court behind me. The trim is black, the giant, triple garage doors a smoky glass, though you can't see through it.

We continue past the driveway, up the giant, square steps framed by large pots, white gardenias perfectly rounded inside them.

I hate gardenias and the white does nothing for the house.

I pause when the front door is opened and Elena stands inside, a binder in her hand and a kind curl to her lips.

228

"Hello, Jameson."

"Elena." I offer a smile. "Nice to see you."

She nods, stepping back as Anthony leads us inside.

I scan the walls, surprised by the life inside the place.

The couches are wide and deep set, as if meant for movie nights or comfort rather than for show, as the ones in my living room are. The ceiling is high, and the light natural.

The walls are a soft gray, the trim stark white, and giant art pieces cover the walls. It's bright and inviting.

Anthony squeezes my hand and I turn my eyes to his.

"Do you like it?" he asks.

"It's beautiful."

He pulls me along, up a set of wooden plank spaced stairs to the second story.

There are doors on both the left and right side, a slider that leads to the front balcony behind us and a giant window at the back.

Anthony releases me and steps ahead, but I'm close behind. I get as close as possible and my eyes widen.

The light shines in, the sun high this time of day, and beaming through the loft-like space, creating a tranquil setting.

I step up to the glass, careful not to touch and leave fingerprints behind. "Wow."

The ocean is just below the hillside, the house at the deepest point of the cul-de-sac, so there are no neighbors to see inside, no private back access for others to look up and through the glass. It's just pure ocean for miles.

A low rumble sounds around me, and I turn, my eyes sliding to an electric fireplace running along the mantel.

Anthony sets the remote down, slowly peeling his suit jacket from his body next, his eyes intent and on me.

He tosses it over the back of the chair and slowly stalks

toward me.

I know what the need for affirmation looks like, and it's written over every inch of his face, so while I'm tempted to move, I know better than to actually do so.

But over his shoulder, something catches my attention, and my eyes follow.

Pearls.

An iridescent vase full of them.

A frown begins to build, but I refocus when Anthony's hands land on my biceps.

"This is my home." He gauges me. "Soon, it will be yours too."

An anxious laugh slips, but I play it off as well as I can, and repeat what I already said because I've got nothing else. "It's beautiful."

"You, Jameson, are beautiful." The look in his eyes shifts and I prepare myself for what follows.

He leans in, and I close my eyes as Anthony presses his lips against mine.

An unexpected, alarming hint of guilt warms my stomach and my features pull. My eyes fly open and I almost blanch when I find Anthony studying my expression, as if he never closed his own.

He straightens and while I quirk my lips upward, his point down.

He nods, sighs, and steps toward the small glass end table, pouring himself a glass of scotch from the crystal decanter, turning to me once more.

I smile, but his facial expression doesn't budge.

It's blank.

"Elena," he calls, and soft footsteps pad on the stairs behind us.

I begin to turn, but he grips my chin. I expect him to

tell her to have our meal brought up here or something along those lines, but he stands there swirling his glass and tips his head slightly.

For the first time, he inspects my cheek, his grip on my face tightening, borderline bruising, and my eyes narrow, but his hand falls in the next second.

"Get the car ready to take Miss Filano home, lunch is canceled for today." He takes a slow sip of his dark liquor.

My blood pressure rises as I stare him in the eye, a million demands flickering within his.

Anthony gives his back to me, walking toward the fireplace, so I turn and make my way down the stairs, but I only get to the third when his words ring out behind me. "Next time you decide to change your hair, let me know beforehand."

My head jerks over my shoulder, and he cocks his head, a dead look in his eyes as he says, "I want you to appear naturally beautiful and moves like that are proof that you are not."

I open my mouth, my fist clenching the railing, and he watches me through sharp eyes, as if he's daring me to object.

He takes another sip.

Any means necessary.

I smile. "Enjoy your afternoon, Anthony."

His chin lifts slightly. "See you soon, sweetheart."

I leave, and the entire ride home I can't help but heed his goodbye as a threat.

I'm in a shit mood for days after my 'date' with Anthony.

Thankfully, it's a short schedule at school all week as the student committee prepares for the upcoming dance. Every day of the week it's pretty much princess prep once the bell rings.

Monday, all of us girls meet for facials and salt scrubs. Tuesday afternoon, it's mani-pedis. Wednesday is for waxing and today, final fittings at the boutique.

I managed to get out of the trip to the inner city since I lied and said my dress was on its way. Little did I know but should have fully expected my mother had it covered, and a golden gown arrived late Monday night. What I was unable to escape was the private premiere party at Jules' house for her mom's next film.

Every release, the night before the red-carpet event, her mom arranges for Jules and Amy's friends to come over for the 'privilege' of early viewing. Everyone who shows has to sign a waiver, agreeing not to talk about it until the following day, when they are required to blast it over social media.

I didn't sign, but her mom only smiled my way, so I assume she knows my mom would lawyer her ass if she even thought to ask me for my signature.

The movie is a good forty minutes in, Jules is trashed, Dax disappeared twenty minutes ago, and Cali is engrossed in her phone. Scott has passed out beside me and I'm more than ready to get out of here, so when Beretta texts to say he 'needs' to pick me up, I say okay.

I step onto the balcony, my eyes on the street ahead.

Mere minutes pass when headlights come around the corner, and an unexpected sigh escapes.

A mocking laugh fills the air behind me, and I spin, squinting.

Amy slips from the dark corner of the patio, a nasty grin on her face.

"You're really enjoying yourself, aren't you?" She laughs again. "Being their whore, keeping your secret? Or should I say... secrets."

My shoulder blades tighten, but I keep my expression blank as I turn to face her, the roar of the engine now at my back.

She eyes me a long moment, her head tilting to the side as a smile spreads along her lips.

"What do you want, Amy?"

"I'm trying to figure out if you really are as clueless as you seem, because, if so, that's just... tragic."

My fists clench, but I hide them behind my back. "I can ask if you can join in, if that's why you care, or why you watch them from across the room every chance you get. Waiting to be seen, are we?"

"Oh, honey." Her smile surprises me, but I don't show it. "I've been seen, and clearly you've had them."

This time, my eyes narrow. "Clearly I have."

She damn near giggles, creeping closer.

"But have you had *him* alone?" She blocks the doorway, her head tipped to the side, her tone low and illicit. "Do you know what makes him tick, what he likes... how he likes it?" Another laugh, and then a whispered, "No, I don't think you do."

She steps around me, spreads her hands out on the beam in front of her, staring down at the two boys waiting for me just below. "Have fun, Jameson." Her eyes cut over her shoulder, locking onto mine. "I can't wait to watch this blow up in your face. And it will."

I frown at her, but she doesn't see it.

She's stuck on the little sports car below.

Her words spin in my head as I slip out the front door and make my way to the curb, where Beretta stands beside the open door.

"Hurry, he's going to need us," he says, jerking his head for me to climb in the back.

I do, but don't bother asking where he is.

All I know is 'he'... isn't here.

We started at Beretta's, but when Ransom called them to say he would be longer than planned, we left for my house.

The boys moved Monti's video game console into my room and have been playing an obnoxious shooting game for the last half hour while I finish up homework for my English class.

The boys are as lost in their online world as I am in modern-day literature so we don't hear him walk in.

We don't realize he's here until my bedroom door is slammed shut.

I jolt, my laptop flipping off the pillow I had it perched on, my head snapping to the right as my legs slip over the edge of the bed.

Ransom leans against the wall directly beside it, his hand reaching over to twist the lock, trapping us inside. His head is dropped against the frame, and he stares down the length of his nose, right at me.

I hardly register the TV being shut off, but I do glance over my shoulder when my shutters are pushed closed, every trace of natural light fading around me. I meet Beretta's gaze as he draws the curtains shut, and then all that's left is the glow from my light.

My toes burrow in the carpet at my feet, and then Arsen is in front of me.

His hand glides up my neck, and when I take a deep breath, he nods, stepping back.

I stand and Ransom pushes off the door.

His body is weighted, sagging, but his eyes are wild and raking over mine like he's famished and only I can satisfy the hunger burning inside him. The need radiating off of him. The desperation thumping in the veins of his neck.

Goose bumps form along my legs as his focus falls to the satin of my lounge shorts, and his teeth sink into his bottom lip.

My ribs constrict, my core muscles clenching.

He tears his shirt from his body, stretching his shoulders out wide, but he quickly falls against the door, and slowly, his friends glide closer.

"Take off her top," he rasps, and his words are felt between my legs.

My body twitches, but when it's Beretta's hands that fall over my shoulders from behind, a grating voice seeps in, hijacking a moment that should be mine. Ours.

Have you had him alone?

Beretta's fingers float along my sides, to the hem of my shirt, and slowly, he pushes the soft fabric up and over my breasts.

Ransom's nostrils flare, a mix of anger and envy, a hint of something else.

Do you know what makes him tick?

My top is lifted over my shoulders, and as my hair slips free, spilling over my chest, Ransom's hands wrap around the buckle of his belt, pushing. Squeezing.

Arsen slips closer and my eyes slide his way.

His smile is small, gentle and he looks to his friend.

Have you had him alone...

My eyes drop to the floor, realization weighing me down.

She has.

Amy.

She's had Ransom alone, just him and her.

She knows what he likes, how he likes it...

Just him and her.

That's what she was hinting at, isn't it?

My skin prickles, frustration I have no business feeling sweeping over me. Bitterness I've never felt creeps in, doubt I've never experienced right behind it.

I'm hot all over, irritated.

Is this what jealousy feels like?

Heat in your chest, a nasty swirl low in your abdomen, a queasiness that pisses you off?

I jolt when knuckles find my chin, guiding my head up, but I wait until the last absolute second to raise my eyes.

Arsen's thumb lifts, tenderly gliding along my lip.

"The shorts, Arsen. Take off the shorts."

Arsen steps closer, pausing dead in his tracks when I say, "no."

I spin, facing Ransom.

The hand gripping his unfastened belt, ready to yank it free, freezes in place.

I stare him dead in the eye, witnessing his eyes sharpen with every second that passes.

I don't have to look behind me to know Beretta and Arsen are frozen in place, I can see them from the corner of my eye, but I don't pause.

I walk closer to Ransom, and with each step I take, his muscles grow stiffer, his gaze snapping from me to his buddies and back.

"No?" he rasps.

I shake my head, stopping two feet in front of him. "Not him. You."

His eyes tighten in protest, but then they fall to my body, slowly devouring every inch, every curve.

His want is clear, undeniable and straining against the briefs peeking from the open zipper of his black jeans.

My pulse jumps, a flair of expectation flickering low in my belly. The stupid thoughts from moments ago evaporating as he brings himself closer.

He takes slow steps, each one eliciting something deeper inside me. It's torture, waiting for him to reach me, to be close enough to reach *for* me, but then he's right there.

His chest brushing mine, causing my nipples to harden beneath my bra.

His breathing grows shallow, labored, and the pit of my stomach tingles, the need building inside me overwhelming.

Our eyes lock and a pulsing knot forms in my core.

He reaches out, and my body shivers in anticipation.

With my gaze as his prisoner, he licks his lips, his brows caving as his knuckle comes down on my cheek.

His chest rises, his hand twitching until his thumb meets my lips.

He shuffles even closer, and I would stumble back, if a warm chest wasn't already there to catch my fall.

His lips lower, and he glides them along the tip of his thumb.

My breathing quickens, my head dropping onto Arsen for support.

Right as his thumb slips from between us, his lips land on mine...

And the lights go out.

My eyes, that must have closed for a split second, fly open, my muscles locking. The room may now be a blur, but the situation couldn't have become clearer.

I'm the toy.

Ransom doesn't want me, he just wants to play with me, the same way Anthony will, like a doll he can pull out and dust off as he wishes.

I willingly accepted the role, I know that, so it should be

a relief to realize this, to know I'm simply the girl they chose as their latest game piece and will likely replace tomorrow. As they should.

I'm unkeepable anyway.

Greedy, heated lips, I don't know whose and I don't care, fall on mine and I meet their every sweep with my one. Hands glide along my thighs, and when my shorts are pushed down, I step out with ease, prepared to enjoy every second of what comes next.

Because I am the plaything.

It's not like I can offer them anything else anyway, so yeah. It should be a huge relief, an easy ending.

It really *really* should.

So why do I feel like a bitter ex ready to run on a rampage of twisted proportions?

CHAPTER
Twenty-One

"Man, Mom shot to kill." Monti grins, sliding the last bobby pin into my hair, smoothing the deep part down so it's slick to my head, my curls falling over it and giving Jessica Rabbit a run for her money. "You look like a goddess."

I frown at the light enhanced mirror. "I look like Belle."

"If Belle was a Roman plaything and not a Disney princess."

I glare. Two words I'm sick of hearing.

A car door closing reaches us and my sister walks over to the open window, peeping outside with a grin. "And they're walking up to the door," she singsongs.

I move over to my nightstand, tugging the drawer open. "Tell them I'll be out in a minute."

"Jameson wants to make a grand entrance?" Monti teases, her palm flattening on her chest as she bats her lashes, but then her eyes fall to the heart-shaped crystal in my hand, and her playfulness washes away.

She nods and steps out.

Opening the small trinket, a frown attempts to slide over me as I realize I haven't refilled my prescription this month.

It makes no fucking sense.

I've never felt so much in my life, yet for the first time *in* my life the need to drown it out has evaded me.

It must have, because I still have a handful left... something that has never happened.

I take a deep breath and place a pill under my tongue, my lips pinching together as I move back to the mirror.

A ball gown with heavy garments underneath, the finest silk laid perfectly over and framed just above the hip. Golden, sequined lace draped all around, and of course, the slight train in the back.

A fucking train.

For a high school dance.

This thing is nice enough to be a wedding dress, and likely cost as much as the average one, too.

I trace over every inch of the gown, taking note of the precise tailoring, and when I meet my eyes, it's with a shake of my head.

I glide my palms over my shiny hair.

Pretty little princess.

My fingers trail down my neck.

Silly little plaything.

I grip my own hips, tipping my head to the side.

Pathetic little pawn.

I lick my lips, smiling as I was taught, but a humorless laugh quickly follows.

I look to the ceiling, letting out a long sigh.

Monti calls my name from the hall, my phone beeps with the fifth ignored text of the day, and promptly rings right after, but I don't move. I stand there in the middle of my room, staring at myself.

Anger burns in my chest.

"Screw this."

I move as quickly as I can, but another ten minutes pass before I'm walking into the living room where the others are waiting.

Monti is the first to spot me and her eyes shoot wide, but her laughter replaces it just as quick. "Just..." She shakes her head. "Yes."

Her smile is wide, and she turns it toward the others behind her who now realize I'm standing here.

Light eyes meet mine, and a slow smile curves his lips. "Damn."

I step up to him and he leans in, bringing his mouth to my ear. "Red is your color."

"Thanks, Scott." A smirk pulls at my lips and my chin lifts a little higher. "It was a gift."

To say that I stand out tonight is an understatement and something I failed to consider in my two minutes of having no fucks to give. Obviously, as I was at the start, everyone here is in their best-made ball gowns, Valentinos, and draped in family jewels. I would guarantee the majority of these girls sat in a salon chair for the last six hours, all to get here and compare every inch of themselves to someone else rather than enjoying their night for what it is—an over-the-top high school dance fit for royals, California-style.

It's almost as if, in worlds like ours, we're meant to be pinned against each other, to fight over who wore it best or compete to make sure it's us in the end.

Amy is a perfect example of this; she had no idea what I'd wear tonight, and the girl spared no expense. Her dress is by far the most captivating ball gown of the night... but mine is far from a gown, so in her vindictive little mind, I wore this as a way to steal the show when really, I wore it because I wanted to feel like I was running my own.

Not the dance committee who decided the theme.

Not my mom, who picked and shipped the pile of lace on my bedroom floor.

And okay, maybe a little out of spite too, but I'm annoyed, and that nasty little fact only annoys me further.

Maybe Amy does know Ransom as well as she claims, because she too wears red. She's draped in it from neck to toe, and the custom piece is nothing like the one she was having tailored the day I was with them.

I wonder if hers was a gift, too?

Something sour coats my mouth and I reach for the flask hanging from Scott's fingers.

He cuts me a quick, approving grin and goes back to his conversation.

I swirl the too sweet whiskey in my mouth, reveling in the burn, holding on to it as long as I can stand, before forcing it down my throat and passing it back. As I lick my lips, my eyes catch Amy's for the fiftieth time tonight, and this time, I flip her off for the hell of it.

She purses her lips and goes back to what she's been doing for the last few hours—glancing from me to the door, from the door to me, to the bathroom and toward every dark corner in this place, knowing if they were here, she'd find them in one of those three spots. But they're not.

They had said several weeks ago that they wouldn't be. Maybe it's not their thing, or maybe they couldn't meet dress codes—black jeans would never make it through the door. Of course, if they wanted to, they'd find a way. It's what they do, get their way. They did with me.

Several times now.

Not that I complained.

(I'm just a dumb girl who had to go and accidentally

want a little more of the one who occupies her dreams at night.)

Scott turns to me, a fake gold crown hanging half off of his head, a drunken grin written along his lips as he tosses his arm over my shoulder. "Ready?"

I nod, glancing from him to Cali and Jules as they walk up with several others trailing behind.

Scott holds the flask up once more, a sly smile on his face, and I grab it from him, taking another drink as we slip through the open double doors.

Cali and Jules squeal, grabbing on to my free arm with excitement, as if me joining in on their fun tonight is the best thing ever. To them, I'm on board to party, but really, I'm searching for numbness I used to possess naturally. Daily. Around the damn clock.

But it evades me, instead forcing me into a pathetic little part of my mind where I'm all the things I never wanted to be.

Needy.

Greedy.

Among other things.

But this...

I look around the party bus the others rented to take us a whole 3 miles and grab one of the personal shots from the ice bar as I make my way to a seat. I twist the top on the tiny bottle, eyeing the golden liquid in my palm. My head is already getting fuzzy, and I'm grateful for it.

A small grin forms on my lips and I drink it in one go. *This should help.*

Cali lifts her phone, pressing her lips to my cheek while I blow kisses at the screen, a bottle in my left hand, sucker in my right.

Only when I place the lollipop between my lips and Cali giggles, saying something about my tongue game, do I realize she's not taking a picture but recording.

I laugh, bending at the waist to get out of the shot and she giggles, moving it along the group instead.

Scott comes up behind me, his smile disappearing into my neck, only to steal the liquor from my hand.

I roll my eyes, pushing to my feet, and chuckling at myself when I nearly lose my balance, but Dax is there to catch my fall.

He smiles. "Look who decided to let loose."

"Look who is really far away from his girlfriend."

Both of us turn to where Jules is already passed out drunk, sleeping on her folded arms on Scott's dinette table.

He sighs, his shoulders sagging. "Yeah, I should get her into the spare bedroom."

I pat at his chest and free myself, moving over to the deck's edge.

I bob around to the music, tipping my head back and forth and raising my arms in the air, only to drag them back down, but my hand hits the ledge and the glass I didn't realize I grabbed on my way over slips from my palm, falling to the floor beneath it with a distant crash.

Laughing, I lean for a better look and several others make their way over.

"It was just a glass." I look their way, but their eyes aren't on me.

They're focused on the vineyard below.

Facing forward, I squint, trying to see through the night, but the stars aren't so bright this evening.

And then the liquor-induced fire swirling in my stomach doubles, but for a very different reason.

I knew for certain the boys wouldn't show at the dance to see if I went after all, let alone with who. But I was so sure they wouldn't be there, I failed to realize how they didn't have to be.

They'd find out anyway.

The lights go out around us, and the whispers start, the laughter following, though not from everyone. Not from me.

Scott steps up beside me, and then a small light appears. It's fairly far, way out in the middle of the grapevines.

It's a low flicker, but it flashes across the face of a demon in the flesh.

My hands fly to my abdomen as a pair of fluorescent blues glow in the distance. I stop breathing when two more pairs emerge to the right.

And then that flicker grows... into full-fledged flames.

Ransom jams the flaming stick into the ground, dead in the center of the vineyard.

His eyes slice to mine, and then they're running at warp speeds, all in different directions...

Shit.

CHAPTER
Twenty-Two

I spin, bumping arms with other girls as they panic, pushing closer to the railing in an attempt to get a better view of the space behind me. Scott, Dax, and every other guy here dashes around the side, racing to get to the ground before the fire burns lower, reaching the vineyards that surround it and pumped for a fight.

But they're all fools.

The boys aren't down there hiding in the darkness.

They're on the way up.

I shove through a few people, pulling my pumps off for better balance. I trip, bouncing on the heel of one foot as I try to steady myself, and the moment I get myself straight, my head flies up and I jerk to a stop.

The air in my lungs evaporates, every organ in my body shriveling at the sight before me.

Ransom stands as tall and sturdy as a stallion, his shoulders broad and stance wide. Dripping in black, his hood covers his hair, effectively shadowing his face as he intended, his glowing gaze glaring down into mine.

His lips are smashed firm, his jaw ground tight and ticking, his pulse wild and uncontrolled. Sharp.

But his chest doesn't rise and fall.

I would almost swear he was a zombie, dead on his feet, if he weren't standing here right now. He looks dead, the way I wish to feel but am unable.

Not anymore.

Not since him.

He pushes closer, and I shuffle backward.

Back onto the patio deck, where the other girls have finally realized we're no longer alone up here.

The shock is clear and loud, the gasps and giggles following, but the excitement doesn't last long. It fades into the darkness around us, or maybe only for me as all that's left is him, angry and an inch away.

I open my mouth, but nothing comes out.

He shoves against me, my body thumping against the railing and blocked from escaping by his.

"Jameson..." Cali calls, her voice hesitant. Unsure.

But I ignore her and so does he, if he heard her at all.

He's fuming, his body flexing over and over again.

Scott's shouts reach us from below, he screams for someone to grab the hose, barking for another to check the right side of the field.

Ransom's eyes snap over my shoulder, toward the vineyards, and then he flicks his gaze to the deep plunge neck of my dress, to the high slit over my thigh.

Ah, of course.

It's what I'm wearing that's pushed him to show up tonight.

Not who I came with, why I ignored them all day.

Why I'm chasing a strong buzz, seeking comfort I shouldn't and had never needed before he came in and warped my mind.

The stupid fucking dress is his concern, because *how dare I...*

My lips part with a low, drunken chuckle and I relax. Lifting my hands, I glide them along the cool metal behind me until my arms are stretched to their full length. I push up onto my toes, keeping my knee bent so the fabric slides off my skin, completely baring the smoothness there for any who wish to look.

I jerk when his hand darts out, gripping the material at its deepest V point and twists, balling it into his fist.

"This." His voice is crisp, fixed, but only for me. "Is mine."

"It was a gift."

His knuckles press into my breastbone, his head lifting slightly, allowing me a somewhat better look. "I'm not talking about the fucking dress."

I nearly choke on air, my eyes widening, only to narrow a moment later.

Me?

A heavy ache pushes against my ribs, but I don't show it.

His?

"Yeah, mine." He's somehow closer. "The girl and what she's wearing." His wild eyes pop up. "Mine."

I swallow.

Deny, deny, deny.

Love kills.

"You can have the dress—"

"I have the girl," he snaps, my words clogging in my throat as the pad of his finger taps at my temple. "I'm in here."

The hand gripping my top shifts, his knuckle now pressing near my left breast where my treacherous heart beats against him, as if begging to be heard or felt or any other stupid thing it knows I won't want to ask for. "Getting close to here."

His brows raise as he dares to slip beneath my dress, and right as a flash of fake blonde makes herself seen in the distance, purposely rounding us like a thirsty little vulture. "Been here—"

"Have you?" flies from me as I fight to slam the walls back into place, over my mind, my heart, and everything since he's all over me, bleeding into the wounds I've kept patched with salon trips and smiles.

He freezes.

"'Cause I'm not so sure," I force out. "Maybe it was your friends who slipped in—"

"Careful, baby." His low, almost wounded rasp stings, but I hide it.

I have to.

This is too much.

And he's a liar.

I'm a fucking toy, not good enough to look in the eye when he touches me.

Not worth the sight of desire.

A dark, dirty, damaged little secret.

My head falls back on a mocking laugh, and his muscles grow tenser.

I lock my eyes on his.

His gaze narrows, and my god, the pain in his harsh whisper. "Don't."

But I have to...

"Look at you." I shake my head, speaking slowly in an attempt to keep from slurring my words. "Showing up tonight and acting the part of what, exactly? The disrespected wannabe alpha? Is your pride bruised?" I lean into him and his body twitches in anger.

"I know you get jealous. I see it in your eyes when I lay my head on Arsen's chest, or when I smile at Beretta. Your jaw gets tight, like it is now, and you—"

"If you really think I don't trust them with every fucking thing I own, I am, and I'll be, you're mistaken," he hisses frankly. "There is no rift in our water and there never will be." His eyes shift between mine. "But what about you, hmm? Is the ground beneath your feet starting to shake? Is your ocean on the edge of a tsunami, ready to spill over until all that's left is a mess of broken parts?"

"Screw you."

He acts as if I didn't speak. "Better be careful, Trouble, you might want to run soon. You wouldn't want Scott to realize how you like extra whipped cream on your coffee, or how your toes curl in your heels when you're nervous or anxious... or wanting."

My pulse jumps in my throat. "Shut up."

"You wouldn't want him to notice the way your lips curl left when you fight a smile, and how you love it when—"

"I saw you" rushes from my mouth, the need for him to stop talking higher than I'll admit.

It works, distracting his train of thought.

His mouth slowly closes, and his eyes grow quizzical.

I steady my breathing and summon a bitchy carelessness I struggle to find. "In the park, with the blonde. And I know you fucked Amy."

As if his body is dropped in arctic waters, his limbs lock up, freezing him in place, and the struck state he's in, the shock and lack of denial makes it easier to continue.

"You clearly have a type and maybe I'm just not it, being a brunette and all." I blink obnoxiously. "I might be wearing a dress you gave me, but I'm not yours." I shake my head, the alcohol helping keep my expression blank. "I could never be yours." I grin like a wicked bitch while my mind screams *even if I want to be.*

I want to be.

But this isn't real, it's a game. He plays games, I learned this day one.

"You should go." I nod, pushing him away, but he doesn't move an inch. "You don't belong here."

His jaw clenches and in the distance, it's easy to hear the guys rushing back this way, there's stomping all around, coming from both sides, from behind him.

I lift my chin, summoning every ounce of strength to keep it from trembling. "Get out of here, blackout. This isn't your world."

Something flashes in his eyes and I wait for him to be cold and callous, to go for the throat and drag that metaphorical, jagged blade straight across.

That is what I hope for, what I want, but I don't get it.

I get something much, much worse.

He gets in my face and he stares me dead in the eye, somehow, though he wears his glow-in-the-dark contacts, it's my favorite shade of blue I'm staring into.

"You're right," he rasps, his fingers discreetly, subconsciously, playing with pieces of my hair. "This isn't my world, but if you think mine isn't where you belong, you're dead fucking wrong."

I suck in a desperate breath, and then I gasp as Ransom shifts, grips the railing and hops over the side.

I scream, bending to look over the ledge.

He's gripping the crossing bars beneath it, using them to break his fall. He drops to his feet with ease, and not a second before Scott, along with every other guy here, is surrounding me in an attempt to grab him.

But again. They're fools.

As if they didn't get them all to the bottom as they wanted, when they wanted, and got them all back to the top just the same.

Beretta appears, and while it's dark, and all you can spot is the glow of their eyes, I know he grins at Ransom's side.

He flips them off as they scream and shout at the 'punks' below, but they keep on walking toward the end of the property, where Arsen now stands, waiting.

Ransom turns, facing this way.

He tips his head and I know he's looking at me, and only then do I realize Scott is behind me, his arms locked on the railing at my sides.

Ransom pulls something from beneath his hood, and everyone gasps when a blue flicker glows in the distance.

He doesn't hesitate but cocks his head to the opposite side as he lights the vines on fire and panic begins all over again, but this time, for real as the dry branches go up in flames in an instant.

My hands fly to my mouth and by the time I look back to where the boys had stood…

They're gone.

CHAPTER
Twenty-Three

The fire department arrived within seven minutes and Scott and the others, all intoxicated, were somehow able to use the well water on the land to stop the spread, or so they continue to boast.

Really, they're lucky Ransom chose the row he did. The outer row, where the wind blew opposite of the others and was located closest to their water supply.

This could have been bad really, everyone is drunk and has been drinking for hours already, so they're idiots for what they did.

It was reckless and dumb and could land them in jail.

Everyone here likely assumes they don't care, but I know that's untrue.

I don't know what the hell Ransom was thinking tonight. This could be bad for him; it could screw up a lot more than I know.

But I try and force myself not to care, while also eavesdropping as much as I can when the officers ask around for statements.

So far, nobody has given one of merit.

It was too dark to see...

By now, most everyone has gone home, and my sister and Tanner have just pulled up, but I don't make it to the curb before Scott is slipping in front of me.

His eyes are pinched tight at the edges, but his touch is gentle as he grabs my left hand, my heels dangling from my right, and pulls me into him.

I lift the corner of my mouth and his free fingers glide into my hair.

I tense, my body hating the feeling of another's touch there, but my mind screams it's no big deal, that it shouldn't be. He either doesn't notice, or he pretends not to.

"Thanks for being my date tonight," he says.

I nod. "Kind of funny, how I only texted you last night and you still didn't have one."

He smirks. "I had one, just had to wait for her to realize she did too."

A low laugh leaves me, and I tip my head slightly.

"I was hoping you'd stay, planned for it really," he admits.

"Yeah, I think you'll be busy for a while." I motion toward the firetrucks still lining the street, finishing up whatever it is they have to do.

He nods, and when he leans in, my chest clenches.

I close my eyes, ready for it, desperate to erase the last lips that landed on mine, but my head decides to turn away without permission, and my eyes fly open when his mouth freezes on my cheek.

Slowly, he pulls back, a quizzical narrow of his eyes, but he shakes it off, drops my hand and licks his lips. He forces a grin. "See you Monday."

"Yep." *Smile*.

I step around him, slide into the back seat and Tanner shuts the door behind me.

My sister starts talking and I slice my eyes to hers. I tear open my purse, pull out, and slip my earbuds into my ears, cranking the music up as high as it allows.

I don't even know what's playing. I don't hear it, but I don't hear her either.

She blinks, a frown tugging at her brows as she drops against the seat, skating her eyes past mine every few minutes.

When we walk into the house, I head for my room, but her soft hand lands on my elbow and I just can't.

I whip around, tearing my earbud from my ear.

"What Monti?!" I shout, tossing my shoes to the floor. "What the fuck do you want?! You want to ask how I am, how it went, what the fuck happened?! Why I shed the dress Mom sent me and wore one a guy who likes to fuck with my head gave me?! Go ahead, sister! Ask!" I scream, stalking toward her, but when she says nothing, I get angrier. I shove at her chest and she stumbles back. "Fucking ask! Talk! Say something!"

Her face falls, a blanket of remorse covering her from head to toe, and tears fill her eyes. "J..."

My teeth begin to chatter, so I clamp them shut, and it aches. My jaw, my muscles. My entire fucking body.

She reaches for me, tears pooling in her eyes.

I slap her clear across the face, revel at the shock in her eyes, and tears roll down her cheeks.

"You're seriously going to cry?" I scream, shoving her as she goes to cup her cheek and she falls against the wall. "Are you pretending like you feel bad for being the shittiest sister on the fucking planet? The worthless daughter who couldn't even do her fucking part?!" I seethe, my limbs shaking, but something behind my ribs cracks so I try to crack something in her.

I stand tall, clear my face of all emotion and take a step

back.

"You're as pathetic as Dad was. Weak and useless." I try to take a breath, but my lungs refuse the air, so I force a quick, "Go cry for someone who gives a shit," and back away as quickly as I can and get the hell out.

I lock myself in my room and the walls begin to spin.

Swatches of gold and glamor funneling around, cutting off my airway and leaving my lungs starved.

I drop to my knees, my head falling into my hands as moisture threatens to slip from my eyes.

But I don't let it.

I can't.

Because who the hell do I have to cry for, myself? In pity over a situation I created?

Maybe I'm the one who is pathetic.

And damaged.

And so so screwed.

My door stayed locked all night and day the remainder of the weekend. I played music at deafening volumes that did horrible things for my massive hangover, and if Monti tried to knock, I didn't hear it. If the doorbell rang, oh fucking well.

But it's Monday now, so I have to smile and move along like all is well in this fucked-up world of spoiled rich kids and the shit we deal with behind closed doors.

Speaking of closed doors, I open mine to find Monti sitting outside of it.

She jolts, jumping to her feet, looking as if she hasn't slept since I left her in the hall.

Her cheek is stained a light red in color and a twinge of guilt pokes at me, but I push it away.

It does no good to feel bad for the things we do, that's

just our own conscious trying to justify our actions, but it's an action that came from us. I did something, so that means, at that time, in that moment, I meant it. To take it back now is to try and save myself from the shame or whatever you want to call it that comes with facing it.

The reality of the situation is I slapped my sister because she cracked, showed her guilt, which forced me to face the facts I no longer seem to be able to fight off.

I'm angry with her.

Livid with her.

I might even hate her.

More pressure falls on my chest, and she senses it, offers a small smile and walks away, but not before pointing to the steaming latte left in the place she stood from.

I kick it over and get the hell out.

I wait until the bell rings to enter the school and avoid eye contact as much as possible throughout the day, but when lunch rolls around, I'm forced to call on my smile, at least for a few minutes until everyone settles into their own conversations and I'm able to pretend to be reading over my French paper on my phone.

That is until the space across from me is filled by a bleach blonde with dark chunks underneath that look like shit.

Her gaze is burning into my skin, so I snap mine up.

She glares, sipping on her smoothie like a prissy little bitch.

Of course, she waits until I look down to lean forward, bringing herself closer to me. With a quick glance down the table, she whispers, "We warned you they were psychotic. A waste of space that will never belong."

"You're just mad he stopped letting you suck his dick."

She gasps and sharp inhales sound around the table,

people having only caught my response but completely clueless as to what we're talking about.

Amy beams a bright, instant red.

"Wait, what are we talking about?" Cali leans closer while Jules seeming anxious, sinks into herself.

Amy glares, an instant 'nothing' flying from her.

I sit forward, not allowing her to backtrack. "We're talking about Amy slumming it." I use words bound to eat at her.

"You bitch," she shouts, loud enough to turn heads as she shoots to her feet. "Like you're one to talk."

"There's a difference. I'm not ashamed."

Her shoulders draw up, her tiny fists balling up at her sides. "You might have a good family name to stand behind, but you are nothing like us. You're trash. Just like your sister, just like them."

I fly to my feet, launching the contents of my coffee cup all over her.

Those at the table shriek, and Amy hops back, shocked with her palms in the air and I swiftly round the table getting in her face.

"You're lucky it's cooled down or your skin would be on fire," I snap.

"You are so—"

"What?" I goad her. "Dead?" I walk into her, forcing her steps backward. "Please. You're more than weak-minded and you know it."

Amy growls, shoving me in the chest, and I stumble back a step, but push back twice as hard until she's falling into the girls sitting near us.

People around us begin to shout, and I only get a foot closer before Scott is slipping between us.

Amy reaches past him, so I flip the cup on the table at

her, and it sprays over several people.

She gasps again and I dart for her, but Scott grabs me by the arms and walks me backward.

We only make it a half step before he's tackled into the table, and I'm jerked back in the same second.

The table, with several students still sitting at the far end of it, grinds along the flooring with an echoed, grating sound.

Students scream and scramble to get away as Ransom lays hit after hit into Scott's ribs. Scott gets his arms locked around Ransom's head, grinning in premature triumph through the pain, but Ransom lifts and slams him into the edge of the table, the sharpest corner digging into his back.

He lets out a loud wail that is nothing compared to the echoed whack of Ransom's skull as it comes straight down onto the tabletop, something he knew would happen when he went for the move yet followed through with anyway.

Scott's ribs may have been snapped in two, and as Ransom planned, he's released. He tears himself away, and lifting his foot, he more shoves Scott than kicks him to the ground. To Ransom's feet.

Forcing the self-proclaimed king to look up at one far more worthy.

"Touch her again, I'll rip your fucking arms off and feed them to the sharks."

Scott's eyes narrow, snapping to me, but Arsen steps up, blocking his view, Beretta now standing behind Scott, not that he realizes it.

I jerk back, grab my things and whip around to get the hell away, but Amy slips in front of me again.

"Amy, I swear to God—"

"Look at the problems you've caused!" she snaps.

"You should be happy! It blew up!" I bark. "Just like

you said!"

She laughs, loud and instant, and my muscles coil at the malicious sound.

"Oh man, this is..." She trails off, her laughter genuine in a hateful, cruel witch way. "God, you think this is what I was referring to?" She grins, true glee written across her. "Maybe spend less time hating our world, *Jamie,* and more time living in it."

My body locks, and her smile spreads wider.

Jamie.

She said Jamie...

Her hip pops out. "You'd be surprised what you can find out, learn, or realize by simply opening those hazel eyes," she mocks.

I dart for her, the tips of my fingers coming in contact with her hair, but Dax slips in front of me, though he keeps his hands up high.

"Don't do this." He shakes his head.

"Are you serious, Dax?" Jules shouts, and we both look her way.

She spins on her heels and storms out of the dining hall.

With a low curse, he chases her, and I dart forward, grabbing her wrist as I yank her to me. Her loud shriek has footsteps stomping our way.

I tug harder, and she scratches at my forearms, but I don't feel a thing. "Why did you call me that?!"

"You're crazy!" she screams, and I'm torn off by campus security. I kick at her, but she jumps to the side just in time.

She inspects her puny little wrist, fuming. "Screw you! You're psycho! Just like them!"

I jerk in the man's hold, but he doesn't let go, and then I'm torn away by a completely different set.

Large, strong hands grip my arms, pushing me to the side and out, walking us toward the door.

I look over my shoulder and swallow.

Blood runs down the center of Ransom's forehead, and it's as if he doesn't realize there's a gash at his hairline.

Security comes toward me, but Beretta slips in front of the man, lifting his arms and cocking his head. "Don't even think about it."

It's one man against three, so all he can do is shake his head and move to check Scott, but Scott, of course, jerks away from him, standing tall as if his ribs aren't on fire.

He steps out, his friends at his back, eyes hard and on me.

I don't realize I'm taking backward steps, away from all these people and closer to the ones who have become mine.

Scott takes small shuffles toward me. "Remember what I said about there being a difference?" He spits blood to the floor, raising a brow.

There's a difference between fucking *and fucking up...*

His chin lowers. "This is it."

My stomach turns, my pulse pounding hard at my temples.

I take a deep breath, half glancing over my shoulder without actually looking, and with a fixed expression and a straight spine, I go to Scott.

The pull behind me is strong, an almost overpowering tension that grows tighter and tighter, curling over my every limb and adding strain to my already heavy steps.

He tries to hold his smirk in, but his arrogance is beyond his control and it slips.

I reach out, placing my hand on the wall beside him, and the moment he shuffles in, my fingers curl over the championship poster on the wall, the one he's kneeling proudly in.

I tear it from the wall.

He jolts for me before he realizes what he's doing, and a wall of muscle is suddenly at my sides, at my back, wrapping around my middle and walking us backward as I crumple the poster between my hands, tossing it at Scott's feet.

Anger has his limbs trembling, but he scoffs, throws his hands out as if he doesn't give a shit, and truth is, he doesn't. Not really.

It's a small wound to an overflowing ego, patched the moment it was made.

I'm led out the door and only once we're out of sight of everyone else, does Ransom release me.

He steps back, but not far, and when I refuse to meet his eyes, his knuckles move under my chin, forcing mine to his.

Blood still rolls gingerly down his forehead, over his brow and down the curve of his nose, but he doesn't seem to care.

He stares me in the eyes, searching for a sign of something, and when the edges of his soften and his knuckle is replaced with the soft swipes of his thumb, I squeeze mine closed.

This is so messed up.

How did I get here?

How did we get here?

I pull away and, at first, it seems like he'll refuse to let go, but then his hand falls.

The space I've created leaves room for my anger to return, but I'm not the only one. Ransom's gaze is sharp now, his jaw grinding as he glares at me.

Good. That's good.

If he's forcing me to feel, anger is the emotion I prefer, I'll take fire in my veins over an unyielding weight in my chest all day long.

Ransom jerks away, taking wide, furious strides from us, not stopping until he's at Arsen's passenger door with his head twisted in the opposite direction.

Arsen frowns, holding his hand out toward me, and I know what he wants, so I dig my keys from my bag, dropping them in his palm. But as I start toward my car, Beretta wraps his arm around me and everyone swaps.

Arsen and Ransom leave in my car while Beretta and I climb inside the other.

I don't speak or glance toward him until I realize we passed my neighborhood and are headed toward Balboa Pier.

He doesn't bother finding a parking spot, but cruises right up on the sidewalk.

He parks five feet from the door of Newport Coffee Company and kills the engine, stepping out without acknowledging me.

My leg bounces, the stubborn part of me wishing to stay right here, but I too jump out, and stomp my way inside the shop.

In my peripheral, his lips curve, but he glances the opposite way to hide it, and within minutes, we're back inside the vehicle.

As we pull up to my house, I find my car inside the garage, the door left open and Beretta pulls up beside it, locking us inside.

Inside, Beretta nods toward the back deck, so I follow his lead, stepping up to look out over the ocean.

His face is pinched tight, as if he's unsure what to say or how to say it, but a long, pained sigh leaves him.

"It's not jealousy," he finally says, meeting my eyes while keeping his head forward. "When he sees us with you. It's not jealousy. It's anger. Defeat." Another sigh, and a sad, quiet chuckle. "It's frustration, but not with you. With himself. He's angry and sad and frustrated *with himself*."

"Beretta—"

"He wants you, Jameson," he cuts me off. "More than he's ever wanted anyone. He craves you, and he hasn't craved anything in a long time and even when he did, it was just a guy being a guy and looking to hook up. It was nothing compared to the way he wants you."

"That's easy to say."

"No. It's not," he stresses with a bit of a bite. "It's really fucking not, but I'm telling you because I don't know if he can. I think he would, eventually, but only once he officially snaps and has handed every guy in this town their ass when you get stubborn and run their way."

"That's not fair."

"It's the truth," he throws back. "Jameson..." He licks his lips, looking off, and when his eyes come back, they're steady, clear, and piercing. "The girl you saw him with in the park, that was his sister."

My chest clenches.

Of course it was.

He was tender and sweet, a little helpless and heartbroken.

Beretta keeps my attention. "Jameson, Ransom can't... execute. He hasn't been able to since everything with his sister," he shares somberly. "His shame is like nothing I've ever seen."

Unease weighs on my lungs. "Shame?"

His brows dig in. "Over what he was doing while she was fighting for her life."

My stomach drops to my feet, and I grab on to the railing for support as it becomes clear.

"He was with a girl."

"He was with Amy."

My fingers claw at my top, clenching.

Beretta's gaze sharpens, pain and a heavy hint of hope within them. "He was fucking Amy, for the *first* and *only* time, while his sister was on the operating table."

Oh god.

I feel sick for him.

"He needs, but he can't seem to get past his mind. Something disconnects, and he shuts down." Beretta stands tall, honored. "We love him, so we help him."

My mouth opens, and he lowers his chin, waiting for me to connect the pieces.

"You help him…" I trail off. "By being *with* him, being together?"

He nods. "He tries, but he goes numb when he feels himself losing control, or sometimes it's as simple as someone touching him in the act. We don't."

"So, you, or Arsen, fuck the girl, and he..." I stare at him.

"Tries," he explains. "He'll touch, play, depending on where he's at in his head, and when his body goes numb, he backs away. We slip in, handle her, so she's none the wiser, and he listens while doing what no girl can."

He relieves himself.

I shouldn't care right now, this isn't the time, but I can't stop myself.

"Who fucked me?"

His eyes widen, his head pulling back. "Jameson..."

"Never mind," I backtrack quickly, the thought too much. "It's—I don't want to know."

"Have you not been paying attention?" he says suddenly, and my eyes snap back toward him. He steps closer, his hand coming up to gently cup my cheek as he keeps our gazes connected. "Did you not hear anything I was saying?"

"Beretta..." My head aches, it's pounding, and I don't know how to stop it. I don't want to want to hear anything, but I'm a dumb girl, and I do.

"He has never wanted anyone like he wants you," he repeats his earlier words with a calming exhale. "We could feel it, sense him and his need for you. Why do you think we didn't take you that first night, like we normally would?"

"That's kind of an egotistical question to assume you could have," I breathe.

He chuckles, nodding. "Yeah, but we're damn good at convincing." He grins and I too smile a little. "But I'm serious. He held off. He never holds off." Beretta eyes me, waiting to see if I understand, but I don't. "Jameson, he was anxious. You made him anxious, something he hadn't felt in two years. He was damn near foaming at the mouth, that's why we grabbed you. He had to feel you, to touch you in some way, right fucking then, but after that, he needed time to see what you were about, to see where your intrigue would lie."

"What do you mean?"

"I mean, if you wanted in on the game three punks play with pretty, willing rich girls, or if you wanted him." Beretta's hand glides down my jawline, and his lips curl tenderly. "Didn't take long to figure it out."

My chest aches and my mind is a mess as I try to comprehend what he's telling me, to grasp the situation he's trying to lay out for me.

Of him and them.

Of them and me.

Of us.

Oh my god, there is *an us...*

My skin prickles from my neck down to my toes,

realization reaching beneath my ribs and clenching the thing in my chest tight.

Too tight.

This is too much.

I wasn't supposed to... we weren't meant to...

There is an us.

My eyes snap up to Beretta's and slowly, I back away, setting my full, steaming drink on the small table as I pass it.

His brows crash, and he begins to shake his head, to beg me not to run, not to deny what's so clearly understood.

He's ready to slump over, to fall to his knees in defeat, for his friend.

But then I lift my hand, reaching for his and his tightly wrung face falls, and the hopeful look that fills his eyes is nearly heartbreaking.

Beretta doesn't hesitate, he walks straight up to me, runs his fingers over my knuckles, and threads his with mine.

"That first time outside the club..."

Beretta nods, squeezing my hand, and suddenly so many things make sense.

That night wasn't for Ransom. That was for me.

They did that, showed up and took me outside, led me into darkness and brought me out of my mind for me.

To help me escape.

To help me breathe when I felt like I was suffocating.

They were there for me and I didn't even realize it.

I was never just a girl in a game to them.

They care.

Beretta looks toward the house, but he doesn't lead us inside.

I do.

The game room seems farther away than ever, and once we reach it, I find them inside, as I figured they would be.

The French doors are open and Ransom's bent over the pool table, his head turned the opposite way as he sets up his shot, a devastating, lost expression on his handsome face.

Arsen sits in the chair adjacent to him, just inside the room but still close enough to be his shadow of support, pool stick loosely laying between his legs.

We take a single step inside, and as if we're wearing bells, both of their heads turn toward us.

Ransom's body grows visibly rigid, and it tightens the muscles in my own, but Beretta pulls his hand from mine and glides behind me as Ransom slowly straightens his spine.

Arsen looks over my shoulder, right as Beretta's warm breath fans along the slope of my ear. His fingertips feather down my arms, making me shiver, but his touch is not for my benefit. It's for the bronzy-haired boy thirty feet before me.

Ransom scowls, his eyes flying from one of us to the next, over and over again.

Behind me, the door is closed, the flick of the lock making my pulse jump.

Ransom's fingers curl tighter over the wooden cue, his frown doubling the longer he stares.

And then Beretta is next to me. So, with my eyes locked onto Ransom's, I lift my hair and turn sideways.

Beretta wastes no time, his fingers finding the zipper of my jumpsuit and the soft sound might as well be broadcasted over the house speakers, it echoes so loudly in my mind.

I spin, slowly allowing my hair to fall back over me, and Ransom's eyes heat, pulsing before me as his chest stretches wide.

I'm prepared to allow it to slide from my body, to stand here in the middle of the day, the sun shining bright and straight through the open French doors, in my bra and panties before them.

Hot blooded males who share women... all to help their friend.

One could look at this and call it capitalizing, but I call it love.

They love each other.

This is what love looks like.

Being there for someone who needs it.

By any means necessary.

And here. We. Go...

CHAPTER
Twenty Four

The soft silk falls to my feet and Ransom's pool cue drops to the floor, and when he rasps my name with far more desperation than I've ever heard it spoken, I walk closer.

"What are you doing, Trouble?" he rasps, a wretched expression on his face.

Beretta moves ahead of me, placing himself at Ransom's side, and he grips his friend's shoulder when his body begins to quake.

He whispers something in Ransom's ear that has his tongue gliding along his lips, and on my left, Arsen pushes to his feet.

No one stops him as he makes his way to me, and I don't look away from the blue eyes glued to mine.

Arsen's fingertips come up, running along my collarbone, and he keeps them there, trailing them along my skin as he rounds me, tipping my head to the side as he does.

I gasp as he presses hard into my back, my body lurching forward the slightest bit, but he catches me with a strong arm around my waist, only he doesn't keep it there. His hand drops lower until the tip of his pinky slips into the waistband of my thong, and Ransom nearly falls into the seat behind him, Beretta still at his side, holding on to him. Squeezing.

I shiver when his free hand meets my spine, flicking my bra open without effort and it bounces at my sides, the heaviness of my breasts causing me to slip from the cups, my nipples barely covered beneath the soft material.

Ransom reaches out, gripping on to the edge of the pool table, his face drawn tight.

Using his chin and the same hand, Arsen pushes the straps from my shoulders and my bra falls, but not all the way. The cups' edges catch on my hardened nipples, and Arsen's husky chuckles waft over my skin, making goose bumps rise along my neck.

He helps it off, and I curl my toes in my heels.

My breasts are bared to them.

I should be embarrassed, but I'm not.

I'm burning.

Aching.

And all I want is the boy who can hardly look at me but can't manage to look away either.

Beretta catches my eyes, giving an encouraging nod, so I lift my hands, cupping my own breasts.

The second my hands touch my skin, a moan escapes, and my head falls to Arsen's shoulder, where he welcomes it.

I squeeze myself harder, gliding my hands out until my nipples are slipped between my fingers.

My thighs tighten, my knees bending in to touch each other, and Arsen's pinky slips lower, making its way to my hips.

His thumbs hook over the band, ready to push them down, and I whimper into the air, my eyes locked with Ransom's.

Arsen pulls, but the loud scratch of a chair shoving

backward as Ransom shoots to his feet echoes around us, and Arsen's grin stretches across the heated skin of my shoulder.

He knew it was coming.

On his feet, Ransom's hand flies out, fisting Beretta's shirt as his body begins to shake before us.

My eyes fall to the heavy bulge in his jeans, and when I look back up, he takes a step forward.

And then another.

And another, dragging Beretta with him all the way.

They stop right in front of me, and Beretta's hand wraps around the back of Arsen's neck, their temples touching as they silently watch the two of us.

Ransom's face is drawn tight, and I lift my hands to smooth it away, but he grabs my wrists, hard, punishing, and I gasp, not fighting him as he pushes them behind me and someone else locks them in place.

His fingers trail down the center of my chest, under my breasts, and down my ribs. They bite into my hips, then slip into my underwear.

I suck in a breath, eager, as he presses over my clit, his lips parting, short, quick puffs leaving him as his eyes squeeze shut.

My hands lift, planting on his pecs, and he freezes, his fingers attempting to retract, but like in the darkness of the bathroom, a hand catches his, holding him there, so I push mine higher.

Past the rapid beating of his heart and over the throbbing pulse in his neck, until his face is nestled between my palms.

He takes a slow, jagged breath, and slowly, oh so slowly, his hand begins to work me.

I bring myself closer, the proof of my excitement coating his fingers, my breaths just as shallow as his own.

His eyes peel open, the hand on Beretta's chest prying

itself free, and coming down on my ass. He squeezes, and suddenly Beretta's hand between our bodies is too much for him, for me.

Beretta senses it's time.

He yanks his away, and in the same second, I'm lifted off my feet, spun and set on the edge of the pool table.

My feet lock around his hips and he grips my face.

His eyes are hard, almost angry, and his nostrils flare wildly.

He growls, his lips curling, and then his mouth smashes into mine.

It's hard and demanding and I'm gasping, but he doesn't let me breathe, he takes all I have and gives me all he can.

His tongue is raring, fighting to memorize my every taste, every swipe more purposeful, more controlled.

Just... more by every sense of the word.

My body is the one vibrating now and from nothing but his kiss.

But it's not just his kiss.

It's the way the sun beams off the side of his face, the cuts in his forehead, and harsh lines along his brows. It's the way he takes what he wants and with pride, with desire.

Desperation.

Our eyes seem to open at the same time and still he doesn't tear away.

He grips me harder, staring into my eyes as his darken before me, a majestic, mayhem blue.

He stares like I'm not real, as if I'm not naked and latched to him, as if he doesn't believe he's the one holding on to me. Kissing me, though his mouth hasn't stopped moving, but his lips stay pressed on mine.

We pant, drawing in short spurts of air through the tiny space our lips leave room for.

He kicks his shoes off, rips his belt open and allows his pants to fall open slightly. He tears his shirt over his head and my hands waste not a second, exploring his naked skin once again, and while his muscles flex, he doesn't pull away.

He wraps my hair around his fist and tugs my head to the side, kissing and flicking his tongue along and over me, and then he's lifting me again, curving us around the table vertically, and the moment he sets me down, his fingers are inside my pussy.

A long, husky moan pushes past my lips and he groans, pressing his cock into my inner thigh.

I reach down, freeing him from his boxers and he locks up on me. Everything in him tenses, and he grips my wrist as I wrap my fingers around his thickness, but then his forehead falls to my shoulder, and my free hand sinks into his hair.

It's okay, Ransom...

I pull and he growls, shifting and biting at my lip.

Slowly, I pump him a little faster when his muscles loosen in response, readying him for more.

His pants are kicked to the side, boxers with them, and I'm scooted to the edge of the table, his cock aligned with my entrance, one of his strong hands on my hips, the other making its way up my spine until he's casing my neck in his palm.

He's ready, the head of his cock applying pressure at my entrance, flexing with eagerness and with one more small tug of his hair, he pushes the tip inside.

I beg for more, lifting my hips, but he holds me still, and my entire body breaks out in chills when the corner of his mouth curves up.

He gives me his wicked smirk and an airy chuckle leaves me.

My god, look at him.

He's rugged perfection.

He licks his lips, glides his along mine and pulls back again.

"I'm gonna show you something," he rasps, his hold on me tightening. "You're going to like it, but you'll never see it again," he promises, lowering his chin.

My core twists in eagerness, and I hastily nod. Upon my answer to his implied question, I'm torturously rewarded with another inch of him.

My body clenches around him, pleading, and that grin of his deepens.

He dips in, keeping his body close to mine as he begins to lay me all the way back. "Close your eyes, baby, and when you feel my teeth... open."

I swallow, proof of my pleasure coating his cock as I do what he asks, and he moans as if he can feel it, what he does to me.

My skin meets the soft felt of the table, my shoulders level with its edge, my head completely off and hanging upside down. He dips his hands in my hair, tugs with a slight groan, and then releases it, allowing it to fall, the ends likely teasing at the floor beneath.

The heat of his body hovers above me, and my nipples ache to be touched. My hands lift, gliding across them, and I grin at his sharp intake of breath.

His lips fall to my breastbone, and he kisses his way down, his nose pushing my left hand out of the way, so he can swirl his tongue around the sensitive point. He hesitates, mouth open, warm breath blowing over the cool spot and sending a chill through me.

And then he bites.

My eyes fly open, and the moment they do, I gasp, my thighs clamping around him.

Beretta stands behind Arsen at the opposite end of the room, his palms skating down his body until he reaches the waist of his jeans. Beretta says something into Arsen's ear when he slips his hand inside his boxers, cupping Arsen, and Arsen's low moan reaches us.

He yanks away, driving Beretta backward until he's hitting the wall, and gently slams himself into him.

Beretta chuckles but quickly spins them again, and Arsen settles in place, his stance widening the slightest bit.

One of Arsen's hands slides into Beretta's hair, his mouth falling to his ear, as the other plants firmly on his shoulder, pushing him to his knees.

Beretta drops willingly, locking his fingers with Arsen's on the way down.

I hold my breath as Beretta leans in, and while I can't see in front of him, I know the moment he's pulled him into his mouth.

Arsen's head falls back to the wall, his free hand moving to cup Beretta's face, and then his lids flick open, meeting mine.

Arsen winks, closes his eyes, and Ransom chooses that exact moment to push all the way inside me.

My back flies off the table and he uses the gap to slide his hands underneath, pulling me up. He backs up, lowering us onto the chair, my heels straight on the carpet at our sides, his legs stretched out in front of him, my breasts in his face.

I sink into him, and he growls, pushing my hips back and forth, grinding me on his cock rather than bouncing me up and down on top of him.

He wants to feel me, to *fill* me, fully and completely.

My eyes hold his, my palms flattening on his chest. I slide them up and over his shoulders and back, before driving my fingers into his hair and gently tugging on the length on top.

His hands have come up, now hugging my body to his, and when I press deeper, using my right hand and the chair as leverage, his muscles flex, his cock swelling inside me, and he starts to shake.

His eyes clench closed, and his hands fly from me, pressing at my ribs, ready to push me away as a deep frown pulls at his forehead, but I quickly drop mine to his. Breathing against his mouth, my body trembles too, but only because my orgasm is mounting just as his is.

I can't lose this; I need to come.

I need him to come, and I want to be the one to do it and know that I did.

I kiss him slowly, flattening my chest to his, leaving no room to escape, and after a moment, his mouth moves with mine.

Slow, at first, and then faster, more urgent, and then whatever hold his mind has over him, it breaks.

He's grunting and growling and thrusting up into me with such a power I know my inner thighs will be bruised. He allows no room between us, keeping himself buried inside me as deeply as possible and when he's about to come, he flies from the chair, my ass in his rough palms as he spins us, pinning me to the wall.

He grips my chin, driving his tongue into my mouth as his cock works my body into a frenzy, with deep, full strokes.

I come around him and he bites at my lip, his entire face morphing as he does the same, but as he fills me, those eyes open.

And soften.

Promise more than I can understand.

His muscles ease, and slowly, his weight becomes mine.

And then he twirls us again, carries me through the house, out into the back yard, and lowers our naked bodies into the hot tub. He reaches behind him, pulls my heels from my feet and sets them on the cement beside us. My legs fall from around him, and he sits back against the jet, entwining my fingers with his so he can pull me forward.

His eyes fall to my breasts, but his hands lower to my hips and as his gaze meets mine again, he gently turns me, tugging me down onto his lap.

He doesn't say a word but holds me still while I memorize the way his heart races, noting how long it takes for it to settle and beat in rhythm with mine.

I close my eyes, but then the slash of water has them flying back open, and my mouth gapes as the boys lower into the hot water with us, both as naked as we are.

They sink against the jets, lay their heads back and close their eyes.

I laugh, loudly.

And then suggest we order in.

CHAPTER
Twenty-Five

Ransom and the boys don't leave, but take turns showering and then slip into extra clothes they find in the trunk of Arsen's car. We didn't end up ordering in because I learned something new today.

Beretta cooks. He said his mom taught him, so he slipped into our ridiculous kitchen built for a damn Master Chef when no one in my family cooks beyond the basics, and even then, it's only Monti or myself making a quick batch of eggs or something if we're bored and Gennie hasn't made her stop yet. My mom hasn't so much as poured her own cup of coffee since, well, ever, as far as I know.

After we ate, we headed to my room, the boys started playing video games while I caught up on some classwork. We've been relaxing, watching random TV for the last hour or so, and I can't stop glancing toward Beretta.

He sits with his back angled in the curve of the chaise, one leg bent, the other stretched along the velvety material. His left arm is draped along the back of it, the remote sitting loosely in his palm while the fingers on his right hand glide along Arsen's naked neck, who sits on the carpet just before him, his back pressed against the thing, both absentmindedly watching TV.

"Seem obvious now?" Ransom whispers beside me.

I don't look away from the two, but nod.

"Yeah," I say quietly. It does.

The looks, the sound of lips locked in the dark bathroom that day...

"At Beretta's when they were boxing..."

Ransom chuckles softly. "Oh yeah, they almost went for it." He grins, and I look up, meeting his eyes. "Arsen gets horny when they box. Every time."

I laugh silently, lowering my head back down.

We're lying on my bed, him pushed up on the headboard, while I'm perched on a pillow under his right arm.

They seem so content, calm and... complete, as if they need nothing else in the world, when they don't have much to begin with.

Or maybe they believe they have everything because they have each other?

It's such a dangerous ideal, happiness.

"Do they love each other?" I wonder.

"They're it for each other, if that's what you mean."

I nod, maybe that's what I mean.

Beretta's hand falls over Arsen's shoulder, and Arsen lifts his, lacing their fingers together.

"They've never been like this in front of me," I speak softly, a small smile on my face.

"You saw one suck the other's dick; I'd say they're comfortable around you."

I gape, flopping onto my back with a laugh that's a little louder than I meant for it to be, and the others look our way curiously.

But as they stare, a tenderness slips over them both.

Their eyes meet mine, moving to Ransom's, and as if

they're one, they both nod, small curls hitching the corners of their mouths and then turn back to the screen.

Something cracks in my chest and I flick my gaze to the TV, uneasy.

This is... a lot.

Because for the first time in maybe ever, I too have a sense of comfort, of calm, and it's nearly enough for a part of me to want to kick them out, but the larger part, the buried, reckless part—the part that I got from my real father—never wants to leave this room.

That part wants to hold on to the boy at my side and give him things I'm not so sure I'm capable of, but he makes me wish I were.

He makes me want to be.

He makes me wish I was in control of what I want.

Ransom has never expected a thing of me, was there when he had no reason to be, and seems to enjoy the messed-up side of who I am. He doesn't bend at my will, but he doesn't discount my voice either.

Ransom being Ransom senses when I slip inside my mind and get lost there.

He scoots lower on the bed until his eyes are level with mine.

Perched on his elbow, he stares down at me.

He's incredibly sexy, far from pretty, but rough and alluring in only a way he can accomplish.

Without realizing, my hand lifts, my fingertips ghosting over the edge of his sharp jaw, and he dips his head, so his lower lip can get a taste of me.

His blue eyes search mine, for what I'm not sure, but I think he finds it as his mouth curves with rawness, softening his features.

"Beretta told you," he whispers.

My ribs constrict. I'm not sure if he's talking about his sister or about his own struggles, and I know there is more to be told, but I nod.

"You know it was only me, right? That they were never inside you? It was only me."

He scowls at his own words, as if pained by guilt or embarrassment, but I reach up and wipe it away with my thumb.

"Yeah, I know," I breathe, and attempt to settle him a little. "...but they did touch me."

I fight my grin, but it spreads rapidly, and Ransom growls playfully, gripping my hand before it can fall and pinning it above my head as he climbs on top of me.

My legs decide to fall open for him and he eases between them, his cock hard and ready and gliding along the thin fabric of my sleep shorts.

He grips the blanket, tugging it up over our heads, and I briefly register the lights in the room dimming as the volume on the TV grows louder.

Ransom smirks, freeing himself from his sweats and pushing my shorts aside, the head of his hard-on teasing my entrance.

"You shouldn't have let me fuck you."

I push into him, sucking in his tip and trying for more of his length. "Why not?" I pant.

"Because I don't see how I can ever stop." He stares at me, right into my eyes.

My sharp ache hits my ribs, twisting and tightening my lungs, but it's confusing because my mind is full of him.

He said he can't stop, but it's only the end of October.

We have time for this.

For us.

My palms plant on his chest, wrapping around his back,

and I pull him to me, whispering against his lips, "So don't."

―――――

Closing the door behind him, Ransom reaches over, lifting his backpack and my bag from the back seat, but when I reach out for it, he glares and hooks it over his arm.

Grinning. Face forward, we head toward the school. With Arsen and Beretta at our sides, we climb the first steps, where Scott, Dax, and a few others stand, chatting. Amy and Sammie among them.

I wait for Ransom to grow stiff at my side, but he doesn't, not even when their heads do a double take as they notice we're approaching.

Amy is trying to keep from frowning, but a smirk plays on her face, as if she's still winning—as if this is a contest—since she had him alone and assumes I haven't.

Sure, she screwed him once where no one could see, but there's a difference.

She never *had* him; she merely fucked him.

I've had him twice and I *have* him now.

Ransom chooses the moment we are but two steps from passing them to slip his hand into mine, pull it to his lips and bite at my knuckles.

I couldn't hold my grin in if I tried, and I don't care to.

I do meet Amy's eyes, and I could laugh at the wide, sheer shock in them.

I lift my hand, waving with my fingers like a spiteful bitch, but I don't care.

Yesterday, I made a choice in front of everyone, my place in their world, *my* world, or another.

I chose them.

I chose him.

The thing about spoiled, holier-than-thou teenagers is

they never acknowledge a loss for what it is, but pretend the situation, whatever it may be, is the one they favor.

The boys and I have become invisible, or so the others wish us to believe, when it's obvious they stare from the corners of their eyes, continuing to do so as the day goes on.

At lunch, when Ransom's body frames mine on the back of the bench-style seat, they make it a point to face the opposite direction. They couldn't possibly be caught staring, that would be admitting it bothers them that I'm no longer sitting at their table where, as the unspoken rule goes, my bank account deems I belong.

Cali and Jules seem to be the exception, but even so, they stick to 'their people'.

I look from Arsen to Beretta, who sit close to each other, laughing and joking, and Arsen catches my eye, nodding his chin, so Beretta turns to look at me, but he can't keep himself from looking up at Ransom.

I'm not sure what he sees, but he grins, and then gives his attention to me.

"Yes, Trouble?" He smiles and mine follows.

"You know," I begin, replaying the sight of them yesterday. "I kind of thought you'd be the alpha."

Beretta laughs loudly, his grin deepening. "I can be, if he wants me to be." His smirk is as naughty as a man can muster, and I almost blush. "But I am a lover and he's aggressive, but in a good way."

I pull my lips in, nodding. "So..."

Arsen chuckles, pushing on Beretta's chest so that he leans his back against the table, allowing Arsen to see me better.

Beretta's smile is teasing. "You must have a sex question, your chest is getting red. You embarrassed?"

"No!" I laugh. "I'm not... but do you care if I ask

something, though?"

They grin at each other, looking back with a shrug. "Go for it."

"When you aren't with Ransom, like when he no longer needs your help, will you still sleep with women, or do you guys already, when it's just you two?"

His eyes snap up, meeting Ransom's, a small frown builds along his brows, but it smooths when he looks back at me.

Ransom's hands fall from my thighs, but I wait for the answer.

"We would if we wanted to." He glances at Arsen quickly. "It hasn't been about any of that, but with you, we realized it could be enjoyable, and I'm not talking nutting at the end," he says unabashedly. "That part's natural, but to actually feel good, to be excited and want to please? We've never gotten that outside of us." He shrugs. "So, if we want to fuck with an added person, we will, and when we're done, we'll still be us. It's not a plan, but we have no reason to limit ourselves. We know what matters, so we'll do what we want when we want."

God, the freedom in that statement.

Envy forms a knot in my abdomen, twisting.

"So, what if you find a girl you want to keep?"

They both laugh, but, again, share a look and shrug.

"Then we keep her, I guess." Beretta's grin is wide, teasing. "But so far, the only one we'd consider isn't up for grabs." He laughs, and both their eyes lift to Ransom's as they climb from the table, and only a second before the bell rings. "And by the looks of it, that girl is in *trouble*."

I frown and they smile wider, both walking away.

I glide forward on the seat, pushing to my feet as I grab my bag, but when I turn to Ransom, and he hasn't moved, I pause.

A deep glower stains his forehead and his eyes pin mine.

"What?"

He licks his lips, looking off a moment and back in the next.

"If you think I'll be fucking anyone who isn't you, you're wrong." He rises to his feet, placing himself in front of me, his hand burying in my hair, right here in the middle of the dining hall, without a care. Without pause, though there is a slight shake to his hands.

My stomach flips, a strange tingling sensation spreading along my face.

He kisses me, and not gently either, but short and harshly, and when he pulls back, he adds simply, "And if you think you will be, you're very fucking wrong."

I don't know what my face looks like, but he laughs, wraps his arm around my shoulder and leads us to cooking class.

At my seat, he nudges my knees apart, stepping between them with his hands in my hair.

His eyes tighten suddenly, falling to the floor. "What are you doing after school?"

I shrug and say, "Nothing."

"I want to take you with me."

Suspicious, my mouth curls into a grin. "Where to?"

He licks his lips, his gaze snaps to mine. "To see my sister."

I freeze, my throat growing thick.

"What?" My question is nearly inaudible.

Ransom stands tall, waiting, but all I can manage is a nod, and slowly, he nods back.

He turns and walks away, but he doesn't go back to his

seat.

He slips out the door.

The others watch him go, both making their way to me, scowls in place.

"He wants me to go with him after school," I share, slightly panicked. "To see his sister."

Shock wrinkles their foreheads, but it's quickly followed by soft smiles.

Beretta taps on the desk. "In case you were wondering, that's fucking huge."

My brows cave and they chuckle.

Class begins, but I can't focus, forcing Arsen to carry us today.

All I can think about is Ransom and what this means.

Stepping inside the tall white building, we're greeted by a middle-aged woman who must recognize Ransom.

Her eyes soften, and she sets a small clipboard down in front of us.

Ransom grabs a pen and the woman looks to me.

"Hi, can I help you?" She smiles welcomingly.

I stiffen and Ransom's eyes snap up.

"She's with me," he tells her.

The woman's grin seems to double in size. "I'm so sorry, I didn't realize. Sienna will be so happy to have her here."

Sienna.

My lips curve.

That's her name.

"In the garden, Mr. Rossi?"

Ransom nods, setting the pen down, and I glance at the form. It's labeled Rossi 242, her room number maybe, and the sheet is nearly full of visitor sign-ins, each one the exact same. His.

His hand slips into mine and he walks us around the entryway and out through the large double door that leads to a mini pond and outdoor recreation-like area.

There're a few tables and benches scattered around, a few other patients visiting with family members or friends, a small snack hut and a wall of board games that have been put to use for some time now, their boxes are faded, torn at each edge.

"He never comes to see her." He frowns, grabbing my free hand and lacing it into his other one. He looks to me. "You saw the form."

I shrug a shoulder, wrapping my hand around his bicep.

"He's a dick, can only be bothered when they make him, when he has to sign orders and shit he can't do by email, and even then, he complains about missing work. I can't wait to get her out of here," he admits a moment later.

"What do you mean?"

We lower onto one of the benches, and he stares at the door we stepped out of. "He put her in this place because he doesn't want to take care of her. She was in the hospital for over a month after the accident, and then, bam. Straight here, like she hadn't already lost enough."

"Do you think she's unhappy here?" I ask.

He shrugs. "She says she's fine and I think they're good to her, but still, they're not her family. They're strangers and she's young. I'm sure she gets scared sometimes, but she hasn't said out loud and she wouldn't. She doesn't like to worry me," he scoffs, his jaw clenching and he flies off the bench, a long exhale escaping him. "I know she needs real care but for the price he pays to keep her here, we could have someone at home for her. It's a fucking miracle he's paying for this place, even if it is her money to begin with."

His eyes fall to the ground, his jaw clenched angrily. "I've watched him step into her room here, listen to her nurse, sign whatever got him here, and just... walk out, like she can't see or hear or feel. Like she can't fucking speak." His muscles clench and release over and over. "Sometimes I wish she would yell at him, but I get why she doesn't. She knows he wouldn't care; he makes that clear to her when he doesn't even look her way."

"He's an asshole," I force out.

Ransom chuckles, but it's heavy. "Yeah, he is." His eyes find mine, and slowly roam along my face as he slides closer, lifting my chin slightly.

"He'd hate you," he says quietly, and my shoulders stretch. "He'd hate you because I don't."

Something settles over me and a sense of self-preservation knocks at the back of my mind, but I don't answer.

Even if I did, it would be a Ransom shaped silhouette standing on the other side of it.

He was right before, a piece of him has found its way into every part of me. Even the ugly parts I hide.

I don't know how or when it happened, and I can't claim to care.

I like who I am with him.

Without him, I'm not sure I exist.

Ransom's eyes soften as he stares at me, but then they lift over my shoulder and his entire being transforms.

The anger is gone, the heartache no longer lingering.

He smiles same as I witnessed that day I saw him in the park with her.

I'm almost nervous to look but then the foot of her chair comes into view and slowly I turn, watching as Ransom leans in to hug her, gently kissing her cheek.

She is young, maybe fifteen, and beautiful. Her hair, the most striking shade of blonde and her eyes, the exact shade of her brother's.

She sits up in her wheelchair with the help of padded straps around her legs, chest, and her left arm. Her fingers tap at the right handle in which her palm lays flat and she tips her chin the slightest bit, her eyes sliding from me to her brother and back again.

Nervousness comes alive in my stomach like never before and I'm tempted to smile and exit, but I won't. Emotions don't come easy for me, but no part of this can possibly be easy on him, so I have to suck it up and open myself up to the terrifying feelings taking over me.

"Hi, Sienna." I smile softly. "I'm Jameson."

It takes several moments, but her blue eyes move back to Ransom, holding.

His grin is small, and a low chuckle leaves him. "She knows who you are."

My mouth runs dry as I stare at his profile.

This is insane. I'm overwhelmed and in need of a little blue pill pronto. Even as I think it, I know how weak I sound, because how pathetic are my worries compared to theirs?

I want to run, but I sense her eyes on me once more and he said she knows who I am, so he must have shared my name, if nothing else, so, for him, I swallow the overwhelming emotion threatening to consume me.

I turn to Sienna, holding my breath when her lips part and she speaks.

"How do you put up with him?" she teases, her tone soft yet holding a hint of a rasp and she lifts her right arm up a few inches, pointing his way.

My heart pounds wildly in my chest, and her lips curl as

her brother's did. It's subtler, a little less even, but it's there, and I can't help the airy laugh that follows.

I swallow and realize this is what she wants, to sit and be the little sister of the boy who brought a girl to meet her. Everything else forgotten, as it should be.

So, I smile wider, a smile that comes easy as I widen my eyes playfully. "Oh, it's not easy." I joke back with her, and in my peripheral, Ransom's shoulders ease creating a warmth deep in my chest. "Did he tell you what he did to me the first day we met?"

Her lips twitch and she gives the slightest shake of her head.

I cross my legs and start from the beginning.

CHAPTER
Twenty-Six

As we walk up the school steps Tuesday morning, Cali comes bursting through the doors, tears pouring down her cheeks. "Jameson!" She spots me.

My nerves tighten as she moves toward me.

"Jameson! Oh my god, I've called you three times!" she sobs.

I slip from under Ransom's arm, meeting her in the middle of the hall.

"What's wrong?"

"It's Jules!" she cries. "She didn't answer her phone or the door this morning, so I thought she was playing hooky with Dax, but then I got here and he was here and she never showed, so I called her mom. Her mom was mad, but she went home to check and she... she found her in a pile of her own vomit. Jameson, she's in the hospital getting her stomach pumped."

"Alcohol poisoning?"

Cali nods, her arms wrapping around me.

"We need to go."

"My driver is picking my brother up from the airport," she shares. "And the others left already, but I had to come find you."

"Shit, I didn't drive either, I..."

My eyes fly to Ransom, and whether he realizes it or not, he's backing away, a lost look in his eyes.

Alcohol and the hospital.

Damn it.

I turn back. "We'll Uber."

"No."

Both our heads snap to Ransom.

He frowns down the hall. "We got you."

Arsen and Beretta, having held back at the car a second longer, reach us then, keeping their expressions as blank as Ransom's when they spot Cali—they give others no insight as to where their minds are.

Cali's spine shoots straight, and she turns away, wiping at her tears, and they scoff, shaking their heads at her.

I grab her hands, gently pulling them down, and she grows uneasy.

"Come on, you can worry about that later. Let's get going, okay?" I nod, and after a moment, she rolls her eyes at herself and nods back.

We follow them outside, and Beretta gives her the front seat, taking the one beside me.

We're at the hospital within fifteen minutes

I get ready to climb out, but Cali simply grabs her bag and waits.

"Hey, uh, princess." Beretta slouches farther in his seat. "The only way that door is getting opened is if you open it yourself."

Cali glances over her shoulder with a small frown, but when she realizes he was speaking to her and what exactly he had said, her cheeks tint pink.

Arsen swallows a chuckle, laughing when Beretta reaches between the seats and nudges his head.

Cali looks around the car, from them to me. To them. "Cali..."

She brings her eyes to mine, and I lift my brows.

"Shit, yeah, right. Sorry." She looks around for the handle and then pushes the door open.

It's bouncing back, about to smash her legs as she climbs out, but Arsen flies over, catching it before it can, and her quiet, completely embarrassed 'thanks' is barely audible.

She doesn't look back again but waits for me to fall in line beside her. The boys tell me to call them when I'm done, and we head inside.

Jules and Amy's mom is pacing the hall when we get to the correct floor, and relief washes over her when she notices our arrival.

"Oh, thank god!" She smiles tightly, coming to us.

She grabs both our shoulders but focuses on Cali. "She'll need you when she wakes up, God knows she won't care to see me." Tears fill her eyes, and I look away.

"Do you know what happened?" Cali asks her.

"She drank too much is the simple answer, the rest..." Her eyes dart up, hardening, and when we turn to look, it's Amy we find.

She cries silently, tucked into the farthest corner, alone, while her twin is fighting for consciousness.

"Let's wait for her to wake, and just... be here when she does." She says this more to herself, releasing us and answering her phone as it rings.

An hour or more of silence passes before a doctor comes out to say she's doing better now, but we still can't go inside. They've had to put her under a seventy-two-hour watch, and she's not allowed visitors until the time is up.

We stay sitting with the family and Dax for another hour or so, but then Cali turns to me. "Let's just go."

I begin to shake my head, but she stops me.

"Really, let's go. We can't see her anyway and it will only stress her out if she knows we're all out here waiting for her. Besides, Dax's here." She turns to him and he looks up from where his face was buried in his hands, his eyes red as if he were hiding his emotions. "You'll call us if they tell you anything else?"

He nods. "I'm not going anywhere," he says as he gets up and walks away from everyone, but we know what he means.

We make our way downstairs and out the front door to find the boys are in the exact place we left them.

They never did pull away.

A smile graces my lips, and we climb inside, dropping Cali at her house before heading back to mine.

Ransom shifts us both, pulling my upper half to his chest as he rests sideways, and I lift my legs onto the seat.

I close my eyes, focusing on the touch of his hands as he runs them through my hair.

It's relaxing, calming.

He's addicting.

But bubbles are meant to be popped, and the one we placed ourselves in was thin from the start, so when Beretta's troubled "heads up" is spoken, I should have known the needle was close and pointed our way.

Ransom's body grows tense beneath me, his hands freezing in my hair, and my eyes open.

Slowly, I sit up, realizing we're on my street, a car-length distance away from my driveway.

My driveway... that my mother stands directly in the center of.

Waiting.

"Oh shit."

Arsen slows to a stop. Her deep frown is usually vacant, but currently her severely pissed-off eyes fall on mine. She doesn't spare the boys a glance and she doesn't wait for me to climb from the car.

She gracefully turns on her heels and walks inside, knowing full well I'll follow... like a good little daughter would.

I silently climb from the car, spinning to face them, but I don't know what to say.

Turns out, I don't have to.

They understand.

Ransom pushes up in the back seat and grabs my hand, tugging me to him.

He grips my chin, jerking his head toward my house. "Go."

I hesitate, and he nods, letting me know they're fine, and they don't have to remind me they're only a call away because I already know.

My palm falls to his chest and I take a deep breath.

I head inside, prepared for her wrath, and counting down the minutes until she's gone again, but as I pass through the threshold of the door, dread cools my veins.

Her luggage is lined along the floor in perfect precision, the golden LV logo shining with pathetic pride in our direction, and I beg the universe to offer any other reason for all her things being here, other than what's running through my mind.

She can't possibly be moving back in.

I can't live under the same roof as her, not anymore.

Not since I've been here and remembered what it meant to breathe easy and just... be. No round-the-clock primping staff or stupid social calendar that she herself can't be bothered with but forces us to attend. The Friday dinner parties, Saturday charity balls, and Sunday country club appearances.

Only as I step closer to her, the universe answers my manifested thought with a nasty little twist.

A shiny, golden J, a mirror of the one dangling from my keys, hangs from the side of each piece of luggage, and I realize.

This isn't her set, but mine.

They're the very suitcases that I flew into California with.

My stomach flips. "Mom..."

She blinks, and just like that, the anger is hidden, buried. She smiles. "Sweep your room, dear. Make sure we've got everything you need."

Panic punches me in the gut and my palm flattens over my stomach. "Mom, I'm not going back to Florida."

She laughs, waving me off nonchalantly. "Of course, you're not, don't be silly."

My mouth opens, but nothing comes out, and she sighs, her smile still there but close-lipped. She walks to me, failing to hide her disappointment in my singularly layered foundation.

"You are not going back to Florida, Jameson," she assures me, and my shoulders settle, but then she speaks again, and this time with a fixed smile. "You are moving in with Anthony."

I'm almost positive I stand frozen, unblinking for far longer than should be possible, but when Tanner suddenly appears and begins rolling my suitcases out the door, I snap out of it.

Rather loudly, in fact.

"Are you *fucking* kidding me?!" I scream. "Tell me you're actually joking. This has to be a joke."

She folds her hands behind her back, rounding the table as she would a desk in a courtroom. Her eyes are calm, her shoulders strong and face as smooth as Botox can accomplish.

"Did you see Anthony this weekend?" she asks.

"Oh course, I—" I snap, but my mind freezes. Wait.

After the dance, everything with Ransom, I needed a damn day.

One day, and I...

My eyes meet my mother's, and she juts her chin and I know exactly what she's repeating in her mind.

Your choices decide your consequence...

She's serious.

"You really think I'm going to go live with a man I hardly know—"

"What better way to get to know him?"

"I'm not supposed to marry him until next summer!" I shout. "Next. Summer. Mom, what happens if this backfires on you, and he decides he doesn't want me in that time?"

She says nothing and my breathing grows rapid.

I shake my head. "I'll leave," I tell her. "When you go back to Florida, I'll be back here, and what are you going to do, come home again?" A humorless laugh escapes me. "We both know how long that will last. You can't possibly miss work for more than a nonstop flight's time, can you?"

In my mind, I won, and everything is fine, but she doesn't look shocked or upset. She's not at a loss.

I know my mother's lawyer face, the one she uses when she's caught off guard, scrambling in her mind for a way to flip things in her favor. It would likely rival the Grim Reaper's dead eyes, as if she holds a secret that you're not privy to, as if she already has you on the hook and you don't know it, but the intense way her green eyes pierce yours makes you more inclined to confess your darkest secrets.

She would have a heart attack if she knew mine.

But that isn't the face I'm getting.

What I get is a small grin, one that screams what we've always known, yet again.

I am my mother's daughter, and she knows my moves before I make them. It's all right there, written in the gleam of her eyes.

She lifts her purse from the kitchen table, her nose turning up when she sees the slight ring of a cup shimmering on the glass top.

She focuses on her phone, speaking to me while tending to things much more important, her emails. "You'll find your keys no longer work, nor your code, and your cards are no longer active. A new one has been ordered and there's two thousand dollars in an envelope in the side pocket of your traveler bag to use until it arrives on Monday." Her eyes lift to mine. "The card will be delivered to Anthony's home, your new home."

I try to swallow, but my throat is clogged, so all I manage is a strangled, "Mom."

"Yes, Jameson." She speaks clear, confirming, "Your account is now joined with his. There will be no more delay. No more freedom. No more '*Trouble.* '"

My spine straightens, my eyes narrowing, and she walks toward the door, pausing as her shoulder passes mine.

Her head turns, and she stares me dead in the eye. "Now, get in the fucking car."

CHAPTER
Twenty-Seven

I have no voice.
No fight.
No choice.

I've always done what my mother required of me, and she always appreciated my lack of emotional connection to, well, everything.

I never cried, never complained or got angry.

My nanny told her once she was concerned because I didn't smile unless someone was watching, and I didn't laugh at things that, according to her, a child should.

My mom responded with a question that was left unanswered and consisted of three words. *Isn't she brilliant?*

Gabriella Filano didn't love, but she sure seemed to love my lack of life.

I was dull and uninterested when alone, and when I wasn't alone, I was whatever I was supposed to be.

I never asked for anything and went along with all; my arranged marriage was simply one of the many examples of this.

My mother asks; my mother gets.

That was the rule.

In our house, rules were to be followed and breaking them meant breaking mentally. To do as you please was weak, because it took drive and strength to be what you should, or so she would claim.

To be honest, when the idea of having my life planned out for me was presented, I had no concerns or reservations whatsoever—something my mother banked on, I realize. She knew how I was and packaged her needs with a pretty little bow to ensure I accepted with open arms and the smile she suggested I use when spoken to.

I wanted a clear understanding of my future.

I wanted to protect myself, to remain numb and go through the motions of life rather than risk an ending like my father's.

I wanted all those things, and she knew it, she's the one who forever reminded me of what led Dad to his last day, glorified the idea of impassiveness.

I want none of those things anymore.

Looking around the large space, my eyes travel toward the stairway that leads to the window Anthony and I stood in front of when he brought me here. It will serve as my reminder of how large the world around me is, but how incredibly untouchable it will be from the side I'll be standing.

This isn't happening...

"You can begin redecorating whenever you're ready." My mother spins, looking at me as if she's a realtor and I'm nothing more than a client she's trying to sell a shitty deal to rather than her youngest daughter.

"And while you're clearing things out..." She trails off, dropping her lipstick in her bag. "Be sure *all* the trash goes with it."

"Trash is subjective, Mother, and as far as I'm concerned, you're the filthiest." I shock myself with my words, but I don't care. "Get out."

"Careful, daughter."

"No." I shake my head. "I have no need to be 'careful.'"
I look around this stupid fucking house. "He has all that's
mine now, right? And without a wedding..." I tip my head at
her. "I wonder what he'll do if I step out of line?"

"Jameson—"

"I'll give you credit, Mom. You were pretty damn
thorough, but you didn't think it *all* through, did you? I mean,
why would he bother to buy the cow now, when he's getting
the whole fucking farm for free!"

"Don't be dramatic."

"I'm being dramatic?!" I bellow, and in my peripheral,
a maid scampers by.

Great. A fucking in-house maid?

"You are giving me to a man you hardly know! Leaving
me across the country with no real way of being sure I'm fine,
well guess what, Mother, I am not fine!!! I'm not fine!" My
pulse beats out of control and I feel dizzy. "Are you seriously
going to do this? All because you didn't have a son to leave
your legacy to? We both know you never wanted daughters,
which is why you named us after men!"

"We don't always get what we want, so we adapt," she
says simply, as if any of this is simple.

"You do. You're getting all you want, and for what? For
a second generation of fortune, as if the one you have isn't
enough?! As if your success in one part of the nation isn't
astronomical and more than most people could ever hope
for?! Do you know how many people wish they had even just
a little of what you did to help their families? To give their
families what they need just to survive?" I think of Ransom
and his sister, of Beretta and the fishermen on the pier, of
Arsen and the young, orphan boys he lives with. "Are you

really so greedy for—"

"You know nothing!" she shouts, clipping my words, and my entire body locks.

My mother never shouts.

She *never* loses control.

And yet, her neck is bright red, and her chest rapidly rises. Her eyes are narrowed in uproar, and her knuckles are growing white around her handbag.

I stagger back, my hand slapping over my mouth. "Holy shit," I mumble into my skin, slowly dragging my hand down.

"That's... not what this is about, is it? You're not telling me everything." I spin, my fingertips lifting to my temples as I pace. "Mom, what are you not telling me?"

"Hush."

"Do I not deserve to know who I'm living with?!" I scream, whipping around with a glare. "What kind of mother—"

"I said SHUT UP!" she snaps, louder than before, but it knocks her back into her comfort zone.

Again, at her foreign tone, I straighten before I can stop it.

"As I said, you know nothing, and there is nothing you *need* to know." She takes a calming breath, tugs her blazer down, and pushes her hair over her shoulder. "You will do as you're told, Jameson, and you will see, you *will* be happy."

Her voice grows quieter, and her eyes seem to soften as she steps toward me.

My body is so confused on what to do and my mind is all over the place. Parts of me I never knew existed ache, and it's not on the surface.

It's inside.

Something is wrong.

Something's breaking.

Am I breaking?

"Sweetheart." My mother's soft whisper draws my attention, and when her palm touches my cheek, I jolt, my eyes lifting to hers. "It's okay."

"Mom..." I grip her wrists, subconsciously seeking her affection.

"You want this," she promises, nodding as if she's coaxing me along. "Trust it. You know you're attracted to him, and he to you. Everything will be okay."

"No." I shake my head.

"Yes."

"Mom..." I swallow, my lungs strained and muscles coiling beneath my skin, twitching and aching as I open myself up to my mother, confessing something for the very first time. "I need more."

Her thumbs stroke my cheek, and she whispers, "No, honey, you don't."

CHAPTER
Twenty-Eight

y mother's parting instructions are for me to familiarize myself with the home and to prepare for Anthony's arrival. By prepare, she means pretty myself up, but even if I wanted to, there's no time left for that.

She hasn't even made it to the driveway, and he's already stepping from his car.

My heart screams for me to run, but my feet don't get the message, and then Anthony's standing just outside the entrance, his phone to his ear.

His voice carries through the grand doors as he argues with the person on the other line, threatening to take their name off of a party list, knowing that taking a man's access to the world he believes he belongs is the quickest way to get what you want. I could almost roll my eyes if I wasn't already spinning in my head.

More words are mumbled, followed by a hard demand and snapped 'not a minute past,' and then he's walking in, a perfect grin already in place, blue eyes bright and shining.

"Wow." His smile seems to spread. "I didn't expect walking inside to find you waiting for me to feel so exciting."

That makes one of us.

I force my mouth to curve up, my eyes trailing his every move as he slips his jacket from his back and that maid I spotted earlier comes out of nowhere and sweeps it from his hold, the two not once making eye contact.

He pulls his wallet from his pocket and sets it on top of the square crystal bowl on the table near the door and turns to me with his hands in his pockets.

He smiles, stepping closer. "You seem a bit stunned."

A quick laugh leaves me. "Yeah, I'm definitely surprised, but my mother is nothing if not stealthily shocking."

It takes effort not to look away.

He nods, three feet from me now. "On our last few outings, I had suggested a little more for us, but maybe I was too subtle."

His eyes hold on mine and I can read what he's not saying.

Maybe he was too subtle or *maybe* I wasn't paying attention.

Maybe I was occupied.

My skin prickles as I realize. "You asked for this..."

His lips curl into a full smile, teeth and all. "I did."

"Why?" I can't keep from asking.

His brows snap together, but it's too late to backtrack, so I wait for an explanation that never comes.

His demeanor shifts and his attention moves to my luggage, the pieces lined exactly as they were on the floor of my home, now in his.

I don't even know what's inside them.

Anthony licks his lips. "There's a room down here in the back part of the house. Gorgeous view for a gorgeous girl." He lifts the golden J in his palm, flipping it over to inspect the back.

"They're real," I offer since he seems intent on knowing.

His eyes lift to mine and he walks into the kitchen area, where a glass, a third of the way filled with golden liquid, sits waiting for him. "Nana will get things moved for you. If you'd like her to unpack for you, she will. If you're particular about where things go, let her know and she'll do all she can to make you happy, as will I."

"Coffee makes me happy," I throw out, pushing back how ridiculous this entire situation is for a moment, just to see his reaction.

Because fuck tea.

Fuck everything.

Why am I doing this? I should leave...

Anthony's glass halts at his lips, and surprisingly, he chuckles, walking toward me with kind eyes and soft steps.

I don't flinch when his palm lifts, gently falling to my cheek. "Tell me what you like, and I'll have it delivered for you."

Someone already knows what I like.

A sharp pain hits my ribs.

"All I want, sweetheart, is to be everything you want," he says.

You could never be.

"I have some work to do, but if you prefer, I put it off to help you get comfortable, I will."

"No," I say, maybe too quickly and the edges of his eyes tighten, though he tries to hide it. I clear my throat, smiling. "No, I'll be fine. I won't lie, this is a change I wasn't prepared for, but I'll settle in fine. Do what you need to and I'll... go find my room." I push my tongue into the back of my teeth, my tolerance for this nightmare nearly peaking.

I might lose it if I can't find a solo moment to breathe soon.

He nods, and I don't miss the way the pads of his fingers search my skin where the cut once was.

Anger flares in my abdomen, but I keep the sugary tone he expects. "It healed enough to hide."

His eyes glide to mine again and he nods slowly.

"And once again, she's perfection," he whispers, letting his hand fall as he steps past me, but before he rounds the corner, he pauses. "I'll be home the remainder of the day, and I'll already be at the office by the time you leave for class in the morning, but tomorrow night, we'll celebrate."

"We don't have to." I shake my head. *Please, no.* "We have... plenty more nights for that."

"We will, yes, but you will only have one eighteenth birthday."

My face falls and he brings his glass to his lips. "Our guests will begin arriving at seven, be sure you're ready." He turns and walks away.

And I'm left standing in the middle of the room having no fucking clue where to go from here.

But I know where I won't be going, and that's to school tomorrow.

I didn't sleep more than an hour or two and all the time I sat awake did me no good. I couldn't form a single thought and staring at myself in the giant mirror across from this ridiculous bed, only seems to fog my mind more.

The girl in the mirror, she was beginning to recognize herself not twenty-four hours ago, but she's fading to black now.

Suffocating.

Sinking.

This is why I kept my relationships at face value.

I hate the way my body feels, as if it's tied to a tower, suspended so high that the air's too dense to breathe, the clouds too countless to find my way through, the harsh wind a cool slap in the face.

There is no escape, this house is my tower, and the hand that sweeps across my skin is my own, a desperate attempt to hold on to the girl within, whoever the hell she is.

The perfect daughter?

The playful paramour?

The desolate doll.

I need to get out of here.

I need to see Ransom.

As if my mother has not only the power to dictate my life but the ability to read my thoughts, her curt tone breaks through, pulling me from my mind and placing herself inside it.

I turn toward the door, knowing she'll be headed for it soon enough, so while I have a second, I call Cali to see if she heard anything about Jules. She shares she's awake and in recovery, but nothing else has changed. We still can't see or talk to her.

"I'm staying home, I don't want to deal with the questions from people who pretend to care." She yawns into the line.

I nod, my eyes trailing over the massive grandfather clock on the wall opposite of the foreign bed I'm sitting in. "Yeah, I'm not going either."

"It will mean a lot to her to know that you're checking on her," she shares.

I grip my phone tighter, pulling at the small thread hanging from the hem of my leggings. "Have I been that shitty lately?"

"Not shitty, but you did drop us pretty fast. At least we

know why now, though."

When I don't say anything, she quietly adds, "You know we don't care, right? About you and, you know, those guys."

"They have names."

She chuckles sleepily. "Yeah, they do, but after the way your back seat bestie looked at me yesterday, I think I'll take a page from Harry Potter and fear speaking his name aloud."

I scoff, a small smile tugging at my lips, but my muscles ache beneath my skin. My mother's voice grows closer, so I tug myself up.

"Want to come over, watch some Kardashians or something?" Cali offers.

I know I'm messed up in the head when that sounds amazing.

"I can't." I put the phone on speaker and set it on top of the dresser, tightening my ponytail and running my fingers under my eyes, patting at the puffiness my sleepless night gifted me. "I have to go, and I might not be around to answer calls today, but I'll check my messages when I can."

"Well, unless Jules can sweet talk her way out of the hospital's regulation of the mandatory psycho watch, I say you'll be missing nothing."

"True. Okay, talk to you later." I hang up, stuff my phone in my closest bag and open the bedroom door to find my mom headed right for me, a glam team silently following.

"What, you have a key to his house?"

"Your house?" she corrects but waves me off and steps inside the giant space. "No, I don't have a key, but you have a maid, and maid's open doors when someone knocks." She spins on her heels. "I called you three times."

"I know. I'm the one who hit ignore."

She looks over my shoulder. "Come in, set up. We'll be

right back."

She steps out and with a roll of my eyes, I follow her into the kitchen where an espresso machine is being set up in the corner.

A hint of satisfaction twitches at my lips, but it's an extremely low win at this point.

"I thought you were strong, Jameson? Tough."

"I am."

"No, you're not. You're standing here acting like a child and pitying yourself. You're not a prisoner here, Jameson. It's simply a new place to call home. Nothing changes in your contract." She shakes her head and tries a different approach. "You are the one who wanted this." She slips closer, reminding me of the words I once spoke to her, but standing here, I can't remember if they were ever even mine, or if they were planted like a seed, and called upon at the precise moment she planned for, the skill she's perfected that's led her to courtroom victories, time and time again.

She's a cold woman, and she never should have been blessed with children, let alone daughters—a fact she'd agree upon.

I shake my head. "My dad would be so disappointed in you."

"Yes, well." She nods. "The weak always are."

Her blatant disregard for her deceased husband is sickening and steals the air from my lungs, but she either doesn't notice or doesn't care as she goes to turn away.

"Are you not going to tell me Happy Birthday?"

She freezes, her eyes slicing to mine.

"You flew here, passed me off. You're officially free of kin duties now, but would it kill you to smile, and say 'Happy Birthday, Jameson?'"

My mom studies me curiously, slowly turning to face

me once more. "Honey, please don't tell me you went and turned into your sister?"

My eyes widen. "Are you serious right now?"

"Are you?" she counters. "Have you truly strayed *so far* that you now need the validation in the form of an adolescent's wasted wish?"

"Do you hear yourself?!" I shriek. "Can you even see me?! Am I fucking invisible!" I clutch my chest. "I tried to open up to you yesterday, something I have never done, and you basically spit in my face! You're my mother! Can you not see that I'm not okay?!"

My mother sighs. "Jameson, keep your voice down—"

"Fuck off!" I throw my hand out, sending everything on the counter crashing to the floor, and everyone else in the room quickly rushes out of it.

"Fuck. Off!" I scream. "This is your fault! Everything is your fault, I—" I break off in a numb chuckle, my hand flying up to my forehead as I look away. "I'm broken. I'm... I'm a fucking mess."

I snap forward, jerking toward her but the woman doesn't so much as flinch. "You told me to feel was to fall flat on my face, but you had it all wrong. To fight what you feel is so much worse because there are things you can't push away, and then everything you've fought off for so long comes raging like a fucking hurricane, suffocating you from the inside out. I can't think straight. I can't sleep or eat. I fuck up over and over again, running from what's real because I'm too messed up to recognize it."

I glare at my mother.

"I don't even know how to let someone love me, let alone love someone back." Thick, unrelenting claws curl beneath my rips, tugging and tearing, yanking.

Everything hurts.

"You ruined me," I croak.

"My god... Jameson," my mother whispers, and there's another crack somewhere. Everywhere.

The corner of her mouth lifts the smallest bit, her left arm coming up and gently brushing my cheek. "Take a Xanax already."

Her hand falls, and with it, my heart hits my feet. I stumble backward, hitting my hip on the kitchen island, but she doesn't notice.

She's already walking away, but I'm frozen in the spot, spinning and spinning. I might vomit.

I don't know how long I stand there, but I'm still attempting to remember how to breathe when a soft palm lands over mine on the countertop I don't remember grabbing on to.

The hand is small, telling of age, and I lift my eyes to find the softest shade of brown.

Nana, the housemaid, stands there, a steaming cappuccino in her free hand. She lowers it to the countertop with an encouraging smile. "I'm happy to have whatever you wish ready for you when you wish, but something tells me you'd like to know how to work the machine on your own?"

I nod, struggling to find my voice.

"Good, and it will keep you from them a while longer." She tips her chin with a smile.

A low, unexpected chuckle escapes, and we take as long as possible to go over the instructions on the espresso machine, but eventually, I make it into the room where everyone waits on me.

My mother barks instructions and I play like porcelain, cold and lifeless, unmistakably still with my spine straight, neck stretched, and chin high as they turn me into whatever she sees fit.

I'm primped and pressed, and when the clock hits six-forty-one, my lipstick is applied for me.

She nods in approval of the royal blue dress she surely picked out.

It hits mid-thigh, lies elegantly over my skin with long sleeves and a cross-over cut in the front. I have no cleavage showing, but my shape is accentuated as intended. My pumps are nude, bangles golden, hoop earrings a perfect match.

"Well, my job is done." She smiles, proud of herself.

"Yeah, as of last night, when you used me to your advantage."

"I didn't—"

"Save it, Mother. I'm here, I'm all dolled up, as intended. You can go now."

"You better shape up, Jameson Jole, or we all lose."

"Lose what, Mother?"

She stands tall. "There is nothing for you to worry about."

Yeah, nothing. Only the shredding of the thing I swore I never needed but now beats for someone else completely.

Shaking my head, I reach past her, taking the glass of champagne Nana offered. I finish it off in one drink before trading it for another and then lean forward, inspecting my red lips in the mirror.

"Hey, Nana?" I step around my mom.

Nana steps from the corner. "Yes, dear?"

My eyes flick over my mom and while I ache on the inside, I remember all my years of training at her hand and manage to hide every facet of it, pulling out a sunny, socialite smile, as she so adores.

"Show my mother out the back door. Mr. Blanca has guests arriving soon, and I'm afraid she didn't make the list."

I step from the room as quickly as possible as the false

bravado is slipping and slipping fast.

My palm flattens on the wall and I close my eyes, fighting for a deep breath. When I open them, I find Anthony standing there, staring right at me.

He watches me closely as he approaches, nodding his head in approval when he finally does allow his gaze to travel over me.

He takes my hand and I let him, my thumb twitching when his lips fall to my knuckles.

His eyes come up, and I don't mean to, but I pull back when his fingers reach for my hair.

Something flashes over him, but he smiles. "I hope you're ready for your birthday dinner, Jameson. I'm going to do everything in my power to make it a memorable one." His grip on my hand tightens, my knuckles grinding together slightly to the point of pain, but I bite into my cheek to hide it. When he finally releases me, I'm given his back.

The moment he's out of sight, I turn, lifting my hand to inspect the area. It's red and throbbing, but the shading will fade and all I'll have to do is avoid the use of it. People will be none the wiser.

I just have to get through tonight, and tomorrow I'll have a clearer mind to figure out what the hell I'm going to do next.

Opening and closing my palm once just to be sure nothing is broken, I hiss, and a slight shuffle catches my attention. My head snaps as my arms fly to my sides.

My mother stands there, tucked into the corner, but her eyes don't meet mine.

They're frozen on my hand.

"Tell me, Mother, is a man like that worthy of your name?"

Her eyes begin to lift, but I don't stand there to find out

what's within them because it doesn't matter.
She's about to leave and I don't get to.

CHAPTER
Twenty Nine

The furniture in the great room has been moved in favor of small cocktail tables and random seating is scattered throughout.

The music is low and some classical bullshit the rich only listen to because some uppity asshole along the way decided it was to be part of the process.

The hors d'oeuvre table is fit for a rabbit cage and the gift table could rival a mall's Christmas display, but I smile and play polite as I'm introduced to Anthony's staff and who the hell ever the rest of these people are.

I know I sound like an ungrateful brat, maybe he's trying to be nice and he absolutely didn't have to do any of this, but considering the circumstances, I have not a grateful bone in my body.

My soul purpose is getting through this evening so I can slip back inside the room I've been assigned.

I'm basically Anthony's shadow for the night, stuck to his side to smile, to play polite, and to laugh at jokes I don't get while making small talk with women I'll never fit in with. We didn't discuss a story to share with his crowd, so I let him tell a tale of how we met through mutual friends and our connection was instant.

It's true if the friend is my mother and the contract

she put together within a few days' time counts as the connection.

Either way...

Smile, smile, smile.

Thankfully, Anthony's friends are his coworkers who all have work tomorrow, so they're out by eleven-thirty.

As he closes the door behind the last guest, I spin away, but he catches my hand and walks me up the stairs.

"I have a gift for you," he shares. "I was planning on waiting, but the circumstance doesn't quite allow for it."

"You didn't need to get me anything, Anthony. I appreciate you setting this up for me tonight." Lie.

"Of course, I figure it's best we start off on a strong foot, one where we understand each other."

I try to play coy, but suspicion swims in my gut. "Should I be following what you're saying?"

"A better question, I think, would be, do you think you should?" he counters, lowering into his chair, leaving me standing before him.

"I get the feeling you wish the answer were yes."

"But it's not." He cocks his head. "Is it?"

"Is this some sort of game to you?" I suspect. "We have a contract for the end of the year, you agreed to separate lives until then, and I think our Sunday afternoons have gone well enough, minus almost being turned into fish bait. So why the change, why bring me here, and what was the point of this entire evening?"

His eyes slowly narrow. "I told you before, I want to be—"

"Everything I want, yeah I heard, but you could have worked to achieve that later. Why am I here, Anthony? My mom breaks contracts for no one."

The smile he wore along with the kindness of his gaze

is gone, and he faces me fully. He reaches into the drawer on the small side table beside him and tosses a small piece of paper onto the ottoman before him, nodding his head for me to grab it.

I do, and as I open it up, my heart both sinks and flips.

It's my note from Arsen, the one he left me the day Anthony showed up at my school unannounced, the note that, after the yacht went up in flames, was missing from my purse pocket.

My eyes snap up, locking with his, and he reaches in again, tossing out the keys to my new car—my mom must have given them to him.

Following that, a clip from the *Daily Pilot*.

The headline reads, "Misfortune at Gentry Vineyards." An accompanying photo of charred vines following.

"Were you having me followed?"

"No, actually. That's where things get interesting." He cocks his head. "Did you know my father died when I was young, too, of course mine didn't go out quite the same as yours." He doesn't wait for an answer. "My mother, like yours, was quite the cold-hearted bitch who remarried quickly. That's not why she's cold-hearted, but a fact is a fact. She took her new husband's name, I kept mine."

"Why are you telling me this?"

"What, is this not what they call pillow talk?" he mocks, but then he looks to his watch and a grin takes over. "I'm kidding. I'm telling you this, so that you understand, what happens next falls solely on your shoulders."

A door slams downstairs, the hinges rattling and echoing with the help of the vaulted ceilings of this place.

"Ah," Anthony drawls, slowly pushing to stand. "Perfect timing."

Feet pound heavy against the stairs, and as they grow

closer, my skin begins to prick.

Anthony's smile is vicious, and it only keeps growing.

"I'm here, motherfucker, where you at?" comes from the first floor.

Ice fills my veins and I grow lightheaded, slowly spinning where I stand.

The first thing to come into view is a mess of hair, and then a face wound tight with anger followed by a hoodie as black as night.

Eyes lift, connecting with mine, and shock drains the blood from my face, but the sight before me has nothing on the greeting that follows.

"Hello, brother."

CHAPTER
Thirty

*M*y hands come up, freezing in the air as I try to work through the warped world I've clearly entered.

The one where my man is related to the man I'm supposed to marry.

This can't possibly be happening...

Ransom, still frozen on the last step of the stairwell, blinks hard. "What the fuck is going on?" he draws slowly, his gaze never leaving mine, but I know he watches his brother from the corner of his eye.

"You tell me," I manage to rasp, though it doesn't sound like a question, because Anthony said brother.

Ransom is here.

Anthony is his brother.

Anthony, the guy I'm contracted to marry, is the man who Ransom tried to fight in the club that night because he was blowing their money, money they need for his sister. That's the familiar scent I recognized, his cologne.

He's the man who locked his sister away with strangers, *their* sister, and the person he was on the phone with yesterday was Ransom, threatening his visits with Sienna if he didn't show up here tonight, at the exact time he planned.

The stroke of fucking midnight, like some twisted fatal princess shit.

This is twisted.

And fatal.

But for who?

Us?

Jesus, which 'us'?!

My airway begins to close as I stare into the eyes of the only person I've ever truly wanted, knowing our relationship, that was condemned at the start, has just met its catapult.

But the real question is, who holds the hammer?

Maybe I was the ultimate pawn, played by not one blue-eyed bastard, but two.

My thoughts must mirror my expression as Ransom breaks from his frozen state.

"Baby, no." He darts forward, right for me, but Anthony makes a really stupid move, one that goes to show he doesn't know his brother at all.

He shoves me to the side.

Everything inside me locks, panic curling, pulling at my every nerve, but it has nothing to do with being pushed, and everything to do with what I know, without a doubt, comes next.

Ransom snaps.

He flies forward, grips Anthony by the neck, and kicks his legs from beneath him before he has a chance to blink, let alone fight back.

His skull slams against the hardwood and Ransom comes down on top of him, giving him not a moment to recover, but slamming his fist right into his jaw.

Blood spills from his lips, but Anthony laughs from beneath him, the sound a gargled mess.

"Baby, huh?" Anthony seethes, and he seems to cave, his muscles loosening.

But Ransom must be used to this, because he angles his body and as he does, Anthony's arms come up under his.

"Fuck you," Ransom growls, jerking to try to free himself.

With his right foot planted flat on the floor, Anthony lifts his right hip, using the momentum and position to flip them over, but with the way Ransom adjusted, they do a full toddler version of tumbling.

Both break apart for a split second and Anthony reaches up, gripping the glass he was drinking from.

"Ransom watch out!" I scream.

His hand comes up just in time to catch Anthony's wrist and he slams his forehead into his.

They both manage to scramble to their feet, and this time, Anthony lands a punch across his brother's face. Ransom's head jerks to the side on impact, but he comes right back, swinging wildly with both hands, forcing his feet backward until his lower half hits a wooden chest.

"What the fuck is this?!" Ransom shouts. "What did you do?" His eyes slice to mine.

His gaze falls to my dress then, as if he's only noticed I'm made-up, and his head tips the tiniest bit, small creases forming between his eyes. "Wait... it's him? He's the one who—" he cuts himself off, putting the pieces together.

Anthony takes advantage of his distracted state. He lifts his foot, kicking Ransom right in the stomach and he stumbles backward, hits the small table and the case on top of it crashes to the floor.

Hundreds of pearls spill over the floor. They roll in every direction, down the hall and the stairs, over the slatted railing, the hard pings echoing as they bounce along the first floor.

"Fuck," he ground out. He squeezes his hair with his hands, his eyes clamped shut as he shakes his head, an angry growl slipping past him. "Fuck!"

In that moment, I know the answer to my question.

Anthony Blanca holds all we have in the palm of his hands, and he knows it. He's known it for a while now, but Ransom had not a clue.

This wasn't his plan.

I'm not a board piece in a game of Family Feud, at least not where he's concerned.

My pulse leaps in my chest, deep beneath my ribs. It's the part of me I swore, time and time again, didn't work properly, yet I now know the truth.

It didn't work because it had yet to be charged, but it beats wildly now, aches deeply for the boy in front of me and I don't even know why.

That might be a lie.

It might be because I'm not sure where we go from here.

Needles prick in my throat and I think I whisper his name, but I can't be sure as his head never lifts. He doesn't step from the corner he's backed himself into.

Anthony coughs, and my eyes fly his way.

He shakes his head, glaring at his brother, a heavy scoff leaving him. "Weak little fucker. Always were. Let me lay this out for you now. Ransom, I will give you the house and the inheritance—"

"Fuck the house, fuck money, and fuck you!" he bellows, swiping a hand across the table and sending everything on top of it crashing to the floor. "*She* is mine. Try and take her, I fucking dare you."

I wait for Anthony to shout back, sure that he will, but

a foul chuckle is what follows, and somehow, I know it's worse.

My ribs cave, my stomach hollowing.

"I wasn't finished." Anthony cocks his head, and the gambit fucking falls. "But maybe I'll start backward so you get the full picture." He grins wickedly. "Jameson will be my wife—"

Ransom scoffs, shaking his head. "Fuck you, she will."

"And once she is," he continues as if Ransom never spoke, "I no longer need the rest. The house will be yours, the trust, but most importantly, or so you seem to believe, I will sign complete conservatorship over to you."

Ransom's face falls, he turns white, stumbles over his own two feet, and drops against the wall, his back sliding down it until his ass hits the ground.

"There we go, you're getting it now, though, I admit, I'm a bit surprised by the dramatic reaction."

"Fuck you," Ransom breathes. It's hardly audible, but it's there.

"It works in my favor though, because now you know. There's no reason to fight me anymore. You'll soon have everything you ever wanted."

It dawns on me, and I don't realize I've whispered her name until Anthony's scoff reaches me.

"Yet another surprise, you do know about our dear sister, so you must know how much Ransom cares for the girl." Anthony's disregard for her, as if she's a thing rather than a person, is sickening.

"On the off chance that it needs to be said aloud..." He trails off as his phone rings and he bends, grabbing it from where it must have fallen from his pocket, his eyes slicing to mine. "Every decision surrounding her, will be his, the moment *you*... are completely mine."

My knees weaken, and I have to grip the arm of the chair as not to fall, and Anthony's laugh deepens.

"It's funny, you'd think I planned this out." He dabs at the blood on his lip. "Do we call it coincidence, or fate?" the asshole adds, adjusting his button-up. "I'll give you ten minutes to fill him in on our contract, and only because I know he's incapable of touching you."

If only he knew...

"You're a prick," I manage to rasp.

"Ten fucking minutes, Jameson. Don't test me. You have no idea what I know, what I have, and what I can accomplish with it."

Anthony's angry steps carry him away and I move closer to Ransom, dropping onto my knees in front of him.

My hands fall to his shoulders and he jerks, trying to push me away, but I grip his face, forcing his gaze to mine.

He blinks, a dead look in his eyes, but when I span my fingers out along his skin, he blinks again, and an entirely different expression takes over.

Pure desperate need.

The need to be close, to feel a connection.

My blood runs warm.

His left hand comes up to cup my face, and he strokes my skin there, desire boiling in his hooded gaze and sparking my own deep within me.

Suddenly he's gripping my hips, tugging me onto his lap.

My eyes widen and I jerk away, try and glance in the direction Anthony disappeared, but he doesn't allow it.

He grabs handfuls of my hair, holding them stiff and straight, tugging them hard, so I can't turn my head, his hips pushing up, letting me know how hard he is, that he needs me. Here. Now.

"He might hear."

"Fuck him."

"But he'll screw with you—"

"Shhh," he cuts me off, a broken smile on his lips.

He wants me to know he's fucked up, getting lost in his mind, and instead, he wants to get lost in me.

I feel the same. The last few days have been overbearingly heavy.

I need him too.

"My mom, she—"

"No, baby." He shakes his head, one hand sliding into my hair and tugging me closer, the other squeezing my upper thigh. "Show me."

He pushes my dress up to my hips, his eyes low and heavy, weighted and worn. "Fuck everyone by fucking me. Now. Slow."

My core clenches and he grinds into me.

"Let me inside," he whispers, his lips aligned with mine, waiting for more and on the verge of taking it. "Let me have what's mine."

Desire surges through me, and my clit begins to throb.

Ransom groans, his tongue gliding along my lips, and my eyes nearly roll back. "I can feel how wet you are for me, baby, right through my fucking jeans," he growls, his hold tightening.

My fingers fly to his belt, desperate to get the thing open. I don't take the time to get it off and he doesn't waste a single second.

My panties are torn from my body and I'm lifted and lowered onto him.

I moan instantly, taking his cock and wanting more of it.

I grind into him.

"I've been thinking about your cunt, baby." He groans, not bothering to keep himself quiet, rolling my hips into him the way he wants it. "About how it squeezes me, tugs on me. Fucking loves on me."

I shiver and his hand finds my spine.

He presses there, rolling with me as he thrusts up into me. My palms flatten on the wall at his back and I lift a little.

He knows what I want, he scoots down slightly and I drop, taking him deeper with a gasped moan.

I ride him, reveling at the feeling of his cock swelling inside me and he lets his head fall back, his eyes closing, lips parted and panting.

He's feeling all of me, seeing me behind closed lids.

But then he begins to shake, so I press firmer, placing my lips on his and breathing for us both. I set the pace and after a few tense moments, he slowly follows.

His thigh muscles begin to clench, and I press harder, move faster, and he buries his face in my neck as he comes.

He grunts, low and deep, his body twitching, palms squeezing.

I hold him there and he me, massaging my back and running his hands along my body.

His lips find my ear, buried half in my hair, and he whispers, "Happy Birthday to my girl."

Instant, bone deep aches zip through me, but I can't pinpoint where I'm hurting.

Maybe everywhere.

All over.

He pulls back, looking into my eyes with a twisted expression.

"I tried to call, we all did," he tells me, and I know this. I ignored his calls too.

"We had something for you. Arsen made you a cake

and B wanted to bring you coffee and pasta."

I don't know what to say, so I say nothing.

"I'm going to tell you something," he rasps. "And you're going to panic, stress, and you'll probably make a mistake after, but we'll get over it."

"Ransom—"

"I love you. For real love you." He fists my hair, a heart-wrenching tenderness written across him. "Bottom of the fucking ocean, love you, Trouble, and you're not going to say it back, but I don't need you to. I already know."

I swallow, shaking my head. "Ransom..."

"You don't know what it means to love, you don't understand it, but I fucking feel it. When you look at me, when you touch me."

"We can't do this," I breathe brokenly.

"Let him catch us," he rasps, his hips shifting beneath me. "I can't stop needing you. I fucking want you, always."

"That's not what I mean." My throat aches with loss and he's still beneath me. I can't imagine the pain that follows.

"I mean this." I try to pull back, but his hands fly to my hips and hold.

"This," he deadpans.

"Us."

His muscles grow tense, eyes tightening. It takes him several seconds to speak and when he does, it's heartbreaking. "There is no 'doing this.' It's done."

He adjusts, leaning forward with his brows raised high.

Footsteps fall in the distance, and Ransom's eyes snap over my shoulder.

I quickly jump up, backing away as I fix my dress, and with a pointed expression, he does the same.

With slow, predatory steps, he advances on me. "If you think I'll let you walk away, you're wrong."

Acid coats my tongue, but in this moment, my mother would be proud.

I lift my chin, a cold, callousness washing over me, making me appear numb and indifferent when really my body is on fire. Everything inside me is burning.

"If you think you can stop me, you're wrong."

His eyes flash, his chest heaving, but he gives a curt nod, walks past, and stops two feet from his brother.

"You can have everything that's rightfully mine, it means nothing to me, but try to take her, and I will kill you." Ransom's promise sends a tremor down my spine.

Anthony, the bastard, laughs, sticks his hands in his pockets, and cocks his head. "If you do, make sure you're successful this time because it will be your ass if you are not. I won't stick my neck out for you again."

"Fuck. You." Anger courses through Ransom's very being and his body vibrates where it stands.

His eyes slice to mine, holding as he slams his shoulder into his brother as he passes. He charges down the stairs and out the front door.

The hinges rattle and it shakes the vessels to my heart, threatening to tear them from the heavy beating organ and ending me right here, or at least that's the way it feels.

But then I realize what he's just said...

Again.

Subconsciously, my eyes fly along the floor, at the mess made during their spat. Pieces of the iridescent vase gleam around the room, the one that caught my attention the day Anthony brought me here, taunting me without my knowledge with what he knew was coming.

"Ah, yes, the pearls." Anthony rounds where I stand, using the bottom of his shoe to send several rolling out of his path.

He pours himself a scotch, swirling it in his cup with a small, vile smile.

"See," he begins. "Sienna loved the ocean. Our family knew this man who worked near the pier, owned this little shop. You go in, pick an oyster, and hope something worthy is inside. She would walk there every day after school, buy herself a bundle, come home and add whatever she found to that exact vase. I guess you could call it her... life's work." He grins and horror crosses my face.

"She never found one worth a damn," he adds. "But she kept going and going, hoping. It's in our blood, gambling." He shakes his head. "All she wanted was one perfect pearl, but she never got it."

My temples throb, and he looks to me.

"The yacht."

"The yacht, the imperfection hidden under your makeup." He lifts his glass to his lips, taking a small sip.

Ransom blew up the yacht, set it aflame, as he did my car, the Bonzi tree Cali told me about, Scott's grapevines...

"He's unstable, of course you would be too if you were the reason your sister was dead, but alive."

A chill runs through me, and I pale, my eyes snapping to his.

He squints, and a low chuckle leaves him. "Oh, you didn't know?" He walks closer, fully entertaining himself, and with every step he takes, my lungs shrivel a little more. "Why do you think he doesn't drive?"

"No."

"Doesn't drink?"

"Stop."

"It's because he climbed behind the wheel with his precious baby sister in the passenger seat."

My palm flattens on my stomach. "I said stop."

"And when he took a corner, he took it wide. Flew right over the center median. *Right* into oncoming traffic."

Oh my god, this is how it happened.

She wasn't hit by a drunk driver; she was in the car with one.

But it wasn't Ransom, I know this, because Ransom would never leave his sister after a moment like that, and he was with Amy just after it happened.

It was Anthony.

Anthony wrecked with his little sister in the car and found a way to get Ransom to take the blame.

No wonder Sienna doesn't care or try to speak to him.

I'm sure she's angry, but more than that, it must be painful to be the one ignored, to be the one someone else turned their back on as if you're the one at fault.

Anthony claps his hands together, and I jump, snapping out of my thoughts.

He chuckles, shakes his head and begins to walk away, but the rev of an engine reaches our ears.

It grows loud, and then louder, and Anthony's face falls in an instant.

He slams his glass down and runs across the room.

I spin, following, forced to jog to keep up.

He throws the double doors open and flies out onto the front balcony, grips the railing, and screams, "What the fuck are you doing?!"

I reach the edge, my hands flying to my mouth when I spot Beretta and Arsen at the end of the driveway, Ransom standing just outside the open door of my Camaro.

My toes bend in my heels, and I stop breathing.

Ransom's hood is up, nothing but a slight glow coming from him, his eyes, the night a bit too bright to make them pop, but then behind us, the lights go out.

Anthony growls. "Don't play your fucking games with me."

Ransom's foot slips inside the car, and again, he revs the engine.

"Ransom!" Anthony screams.

And then Ransom climbs behind the wheel.

He hits the gas to the floor, the wheels spinning and smoking, and then the house rattles as the convertible crashes through the glass garage.

Anthony jolts back, shouts, but my eyes remain locked on the group below.

Beretta and Arsen step forward, and through the smoke, Ransom appears.

He walks backward until he's standing in the middle of the boys, all three staring in our direction.

My body aches, a sense of betrayal wrapping around my ribs, squeezing, but I hide it, slowly spinning on my heels.

"So much for not driving." I wait until Anthony's enraged eyes meet mine and add, "I wonder what else about him you've underestimated?"

I leave him standing there and go back to the tower he stuffed me in, his blood smeared on my arm, his brother's cum spreading along my inner thighs.

I understand my mother more than ever now, why she continues to feel nothing. It's because, at the end of the day, burying your weakness does nothing but manifest it, and then the universe gives you what you fear, so the answer is to feel nothing.

A cruel fate at its finest.

CHAPTER
Thirty-One

I wake up to the bedroom door opening and look over to find Monti standing there, Nana at her side.

Nana offers a small smile, and I nod, letting her know it's fine.

Monti's shoulders visibly relax, and she wrings her hands together. "Um, she offered to make us lattes..."

"You can make me a latte, Nana." I stare at my sister, and she drops her eyes to the floor. "My sister prefers a cappuccino."

Monti's head darts up, and tears brim within them.

Nana nods, slowly backing from the room, and Monti steps in farther.

Her eyes roam the space, but she doesn't comment.

"I came home from classes to find your bedroom pretty close to bare, and I thought for sure I lost my sister again." She sits on the edge of my bed, her eyes moving to mine. "But then I realized I never really had her, because I'm a mega fuckup and she's... perfection."

"Fuck off, Monti."

She nods. "You don't see it, you never have and you *hate* the idea of perfection, but it's just who you are. You are envy at its finest."

"Yeah," I mock myself. "Dozens of girls are sitting around wishing they could swap places with me." I roll my eyes.

Monti sighs.

"I had to threaten Tanner to get the GPS coordinates to find you. Mom wouldn't tell me shit." Her eyes shift between mine. "Will you?"

"What's there to tell? You failed to do what Mom asked of you, and here I am, picking up your slack." Slowly dying inside.

Monti nods, thanking Nana when she slips in, passing off our drinks.

I know I'm being unfair, and I know had Monti done what our mother asked, I would simply have been passed off to the next man she plunked from the pack. But still.

I can't seem to let it go, not yet.

Monti sets her drink down, pulling a long silver box with a small red bow from her bag, and sets it in the space between us.

My eyes lift to hers and she half smiles. "I was going to give this to you last night, but you never came home."

I eye the box, bringing my warm drink to my lips. "What is it?"

"A gift."

I look to her with a blank expression, and she chuckles, then she takes a heavy breath.

"I owe you more than I've given you," she tells me, pulling the top off of the box to reveal what's inside.

I stare at the small copper key, knowing exactly where it fits.

"Where did you get that?"

"I stole it," she admits. "I snuck into Mom's office back in Florida the night before she sent me here. If I was coming home, I knew I had to take it with me."

I grind my teeth together, closing my eyes.

"Gifts can change your life, Jameson, but in order for that to happen, you have to be willing to accept them and decide if you're ready for what's on the other side, because there will be no going back."

My gaze snaps to hers, and a slow frown builds when she tucks my hair behind my ear, a sad smile on her lips.

I clench my teeth, fighting back my words.

My sister and I don't speak like this; we don't open up and share things between us, but she's here now, trying.

Would it kill me to try too?

I take another small sip.

"You're a Filano," she says simply. "We never lose."

"You lost, Monti," I remind her. "Mom and Dad will hardly look at you. I'm... apparently more pissed off at you than I realized." Guilt weighs on me, but it's the truth and I didn't see it until emotions I buried began to resurface with a vengeance.

"Like I said" —tears soften her tone and I retreat a little— "there's no going back. I made a choice, and to be honest, it's really, really hard," she cries, looking away as her hand comes up to dab at her eyes. "But I would be lying if I said it was the wrong one."

She sniffles, turning back to me. "I'm fucked up, J. I know that. I still kill myself trying to find perfection and I know it's some sick and twisted mommy and daddy issues. I might never be 'okay,' if I'm being honest. Who knows, but what I do know is you're stronger than I am, Jameson," she whispers, and my chest tightens.

"You're a force, sister." She leans forward, locking our eyes for a long, hard moment. "Maybe it's time to let every asshole know how fierce you really are."

I swallow, set my cup down and stand, her eyes trailing me as I walk over to my bedroom door and open it.

I turn to her.

"I could do that, but I won't." I open the door and step to the side. "I do believe you were brave to take your life into your own hands, Monti. I know that took courage, but I can't be so selfish. I would ruin someone in a way you don't understand if I were."

Monti lowers her eyes to the floor, making her way to me.

She pauses beside me, her eyes full of moisture, cheeks tear-stained. She smiles lovingly.

"See," she whispers. "You're stronger than me. You don't want to ruin anyone else, so instead, you'll ruin yourself." Her words sting, but her intention isn't to hurt.

She understands, but she hates it.

"Love you, J. Happy late Birthday." She touches my shoulder and walks out.

It takes everything in me to hold strong, to keep the hurricane brewing in my gut at bay but losing it will do nothing for me.

I throw myself into the shower, and when I step out, I'm shocked to find Monti is still here, but I don't show it. I keep my face blank as she stands, and lower into the vanity seat.

She steps up behind me, and we never once meet each other's eyes as she reaches for my comb and begins running it through my hair. She braids, twists and pins it, giving me two Dutch braids, the ends twisted and tucked under.

When she's done, I stand, step into my dress and she zips it.

I slide on a pair of four-inch heels to offset the six-inch pair I wore yesterday and face the mirror. She steps back and

I straighten my spine, pulling my shoulders back as I lift my chin.

This is who I am.

A porcelain trophy.

Anthony chooses that moment to walk in, and with his entry, Monti makes her exit.

Anthony walks over to my window, looking out over the ocean. "Remember that district attorney in Naples? The one who transferred out not long before your parents first attempted to trade your sister to him?"

I didn't know about the transfer, but how could I forget the rest. "Of course, I do."

I turn to face him, but he remains focused out the window.

"Do you know why she was forced to make such an offer?"

A slight frown forms between my brows. "Because he threatened her."

"Yes, but with what?" he leads.

I cross my arms, uneasy. "Clearly you are aware, so what's the point of this?"

"I am." He finally faces me, his blue eyes sharp. "But I don't think you are. I don't think you ever stopped to think about it, because if you had, you would have known there was more to you and me. You would have done better in upholding your end of our deal."

"Our deal was to get to know each other and move forward at the end of my school year."

"And you didn't think falling for someone else along the way would jeopardize everything?" He angles his head. "Your mother assured me you weren't the type, but mothers are often unaware, especially busy ones like her, so I had to be extra cautious."

"So, you did have me followed."

"I kept my eyes open, was all. I'm a lawyer, a great one. It's my job to see all the signs and, sweetheart, you had many."

"I guess neither of us are who the other thought."

He nods. "What did your mother tell you of our arrangement, Jameson?"

I lick my lips and shrug. What point is there to lie now?

"She said she believed in you, that with you as senior partner, the firm would have a new kind of power, and power is everything to her. She wanted someone to take over who was as cutthroat as her, and she needed my help to secure it." *Or her life's work would die with her, and that would be incredibly selfish of me to be the very cause of such a misfortune.* I force myself not to swallow. "I'd say she met her match."

Anthony buttons up his suit jacket. "All true, yes, but what she didn't tell you is I'm the one who went to her."

"Does that matter?"

"Since that one meeting led to you standing in front of me now, yes." He pauses, for effect, I'm sure. "See, the DA, I found, had threatened your mother with who knows what, but she was able to pay him off in the end, which told me the man didn't have what he needed to back her into a corner."

"And you did."

He nods.

I'm hit with a wave of nausea.

I knew it.

I take a deep breath, shaking my head. "How did you know about any of this?"

"I'm young, hungry, and ambitious. I knew I needed to find a way to catapult myself and it just so happened the queen of my world had spawned not one, but two princesses."

"You stalked my family."

"Again, all I did was pay attention. Very close attention, until what I needed fell into my lap." He sits on the edge of the dresser, watching me closely.

"See, your mom began taking more and more cases when she made her name by doing the opposite. She never kept a full schedule, because she refused to lose. She made sure she had the time she needed to put in the work, cover every avenue to ensure she was victorious every time she stepped out of that courtroom. As we both know, she was. But then suddenly, she was all over the docket, case after case, and what do you know… still on an unbelievable winning streak.

"I flew down to Florida to find out how, and before I came back, I had a Filano of my own." He grins, proud. "With a file that held the proof that your mom had added to her resume. She suddenly had an entirely new bankroll coming in and a good chunk went right back out, to a dirty PI. A man with known mafia ties whose job was to find and bury evidence, to make sure she won by—"

"Any means necessary," I whisper.

Anthony smiles. "Exactly. I watched as her client list flipped from high profile, secretly dirty politicians to suddenly every notorious criminal of the last decade. It's genius, really, the big money always comes from the ones with the most to lose, and if you can win, you get paid." He nods. "And we both know your mother always wins."

That she does.

"So now you see, her entire career will go up in flames if I were to share what I have. Every case she has ever worked on could be reopened and she, as well as your stepfather, would likely spend the rest of their lives in prison, maybe even have their assets frozen should someone decide the money she's been paid was blood money."

Anthony chuckles, and I feel sick.

"So, if you're willing to be the reason for all that, as well as the one thing that keeps Ransom from getting some parts of his life back, then, by all means, continue as you are, but something tells me you're smarter than that." He walks over to me and when I try to turn away, he grips my arm, his other hand pinching my chin between his thumb and pointer finger. "A little sacrifice can go a long, long way. We can go back to the way we were before. I'll be all you wish me to be, and you'll be in my bed," he whispers, lowering his head.

I jerk, and he squeezes tighter, pressing his lips to mine.

"My brother can't do half of what I can, sweetheart," he rasps. "All you have to do is allow me to prove it."

This can turn bad fast, so I force my muscles to ease, my pulse to calm, my eyes to soften, and it takes everything in me to lift a palm and place it on his chest.

I pretend to surrender to him.

His gaze holds mine a moment, and then he nods, his grip now gentle and sliding to my cheek.

He smiles softly, and it's almost terrifying how quickly his behavior shifts. "Your new driver is outside, ready to take you to class."

I nod and squeeze my eyes closed when he kisses my cheek, walking out.

The second he's gone, a loud cry slips from me, and my hand slams over my lips, but nothing else follows.

It's just a sound.

I'm fine.

I suck in a shaky breath, spin, and walk out the door.

As I climb into the back seat of the town car, the driver pokes his head inside with a smile, and I recognize him by the mustache on his face. He's the man who got in Arsen's face at the club that night.

"Long time, no see." He chuckles, holding out my phone.

I glare, subconsciously touching the side of my purse where I last knew it to be.

"He took it last night, just in case. I'm Mr. Banks to most people, but you can call me Charles." He closes the door.

I power my phone on, and immediately, it begins to ding over and over again. I quickly turn off the sound and wait until all the missed messages finish coming through.

I hesitate over Ransom's name, over Beretta's and Arsen's, and my heart weeps wildly, threatening to burst through my chest it pounds so vigorously.

I can see the first few words of the most recent messages and all have one word in common...

Please.

My grip tightens on my phone and I squeeze my eyes closed, but not a second passes before it begins to ring.

I jerk, a queasiness taking over my stomach as I fight looking at the screen. Instead, I go to power it off, but as I swipe the screen, I accidentally catch a glimpse of the name, finding it's Cali's.

With a low sigh, I answer, and the moment she speaks, I wish I wouldn't have.

I wish I would have stayed in my prison a day longer.

No phone.

No outside world.

No one but me.

Because, as Cali cries into my ear, her words nearly incoherent, she's so distraught, I'm reminded I'm not the only one whose reality can sometimes feel as if it's too much to bear.

Devastatingly, Jules could no longer take hers.

CHAPTER
Thirty-Two

After getting approval from Anthony, *Mr. Banks* drove me to Jules' house, where Cali and others have already begun to gather. There are at least a dozen cars parked out front and the side gate is open, several students coming in and out.

I text Cali that I'm here, and within seconds, she's charging out the front door, so I quickly climb out, just in time to catch her when she falls against me, her cries nearly doubling.

I hug her back, but I don't speak because I have no idea what to say or how to say it.

I didn't know Jules was hurting the way she must have been, I didn't know she felt so alone or overwhelmed. I was judgmental and assumed she began drinking heavier because she simply felt like partying.

She always seemed happy, but maybe I should have seen through her facade since I'm so good at hiding myself.

My limbs begin to tingle, an uncomfortable sense of desperation overtaking me, only I don't know what to do about it, so I stand there and let Cali cry until she's ready to pause.

When she pulls back, she shakes her head, grabs my hand and offers a small wave to my driver.

He steps onto the curb with us, and I freeze, gently pulling my hand free from Cali's, stepping closer to him.

"I don't need a fucking babysitter. You are not following me inside," I hiss.

Charles frowns, hitting the alarm button on the remote. "I've been driving for the twins' father for five years, beautiful. How do you think their daughter knew about you and Anthony?" He lifts a brow angrily. "I'll go inside if I damn well please."

I suck in a quick breath and he scoffs, shaking his head.

He steps around us and I follow behind him with a frown, but I quickly forget about him and focus on my friend.

As we walk through the front door, someone begins to shout, and as we come around the corner, we witness Amy being thrown around by her mom, the photo on the wall behind her swaying, but it's caught by another student before it falls on top of her.

Mrs. Marino picks up a pile of roses from the floor and heaves them at her daughter, blood dripping down her arms as she cries hysterically.

Amy stands there, frozen, as Dax steps toward Mrs. Marino, trying to soothe her, but she lashes out at him, too.

"This is all your fault," she cries hysterically, her body beginning to sag to the floor, but Dax catches her, lowering with her, and she wails, punching at his chest as he tries not to lose complete control himself.

But his tears fall, his eyes already swollen and puffy.

"Get away from me!" she cries, breaking before us all. "How am I supposed to look at you every day?!" she wails, her body slumping more. "My baby. My little girl." She completely breaks.

Tears pour from Amy's eyes, but she says nothing, her hands frozen flat on the wall, pieces of flower and stem stuck to the front of her.

Mr. Marino runs around the corner then, spotting them both. He jerks from right to left, unsure of who to go to first, but he decides quickly. He reaches for his daughter, but Amy pushes off the wall and runs away.

Mr. Marino drops onto the floor beside his wife and pulls her into his lap.

Another family member comes in, ushering all the students and others standing around from the room, but Dax can't seem to get himself off the floor.

He screams into his palms, his body bent over, forehead on the marble flooring beneath him, and my throat clogs.

Cali releases me and flies for him, falling to his side, and the moment her hands touch his back, he accepts her comfort, wrapping his arms around her.

I stand there, witness to a family's world crashing to the ground around them and sickened by a fleeting thought that comes along with it.

I bite into my cheek, fighting as hard as I can to push everything away.

I need some air, so I climb the stairs and head out to the balcony, moving to the farthest corner, resting my elbows on the ledge.

"This is so fucked up," I whisper.

"Yeah."

I jerk around, finding Amy tucked into the back side corner, hidden by the furniture and curled into a ball, her arms wrapped around her pulled-in knees, a joint between her fingers. "It is," she adds, tears still silently falling from her face.

My muscles freeze and I'm conflicted on what to do,

but then Amy's chin falls to her chest and her body starts to shake with sobs.

"My mom can't even look at me," she gasps. "Wait until she's ready to read Jules' diary." Her eyes slam closed, and she shakes her head.

My jaw muscles flex and I walk a little closer to her.

"Once she does, she'll make me leave. She's... they'll both hate me." Her head lifts. "I dyed my hair so that me and..." She can't say her twin's name. "So that we could have something of our own, so people would stop looking at us and calling us by the wrong names..." She trails off, looking away. "I had to buy a wig."

A frown forms along my forehead.

"And I waited in her room." She swallows. "I knew what time he would get here. I just wanted to see how long it would take him to notice, to see if he really saw her like she saw him. If he loved her like she loved him."

My face falls as I realize what she's saying. "Amy..."

"He didn't even know," she whispers. "He was so... gentle and..."

"Loving," I snap before I realize I'm saying it.

Amy nods, lifting her eyes to mine. "Nobody has ever touched me like that."

"Jesus, fucking Christ." My hands come up, swiping down my face, and I shake my head. "He wasn't yours to take. She loved him. You... you tricked him."

Amy nods, her face slowly caving as every inch of her tightens in anguish and her cries grow uncontrollable, her words hiccupped through tears and chokes. "I just wanted to see if he would know, if he really loved her because if he did, he would know, right? I didn't mean to keep going, I... and when she walked in..."

"Oh my god, she saw," I breathe, my stomach

threatening to empty itself.

"Dax, he... he broke down, fell to his knees and Jules she felt like ... like *nothing*. She started to wonder if maybe he didn't love her like she thought, but he did. He loved her so much. I... I had the lights low, the wig. Her clothes, but none of that mattered to her. Something happened in her mind that day and..." she wails. "Oh my god, I killed my sister. My twin. How can I ever look at myself in the mirror again? I did this. I'm a fucking monster!"

She jumps up suddenly, running to the railing, and my eyes shoot wide.

"Amy!" I throw myself forward, grabbing a piece of her shirt, and it tears from its threading. "Amy, Stop!"

I grab her around the waist and yank her backward as she kicks and screams and then she too cracks.

Breaks.

She falls to the floor, desperate screams echoing around us.

The only thing I can do is hug her back, so I do.

I want to tell her it wasn't her fault, that she must have been dealing with things she didn't know how to share or maybe feared to try.

There are so many things that could have contributed to the tragedy of this morning, but we may never know what those are, and we may never understand. All we can do is love her for who she was and miss her for the girl we knew.

My chest aches, but I push it away.

Dad.

I'm seconds from a mental breakdown, ready to run.

Thankfully, her parents are flying around the corner in the next moment, pulling her into their arms.

I back away, rushing down the stairs and out the door. I don't pause when Cali calls my name, and I don't look around for Charles.

I charge out the front door, down the driveway and into the street, but I'm flanked, stopped dead in my tracks. All the air is lifted from my lungs, yet in a senseless twist, I somehow feel like I can finally breathe.

And I fall into him.

Ransom's arms wrap tightly around me, barricading me into his chest. His heart thumps steadily against the palm of my hand, as if it's speaking directly to me, reaching beyond reason and willing my body to respond. A shiver runs through me and everything boiling inside me settles in an instant, but the moment it does, my mind is triggered, panic flares, and I feel lightheaded all over again.

It's too much.

Too many things too fast.

I don't know how to feel and I sure as hell have no idea how to process what I am.

I'm pissed and confused and worried. I'm scared and unsure and sad.

I'm so, so sad.

Everything is out of sorts; nothing is right or fair or in line.

It's messy.

It's everything I never wanted.

So how is the boy holding on to me all I could ever need?

At that thought, I shove away.

He wasn't expecting it, so I'm able to get a few steps before he's sliding into me again.

"Jameson, don't," he warns.

"You shouldn't be here."

"Yes, I should. My girl needs me, and she proved that by diving right into my arms." He reaches for me. "Baby, come here—"

"No." My nose begins to sting, but I clench my teeth to hold strong. "My mistake."

He shakes his head. "Don't do this. Don't go backward."

"It's time for us to face the facts, this was fun, but that's all it was ever supposed to be."

"Fuck supposed to be, we're way past that."

"I told you what my future looked like long ago."

"That was before your future became mine."

A heavy ache stabs at my chest.

We both know it's the only answer, so why is he fighting me?

"Ransom." Raw grief coats my throat, but I don't allow it to be heard. "It's happening."

"Bullshit it is," he fires back. "Listen to me. *Stop* fucking doing things for the benefit of other people. Stop saving everyone else's ass. Do what you want for you, Jameson." He gets in my face, begging, pleading. "Get in the fucking car with me, baby. Say fuck it. Fuck your mom and fuck him."

"And fuck your sister?" I say coldly.

Ransom's eyes harden, but pain darkens the brilliant blue.

That was harsh, way too cruel, I know, but asking me to do such a thing as leaving Anthony is to destroy Ransom in a different way.

I could never put myself in the same category as his sister.

His blood. His family.

His face is caved, clenched tight and it's almost enough for me to reach out and touch him, but I don't.

"If you are standing here, trying to tell me you're planning to go through with this garbage for me, I'm going to lose my fucking mind. I know you think caring about someone means being who they want and doing what they ask, but that's so fucking wrong it's not even funny." Ransom shakes his head.

A nauseating, sinking feeling weighs down my body. "You can't stop me."

"Trust me when I say, I can, and I will." He grabs my arms with firm hands, his blue eyes piercing mine. "I already knew it would be an uphill battle helping my sister, and I've been climbing it for almost two years now. I won't stop, but this is about me and you."

"This isn't open for discussion." I shake my head. "I told you, love kills." *Isn't today a tragic reminder of that?* "I lost my dad a long time ago, if I don't do this, Anthony will ruin everything. I will lose my family."

"You mean the people who have no regard for what makes you happy? Who are willing to trade you like a fucking stock?" He tilts my head up. "Don't you get it, Trouble?" Ransom whispers, his thumb coming up to glide along my cheek. "*I am* your family, and you're killing *me*."

The back of my eyelids burn; a choking sound slipping from me before I can stop it and I begin to retreat.

He steps toward me, but suddenly Arsen is on his right, Beretta slowly appearing at his left. They don't face me, but instead towards their friend, and when their hands fall on his shoulders, he slumps where he stands.

I quickly step around them, but as I get a few houses down, speed walking is no longer working, so I pull my heels from my feet and throw them in the grass. Barefoot, I run as fast as my body is able, as far as I can go without stopping.

I run for miles, walk for more, and when a car horn blares in my ears, I jolt, blinking for what feels like the first time.

I glance around, finding I'm standing in the middle of

the street.

The car pulls up, and the woman inside asks if I'm okay, so I nod and make my way to the sidewalk, where two wrought-iron gates are pushed open, flowers lining the edges and a stone wall is stretching several hundred feet on both sides.

I look across the cream-colored wall, reading the big, bold letters along it.

Pacific View Memorial Park.

I have no idea how long I stand outside the gate staring, barefoot, but suddenly, my sister is beside me, her hand slipping into mine.

She doesn't speak, and I don't look at her, but together, we make our way through the entrance.

She leads me through a garden, around a water fountain, into a short iron gate, mimicking the one on the outside, and suddenly, I'm staring into my father's hazel eyes.

My vision grows foggy, but I don't blink, and then Monti lets go of me. Once she does, she folds my fist closed, and I know what she's left inside.

The key.

My father's headstone is one to be admired.

It's four feet tall and diamond-shaped, the photo in the center one of him holding me in his right hand, Monti in the left.

At the bottom of the design, there is the large stone box that this key and this key alone can unlock. Engraved along the top are the words *free thyself today, love thyself tomorrow.*

There's a peace dove carrying a sword beneath it to symbolize the end of war.

My father's war came from within, and one day, it took

over. He brought his battle to an end the only way he knew how.

And I've spent my entire life hating him for it, judging something I didn't fully understand because it was easier than believing I wasn't enough to keep him here.

I know now it was never about me or my sister, it was never really even about my mom.

It was about him, and I can't fault him for that.

I don't want to.

I want to miss him, but I don't know how.

And I want to love.

I want to feel.

I want Ransom.

I can't stop it, everything inside me shatters.

My dad, my friend, my future, all gone.

Sobs rack through me at an unyielding pace, shaking my body and stealing my breath. Tears heat my cheeks and when my sister pulls me into her, I don't fight it.

I hug her to me.

But that's not what shocks me.

It's when my mother's hand suddenly appears on my shoulder, and I look up to find moisture building in her eyes, our stepdad standing at her side.

She lowers to the grass, white pants and all, and both Monti and I freeze.

But only for a moment, and then we fall into her arms.

CHAPTER
Thirty-Three

It's after three in the morning when there's a knock on my bedroom door, but I ignore it, listening to the waves in the distance, the cold air coming through my open bay doors, bringing goose bumps to my skin.

I look over my shoulder as it opens to find my mom standing there, her pantsuit still on, hair perfectly in place, and I would almost say her makeup was freshly applied.

She hesitates, taking cautious steps inside, and joins me on my bed.

"I'm really sorry about Juliet," she says quietly.

My eyes fall to my comforter, and she understands it for what it is.

We can't pretend sitting here like this is a comfortable feeling when we both know it's not.

It's awkward and, frankly, the sight of her pisses me off, but she is here, which is more than I would expect. I admit it wasn't horrible, having her show up for me today. Honestly, it might have been the motherliest thing she's ever done.

Yes, I know Monti had to have called her and I have a feeling I know who found a way to get in touch with Monti, but who cares. They both came to me in a moment I never would have reached out, and I appreciate that. I probably would have turned around and went home this afternoon had Monti not led me inside.

I needed to go inside.

I needed to apologize to my dad for all the years I refused to think of him. Maybe I would have loved him if I had allowed myself to miss him.

My mom stands, facing me once she reaches my door. "We'll wake in the same world tomorrow, Jameson," she says calmly, and I hear her loud and clear.

Nothing about my life truly changed today, even though everything about me seems to have.

"Yeah, Mom." I glide my thumbnail along my open palm. "I know."

She nods, smoothing her jacket down, her eyes snapping to the flashing screen of my phone on my nightstand, spotting Anthony's name on the screen. "He keeps calling."

"He does."

"Right, well, tomorrow is tomorrow, and tonight is... tonight."

I frown, and she shifts her body sideways, pushing my door open farther.

Balloons fill the entryway not a second later, and then Beretta's face comes into view.

A harsh breath leaves me and only right then do I realize how much I needed someone I care for.

I push up onto my knees, and he comes right for me, ditching the giant red and white bouquet. I throw my arms around him, burying my face in his neck, but I'm stolen a second later.

I'm met with Arsen's smile and my own spreads, emotion clogging my throat. I lay my head against his chest, locking my arms around his waist, but then a hand falls to my lower back and my eyes dart up, locking on Arsen's.

He nods encouragingly, pushing my hair over my shoulder, and slowly I turn around, my gaze colliding with my favorite person.

"Ransom..." I breathe.

He sits on my bed, staring, waiting for me to be the one, and he should.

It's my turn.

I step up to him, and his legs open, making room for me. Even though the sleeves of my sweater cover half my hands, I bring them to his face, tilting his head up and holding his eyes to mine.

I lower my forehead to his, and the corner of his mouth lifts.

He can't handle it anymore, and his arms fly around me, pulling me into him as he scoots to the very edge. My thumbs glide along his lips, and he presses a gentle kiss there, making my own lips curve to one side.

My chest begins to rise and fall rapidly, and his grin turns to a smirk.

A low laugh leaves me, but something calls me to look back again and when I do, I find my mother still standing there, a small frown on her face.

When her eyes meet mine, though, it's gone. She tries to smile but can't manage it, and she holds her finger up, slowly stepping from the door.

I look to Ransom briefly, but then she comes back in, a glass, rectangular box in her hands.

She walks over, and with the slightest caution, she places it on my nightstand.

Our eyes meet.

"What is it?"

She gives the easy answer, the one I already know. "It's what that key your sister stole led to."

I spot the golden J and M on the top of the box, and my gaze flies back to her.

She lifts a shoulder. "Not everything I gave you was for pretentious reasons."

A quiet laugh leaves me, and her lips twitch.

The moment, if we had one, is gone as fast as it came. She taps her fingers along the box once more, quickly walking out of my room, and closing the door behind her.

Not a second after she's gone does Beretta literally run to lock it.

We all chuckle and the boys jump on the bed, lifting and placing me in the center of it, the cake I didn't see them carrying right in front of me, 'Trouble' scrawled across the center.

Ransom moves behind me, while Arsen sticks a couple candles in, Beretta lighting them as he goes.

I don't know why, but I grow nervous and then they're singing.

My smile couldn't be bigger. I bring my hand up to hide it in my sleeve, but Ransom pulls it down, pressing his cheek to mine.

"Make a wish, Trouble." Beretta grins.

His words are intended to be fun, all part of the process, but a heavy sense of despair slips over me and they sense it.

The cake is moved from the bed, and with the two guys at the foot of it, Ransom at my back, I tell them everything, starting from the moment my mom told me what she needed and expected of me.

I share every word that came from Anthony, everything that's happened with him, and all the shit from today with Amy.

I tell them about the gravesite today with my sister, and how my mom showed up, shocking us both.

When I'm done, they don't judge or try to justify anyone's actions.

They don't try to pacify me in any way.

They don't care about any of that, they only care about the way I'm handling it, how I'm feeling.

And I'm feeling a lot.

Too much.

I stand from the bed and they follow my every move.

I don't want to bury anything, and I don't want to hide, but I do want to let go.

I want to cut it all out while we can, so all that's left is what matters most.

Us.

Me and Ransom.

Beretta and Arsen.

And nothing else.

I meet Ransom's liquid eyes.

I turn off the lights.

Someone starts some music.

My man finds me in the dark.

He knows what I need, and he doesn't make me wait.

He gets right to it, drives me against the wall, pins my hands high over my head, and grinds his hips into me. I fight for his lips, but he denies me, instead kissing and sucking on my neck.

Using one hand to keep mine pinned, his other pushes my underwear and sleep shorts from my body, and instead of letting me free to take off my top, he dips beneath it, teasing and twisting my nipples until I'm a whimpering mess.

Only then does he release me and tears my shirt from my body.

I try to undress him, but he grabs my wrists, halting me.

"Not yet, baby." His hands fall to my breasts, massaging, squeezing and then he spins me around, plants my hands flat on the wall and lifts me from behind, his hands wrapped around my thighs from underneath, spreading me open completely.

He walks forward, so the edge of my knees meet the wall.

"Put your fingers where you want me," he rasps. His teeth scraping my shoulder.

I don't hesitate, my fingers slip between my legs.

The way he's holding me, I'm wide open, able to easily find the spot that's most needy.

I rub along the sides first, teasing myself, and my thighs clench. I pinch my clit, rubbing and rolling, and soon, my hips are chasing the feeling.

"Ransom, please," I moan.

He growls, biting me. "Come, baby. Come and I'll fill you with mine."

My pussy clenches. Leaning farther into him, I slide a finger inside, rubbing, and my head falls to his shoulder.

Low, deep moans flow from the other side of the room and my lips curve as my body convulses.

Ransom squeezes, but he gives me no time to come down.

He lowers my legs and spins me, but he doesn't take us to the bed, he hooks one of my wobbly legs over his shoulder and buries his face in my pussy.

He groans against me, sucking and flicking his tongue between his lips and my body starts to shake, the aftershock orgasm far more powerful than the first.

I moan loudly, but I don't care.

I grind on his face, and when I'm about to come, I

pull back, shove him when he isn't expecting it and slam my mouth to his.

He chuckles, wincing when I bite his lip, and then he's tearing off his belt, shoving down his jeans, flipping us.

I chuckle, but it turns into a deep moan when he shoves inside me in one, full deep thrust and my back flies off the carpet.

"Now you can wait to come when I do," he tells me.

I squeeze him with my pussy in protest, and he laughs into my mouth, his tongue sharing my flavor with me.

"Pout, baby, and I'll give you a real reason," he teases.

I pull my legs all the way back, and he groans.

"Fuck."

His thrusts grow quicker, harder, wilder.

He slams into me over and over.

But when he's about to come, he pulls out.

His cock is thick and dripping, and he glides it down, his eyes flicking up to mine as he meets my ass.

I tense at first, but he massages my thighs and I open up.

His pointer and middle fingers slip inside my pussy, slowly working in and out while the head of his cock pushes against my ass.

I groan, long and low, wishing he were close enough to kiss.

His other hand comes up, rubbing on my clit, and applying pressure to my hole all at once but he doesn't try to push inside.

My muscles clench, and he quickly slips back inside me.

He comes instantly, the fingers circling my clit shaking vigorously, but on purpose. That combined sends a tremor down my body.

My orgasm rips through every part of me, an entirely new kind of heat spreading through my core and up to my abdomen.

My toes feel cramped from curling and my thighs are dead.

Ransom falls on top of me and I wrap my hands around his back, sliding my fingers into his hair.

After a few minutes, the moans on the other side of the room soften to heavy breathing.

Ransom kisses my neck.

"Mine," he whispers his plea.

When I nod, he tenses, pulls back and places his forehead to mine, so I nod again and promise, "By any means necessary."

***

The boys never left, and I wake up in a Ransom and Arsen sandwich, Beretta passed out at the foot of the bed.

My mind begins to race, an anxiousness building behind my ribs, not knowing what the day will bring, but it settles a little when Arsen realizes I'm awake and smiles down at me.

I reach up, pushing his hair from his head, and he closes his eyes, kissing my hand as it falls back into place.

"Do you always wake up first?" I whisper.

He pops a brow and then Ransom is squeezing my hip.

A low laugh leaves me. "So, what, you guys are prone to stalking and watching me sleep?"

Arsen nods with a grin, and I shove at his chest.

I don't realize he's so close to the edge of the bed and he falls over, tumbling to the floor. Laughing, I lean over to look at him, but he darts forward and tugs me down with him.

I smile, but it fades as a loud pounding carries through the house.

The boys hear it too, darting up as I do, and our little bubble pops, everything rushing back.

We look to each other, and then quickly open the door.

Ransom grabs my hand, and Monti is slipping from her room as we pass.

"What's going on?" she yawns, following us forward, but nobody answers.

My stomach swirls, my nerves prickling as I prepare to round the corner. As we do, all five of us come to a full stop.

The sight is overwhelming, and my pulse begins to pound heavy at my temples.

Men and women with dark blue jackets are scattered around the room, flipping cushions and yanking open drawers.

They take the art pieces from the wall and flip the entertainment center on its ass, quickly moving to the next piece of furniture and doing their worst with it.

Our stepdad stands off to the side, glaring at the man who stands in front of him, while three others in matching navy suits surround my mother.

She's sort of terrifying, caged in the center of three massive men, yet she remains the picture of composure, as if she's the lion and they're the hens locked in her very own den.

They're searching the property, keeping her and my dad separated, and I swallow.

This is really happening.

I step forward, and several people in the room finally realize we're standing here. "Mom—"

"Not a word, Jameson," she says calmly as she turns, placing her hands behind her back.

"What the hell is going on?" Monti nearly cries, biting at her nails.

Our dad tries to get to us, but the man in front of him

blocks his path.

One of the detectives begins to read our mom her rights.

That's when I step from the hall, slowly walking toward her, and instantly, her eyes lock with mine.

I knew my mom wasn't a saint, and to be honest, I'm not sure any defense attorney can truly call themselves one. They're all, from my experience, quite detached from morality as a whole, but a liar and a cheat?

A fraud, trading her daughters' lives to save her own? For greed and God knows what else?

I hadn't the slightest idea.

But I know everything now.

The thing about my mother, what Anthony failed to realize, is she has *always* worked with the highest tier criminals. The worst of the worst, the filthiest the world has to offer. We're talking dangerous, deadly, and of course, the highest paying.

So, after twenty years in the business of helping keep criminals on the streets rather than off, my mother has made many, many friends in the lowest of places.

She'll be just fine.

She's the one who said we Filanos fight to the end, and in the end, we refuse to lose.

I couldn't lose, not this time.

Not him.

Never him.

My mother wanted me strong, and she built me that way.

But somewhere along the way, and without me realizing, my strength outgrew hers.

I have no doubt in my mind my mother could sense it, even if it took her some time to admit it to herself.

She knows it well now.

I walk up to her, and while the detectives dart their hands out at first, they lower them when they see I'm not a threat.

I reach over my mother's shoulders as if to hug her, but I don't. I carefully unclip the pearl necklace from her neck and step back.

While her eyes narrow at first, her chin lifts next, and a small smile blooms on her lips. A real one, and my slow smirk follows.

She nods, her words barely above a whisper, "By any means necessary."

Yes, Mother.

Check.

Mate.

CHAPTER
Thirty-Four

My mom trained her daughters well.

We know when to speak and when to keep quiet, so for the last four hours, we sat still, silently watching as a half dozen men and women ripped our home apart, carting box after box out the door, possible 'evidence' tucked inside each one, the contents of the lockbox included.

When the last man leaves, our stepdad follows, and the second the door closes, Beretta locks us on the inside.

Instantly, Monti spins to me, but I throw my hands up, backing away as I will my lungs to open.

"Jameson—"

"I need a minute." I turn, my exhale choppy, making me lightheaded.

I look to my hands, my body trembling in place.

Holy shit.

That just happened.

I press the heels of my palms into my eye sockets and drag my hands down my face as I step out onto the open balcony. Gripping the railing, I lean back, stretching my arms wide and bend at the waist, breathing long and deep a few more times.

I wait for the guilt, expecting it to hit me hard, but I don't feel it the least bit.

I do feel anxious, but I think it stems from a good place as butterflies are erupting in my stomach rather than a rope twisting around it. It's as if opportunity's rising inside of me for the first time, liberating me. My spine tingles, and I inhale through my nose, quickly releasing it through my mouth.

"She said she needs a minute," I hear Beretta say.

"Uh-huh, yeah. Down, boy. That's my sister," Monti snaps. "I think I know what she needs."

"And I know what she likes," he fires back. "And one thing she likes is to be left alone when she asks."

Ransom's hand falls on my back and I straighten, shifting slightly to lean my left shoulder against his chest. My head tips, my temple resting at his chin. I close my eyes, but they open when feet pad closer.

Wide-eyed, Monti joins us on the balcony, crossing her arms as the ocean chill reaches her skin. "What am I missing?" she asks, shaking her head. "Jameson, what the *hell* just happened?" There's no anger in her tone, only confusion and shock, both understandable.

I feel the same, but not in the same context.

Confused about what to do now.

Shocked at how quickly things have happened.

Last night, something was keeping me awake and I knew exactly what it was, just as I knew my mom never did anything without a reason. My gut told me her leaving the little box on my nightstand was no different; she wanted me to open it.

I was forced to face how sensitive time truly is earlier that morning, so I took no chances.

I opened the lockbox and sat awake for several hours, reading over as many of the documents tucked inside it as I could, trying to make sense of what I was looking at. Once I got to the final document, I woke up the boys.

Everything clicked, and I had to decide where to go from there.

In the end, and with Ransom in my corner, there was only one direction that would do. I think my mom knew it as well as I did, and I would bet it's why she gave it to me in the first place.

Whether she liked it or not, my mom saw the fight blooming in me that only comes along with having someone to fight for. For the first time, she wasn't selfish and allowed me to be.

But in true Filano fashion, not without a lesson in strength.

She gave me all I needed, the gun and the bullets, but at the end of the day, I had to be the one to pull the trigger, to take what I want, and pave my own path.

To fight for the future that I desire… the one I deserve.

Not the one she arranged, or the one Monti bailed on, but the ending meant to be mine with the person made for me.

Nothing else mattered anymore, not what my mom had to offer or the money she held over my head. It meant nothing without Ransom, so I made my choice, and it was an easy, clear one.

There was no hesitation and I aimed for the head.

I turned my mother in without a second thought, using information she provided me with. Anonymously.

I have to admit, I didn't anticipate such a quick response, but I guess it's considered high priority when accusations claiming the woman who represents the largest crime ring in the Florida area is as dirty as her client list begins to surface.

So what the hell happened?

I took control.

I reclaimed my life.

I let love in.

I let love win.

I look to Monti. "Her choices determined her consequences."

Monti blinks, and blinks again. "I don't understand."

"The box, Monti. You're the one who gave me the key, told me there was a gift inside. You knew what she had to hide."

"Yeah." She nods, incredulously. "The deed to this house, Dad's will, checks and bonds dated with our eighteenth birthdays."

I push off Ransom. "Wait, what?"

"I had to wait for your birthday to tell you in case she tried to pull something crazy while you were still a minor. I was trying to be cautious."

"Monti, what are you talking about?"

She nods, spinning around, and slowly, we follow her into the house.

Spotting her keys, she darts toward them, but Arsen slips in first, snagging them off the table.

She tugs her head back. "Excuse you?"

"Where you trying to go?" Beretta joins him.

She scoffs, crosses her arms and turns to me.

When I don't speak, her mouth gapes. "J..."

I'm on edge, more so than ever considering, and trust isn't exactly a thing right now, so we have to ask.

"Where *are* you going, Monti?"

"My car." She laughs. "What, you think I have a reason to run? Please." She rolls her eyes, laughing again when none of us move. "Okay, wow. Talk about an alpha and her pack."

"Monti."

She sighs. "I stole everything that was inside the box when Mom walked you to the car at the memorial park, Jameson. Stuffed it down my pants, in fact, and hid it under the hood of my car when we got home. I left it empty."

All at once, we move toward the door.

"Wait, seriously? Hello!" she snaps, but eventually falls in line.

Arsen unlocks the doors, and Beretta pops the hood.

I grab the Ziplock bag full of folded papers.

"We should go in, the neighbors are probably watching," Monti says.

"She's right." Ransom grabs my hand, and we all slip back into the house.

As I open the paperwork, laying it out on the table, Monti points to the top one.

"This is his will, he left everything to us. He had moved the money into trusts months before... you know. And this" —she pulls a pink envelope from the center slapping it on top— "this is the deed to the house."

My eyes snap up to hers and a sad smile pulls at her lips. "It's in our names, J. That's why mom couldn't sell, that's why it's been sitting here, waiting for us. It's ours."

It's ours...

"I called one of Dad's lawyers on this paper, just to see if it was legit, and he said Mom never tried to take any of it. She told him that we'd come to claim what was ours when we were older." She frowns. "She never told us about it because she knew with all he's given us, we could walk away from what she was asking us to do, not needing her. And we don't need her, J. Not to help us get a start in life anyway."

I spin, my mind running as I process everything she's telling me, the paperwork in front of me.

More bombs and hidden secrets.

My mom needed us to do what she asked, to carry on her name *and* so the events of today could be avoided, but she never cared for us to need her.

She would never cut us off. She cared about image too much for that. Sure, she stopped 'dealing' with Monti after Monti refused to be a pawn, never cared to call her personally unless it was in search of me, but her cards were never deactivated, and the bills kept getting paid.

No, this is deeper, a safety net set in place decades ago.

She knew where her career was headed.

A low laugh escapes as it hits me and I fall into the chair. Dropping my head back, I stare at the ceiling.

"She did all this because she needed a leg up. It's how she'll blindside everyone the minute they think they've got her, and she will wait until that very last second, let them nearly celebrate, and then, bam. Knock them on their ass." It's her specialty.

My god, Mother, you're an evil fucking genius.

I tap my fingers against the wooden tabletop, my eyes popping up to Ransom, to Beretta and Arsen, but they settle on my sister.

"What is it?" Monti lowers into the chair beside me.

"She handed me every single piece of evidence against her. Contracts and photographers, tapes that must have been recorded conversations and journal logs, USB drives, and computer chips. Everything you can imagine."

"Why would she do that?"

One reason is because she found a hint of compassion and shed it on me, but even that she could only risk for one reason.

"Because this is *our house*, Monti." I nearly laugh as I push to my feet. "And she knew the search warrant issued would be for the residence of Gabriella Filano."

Monti's face falls. "Holy shit."

I nod. "Everything they found today, all the evidence they collected..."

"It's inadmissible, collected illegally." Her hands come up to cover her mouth. "They'll have to throw it all out. This will never even make it to trial."

"She'll be back at work in no time."

"Savage," Beretta absentmindedly whispers and our light chuckles follow.

"Holy shit, this is crazy. You think Dad knows?" Monti wonders.

"He was as calm as she was. He must."

"But like, this is it now? We're done caring what she thinks? No more weekly reports on our lives? We're taking this shit to the bank, literally, and cutting the ties that allow her to control us?" Monti steps toward me. "J, are you free?"

As if Anthony heard her question from wherever he is, my phone rings down the hall and I know it's him, ready to threaten us with the only pull he has left, guardianship over Sienna. But I never would have flipped his blackmail on him if there were even the slightest chance he would still have the power to turn Ransom's world upside down.

Anthony Blanca is about to fall, but unlike my mother, his knees will hit the floor.

Soon, but not yet.

We have an email set up to auto send three days from now at four a.m. on the dot. So, if it happens as it did with my mother, as soon as the sun rises that day, the police should be pulling up to Admiral Law, where they'll find dozens of 'stolen,' sensitive case files. Files Anthony paid a guy to steal in order to collect dirt on my mother for his big extortion plan.

Little did he know, the man he paid to spy on my mother, worked for her, so she passed over the requested files with a smile.

She knew all along what he had on her, and she made sure her every base was covered should this day ever come.

If she were ever to go down, she was taking him with her.

She was the shark in the water, and Anthony was nothing but one of many minnows.

By default, Anthony will lose guardianship over Sienna, and Ransom, eighteen the day it's set to happen, will finally be the one responsible for her care, just as he's always wished.

A strange sense of heaviness settles over me, but as it does, my lungs seem to expand, and the jumbled mess in my mind dispels.

I turn to Ransom, and his hand automatically comes up, gliding into my hair, my smile soft and slowly curving.

"Baby?" His grip tightens.

My mouth hooks higher. "You're not the only one who gets to set the world aflame."

His chuckle is low and rasped.

And then he kisses me.

CHAPTER
Thirty-Five

$\mathcal{J}$ules' parents are having their daughter buried in the same memorial park as my father, and due to the nature of her death, her parents had personal fears and worries surrounding today, what those were we may never know, but as a result, only myself, Dax and Cali are invited to be there with the family.

But as we pull up to the gate, the six of us silently seated in the back of the Marino limo, Mrs. Marino's hand flies to her mouth, and her eyes widen, tears instantly pouring down her cheeks.

The streets are packed from right to left as far as you can see, at all four corners and every which way. Student after student, teacher after teacher, hold flowers and bears, signs, and candles. There is no less than two hundred of our peers.

Some are crying, hugging the person at their sides while others stand silently, watching as we pull into the entrance. As we begin to cross the threshold, Mrs. Marino shouts, "Stop!"

The driver jolts, and we're forced to grab on to the seats, so we don't slide right off of them.

She goes to push the door open, but her husband

grabs her hand, holding her there with wide eyes.

"Honey, they just want to feel close to her too," he tells her, afraid she's going to lash out and lose it.

She might.

Shaking, Mrs. Marino turns to her husband, looks to the rest of us, and then to Amy sitting opposite her.

Amy's head is turned away, her shoulders coiled in, but out of the corner of her eye, she stares at her mother, and when her mother reaches for her hand, Amy darts forward, nearly falling at her mother's feet she's so eager to feel the connection.

My eyes cloud over and look away, as I run my tongue along my teeth to try to hold it together.

My mother has said and done some awful things to me, but when she fell to the ground beside me at my father's grave, none of that mattered, at least not in that moment.

I imagine Amy feels the same.

Mrs. Marino opens the door, and together, she and her family step out and onto the curb. Slowly, Dax, Cali, and I follow.

Cali grips both our hands and together, we hold back, waiting to see what will be said.

"Thank you all for being here with us today," Mrs. Marino manages to say. "I know it means the world to her."

She buries her face in her husband's neck, hugging her daughter to her side.

Mr. Mirano fights to keep his composure, and slowly nods. "Please, join us. Juliet would want that, and we're sorry we didn't realize this before now."

We wait beside the car, allowing the family to slip past us, but as they do, Amy's eyes find mine and there's something inside them, a silent cry maybe, I don't know.

But it has me lifting my hand, and more tears fall from

her eyes as she quickly, almost desperately accepts, as if she were hoping for exactly that.

She clenches my fingers tightly, and each of us linked together in a line, the others slowly shuffling in behind us. We head for the arch of the hill that overlooks the Garden of Valor, where our friend will be laid to rest.

I learned a lot from the tragedy we're facing today.

Love isn't the sole driving force behind our pain. It can add to it, yes, but our pain comes from within. Sometimes it's placed there from experience and other times, some of us have a dark place within us that, no matter what we do, who we have, and how we live, the light never quite reaches it.

Nobody can claim to understand the way one feels, because the reality is, we all feel differently.

We can live through the same exact moments, even side by side, but we don't experience them the same.

I can only hope for the opportunity to hold someone up who feels they can no longer hold themselves up.

I look along the masses and slowly lower into one of the seats along the front row.

Soft music begins to play in the background, and the celebrant takes his place at the podium.

It's a beautiful, devastating morning in Corona Del Mar.

A steaming latte with the lid off and fresh whipped cream added is placed on the railing in front of me, letting me know Ransom is back from his meeting with Sienna's case manager.

With a soft smile, I turn to look at him, and he glides his knuckles along my jawline, slowly tipping my head back.

"You okay?" he whispers.

I nod. "Yeah, I am."

His eyes search mine and a small frown finds its way along his forehead. "With everything, not just today?"

A low sigh leaves me, but it's the good kind.

It's been six days since my mom was carted off in handcuffs, two since Anthony followed suit, granted my mother was already sitting plush in a hotel a city over with the promise not to leave town by the time his black and white ride arrived.

It's been a marathon ever since.

My dad, with the help of one of his judge buddies who 'owed him one,' had Sienna's new guardianship paperwork, naming Ransom in control, expedited, so there would be no lapse in her care.

Monti and I did what she said and went to the bank, claimed our rightful trusts, and officially broke all ties to our mother in that regard.

With Monti's approval, the boys moved in, Ransom in my room, the other two into one of the guest rooms down the hall.

It's not forever, but temporary.

This is our temporary home until we figure out what to do and where to go from here.

"You didn't have to do this, you know." His face caves. "Not for me. We would have found another way."

"There was no other way," I whisper, and then grin. "And I didn't do it for you."

A small chuckle slips past his lips, and he cocks a brow, slipping closer, a soft, low, "Oh, no?" following.

"No." I push up onto my knees, bringing myself closer to him and glide my lips along his. "I did it for me. I did it so I could have all the things I want, like a true ...spoiled little rich girl," I tease, cupping his cheeks, and holding his eyes on mine.

His lips hook in the corner and I place a small kiss there. "I did it because I love you."

Ransom's muscles lock, his jaw clenching beneath my palms.

"And I want you to teach me how to love you right."

He smashes his mouth to mine, bruising and biting. Panting.

When he pulls away, his forehead falls on mine, our gazes locked.

"There is no right, baby. No wrong." He brushes my hair from my face. "Just us."

"I like us," I breathe.

"I know," he teases. "I love you, Jameson."

"I know," I whisper back, making him chuckle.

"You ready to light up the night?" he asks.

I nod, and he tugs me to my feet, grabbing my coffee with his free hand. "Let's do this."

Together, we join the others out front, and we're slipping inside Arsen's car the moment the moon reaches its peak.

I look to Ransom, and he sits back, allowing me to climb into his lap.

The top is down, the wind whipping my hair in both our faces, but I don't care.

I hold his face, my lips twitching when his hands come up to do the same to mine.

"You know how I said I did what I did so I can have all the things I want?" I ask, and he nods. "What I wanted most was for you to have all the things you wanted, which, thankfully, included me. So, it was a win-win on my side."

His eyes tighten, overwhelmed, but in the best way, and he kisses me, deeply and fully.

As the car slows, I climb from his lap, and Arsen kills the lights, slowly pulling to the curb.

"You sure about this?" I whisper.

Ransom nods. "Sienna doesn't want to come back here, home is where we'll make it."

He looks to Arsen and Beretta and both boys reach out gripping his shoulder.

It's like Beretta had indicated before, this place isn't their home and I know now it's not mine either.

Mine is wherever they are.

I smile, nodding, and when Arsen and Beretta move to the popped trunk, we join, grabbing what we need.

Beretta and Arsen place the gas cans all around, and I flick on the torch, but I wait for Ransom to come back and draw a line of gasoline from the front door to the middle of the grass.

He turns to me, rubs the spot on my cheek where my scar lies, and when he nods his chin, I toss it, and together, we rush to the edge of the driveway.

We watch as his childhood home goes up in flames, and once we're sure it's beyond saving, and the sirens ring out in the distance, we slide inside the black convertible and get the hell out.

Once we get to the cave on the beach, where we planned to wait out the fire tonight, I move the blanket from the floorboard and lift what I hid beneath it.

I set it in Ransom's lap and his every muscle locks beside me.

Ransom's face smooths as he stares at it, slowly taking it into his hands.

His jaw flexes, and slowly, his eyes meet mine. He shakes his head.

"I fired Gennie and hired Nana to care for the house,

asked her to bring this with her." I look to the crystal item, and the golden S I had imprinted on the side. "Nana said she thinks she found nearly every one."

He spins the glass, smiling at the pearls inside it.

Again, his eyes slide to mine. "Jameson..."

"If you think she's going to love to see those, just wait." I grin.

As we step into the gardens, Sienna is already there waiting for us.

The nurse excuses herself and Beretta and Arsen step up first, kissing her gently on the cheek. A small grin forms along her lips, as she places her hand loosely on their hips to hug them back, but as we approach, it begins to fade.

Ransom sees it, and his hand twitches in mine before he releases me, slowly lowering on the bench at her side.

He kisses her forehead, and she closes her eyes.

When she opens them, they remain downcast.

I hold my breath, the air thickening around us.

"What's wrong?" Ransom's voice is hardly a whisper.

"Will you promise me something?" she asks him.

Leaning forward, he lifts her left fingers, slides his palm underneath, so he can hold her hand. "Yes."

"No matter what it is?" she adds.

"I don't like this..." Unease draws his brows together.

"Please, Ransom."

He swallows, but nods.

"Leave me here—"

"Sienna, no—"

"Finish school, and the day you get to walk the stage, come get me."

The muscles in his neck stretch and he shifts closer.

"Ransom, you do so much for me, you're here almost every day." She pauses to take a few breaths before continuing, "You made happen what you said you would. I don't have to worry anymore about what Anthony will do to you."

A strained chuckle leaves him and he shakes his head. "I knew you were worrying about me when I was worrying about you."

Her eyes soften and I imagine if she had use of her left hand, she would squeeze his.

I watch as he squeezes hers.

"Sienna, I can't. I want you with me, you belong with me."

"You promised," she whispers and his face twists. "I'm okay, Ransom. It's only a couple months, do all the things a senior is supposed to do, lame or not," she teases him. "And then we can do what you said. Start fresh somewhere else. As a family."

Her eyes briefly meet mine and my lips twitch.

He pulls in a long breath, sitting up straighter, and with forced movements, her request the sole thought in his mind, he agrees.

It takes him several moments to accept the answer he gave, but once he perceives the happiness in her eyes, it's enough to erase his concerns, at least for right now.

He grins, sitting back and while his shoulders seem to fall, I think it's with ease, not weight. He knows she's okay, and her deciding to stay a little longer lets him know it's the truth, she's being honest, not telling him what he hopes to hear as he thought she might.

His baby sister is okay, and soon, she'll be more than that.

I scoot closer on the bench, and Ransom's right arm falls behind me, bringing me closer to him.

I take a deep breath, nervous for some reason.

"I brought you something."

Sienna looks my way as I pull the long, velvet box from my bag.

I open it, and her lips part, Ransom's hand clamping on my hip in the same moment.

I didn't tell him what my surprise was, only that I had something she would love, and judging by her reaction, I think I was right.

"Oh my god..." she breathes, and her glossy gaze flicks to mine, but only briefly, before falling to my hands again.

"They're Blue Nile, South Sea," I tell her softly, pulling the pearl necklace from its case, the necklace my mother spent more on than I'll ever admit to Sienna, and the same one that I took from around her neck the day she was arrested.

I had it cleaned, polished, and reclasped with a sensitivity link, just in case. It's sixteen inches long and has a total of eighty-five *perfect* pearls.

"Jameson... I can't..." She gets choked up, swallowing hard, and I move to sit on Ransom's lap, so I can be right beside her.

I set the box on the bench and unclip the end.

Tipping my chin, I slightly warn her I'm coming in and she doesn't protest, so as gently as possible, I fit the necklace around her slender neck, then clasp and spin it.

I smile and hers follows, making me laugh slightly and Ransom's chest expands at my back.

With slightly shaky movements she lifts her right arm, her fingers gently running along each pearl.

"Thank you," she whispers. "Thank you for... for everything."

She doesn't have to say it, I know what she means.

She's thanking me for loving her brother, for accepting

her, for the events of the last week, but I should thank her just the same.

And I will, but not today. Today, it's obvious she needed to say those words for herself, so I'll save my gratitude for another time.

And there will be plenty more times to come.

"Okay, gorgeous, where's that new fishpond you told me about?" Beretta wraps his hands around the handles of her chair, and she chuckles.

"Behind the garden," she tells him.

"Behind the garden we go." He grins and Arsen falls in step beside them as they head in that direction.

Slowly, we stand, and Ransom grips my hips, spinning me to face him.

His face is drawn tight, a look of adoration written along his every feature. "That was..."

"The least I could do. I know she wanted a perfect pearl, now she has eighty-five of them."

He chuckles, pulling me in, but he quickly grows serious. "You do know that even if this shit wouldn't have happened with your mom or my brother, that in the end, you'd still be mine, right? No matter what, you would have been with me, even if I had to hide you away?"

My grin is wide and I wrap my arms around his neck, guiding his lips to mine. "Yeah, baby, I know."

I kiss him, and as I do, I find myself where I was before I met him.

Wishing the year would be over already so the end can begin.

Because that's what he is, my end.

My messy, unclear, hopeful future is full of promise.

Full of us.

And our boys.

And Sienna.

And who knows... maybe even Monti, if she's lucky.

I know I am, and tonight, when the lights go out and darkness takes over, I'll show my man how lucky I feel.

And he'll show me just how badly behaved he can be.

Bring on the blackout.

EPILOGUE
Five Years Later

RANSOM

As a kid I wished for a lot of things, but nothing more than to wake up in a different place than the one I went to sleep, so long as my sister's room was still right next door.

When I was in sixth grade, I got my wish.

Our grandfather, who we never knew existed, had passed away and left us what my twelve-year-old self considered a mansion. Just like that, I thought everything would be better, but life only got worse.

My parents were sick with something a home can't heal, and money *can* buy.

The reality of the situation was my sister and I were never enough for the assholes who spawned us and we never would be, but then I met Beretta and Arsen, and suddenly I didn't care anymore.

We were always together. They would stay in with me when no one was home to watch Sienna and brought food from their houses when we had none.

They became my family.

When I almost lost my sister, they were right there the whole time, sat in the ICU waiting room with me day in and day out. All three of us missed most of our sophomore years, fell behind to what felt like the point of no return, but not once did they consider walking out of that hospital when I wasn't the first to push to my feet.

I fell into a bit of darkness after that, and together we tried to break me out, but it was no use. I was smirking on the outside, drowning from within.

And then Jameson Filano came along and every nerve in my body sparked. She lit my ass on fire.

She was a tempest, a gorgeous fucking hailstorm that beat down on my senses until they snapped. She woke me from the nightmare my life shoved me into without trying and completely unaware.

But she was a flame, and I was less than ash.

Once again, that nasty little whisper crept into the back of my mind and screamed I was a fool, that it was a long shot, that a girl like her could never want a guy like me, not for more than a night's play.

That if I wasn't enough for my parents, I could never be enough for her.

I knew the score, understood my place in the world, but I wouldn't let that stop me from trying... and then I looked into her hazel eyes.

All it took was that one time, right there in the dressing room of a store I couldn't afford to piss in.

In her gaze, I didn't find heated intrigue of a society girl faced with a dirty little secret she wanted to cash in on.

I saw a layer of life tacked tight along every edge, a mirage she held high and strong to ensure not a soul could see what was on the other side, but I saw it.

I saw because it mirrored my own.

A desperate need to fucking breathe.

To scream, to be selfish and senseless, and to do it with

her middle fingers held high.

To do all she wanted or do nothing at all and it be okay.

The girl was tired, bored.

Bold.

But she was holding back because the world around her wasn't ready for what she had in her, and she'd repressed life for so long, even she was clueless.

I was not.

I knew what she was capable of and I wanted every bit of it.

I needed to know her, to be hers, and she sure as fuck had to be mine.

It was a slow process, but every time her eyes found mine, I saw a little more, a bit deeper.

And then I had her, tasted her, slid inside her, and if I had a single doubt before, it died that night.

She said she didn't feel, when really, she felt so much she hid it away in fear.

She said she didn't believe in love, yet she fucked like she was made of it.

She loved; she just didn't know it because she had no one to show her what it meant.

I had my sister, my two best friends, so in some ways, I was richer than my little rich girl, but even so, she fell. She loved me long before she realized it.

But my baby knows it now, and I sure as hell will never let her forget it.

"Mr. Rossi."

My head snaps to the priest and across from me, a raspy little chuckle fills the air.

"Your vows, son," he prompts.

The man nods encouragingly, but I shake my head and my girl laughs a little louder, my boys doing the same from my left. They know I don't want to share what's going on inside my head with anyone else.

I squeeze Jameson's hands, my eyes landing on hers again. "Skip to the end," I say to the man.

Jameson's lips curl up high, the red painted along them testing my patience.

She knew what she was doing when she put it on, same as she did when she slid into her dress, a form-fitting thing the exact shade of those perfectly pouty lips.

The devilish piece hides every bit of her skin from me with the exception of her hands and neck, but while I can't say for sure from where I'm standing, I've got a feeling her back might be bare.

My eyes cut over her shoulder, meeting Sienna's as if she'll reveal the answer, but my sister only smiles.

Next thing I know, a matte black band is being slid over my finger and the man at my side says I get to kiss my bride, so I fucking kiss her.

I kiss her like no one is watching when, in fact, they are.

I kiss her like she's mine, because she is, has been, and always will be. The piece of paper we'll get after today makes no difference, she'd have been forever mine without it, but I want it all the same.

I want everything I never thought I'd have, and I want it the way we decide is right. Fuck everyone else and what they think, like, or believe.

This is about us, and yeah, we wanted to get married in the middle of our new club, at the stroke of fucking midnight as a way to rewrite the night our worlds officially crashed five years ago today.

On my baby's birthday.

We have no cake, but we do have espresso flavored

fudge our staff made for us and a couple vases of M&M's courtesy of Beretta.

We aren't having a five-course catered meal, but we did rent out the cafe down the street and made clear anyone who can make it to ten a.m. can join us, on us.

We sure as fuck won't be sleeping tonight.

Jameson shakes her head, her lips parting with a low laugh.

Yeah, she knows what I'm thinking.

Together, we turn and face the others and the room erupts in loud cheers, slams of freshly downed shot glasses and a single popped bottle of champagne that can only have come from where Monti sits beside Cali.

Beretta jerks forward and steals my bride by wrapping his arms around her legs and tearing her from the stage, so I hop down, clapping hands and half hugging Arsen. Just as quickly, we trade places, and then we're stepping in front of Sienna.

She smiles wide, shakily swiping at the tears in her eyes and Jameson leans in, hugs her while whispering something in her ear that has Sienna chuckling.

With a quick wink, Jameson slides away, Monti and Cali rushing her with over-the-top giggles and glitter bombs.

I turn back to my sister, bending down on one knee and gently place my hand over the one she has no feeling in and hold it tightly as I kiss her cheek. "We did it."

She looks around the club, her eyes holding on the giant fluorescent blue and pink sign that reads. *Sienna's Spot.*

It's her design with our black light influence, her signature drink recipes and her passion project.

We've partnered with Lindo Lifts here in the East Bay, and with our cover charge comes a ride to and from the club. We have no parking lot, and the nearest garage is four miles down the road.

Her vision was to provide people with comfort and care and allow them to have a good time and get home safely, for their safety and the safety of others.

So, once she knew what she wanted to do with her future, we finally cashed the check for what the insurance paid out for the house that 'accidentally' caught fire and created what she imagined.

It's been open for three months and has blown our fucking minds.

We have three more under construction as we speak, including one set to open in our hometown one week from now.

It will be the first time we set foot back in that city since the day after graduation when we packed up all our shit and left.

We're near San Francisco now, twenty minutes from the main city and on flat land in the closest thing to country the area has to offer.

We have three homes on our property, one for us, one for the boys, and one for Sienna—only after she insisted, we would have gladly had her in ours forever, but she wanted her own space. Our house is still where everyone gathers, where we eat most nights and four out of seven, the place we all fall asleep.

"No, Ransom." Sienna brings her blue eyes back to mine. "You did it."

"Technically..." Beretta pokes his head between ours. "I did it since, you know, I restored the building," he teases.

Arsen is at our side moments later, and both share the same calm expression.

If someone would have told me five years ago that we, let alone I, would be where we are now, we would have laughed or thrown a punch assuming they were mocking us. We were never supposed to make it.

We were three punk kids with little to no direction.

Now we're three grown men with some college courses under our belts. Arsen and I didn't make it past the first year, but we did apply for a business license after, and with Jameson's help, we passed the tests needed. B and Sienna have certificates from trade school, Beretta in carpentry and Sienna in design.

Jameson took a year off and with the help of an accountant, she and Monti invested most of their dad's money, keeping only the direct checks made out to each of them. She used hers to buy the land we call home and then did what she never thought he had the opportunity to but was groomed her whole life for.

She enrolled at Berkeley, entered as a sophomore thanks to all the whiz kid classes she took in high school. She graduated last year with a degree in finance.

Between the five of us, we've got this whole business shit on point.

We're rolling into life now.

We made it.

For the first time in my life, I'm enough.

I'm more than enough.

And Jameson Filano is the reason.

Jameson

I wash my hands, quickly leaning closer to the mirror once more to make sure I didn't smear my eye makeup and prepare to step back from the bathroom.

It's been hours since my man became my husband and still, we've yet to have a chance to sneak away, but Sienna is now home safe, the lights have begun to dim, and the staff has unlocked the vending machine holding all the glow-in-the-dark body paints, so I know it's close.

But if my husband thinks he's painting me tonight, he's dead wrong, and if Arsen and Beretta think we're sharing the back room for some fun on my wedding night, they're just as fucking crazy.

Right as I'm thinking it, I slip from the door, and not a second after I do the soft fabric gently drops over my head covering my face. My hands are bound together and I'm lifted off my feet by not one, but three sets of hands.

This time I don't kick and scratch, though.

I chuckle, relaxing in their hands and their husky laughs warm my chest.

They still love their games, even though the rules changed a long time ago.

I know we're headed into the back, windowless room before the door is unlocked and I'm carried inside, and I know as they set me down that when I remove the silken sack from my head, they won't be in front of me. Or they will, but I won't see them until they open their eyes.

What they don't know is I had a surprise planned for my husband. I admit, this is almost better.

Maybe I subconsciously expected this tonight, and it's a little thing called full circle, but I know my man, and I know what will follow.

So, I slowly slide the thing off my head, but I keep my eyes closed tight, holding in my laugh, knowing full well the extent of their synchronization. I know they waited exactly five seconds to sharply snap their eyes open to tease me with their glowing gazes.

So when Ransom's sharp demand of "open your eyes, Trouble" comes, my laughter slips free.

I spin and he hears it, but he doesn't see it—this room was purposely designed to block out every single hint of light for nights we wish to play.

An arm shoots out, latching on to mine and I smirk into the darkness.

I could pick his hands out of hundreds by now, so I know it's him, but if I couldn't, the feel of his ring would give him away, and suddenly I'm done teasing.

I spin so Ransom releases me and am now facing in their direction. After an internal count to three, I flick my eyes open.

My core clenches at the short-hissed breaths along the room.

I look from one to the next, meeting their tantalizing, glow-in-the-dark turquoise contacts... with a hot pink pair of my own.

Ransom jerks forward, his rough, strong hands gripping my face tight as he tears me to him.

His excitement strains against his black dress pants, pressing hard against my abdomen and I smile into the darkness.

"Baby," he groans, his palms gliding into my hair.

The boys know what we need, both laughing the second Ransom snaps "Out" and they're already opening the door.

Ransom doesn't wait for it to close but is already clawing at my bare back with one hand, pulling my lips against his with the other.

He kisses me raw, heated, and full, and when his fingers find the zipper of my dress, my mouth curls into a smile he feels. He tugs back, his eyes on mine.

I let him unzip the thing over my ass, but when his

fingertips come up to my shoulders to help the dress from my body, I step back.

He allows it, waiting, knowing more is coming

With slow movements I let it fall from my skin, and he sucks in a harsh breath as it pools around my feet.

The dress didn't allow for a bra, but the pasties I used are star-shaped and the exact shade of hot pink as my eyes are glowing... as is the thong and thigh garment I'm wearing. I've got glow-in-the-dark glitter strategically streaked along the curve of my waist, breasts, and thighs, and Monti helped me out with a small handprint over my ass cheek, so when I turn, he darts forward, molding his hand over the exact spot.

"Fuck me," he groans, burying his face in my neck. "My wife is trying to kill me on my wedding night."

I chuckle, moaning when he bites me there, then licks and kisses, and then I'm hoisted and flipped, set on the edge of the desk.

"Wife." I tip my head farther to the side. "I like the sound of that."

"I know." He sucks my skin, squeezing my breasts in both hands as I work the black suit jacket from his shoulders and follow with the removal of his dress shirt, also black, of course.

His hands come down and he opens up his belt buckle, kicks his shoes from his feet, and steps from his pants. "Wrap those legs around me, baby, and hold on."

"Yes, boss," I tease as I'm lifted from the desktop and carried to the far side of the room.

He likes it, his cock twitching against my center, and I can't help but roll my hips against it in an attempt to ease the ache I too feel, before he gently lays me flat on my back.

The rug is placed in this spot for this very reason velvety soft and slick against my skin.

I let my arms fall back, gliding them along the material as I inhale deeply, enjoying the feel of my man on top of me.

He senses it, the heavy sense of contentment warming my blood in this moment, and his touch grows featherlight, skating along my sides to my cheeks.

He holds me there, and I stretch my arm and fingers, clicking on the wall fireplace beside us.

The flickering of the blue flames illuminates half his face, and it reminds me of that night on the balcony when he first claimed me as his.

I was, am, and will forever be.

The corner of his mouth lifts and a sigh leaves me.

"I love you, Ransom Rossi."

His cock aligns with my entrance, and as he brings his mouth to mine, he pushes inside of me. "I love you, Trouble."

As his head reaches its fullest point, my back lifts from the carpet, and I pull my legs up and over his hips.

His free palm glides under my ass and he lifts me up, angling me as he likes, my ass an inch from the floor.

"Roll those hips for me, baby," he rasps, pressing his lips to mine.

I tear at his hair, forcing his mouth to my chest, tortured by his slow movements while savoring every moment.

In the bedroom, when Ransom is in control, I know I'm in for a long, drawn-out, core-deep orgasm. The kind that builds and builds, making you shake and sweat and beg incoherently, and then explodes a fraction of a second later. The kind that takes over your body and locks every inch of it in place.

He's always liked it slow and deliberate, every twist and curl of his body purposeful and pleasure-seeking.

I love it as it's allowed me to memorize every ridge of his cock, every arch of every muscle in his body, as he has mine.

It's when I'm flipped onto my knees, tugged or climbing onto his lap that things get a little wild.

In every aspect of our lives, he's the half that makes me whole.

My muscles begin to tense and my mind grows hazy.

I moan into the air and he growls against my skin.

"Come for me, my wife," he whispers, his hips gliding in slow, and slamming as he reaches the hilt, driving himself deeper.

My pussy squeezes around him and he chuckles, his mouth coming up to take mine.

His brows crash as he comes, hard and long and he kisses me, panting in my mouth as I cry into his.

I accept his weight as it falls on me, but he only lets me rest a few moments before he flips us, and I'm dead weight on top of him.

He pushes himself so he's sitting up and uses his teeth to remove the pasties from my nipples, pulling them into his mouth quickly.

They pucker before him and his cock rises between my legs.

Ransom drops back, closes his eyes, and crosses his arms behind his head.

"Your turn, Trouble." He smirks. "Work your magic."

So, I do.

Ten in the morning comes a lot faster than it should and we're piling into limos on the way to breakfast.

Everyone was sensible enough to bring a change of clothes, but everything else is left over from the night before.

We walk inside and a smile lights up my face as I look

around.

Ransom and I made no fancy plans. All we did was book the restaurant we like to walk down to after a long night's work, but I knew when my sister said Cali convinced her husband she needed two extra days here, and prior to the wedding, they had something up their sleeves.

The entire country beach vibe of the place is hidden behind sheets of white silk and red rose vine garlands. They hang from the ceiling all throughout and in the hallway down the walls, lights entwined within them.

The tails are covered in black cloths and golden place settings are placed perfectly in front of each chair.

I chuckle when my eyes lift to the back wall and a golden J and R hangs in the center... an A and B smaller and off to the side, as a little joke, I'm sure.

And it's perfect.

Because we wouldn't be anything without them.

They were just as much a part of our journey as we were, if not the reason for it all.

Arsen and Beretta pushed us, tested us, and refused to allow us to hide from what we were capable of.

I think Ransom and I would have found each other either way, but it would have been different, and I would never wish that.

I love us the way we are, and I love the steps it took us to get here, in a room full of people of our choosing, in our timing.

"I thought you might like that."

My muscles tense.

Okay, this is unexpected.

Slowly, I spin around, finding my mom and stepdad standing at the back left corner.

In her finest pantsuit and gold bangles, my mother

walks toward me.

"Jeans, wow." She smiles.

A laugh leaves me and I nod, stepping in and hugging her even though she didn't try for one. I don't clench her tight but I do allow both my arms to wrap around her briefly before stepping back, a chest now right behind me. "I know, who knew they were so comfortable."

"I'm not sure I've ever seen you in jeans."

I grin. "You haven't." It wasn't allowed.

She tips her head, a low sigh leaving her. "Your sister showed me some photos from last night."

I nod, waiting for the passive-aggressive compliment of my dress of choice, location of choice etcetera, etcetera, etcetera...

But dare I say, there is a small hint of pride in her eyes.

Before she's forced to say something that isn't natural to her, I reach out and touch her bicep.

"Thanks, mom. And thank you for being here."

She nods once more and begins to walk away, but something holds her in her spot, and she looks over her shoulder. "I'm sorry I wasn't there last night I... well." She clears her throat and I nod.

I know what she was going to say.

She couldn't be there to watch me get married because she had to work.

When I was younger, I never thought I cared about her workaholic ways, but after everything with Anthony, I realized I was bitter about it, and now that I'm older, settled into my own life, I no longer care. I don't hold it against her, not how she was then or how she continues to be.

My mom is who she is and that's that. Work has and will always come first, period.

It's not sad or disgusting or any other word I may have

used once, or others may think but not say. It's simply reality. I no longer judge her for who she is, I can't and don't fault her for it. I'm simply happy Ransom helped me to realize what I wanted was far from what I had.

I wanted a home where the people within it are more important than the means that placed us inside of it, and that's exactly what I have.

That's the life we've built here, one where any and all other things, no matter what, come second to the people we love.

Ransom is my number one, the boys and Sienna right behind, and the most recent addition, Monti.

She still comes and goes but I've got a sneaky suspicion she won't be going all that often anymore, if at all.

Speaking of Monti...

She slips up, rescuing me from the awkward moment with my mom, directing her and our stepdad to an open seat.

I let my back fall to Ransom's chest as his arms come around me and when I look up, his lips lower, slowly meeting mine for a quick kiss.

"You okay, baby?"

I smile against his mouth, spinning in his arms and hugging him to me. I nod. "I didn't think she'd make it."

"Me either." He tucks my hair behind my ear, meeting my eyes. "But I'm glad she did."

"Yeah," I whisper, looking from where my mom sits beside Arsen to my stepdad, who is leaning over the table asking Beretta about the work he did on our property. "Me too."

Ransom shifts, looking to the right and my gaze follows.

Our employees take up the majority of the tables, a mix of vivacious college students and punk princes and princesses.

Sienna's laugh pulls our eyes her way and Ransom's

chest inflates against mine.

"I'm starting to wonder if Arsen knew what he was doing when he talked you into letting Liam care for her as part of his extern hours." I smile at Sienna and Arsen's foster brother, who snags a blueberry off the fruit tray on the table and gently places it between her lips.

"She's been able to feed herself for nearly four years now," he pouts.

I look up, laughing at the fake annoyance on his face.

He's beyond happy she has someone who seems to enjoy her as much as we do.

I know it's scary for him, to see her look at someone the way she looks at Liam and not know where it will go, if anywhere, but again, maybe Arsen knew what he was doing. I like to think he did.

Liam's been her day nurse for five months now, and it's been weeks since we've seen his car leave after his shift.

Ransom and I join the others, indulge in way too much food, and spend hours we didn't know we'd manage to stay awake for laughing and chatting with our friends.

As my mother readies to leave, she comes to stand opposite of our chairs, and lowers a rectangular white box in front of me.

"Oh, shit. Another box," Beretta whispers, not so quietly and my mother actually laughs.

My eyes widen in surprise and she clears her throat, making me chuckle.

"Open it," she instructs.

So, I lift the top, unveiling a golden key chain, but this time it's not just a J hanging from its end. There is a single, dangling, heart-shaped diamond that glistens from the shine of what's draped beside it. With the lengths of each varying the slightest bit, there are three letters, one representing

Ransom, and two more, a fraction smaller for Beretta and Arsen.

Moisture stings at the backs of my eyes and I lift my gaze to meet my mom's.

"You're the diamond, and they're the reason for which you shine." Her voice cracks the slightest bit, and I offer a small smile.

"It's beautiful, Mom, thank you." I pull the item from its box, gently placing it in my palm for an even closer look, and I hold still when her hand falls over mine, squeezing.

My eyes snap to hers.

"You were beautiful, Jameson. The red suited you well." She jerks her chin.

I swallow, nodding slightly, and her lips pull into a tight smile.

She looks to Sienna with a true kind smile. "That's a beautiful necklace, dear."

I smirk but I'm shocked when my mom pulls another small box from her purse.

"I was going to give these to Jameson today, but I think they're better matched for you."

My mom places the gift just beside Sienna's right hand and while Liam holds it still, Sienna lifts the top.

He gasps, her eyes snapping to my mom's. "I don't..."

"You can, dear. They will match beautifully." She nods, and I hold back moisture from my gaze as I look from the pearl earrings to my mom.

"Thank you so much," Sienna nearly cries.

I mouth the same to my mother and she smiles.

Her and my stepdad say their goodbyes and soon, everyone else is nearly passing out at their tables from a night of no sleep.

We thank the restaurant and pile into the limos once

more.

Beretta lays out across the seat, his head in Arsen's lap, hand in his man's hair, and turns to us. "I love you guys."

"Right back at you, man." Ransom tosses a small pillow at him, but Arsen knocks it away with a grin, dropping back against the seat.

"Tonight at ten?" Beretta asks with a yawn.

Arsen looks from me to Ransom and nods, so we nod right back.

Tonight at ten.

Every single one of us falls asleep on the drive home.

It's after midnight, just twenty-four hours after our wedding, by the time we're pulling onto a dirt road in a little town called Hilmar.

From what we saw on the way in, there's not much here outside of a store or two and what looks to be a school of some sort, which should make this a whole lot simpler than the last time we did something like this.

Like before, Arsen and Beretta grab the gas cans and I flick on the torch while Ransom rounds the small shack looking home to kill the power. This time though, it's Arsen who draws a line of gasoline from the door to the edge of the yard and he who tosses the torch to send the baby up in flames.

But this time we don't run.

We wait until the front door flies open so we can witness the fear as it lights up the man of the hour's face, the moment he realizes he's trapped inside.

His hair, while shining a light silver near his ears, is the same mahogany blonde as the silent man at my right. He seems just as tall as him too, and I'd bet they share the rich navy color eyes as well, not that I care to look into this man's.

Not after what he did to Arsen and Arsen's mother.

It's clear the moment he recognizes his son as his face goes ghostly white, and the flames around him grow larger.

The coward before us turns to run.

We don't know if the asshole ever made it out the back or not, but we know for certain he didn't escape through the front.

With our heads held high, we slide into the black convertible that started it all.

Flames light up the sky behind us and Ransom slips his hand in mine, pulling it to his lips as I smile at the night around us.

This right here, this is the life I was meant for.

Cali and Jules were right all along, these three are a little crazy.

But they're my kind of crazy, and I wouldn't have them any other way.

I look to my husband who already stares down at me and I know what he's thinking as he knows my thoughts mirror his own.

It's Ransom and me forever.

It's Arsen and Beretta always.

It's us evermore.

No matter what.

I had it wrong before.

To hide the heart isn't to salvage the soul, it's to protect it until the person it belongs to comes to claim it as their own and claim it, he did.

Without permission.

Without pause.

And without mercy.

He took what he knew to be his, and I followed suit.

With a smile, I kiss the man I married, and he kisses me right back.

Note from the author

Man, oh man!!
Let me get a little sappy, okay?!
I lived and breathed for this story for months. I never truly
know what or why I am writing something until I get into it,
and once I understood the voices in this particular novel,
I knew it could only be done one way.
No fear. No holding back.

This book is about a girl who dared to look left when
the world told her to look right. It's about courage and
confidence and finding oneself however the hell one needs
to do so. And I wrote this book for THAT reason, because
we all deserve to find who we are.
To be who we wish.
Wo do whatever we want.
To live without shame or fear.
That's what I wanted to give you.
That's what I hope FOR you.

And I hope you loved Jameson and Ransom's story
as much as I enjoyed telling it.

ALSO BY
Meagan Brandy

Shop more titles from Meagan Brandy at

www.meaganbrandy.com

Titles include:

Boys of Brayshaw
Trouble At Brayshaw
Reign Brayshaw
Be My Brayshaw
Break Me

Fake It Til You Break It
Fumbled Hearts
Defenseless Hearts
Wrong For Me

Stay Connected

My newsletter is the BEST way to stay in contact!
You'll get release dates, titles, and fun first!

Sign up at:

https://www.meaganbrandy.com/newsletter

—

Be the FIRST in the know and meet new book friends in my
Facebook readers group. This is a PRIVATE group. Only those in
the group can see posts, comments, and the like!!
Search Meagan Brandy's Reader Group on Facebook!

—

Find EXCLUSIVE merch here:

https://www.teepublic.com/user/meaganbrandy

You can also find her on the following platforms:

Amazon
Instagram
TikTok
Facebook
Twitter
Pinterest
Bookbub
Goodreads

acknowledgements

I couldn't do anything without the support of my family, and this remains true! Forever and always, my boys.

This book took so much out of me, and challenged me in many, many ways. I have to give it to my friend, and newest editor, Rebecca! I hope you know how much I valued your input. You pushed me and understood my vision so well I was mind blown. We made a fantastic team, and I cannot wait to do it again! THANK YOU!

The real MVP, Melissa Teo. You're the super hero people don't get to see but you make my life and job a million times easier/smoother/badass(er? LOL). Never leave me.

Serena and Veronica! Love you girls and I'm so glad to have you on my team.

Lisa and Lindsey! Thank you for dealing with my fearful self and reading early! You made this so much easier for me.

Danielle, thank you for dealing with my 180's in writing! Lol I know it's not easy to go from yin to yang but you're amazing!

Ellie, thank you so much for being quick and efficient! I know I'm all over the place with timeline, so it means so much!

Bloggers and ARC readers! Thank you so much for taking the time to help support my work. It means the world!

My AMAZING readers! You ROCK my socks off!! I couldn't do anything without you. THANK YOU so much!!

ABOUT
The author

USA Today and Wall Street Journal bestselling author Meagan Brandy writes New Adult romance novels with a twist. She is a candy crazed, jukebox junkie who tends to speak in lyrics. Born and raised in California, she is a married mother of three crazy boys who keep her bouncing from one sports field to another, depending on the season, and she wouldn't have it any other way. Starbucks is her best friend and words are her sanity.

Printed in the USA
CPSIA information can be obtained
at www.ICGtesting.com
LVHW020340150524
780334LV00011B/321

9 781088 026793